Little Women

MERMAID EDITION

MEGAN LOIS WHITEHILL

ROCKWATER PRESS, LANCASTER PA

To Elaina

Contents

PART ONE

Little Mermaids

Little Women Mermaid Edition Jo, Meg, Amy, Beth and Marmee Marsh in the Deep Ocean

CHAPTER 1

Mergirl Sisters

"Sea Queen's Day won't be Sea Queen's Day without any presents," grumbled Jo. She nestled down into her seaweed cushion on the cave floor.

"It's so dreadful to be poor!" sighed Meg, looking down at her shabby shell corset.

"I don't think it's fair for some mergirls to have plenty of pretty things. Not while other mergirls have nothing at all," added little Amy, with an injured sniff.

"We've got Father and Mother, and each other." Beth gave thanks from her alcove in the wall.

The four young faces on which the deep sun crystals shone brightened at the cheerful words. They darkened again as Jo moaned, "We haven't got Father, and will not have him for a long time." She didn't say "maybe never," but each silently added it, thinking of Father far away, where the fighting was.

Nobody said anything for a moment. Then Meg said, "You know the reason why Mother proposed not having gifts this Sea Queen's Day? It was because it is going to be a

3

hard Cold Season for everyone. She thinks we ought not to spend sand dollars for pleasure, when our army is suffering so at the Abysmal Trench. We can't do much, but we can make our little sacrifices, and ought to do it gladly. I am afraid I am not glad at all." Meg hugged her tail, as she sorrowed over all the pretty things she wanted.

"But I don't think the little we should spend would do any good. We've each got a sand dollar, and the army wouldn't be much helped by our giving that. I agree to only expect Mother's one gift, and none from any of you, but I do want to buy *The Flounder and the Feather Star* scroll for myself. I've wanted it so long," said Jo, who was a very literary mermaid.

"I planned to spend mine on new music," said Beth. She gave a little sigh, which no one heard but the sea-flowers blooming in the wall pots.

"I will get a nice bottle of squid ink. I need new colors so much," said Amy. Squid ink was the only ink that worked properly underwater, and good quality was difficult to come by.

"Mother didn't say anything about our sand dollars, and she won't wish us to to have a miserable Sea Queen's Day. Let's each buy what we want and have a little fun. I'm sure we work hard enough to earn it," said Jo, toying with her long braid of lavender hair.

The conversation stilled, and the four sisters nestled down, weaving away in the glow of the deep sun crystals. The Cold Season currents made sloshing noises outside their cave dwelling's thick walls. Slosh and crash as they might, they could not get in. Only the warmest, most cheerful water swirled in their parlor. It was a comfortable room, though the seaweed cushions were knotted and the coral fixtures faded. The walls were natural cave-gray, as was the fashion among the merfolk. Merpeople were colorful creatures who collected colorful baubles, corals and jewels and shells. They considered their colors even lovelier in contrast to the dark walls. In the case of the Marsh merfamily's cave, their decorations needed all the contrast they could get. Their coral baseboard, once vibrant magenta, had long since faded to a pastel blush.

The mergirls themselves were bright and beautiful.

Margaret, whom they called Meg, was the oldest of the four. She was sixteen and very pretty. Her body was plump and fair, with violet eyes, and plenty of soft salmon-pink hair, a sweet mouth, and white hands. She was rather vain over her perfectly paddle weed-green tail.

Fifteen-year-old Jo was very long and lanky, and reminded one of a skinny squid whose appendages sprouted too fast. She never seemed to know what to do with her emerald tail, which was energetic and very much in her way. She had a decided mouth, a comical nose, and sharp, silver eyes, which appeared to see everything. Her eyes were by turns fierce, funny, or thoughtful. Her long, lavender hair was her one beauty, but it was usually braided back tightly, to be out of her way. Jo had round shoulders, big hands, and wore her seashells carelessly. She bore the uncomfortable appearance of a mergirl who was rapidly growing into a mermaid and didn't like it.

Elizabeth, or Beth, as everyone called her, was a russet-haired, blue-tailed mergirl of thirteen. She had a shy manner, a timid voice, and a peaceful expression which was seldom disturbed. Her father called her 'my silent little sandfish', and the name perfectly suited her. She seemed to live in a happy Ocean of her own, only swimming out to meet the few whom she trusted and loved.

Amy, though the youngest, was a most important merperson, in her own opinion at least. She was a regular ocean maiden, with crystal-white eyes, and yellow hair curling on her shoulders, pale and slender. She always carried herself like a young mermaid mindful of her manners.

The evening currents drew in, and the sisters set down their weaving for their chores. Beth pinned up their night wraps to comb out any visiting sea bugs or algae crumbs, an important weekly endeavor. Somehow the sight of the clean and cozy night wraps had a good effect upon the mergirls. Mother was swimming home soon, and everyone brightened to welcome her. Meg polished the sun crystal. Amy floated up from her cushion without being asked. Even Jo forgot how tired she was as she swam over to help Beth pick the little creatures out of Mother's night wrap.

"Marmee's wrap is quite worn out. How is she supposed to sleep in this? She must have a new one."

"I thought I'd get her one with my sand dollars," said Beth.

"No, I will!" Amy insisted.

"I'll tell you what we'll do," said Meg, "let's each get her something for Sea Queen's Day, and not buy any presents for ourselves."

"We'll surprise her! What will we get?" exclaimed Jo.

Everyone thought soberly for a minute. Then Meg announced, as if her own pretty hands suggested the idea, "I will give her a nice pair of gloves."

"A vest, best to be had!" shouted Jo.

"An armlet, with colorful beads," said Beth.

"I'll get a tiny perfume sponge. She likes it, and it won't cost much, so I'll have some left to buy my squid ink," added Amy.

When a cheery voice called out from the front door, the mergirls rushed to welcome a motherly mermaid, with flaxen hair and soft eyes. She had a 'can I help you' look about her which was truly delightful. She was not elegantly dressed, but was still a noble-looking mermaid. The mergirls thought that the gray cloak and faded seashells covered the most splendid mother in the Ocean.

"My sweet lovelies, how did your tides come in today? There was so much to do that I didn't swim home for dinner. Has anyone rapped at the door shells, Beth? How is your scale blister, Meg? Jo, you look tired enough to sink. Come and kiss me, Amy."

While making these maternal inquiries, Mrs. Marsh took off her cloak and replaced it with a warm shawl. A cloak or shawl was essential in the Cold Season. Because their vests or shell corsets were always sleeveless, the merfolk relied on such articles to keep their shoulders snug and comfy.

Mrs. Marsh nestled down in the largest seaweed cushion and drew Amy to her lap, preparing to enjoy the happiest moments of her busy day. The mergirls swam about, trying to make things comfortable, each in her own way. Meg assembled crispy kelp sandwiches. Jo set the slate table, over-turning and banging into everything she touched on the way. Beth floated to and fro between the parlor and the kitchen, quiet and busy. Amy gave directions to everyone, as she hovered in the corridor with her hands folded.

As they gathered about the slate slab, Mrs. Marsh said, with particular delight, "I've got a treat for you after supper."

A quick, bright smile leapt from face to face like a streak of silver dolphins. Beth clapped her hands, regardless of the sandwich she held, and Jo tossed up her conch bowl, sobbing, "A letter-in-a-bottle! A letter-in-a-bottle! Three cheers for Father!" Mrs. Marsh grabbed Jo's conch before it floated away.

"Yes, a nice long letter-in-a-bottle. He is well, and thinks he will get through the Cold Season better than we hoped. He sends all sorts of loving wishes for Sea Queen's Day, and a special message to you mergirls," said Mrs. Marsh. She patted her satchel as if she had a treasure hidden there.

"Hurry and get done! Don't stop to simper over your food, Amy," cried Jo. She talked so quickly that she choked and dropped her sandwich. It came apart in the water beside her, the pieces floating about her head.

Beth ate no more, but glided away to nestle in her shadowy alcove and brood over the delight to come.

"It was so splendid for Father to go as chaplain when he was too old to soldier, and not strong enough to fight," said Meg.

"Don't I wish I was old enough to soldier. Or be a nurse, so I could be near Father and help him," exclaimed Jo, with a groan.

"It must be very disagreeable to sleep in a tent, and eat all sorts of bad-tasting things. And not have your dear merfamily nearby," sighed Amy.

"When will he swim home, Marmee?" asked Beth from her alcove, with a little quiver in her voice.

"Not for many seasons, dear, unless he is sick. He will stay and do his work as long as he can. We won't ask him back a minute sooner than he can be spared. Now swim to me and hear the letter-in-a-bottle."

They all drew up to the largest of the deep sun crystals. Mother nestled more deeply into her cushion, with Beth's little blue tail stretched on the floor before her. Meg and Amy hovered, one at each of her shoulders. As Mrs. Marsh uncorked the bottle, Jo drifted as far back as she could. She did not want anyone to see any sign of emotion if the letter-in-a-bottle should happen to be touching.

Very few letters-in-bottles in those hard times were not touching. Especially so were those letters-in-bottles which fathers sent home. In this one, however, he inked little of hardships, dangers or war. He filled it with lively descriptions of camp food, trident drills, and faraway fish. Only at the end did their father's heart overflow with love and longing for the little mergirls at home.

"Give them all my dear love and a kiss. Tell them I think of them by day, pray for them by night, and find my best comfort in their affection at all times. A year seems very long to wait before I see them. Remind them that while we wait we may all work, so that we need not waste these hard days. I know they will remember all I said to them. They will be loving merchildren to you. They will do their duty faithfully, fight their enemies bravely, and balance themselves so beautifully. When I come back to them, I will be fonder and prouder than ever of my little mermaids." Everybody sniffed when they came to that part. Jo wasn't ashamed of the sob that welled in her chest. Amy never minded the tangling of her golden curls as she hid her face in her mother's shoulder. She cried out, "I am a selfish mergirl! But I'll truly try to be better, so he mayn't be disappointed in me when he swims home."

"We all will," declared Meg. "I think too much of my looks and hate to work, but won't anymore, if I can help it."

"I'll try and be what he loves to call me, 'a little mermaid' and not be hurtful and unruly. I'll do my duty here instead of wanting to be somewhere else," said Jo. She thought that controlling her temper at home was a much harder task than spearing an enemy or two near the Abysmal Trench.

Beth said nothing, and swallowed a few tiny sobs. Then she began to weave with all her might, losing no time in doing the duty that lay nearest her. She resolved in her quiet little soul to be all that Father hoped. He would find her well and good when the year brought round his happy return.

Soon their evening drew to a close. They gathered to sing, as usual, before they swam up to their clam shell beds. No one but Beth could get much music out of their old coral harp. She had a way of softly charming the melody out of the brittle strings. Her pleasant accompaniment graced the simple songs they sang. Meg had a voice like a princess, and she and her mother led the little choir. Amy chirped like a clam, and Jo drifted through the notes at her own sweet will. She always came out at the wrong place with a croak or a quaver that spoiled the most pensive tune. They had always gathered together to sing, from the time they could lisp...

and it had become a household custom, for the mother was a born singer. The first sound in the morning was her voice as she swam about the cave, singing like an ocean queen. The last sound at night was the same cheery sound, for the mergirls never grew too old for her familiar lullabies.

CHAPTER 2

Sea Queen's Day

Jo was the first to peek over the rim of her clam shell bed on Sea Queen's Day morning. A sadness settled over her heart that Father would not be there. So she nestled back down, pulled her night wrap over her head, and offered a morning prayer for the soldiers at the Abysmal Trench. Feeling comforted, she remembered to search in the thick folds of her night wrap for her one present from Mother. Mother loved to slip her presents into their clam shells while they slept on Sea Queen's night. Jo's efforts were rewarded when she pulled out a beautiful story-scroll. Jo, ever the reader, hooted and hollered, waking Meg up with a loud "Hurrah!"

Meg rooted through her bed the moment she opened her eyes. She found a little scroll too, one of poems and love. The two sisters congratulated each other and tucked their gifts under their arms. They swam down to the lower chambers, singing carols and laughing. Sea Queen's Day was a joyful celebration, and they greeted it with eager hearts.

The mergirls were delighted to find Nanna-pus cooking

in the kitchen. Nanna-pus was their special nickname for Nesmeralda Nanagoona Nettles. She was the kindly octopus who lived next door. Octopi, along with walruses and dolphins, pick up mer languages quickly, and they frequently socialize with the merfolk. This was the case with Nanna-pus, who had been their neighbor since Meg was born. She was over so often and the mergirls loved her so much, that they insisted on calling her Nanna-pus. Miss Nesmeralda Nanagoona Nettles was just too formal for a creature they considered more merfamily than a friend.

"Where is Mother?" asked Meg.

"Goodness only knows," said Nanna-pus, flipping cakes on the stove with four of her arms at the same time. "Some poor creature came rapping at the door shells, begging up a storm. Your mama swam straight off to help. There never was such a mermaid for giving away food and shells and whatever needs be."

"She will be back soon, I think. So let's help you cook and get everything ready," said Meg.

Some time later, Mrs. Marsh swam in through the front door. "Happy Sea Queen's Day, Marmee! Many of them!" the mergirls all shouted in chorus.

"Happy Sea Queen's Day, my daughters! But I want to say one word before we nestle down to eat. Not far away from here is a poor mermaid with a little newborn merbaby. Six merchildren huddle into one clam shell to keep from freezing, because their cave wall has sprung holes. There is nothing to eat over there. The oldest merboy swam here this morning to tell me they were suffering from hunger and cold. My mergirls, will you give the Hamfin merfamily your breakfast in honor of Sea Queen's Day?"

They were all unusually hungry, having waited nearly all morning. For a moment no one spoke, but only a moment. Then Jo exclaimed impetuously, "I'm so glad you swam home before we began!"

"May I swim along and help carry the things to the poor little merchildren?" asked Beth eagerly.

"I will take the jam and the algae tarts," added Amy, heroically giving up the flavors she most liked.

Meg was already piling the chondus cakes into one big conch bowl.

"I thought you'd do it," said Mrs. Marsh, smiling at her mergirls' generosity. "You will all swim along and help me, and when we return, we will have our ordinary kelp crisp for breakfast, and make it up at dinnertime."

They were soon ready, and the procession swam out. Fortunately it was early, and they swam along the back of the coral reef in order to collect rocks along the way. Few merpeople saw them, and no one laughed at their strange collection of conch bowls and seafloor stones.

The Hamfin's cave was poor, bare and miserable, with broken walls and ragged night wraps. A merbaby wailed, and a group of pale, hungry merchildren shivered in the parlor.

How the big eyes stared and the blue lips smiled as the mergirls swam in.

"A school of angelfish has swum to us!" said the poor mermother, sobbing for joy.

"Not only angelfish, but carpenter fish too," said Jo, and set them to laughing.

In a few minutes it really did seem as if carpenter fish had been at work there. Nanna-pus, who had the longest appendages, set upon fixing the leaking walls. She and Jo did an admirable job with the stones they'd gathered on the way. Meanwhile, Mrs. Marsh gave the mother the chondus cakes and algae tarts, and comforted her with promises of help. Then she swaddled the merbaby's little green tail as tenderly as if it had been her own. The mergirls fed the poor merchildren like so many hungry whale calves. They laughed, talked and told them stories about the Sea Queen's generosity.

"Long ago, when the very first Ocean Queen was just a mergirl," said Meg, recounting the famous story, "She swam over to the window and gave her favorite doll to a poor mergirl begging there. Her parents, lords of their reef, were so touched that they ordered gifts crafted for every merchild, rich and poor."

The Hamfin merchildren giggled through mouthfuls of tart, and looked at Meg as if she were the Queen herself.

The Marsh mergirls had a very happy feast that morning, though they didn't eat any of it. And when they swam away, leaving comfort behind, they were the four merriest merpeople in the whole coral reef. They were merry even though they were hungry little mergirls who gave away their fine food. Joyful even though they ate plain old kelp crisp on Sea Queen's Day morning. "That's being as noble as the Sea Queen, and I like it," said Meg.

Back at their cave dwelling, Mrs. Marsh glided to the upper chambers to gather vests and armlets for the poor Hamfin merfamily. The mergirls took advantage of her absence by arranging her presents on the slate table.

The presents were not a very splendid display, but there was a great deal of love done up in the few little bundles.

The mergirls added heart-of-the-seas blossoms between the gifts, greatly improving the elegance of the setting.

"She's coming! Strike up the music, Beth! Open the door, Amy! Three cheers for Marmee!" shouted Jo, somersaulting about in the cave water. Meg swam down the tunnel to lead Mother by the arm to the cushion of honor.

Beth played her happiest tune, Amy threw open the door, and Meg enacted her escort with great dignity. Mrs. Marsh was both surprised and touched. She smiled as she examined her presents and the little letters-in-bottles which accompanied them. The new gloves went on at once, well-scented with Amy's perfume. She slipped into the vest and armlets, which were a perfect fit.

The excitement had hardly subsided when there was a rap at the front door shells. Nanna-pus sailed into the kitchen, waving six of her legs toward the door, "Food everywhere! Food! Food!"

This surprised everyone. They were even more amazed when they saw nets and chests and shells of food at a quantity unheard of since the departed days of plenty. There was saltwater ice slush—two conch bowls of it, pink and white. Platters of cake and limed sea fruit candies. And in the middle of the table, four grand bouquets of hot water seaflowers.

The mergirls carried it in with tingling tails. When it was all set on the slate table, all they could do was wonder.

"Is it angelfish?" asked Amy.

"Nanna-pus," said Beth.

"Mother did it," added Meg.

"Aunt Marsh was in a good mood and sent the supper," shouted Jo, with a sudden inspiration.

"All wrong. Old Merman Laurence sent it," replied Mrs. Marsh, with an uncorked letter-in-a-bottle in her hand.

"The Laurence merboy's grandfather! What in the Ocean put such a thing into his head? We don't know him!" exclaimed Meg.

"He said he saw your breakfast parade from his window. He is an odd old merman, but that pleased him. He knew my father years ago. He sent me a polite request this afternoon. He wanted to send you a few trifles for Sea Queen's Day. I could not refuse, and so you have a little feast to make up for the kelp crisp breakfast."

"That merboy put it into his head. I know he did! He's a capital fellow, and I wish we could get acquainted. He looks as if he'd like to know us but he's bashful," said Jo. They nestled down and began to eat with *ohs* and *ahs* of satisfaction.

"You mean the merboy who lives in the big cave dwelling next door, don't you?" asked Amy, who was the littlest.

"Yes. When the catfish swam away, he was the merboy who brought her back," said Meg, motherly.

Jo added, mouth full of ice slush, "We talked over the hedge, and were getting on capitally. We talked all about waterball, and so on, when he saw Meg coming, and swam off. I mean to know him some day, for he needs fun, I'm sure he does."

Beth put down her conch bowl and whispered softly, "I wish I could send some fun to Father too. I'm afraid he isn't having such a happy Sea Queen's Day as we are."

CHAPTER 3

Theater in the Attic

They all fell to work the day after Sea Queen's Day. Preparations for the evening theater took all morning and afternoon. They were not rich enough to afford a great outlay for tickets to the Sea Theater. So the mergirls put their wits to work, turning their attic into a playhouse of their own.

Necessity is the mother of invention, and they made whatever they needed. Very clever were some of their productions. They ground corals of many colors and mixed them into sticky sea-clay. The thick paint wasn't as exquisite as squid ink, but they were able to coat driftwood in dozens of different colors. Their sets were resplendent with shiny bits of rock and shells. They even wove elaborate costumes out of old nets and night wraps.

The attic was the scene of many innocent revels. No mermen were admitted, so Jo played male parts to her heart's content. She took immense satisfaction in a sharkbone vest, given to her by a friend, who knew a merlady who knew an actor. This vest, a dove-shell doublet and a driftwood spear were Jo's chief treasures. They appeared on all occasions.

The company's smallness forced the two principal actors to take several parts apiece. They certainly deserved credit for the hard work it took to learn three or four different characters. They whisked in and out of various costumes, and managed the stage besides. This was an excellent drill for their memories. Their acting proved a harmless amusement to occupy many hours which otherwise would have been boring or lonely.

That night, a dozen mergirls nestled into seaweed cushions in front of the stage. They peeped up at the green and yellow home-weaved curtains in eager expectancy. A good deal of rustling and whispering came from behind the curtain. Plus an occasional giggle from Amy. She was apt to fits of laughter in the excitement of the moment. A drum sounded, the curtains floated apart, and the operatic tragedy began.

"A gloomy reef," according to the one playbill, was made from a few painted driftwood sticks in pots and yellow seaweed on the floor. Handfuls of friendly, baby black eels nibbled at the seaweed. They were perfectly tame, Jo had insisted, but added to the look of wild gloom.

A make-believe cave took up much of the stage. This cave was made with blue-painted driftwood for the walls and roof. Inside was the treasure of the production, a small sun crystal covered with jam to make it glow pink. A conch bowl with a lid sat on the glow crystal, and the hunched Sharkman bent over it. The stage was dark and the jam-pink glow of the sun crystal had a fine effect. Especially since more baby black eels escaped from the conch bowl when the Sharkman opened the lid.

A moment was allowed for the first thrill to subside, then Triton, the villain, swam in slowly. A driftwood spear hung at his back. He wore a mysterious gray cloak, a dove-shell doublet and the shark-tooth vest. After swimming to and fro in much agitation, he slapped his emerald tail, and burst out in a wild song. He sang of his hatred for Aquarius and his love for Yara. He resolved to kill the one and win the other. The gruff tones of Triton's voice were very impressive. He gave an occasional shout when his feelings overcame him. The audience applauded the moment the music crescendoed to its finish.

Bowing as one accustomed to public praise, Triton glided to the blue cave. He ordered Sharkman to swim forth with a commanding, "What ho, minion! I need thee!"

Out came Meg, with gray clay matted over her head and shoulders, false teeth and a triangular fin stuck to her back. Triton demanded a magic salve to make Yara adore him. Sharkman, in a fine dramatic melody, promised to make Yara fall in love.

Then Sharkman called out to the fish who had the essential ingredient for the magic salve.

Hither, hither, from caverns dim,
Watery fish, I bid thee swim!
Bring me here, with orca speed,
The sticky oil which I need.
Make it sweet and swift and strong,
Watery fish, come to my song!

A soft strain of music sounded. Then at the back of the cave appeared a gilded, fishy figure with a glittering crown and golden hair. Waving a trident, it sang...

Hither I swim, From caverns dim,
Rub the oil from my scales,
Blame me not if magic fails!

The fishy figure bent to let Sharkman sponge oil off of her left flank. Then she vanished off stage.

Sharkman brewed the salve and handed his conch bowl to Triton. After warbling his thanks, Triton departed. Sharkman informed the audience that Triton had killed a few of his friends in times past. So he has cursed Triton, and intends to thwart his plans. Sharkman belted out a loud song of revenge.

Then the curtain drifted shut. The audience rested and nibbled on kelp crisp while discussing the merits of the play.

A good deal of hammering went on before the curtain rose again. When the masterpiece of stage carpentry came into view, no one murmured at the delay. It was truly superb. A yellow driftwood tower rose to the ceiling. Halfway up appeared a window with a sun crystal glowing pinkly within it. Behind a white curtain appeared Yara in lovely silver seashells. She waited for Aquarius, her love.

Aquarius entered the scene in a gorgeous array, with a conch hat, lavender lovelocks, and the shark-tooth vest, of course. Hovering at the base of the tower, he sang a serenade in melting tones. Yara replied and, after a musical dialogue, consented to swim out to him. Then came the grand effect of the play.

Yara timidly leaned from her window and put her hand on Aquarius's shoulder. She was about to slip out gracefully when "Alas! Alas for Yara!" she forgot to fold in her tail fins. Unable to fit through the window, she tugged on Aquarius. He tugged back, and the whole tower shattered into pieces. The heaviest pieces sunk straight to the stage, burying the unhappy lovers in yellow-painted ruins.

A universal shriek arose from the audience as a golden-headed Yara emerged from the wreck, exclaiming, "I told you so! I told you so!"

With wonderful presence of mind, Sharkman swam in and dragged her out with a whisper, "Don't laugh! Act as if it was supposed to break!" Sharkman ordered Aquarius up, but before he could rise, Triton swam on to the scene. His tail was much shorter and bluer than we'd last seen him, and was of course without the shark-tooth vest.

Triton opened his mouth, then closed it again, evidently forgetting his speech.

Sharkman, still thinking quickly, reminded him, "You've come to give Yara a magic love salve!" Triton squeaked out a little, "Oh yes, I have." Then Aquarius shouted, "You fiend!" And Yara, "Hand me my spear!"

The blue-tailed Triton did not stay and fight, but swam off the stage as fast as his little fins could go. Enemy vanquished, Sharkman blessed the lovers with a song of everlasting marriage and good fortune.

The curtain closed upon the lovers bowing to receive their wedding vows, atop the driftwood rubble. A finale of the most romantic genre.

Tumultuous applause followed, but received an unexpected check. The baby eels, whom Jo had forgotten to collect back into their jars, darted into the audience. Hungry and confused, the babies tried to hide in the mergirls' hair or nibble at their ears. The audience's clapping turned to flailing, as they screamed and pulled at their hair.

Aquarius and Sharkman swam in to the rescue. They collected all the baby eels before anyone—eel or mermaid—was hurt. By the end of the ordeal, everyone was speechless with laughter.

CHAPTER 4

Curls & Corsets

"Jo! Jo! Where are you?" cried Meg at the bottom of the tunnel to the attic.

"Here!" answered a husky voice from above. Meg found her sister sobbing over a scroll on an old cushion of seaweed by a heart-shaped window. This was Jo's favorite refuge. She loved to retire here with half a dozen kelp crisps and a nice story. It was the perfect spot to enjoy the quiet and the company of her goldfish.

As Meg appeared, the goldfish rolled over on its back and fluttered its side fins. Jo rubbed its belly and waited to hear the news.

"Such fun! Only see! A regular invitation-in-a-bottle from Mrs. Gardinia for tomorrow night!" cried Meg. She waved the precious sea paper and then proceeded to read it with mergirlish delight.

"'Mrs. Gardinia is happy to invite Miss Margaret and Miss Josephine to a little dance on New Year's Eve.' Marmee says we should attend. Now what will we wear?"

"What's the use of asking that, when you know we will

wear our seashells, because we haven't got anything else?" answered Jo with her mouth full of crisp.

"If I only had a gold filigree shawl!" sighed Meg. "Mother says I may buy one when I'm eighteen, perhaps, but two years is an everlasting time to wait."

"I'm sure our seashell corsets will do, and they are nice enough for us. Yours are still as good as new, but I forgot the broken shell on the back of mine. Whatever will I do? The break shows badly, and it's too big to mend with filling."

"You must hover with your back to the walls as demurely as you can. Keep the broken shell out of sight. The front shells are all right. I must have a new ribbon for my hair. Marmee will lend me her little pearl comb, and my gloves will do, though they aren't as nice as I'd like."

"My gloves are spoiled from digging in the garden, and I can't get any new ones. So I will have to go without," said Jo, who never troubled herself much about outfits.

"You must have gloves, or I won't be seen with you," cried Meg. "Gloves are more important than anything else. You can't dance without them. If you don't wear them, I should be so mortified."

"Then I won't. I don't care much for formal dancing. It's no fun. I like to lurk about and look for adventures."

"You can't ask Mother for new gloves. They are expensive. You are so careless. Digging in the garden with social gloves! Can't you make them do?"

"I can hold them crumpled up in my hand, so no one will know how stained they are. That's all I can do. No! I'll tell you how we can manage. Each wear one good one and carry a bad one. Don't you see?"

"Your hands are bigger than mine. You will stretch my glove dreadfully," began Meg, whose gloves were a tender point with her.

"Then I'll attend without. I don't care what merpeople say!" cried Jo, taking up her scroll.

"You may have it, you may! Only don't stain it, and do behave nicely. Don't scratch your tail, or stare, or say 'Mackerels and mayhem' will you?"

"Don't worry about me. I'll be as prim as I can and not get into any scrapes, if I can help it. Now swim off and answer your invitation-in-a-bottle, and let me finish this splendid story."

So Meg swam away to 'accept with thanks' and look over her outfit. She sang blithely as she tested ways to fix her salmon-pink hair. Meanwhile Jo finished her story and her four remaining kelp crisps, and then romped with the goldfish.

On New Year's Eve, the parlor was deserted. The two younger mergirls played beauticians. The two older ones were absorbed in the all-important business of 'getting ready for the party'. Simple as the outfits were, there was a great deal of swimming up and down, laughing and talking. Meg wanted a few curls about her face, and mourned that they didn't have a heated curler. Jo offered to swim to her rescue, and led them all to the kitchen. She ordered Meg to float next to the thermal pipes that fed hot water to the stove. Declaring that the pipes were perfectly curl-sized, Jo wrapped several strands of Meg's hair around them. She pinched them in place with a pair of tongs, and assured Meg that she would have perfect ringlets in a jiffy.

"Ought they to smell like that?" asked Beth from her perch on the slate table.

"Of course," replied Jo.

"What an odd smell! It's like molting catfish," observed Amy, smoothing her own pretty curls.

"There, now I'll unwrap them from the pipe, and you'll see ripples of waving ringlets," said Jo, releasing Meg's hair.

She released the hair from the pipe, but no waving ringlets appeared. Salmon-pink hair hung limply in Jo's hand, quite detached from both pipe and head.

Jo tried to hide the burnt hair, but Meg had a handheld mirror. "Oh, oh, oh! What have you done? I'm spoiled! I can't go! My hair, oh, my hair!" she wailed, looking with despair at the uneven frizzle on her forehead.

"Just my luck! You shouldn't have asked me to do it. I always spoil everything. I'm so sorry, but the pipes were too hot. I've made a mess," groaned poor Jo, regarding the baked locks she held in her hands with regret.

"It isn't spoiled. It's just burnt off in the front. Fluff at it, and tie your ribbon so the ends come on your forehead a bit. It will look like the latest fashion. I've seen many mergirls do it so," said Amy consolingly.

"Serves me right for trying to be fancy. I wish I'd let my hair alone," cried Meg.

"I do too. It was so smooth and pretty. But it will soon grow out again," said Beth, coming to kiss and comfort her.

After various lesser mishaps, Meg was finished at last. Then by the united exertions of the entire merfamily, Jo's hair was detangled and her seashells shined.

They looked very well in their simple outfits. Meg in silvery shell, with a blue ribbon, and the pearl comb. Jo in maroon shells, and a turquoise heart-of-the-seas or two for her only ornament. Each put on one nice glove, and carried one soiled one, and all pronounced the effect "quite easy and fine".

"Have a good time, dearies!" said Mrs. Marsh, as the sisters swam daintily from the cave. "Don't eat too much supper, and swim home at eleven when I send Nanna-pus for you." As the mergirls crossed into the thoroughfare, Marmee cried from a window...

"Mergirls, mergirls! Did you remember to polish your tails?"

"Yes, yes, and Meg has perfume on hers," cried Jo. She laughed as they swam on. "Marmee would make sure we had our scales shined even if we were escaping an earthquake."

"It is one of her aristocratic tastes, and quite proper," said Meg. "A real merlady is always known by her shiny shells, nice gloves, and the quality of her scale polish." Meg had a good many little 'aristocratic tastes' of her own.

Some time later, Meg floated in front of the mirror in Mrs. Gardinia's dressing room. "Now don't forget to keep the broken shell out of sight, Jo. Is my pearl on right? And does my hair look very bad?" she asked after a prolonged examination.

"You look sumptuous, but I know I will forget to behave. If you see me doing anything wrong, just remind me with a wink, will you?" replied Jo, adjusting her seashell corset.

"No, winking isn't grown-up at a party. I'll lift my eyebrows if anything is wrong, and nod if you are all right. Now hold your shoulders straight, and swim slowly, and don't shake hands if you are introduced to anyone. It isn't the thing."

"How do you learn all the proper ways? I never can. Isn't that music downright cheerful?"

Down they swam, feeling a trifle timid, for they seldom attended parties. Informal as this little gathering was, it was an event to them. Mrs. Gardinia, a stately old merlady, greeted them kindly at the threshold of their grand hall. The Gardinia merfamily was very rich, and their hall was known far and wide for its good taste. The room was tall as it was wide. Fifty merpeople could dance up and down with ease. A hundred deep sun crystals dotted the curved walls, each framed with ruby or mother of pearl. Their warm glow sparkled over diamond studded balconies, where guests lounged and gossiped.

Mrs. Gardinia handed Jo and Meg over to Sirena, the eldest of her six daughters. Meg knew her and was at ease very soon. Jo didn't care much for lounging or gossip. She drifted away from Meg and Sirena with her back carefully against the wall. She felt as much out of place as a whale calf in a flower garden.

Half a dozen jovial merboys were talking about seahorses in another part of the hall. She longed to swim over and join them, for owning a seahorse was one of the dreams of her life. She indicated her wish to Meg, but the eyebrows went up so alarmingly that she dared not move. No one swam over to talk to her, and she stared at merpeople rather forlornly until the dancing began.

Meg was asked to dance at once, and she twirled to the top of the hall so effortlessly that everyone would think she attended every party. Jo saw a big red-headed merboy swimming toward her place along the wall. Fearing he meant to dance with her, she slipped into a curtained alcove. She intended to watch the dancing through the curtain and enjoy herself in peace. Unfortunately, another bashful merperson had chosen the same refuge. For, as the curtain swayed in the water behind her, she found herself fin to fin with the 'Laurence merboy'.

CHAPTER 5

Laurie's Alcove

"Dear me, I didn't know anyone was here!" stammered Jo, preparing to propel out of the alcove as speedily as she had swum in.

But the merboy laughed and said pleasantly, though he looked a little startled, "Don't mind me. Stay if you like."

"Shan't I disturb you?"

"Not a bit. I only came here because I don't know many merpeople and felt rather strange at first, you know."

"So did I. Don't swim away, please, unless you'd rather."

The merboy nestled down into a cushion and looked at his tail fin until Jo broke the silence. She said, trying to be polite and easy, "I think I've had the pleasure of seeing you before. You live near us, don't you?"

"Next door." He looked up and laughed outright. Jo's prim manner was rather funny when he remembered how they had chatted about waterball when he brought the catfish home.

That put Jo at ease and she laughed too. Then she said,

in her heartiest way, "We did have such a good time over your nice Sea Queen's Day present."

"Grandpa sent it."

"But you put it into his head, didn't you, now?"

"How is your catfish, Miss Marsh?" asked the merboy, trying to look sober while his black eyes shone with fun.

"Nicely, thank you, Mr. Laurence. But I am not Miss Marsh, I'm only Jo," replied the young merlady.

"I'm not Mr. Laurence, I'm only Laurie."

"Laurie Laurence, what an odd name."

"My first name is Theodore, but I don't like it, for the fellows called me Dora. So I made them say Laurie instead."

"I hate my name, too, so sentimental! I wish everyone would say Jo instead of Josephine. How did you make the merboys stop calling you Dora?"

"I thrashed 'em with my tail."

"I can't thrash Aunt Marsh, so I suppose I will have to bear it." And Jo resigned herself with a sigh.

"Don't you like to dance, Miss Jo?" asked Laurie, looking as if he thought the name suited her.

"I like it well enough if it's nowhere fancy, just open ocean and lively company. In a place like this I'm sure to upset something, or crash into merpeople, or do something dreadful. So I keep out of mischief and let Meg do the twirling and whirling. Don't you dance?"

"Sometimes. You see I've been away at the Coastline a good many years, and haven't been around enough yet to know how you do things here."

"The Coastline!" cried Jo. "Oh, tell me about it! I love dearly to hear merpeople describe their travels."

Laurie didn't seem to know where to begin, but Jo's

eager questions soon set him going. He told her how he had been at school in Vera Harbor. "We were close enough to the shore that we could watch baby turtles come into the water for the first time after they hatched. Best of all, sometimes the teachers took us up and let us bob our heads out of the water at night."

"Don't I wish I'd been there!" cried Jo. "Did you see the moon?"

"Yes."

"Can you talk the Coastline language?"

"We were not allowed to speak anything else at Vera Harbor."

"Do say some! I can read it, but can't pronounce it."

"Quaq noma a chee quana quille in roona me?"

"How nicely you do it! Let me see ... you said, 'Who is the young merlady you came with you to the party', didn't you?"

"Va, quille." Laurie nodded.

"It's my sister Margaret, and you knew it was! Do you think she is pretty?"

"Yes, she makes me think of the Coastline mergirls. She looks so fresh and stately pink, and dances like a merlady."

Jo quite glowed with pleasure at this merboyish praise of her sister, and stored it up to repeat to Meg. Both peeked through the curtain at the twirling dancers. They criticized and chatted until they felt like old acquaintances. Laurie's bashfulness soon wore off, for Jo's affected demeanor amused him and set him at ease. Jo was her merry self again, because her broken seashell was forgotten. Nobody lifted their eyebrows at her. She liked the 'Laurence merboy' better than ever. She tried to memorize his looks, so that she might describe him to her sisters. The Marsh mergirls had no brothers and very few male cousins. Merboys were almost unknown creatures to them.

Curly black hair, brown skin, big black eyes, fine teeth, aquamarine tail, tightly packed scales. Longer than I am, very polite for a merboy, and altogether jolly. Wonder how old he is?

It was on the tip of Jo's tongue to ask, but she checked herself in time. With unusual tact, she tried to find out in a round-about way.

"I suppose you are swimming off to college soon? I see you slapping away at your scrolls, no, I mean studying with diligence." And Jo blushed at the dreadful 'slapping' which had escaped her.

Laurie smiled but didn't seem taken back, and answered with a shrug. "Not for a year or two. I won't go before seventeen, anyway."

"Aren't you but fifteen?" asked Jo, looking at the long lad, whom she had imagined seventeen already.

"Sixteen, next month."

"How I wish I was swimming off to college! You don't look as if you like it."

"I hate it! Nothing but slimy scrolls and dull lectures. And I don't like the way merfolk do either, in this part of the Ocean."

"What do you like?"

"To live at the Coastline, and to enjoy myself in my own way."

Jo wanted very much to ask what his own way was, but his black brows looked rather threatening as they knit together. So she changed the subject by saying, as her tail kept time, "That's a splendid Coastline Waltz! Why don't you swim out and try it?"

"If you will swim out too," he answered, with a gallant little bow.

"I can't, for I told Meg I wouldn't, because..." There Jo stopped, and looked undecided whether to tell or to laugh.

"Because, what?"

"You won't tell?"

"Never!"

"Well, I have a bad trick of getting into adventures. And I always chip and nick my shells in the process. I tried and tried to fix the broken shell on my back, and Meg told me to float demurely so no one would see it. You may laugh, if you want to. It is funny, I know."

But Laurie didn't laugh. He studied her for a minute, and the expression on his face puzzled Jo when he said very gently, "Never mind that. I'll tell you how we can manage. There's a long tunnel to the side of this alcove, and we can dance grandly, and no one will see us. Please come."

Jo thanked him and gladly snuck to the tunnel. She wished she had two neat gloves when she saw the nice, gold-trimmed ones her partner wore. The tunnel was empty, and they had a grand Coastline Waltz. Laurie danced well, and taught her the Coastline Twist. It delighted Jo, being always so full of swish and spring.

When the music stopped, they nestled against the wall with their tails tucked under them. Laurie was in the midst of an account of a students' festival at Vera Harbor when Meg appeared in search of her sister. She beckoned, and Jo reluctantly left Laurie to join her in a side room. Meg sank into a cushion, holding her tail and looking drained of color.

"I've pinched my tail. That stupid Coastline Waltz twisted me up so terribly! My partner lost his grip and I sailed into a marble statue. It knocked over and pinched me to the floor with its awful little trident. Right here, where my tail fin is the thinnest. Oh, it aches so, I can hardly move, and I don't know how I'm ever going to get home," she said, clutching her tail and rocking to and fro.

"I knew it looked dangerous to dance with so many merpeople about. I'm sorry. But I don't see what you can do, except get someone to take you home. Or to stay here all night," answered Jo, softly petting the poor tail as she spoke.

"We can't pay for a seahorse sleigh. I dare say we can't find one at all, for most merpeople come in their own, and it's a long way to the public stables, and no one to swim there for us."

"I will."

"No, indeed! It's past nine, and dark as the Abysmal Trench. I can't stay at the Gardinia's all night. Their caves are full. Sirena has some mergirls staying with her. I'll rest until Nanna-pus comes, and then drag myself home the best I can."

"I'll ask Laurie. He will swim to the stables," said Jo, looking relieved as the idea occurred to her.

"Mercy, no! Don't ask or tell anyone. I can't dance anymore, but as soon as supper is over, watch for Nanna-pus and tell me the minute she arrives."

"The guests are swimming to supper now. I'll stay with you. I'd rather."

"No, dear, swim along, and bring me some nourishment. I'm so tired I can't stir."

So Meg nestled deep into the seaweed, and Jo swam blundering away to the dining room. She was so distracted with thoughts of Meg, she first opened the door to a cleaning closet. Then she accidentally swam into a room where old Mr. Gardinia napped on a mother-of-pearl bench. At last she found the food. Darting to the table, she knocked into a pillar and chipped a piece off another one of her seashells.

"Oh, dear, what a blunderbuss I am!" exclaimed Jo, picking up nori cakes for Meg.

"Can I help you?" said a friendly voice. And there was Laurie, with a cake in one hand and a conch of saltwater ice slush in the other.

"I was trying to get something for Meg, who is very tired. And, well, nothing is going my way. So here I am in a nice state," answered Jo, glancing dismally at her chipped corset. Thankfully it was a tiny nick. Still, when Meg saw it, she would have a fit.

"Too bad! I was looking for someone to give this to. May I swim it to your sister?"

"Oh, thank you! I'll show you where she is. I don't offer to take it myself, for I should only get into another scrape if I did."

Jo led the way. As if used to waiting on merladies, Laurie arranged the food neatly on a ledge. Then he fetched a second installment of cake and ice slush for Jo. Laurie was so obliging that even particular Meg pronounced him a 'nice merboy'. They had a merry time over the cakes and other sweets, and were just finishing when Nanna-pus appeared. Meg forgot her tail and rose so quickly that she grabbed the wall with an exclamation of pain.

"It's nothing. I pinched my tail a little, that's all," she explained. Meg used her arms to pull herself along the wall very, very slowly toward the cloakroom. Nanna-pus wrapped her arms about Meg and helped her along.

Jo was at her wits' end. They'd never make it home this

way. Nanna-pus was a tough little creature, but even she couldn't drag Meg so far to their caves. She decided to take the task upon her own tail.

Jo was outside, swimming about in search of a spare seahorse sleigh when Laurie found her. "Ride home with me," he offered. His tutor, Mr. Brooke, had just arrived to bring Laurie home. Mr. Brooke hovered behind Laurie, with two seahorses and no sleigh.

"But we wouldn't fit without a sleigh," began Jo, looking relieved but hesitating to accept the offer.

"Two to a seahorse, truly! Please let me take you home. It's on my way, you know."

That settled it, and Jo gratefully accepted and glided off to fetch the rest of the party. Meg rode on the seahorse behind Laurie's tutor. Jo climbed on Laurie's horse with him. Nanna-pus was fast enough to keep up with the seahorses on her own. Faster, in fact, but she slowed herself down to be a proper escort. So the mergirls rode away feeling very festive and elegant.

"I had a capital time. Did you?" asked Jo, shouting over to Meg on the opposite seahorse.

"Yes, until I hurt myself. Sirena's friend, Ariel Moffin, took a fancy to me, and asked me to come and spend a week with her when Sirena does," answered Meg, cheering up at the thought.

The seahorses picked up speed, and Jo enjoyed the feeling of her hair billowing out behind her. Before she knew it, she was home.

Jo thanked Laurie over and over. Mr. Brooke carried Meg into the parlor and Nanna-pus settled her into a cushion. The merboy and merman rode home, and the littlest sisters darted in to see what was the commotion.

"Tell about the party! Tell about the party!" They shouted until they stuffed their mouths with cake. Jo had smuggled three flavors home for them, with what Meg had called 'a great lack of manners.'

Jo made up for it by massaging a healing salve into Meg's aching tail fin. Meg leaned back and closed her eyes. "I declare, it really seems like being a fine young mermaid to ride home from a party to a personal nurse."

"I don't believe fine young mermaids enjoy themselves a bit more than we do. We have the best adventures," said Jo. Meg thought her sister was quite right.

CHAPTER 6

Long, Hard Days

Now that the holidays were over, it was more difficult than ever for the mergirls to return to their daily life.

"I wish it was Sea Queen's Day or New Year's all the time. Wouldn't it be fun?" answered Jo, yawning dismally.

"We would enjoy ourselves ever so much more than we do now. We could swim to parties, and ride about in sleighs, and read and rest all day. I always envy mergirls who do such things. I'm so fond of luxury," said Meg, trying to decide which of two shabby seashell corsets was the least shabby. She was too disheartened to shine her tail a second time, or dress her salmon pink hair in the most becoming way. The burden of working as governess to four spoiled merchildren seemed heavier than ever.

"I will have to toil and moil all my days, with only little bits of fun now and then. I'm poor and can't enjoy my life as other mergirls do. It's a shame!" She closed her driftwood chest with a thud and swam down to the table, wearing an injured look.

She wasn't the only disagreeable mermaid at breakfast time. Everyone seemed rather out of sorts and inclined to complain. Beth had a headache and lay in the seaweed, trying to comfort herself with the catfish. Amy was fretting because her lessons were not learned, and she couldn't find her favorite colored squid ink. Jo whistled and made a great racket, setting everyone's nerves on edge.

Mrs. Marsh was very busy trying to finish a letter-in-a-bottle, which must be posted at once. Even Nanna-pus had the grumps, for being up late didn't suit her.

"There never was such a cross merfamily!" cried Jo, losing her temper when she ripped her armlet on the door-latch.

"You're the crossest merperson in it!" replied Amy, erasing a wrong answer from her homework.

"Beth, if you don't keep these horrid catfish out of the parlor, I'll have them sold," exclaimed Meg. She tried to get rid of the catfish which had swam up her back and stuck like a barnacle just out of reach.

"Mergirls, mergirls, do be quiet one minute! I must get this off by the early mail. You drive me distracted with your worry," cried Mrs. Marsh, crossing out the third ruined sentence in her inking.

There was a momentary lull, broken by Nanna-pus.

She floated in, laid eight hot chondus cupcakes on the table, one with each arm, and floated out again. These russet-colored cupcakes were a tradition, and the mergirls loved them. Nanna-pus always made them when she was grumpy.

The mergirls particularly appreciated the warm cupcakes on the mornings they swam to work. The poor

things got no other lunch, and they were seldom home
before two in the afternoon.

"Goodbye, Marmee. We are a set of rascals this morning, but we'll swim home regular angelfish. Now then,
Meg!" And Jo swam off to work, pulling her sister out the
door with her.

"The Ocean never saw more ungrateful wretches than
us," said Jo. She took a remorseful satisfaction in the chill
currents of the Cold Season.

"Don't use such dreadful expressions," replied Meg
from the depths of her cloak. She wrapped herself up
tightly against the cold water.

"I like good strong words that mean something,"
replied Jo, folding her arms and pumping her tail.

"Call yourself any names you like, but I am neither a
rascal nor a wretch and I don't choose to be called so."

"You're cross today because you can't nestle in luxury

all the time. Poor dear, just wait until I make my fortune. I will buy you seahorses and saltwater ice slush morning, noon and night. You will attend every dance and dance with every merboy."

"How ridiculous you are, Jo! By the time you make a fortune, I will be so old I'll only dance with the most ancient of mermen." But Meg laughed at the nonsense and felt better in spite of herself.

Jo gave her sister an encouraging tap on the tail fin as they parted for the day, each going a different way. They nibbled at their chondus cupcakes and pulled their cloaks in close. Each mergirl tried to be cheerful in spite of cold water, hard work, and the unsatisfied desires of youth.

Long ago Mr. Marsh lost his fortune in trying to help an unfortunate friend. As the sand dollars ran lower and lower, the two oldest mergirls felt compelled to work. They begged to be allowed to earn a wage. Both parents eventually consented to their desire with a kiss and a prayer.

Margaret found a place as a nursery governess for a rich merfamily. As the oldest, she remembered life when her own merfamily was rich better than her sisters did. Her memories made the change in fortune harder to bear. She tried not to be envious or discontented, but it was difficult. Meg caught frequent glimpses of dainty shell corsets and diamond tiaras. She heard lively gossip about the Sea Theater, dolphin rides, and other merrymaking. She saw sand dollars lavished on trifles which would have been so precious to her. Poor Meg seldom complained, but a sense of injustice crept into her. Sometimes she felt bitter toward everyone.

Jo worked as a companion to Aunt Marsh, who had a

stiff tail and needed someone to wait upon her. To every-one's surprise, she got on remarkably well with her irascible relative.

The real attraction of working with Aunt Marsh was her large library of fine scrolls. The library had been Uncle Marsh's favorite chamber. It was abandoned to stale water and creeping seaweed when he died. Jo remembered how the kind old merman would tell her stories in strange languages and let her build castles out of dictionary scrolls. He loved this chamber, and proudly decorated it with a half dozen marble manatees. All the time and creeping seaweed in the Ocean could not change the joy carved into their faces. Between the cozy cushions, the manatee statues and —best of all—the scrolls themselves, the library was bliss to her.

Jo's life's ambition was to do something very splendid. What it was, she left time to tell. Meanwhile, she felt greatly tormented that she couldn't read or romp as much as she liked. A quick temper, sharp tongue, and restless spirit were always getting her into scrapes. Her life was a series of ups and downs, which were both comic and pathetic.

Beth was too young to work and too shy to attend school. She tried it, but she suffered so much that she did her lessons at home. Now that Father was away and Mother worked, she studied on her own the best she could.

Beth spent her long, quiet days neither lonely nor idle. She had six dolls to dress every morning, for Beth was still a merchild and loved her toys as well as ever.

All her dolls were outcasts or orphans until Beth took them into her care. One forlorn fragment of a doll had once been a merbaby with a demi-pearl smile and poseable tail.

Having led a tempestuous life, the merbaby doll was abandoned in a trash net. Beth snatched it from its fate and cared for it. Because of its poseable tail missing, she swaddled in a night wrap and pretended it was always dreaming peacefully in its bed.

Beth had her troubles as well as the others. She often sorrowed because she couldn't take music lessons or have a fine herringbone harp. She loved music so dearly. She tried so hard to learn at their tuneless old harp, that it did seem as if someone ought to help her. Nobody did, not even Aunt Marsh. Nobody noticed how she sometimes sobbed at the brittle strings. She sang through her days, using her imagination to pretend she had a harp, not a voice.

If anybody had asked Amy what the greatest trial of her life was, she would have answered at once, "My dull, green tail." When she was a merbaby, Jo had accidentally lost her in a coral reef. Amy insisted that the wild climb to get out had ruined her tail forever. All the scale polish in the Ocean could not satisfy its owner. No one minded it but Amy. The tail itself did its best to impress, but she deeply felt the want of a diamond sheen. She painted a whole scroll of twinkling tails to console herself.

"Little Inky," as her sisters called her, had a decided talent for art. She was never so happy as when copying seaflowers or painting portraits of neighborhood fish. Her teachers complained that she covered her homework with dolphins instead of lessons. Even so, she got through her lessons as well as she could. She managed to escape scoldings by being a model of good manners. She was a great favorite with her schoolmates. Besides her drawing, she was talented at language and singing. She could even read Coastline without mispronouncing more than two-thirds of the words. She had a plaintive way of saying, "When Papa was rich we did so-and-so," which was very touching. Her long words were considered 'perfectly elegant' by the mergirls.

Amy was in danger of being spoiled, for everyone complimented her. Her small vanities and selfishnesses were growing nicely.

* * *

"Has anybody got anything to tell? It's been such a dismal day I'm really dying for some amusement," said Meg, as they nestled weaving together that evening.

"I had an odd time with Aunt Marsh today. As it ended well, I'll tell you about it," began Jo, who loved to tell stories. "I was reading that boring *Alluvian's Essays* to her, and droning away as I always do, when she fell asleep. I pulled out a scroll of *Oyster Heaven* to entertain myself while she dozed. I'd just got to where they all tumbled into the Abysmal Trench, when I forgot Aunt Marsh and laughed out loud. She woke up with a wide frown. She told me to read a bit and show what frivolous work I preferred to the worthy and instructive Alluvian. I did my very best, and she liked it, though she denied it.

"I made the trench serpents as interesting as I could. Once I was wicked enough to stop in a thrilling place, and say meekly, 'I'm afraid it tires you, ma'am. Shall I stop now?'"

"She gave me a sharp look and said, 'Finish the chapter, and don't be impertinent, miss.'"

"Did she admit she liked it?" asked Meg.

"Oh, bless you, no! But she let old Alluvian rest for the day. What a pleasant life she might have if only she chose," said Jo.

"That reminds me," said Meg, "that I've got something to tell. It isn't funny, like Jo's story, but I thought about it a good deal as I swam home. At the Kingfish's today, I found everybody in a tempest. One of the merchildren said that her oldest brother had done something dreadful, and Papa had sent him away. I heard Mrs. Kingfish sobbing and Mr. Kingfish talking very loudly. Maj and Maraja turned away their faces when they passed me, so I shouldn't see how red and swollen their eyes were. I didn't ask any questions, of course, but I felt so sorry for them. I was rather glad I hadn't any wild siblings to do dreadful things and disgrace the merfamily."

"I think being disgraced in school is a great deal more awful than anything bad siblings can do," said Amy. She shook her golden curls, as if her experience of life had been a deep one. "Sabrina Puffins swam to school today with a lovely red coral ring. I wanted it dreadfully, and I longed to be her with all my might. Well, she inked a picture of Teacher Wade, with a monstrous nose and a dorsal fin. Then she added the words, 'Young mermaids, my eye is upon you!' coming out of his mouth in a bubble thing. We were laughing over it when all of a sudden his eye was on us, and he ordered Sabrina to bring up her picture. What do you think he did? He took her by the ear—the ear! Just fancy how horrid!—He led her to the recitation platform, and made her hover there half an hour. She had to hold the picture so everyone could see. I never, never should have got over such an agonizing mortification." And Amy went on with her work, in the proud consciousness of the successful utterance of two long words in a row.

Beth spoke up next, "When I swam to the vegetable shop to get some limestone for Nanna-pus, Mr. Laurence was there. He didn't see me. I hid behind the sea celery barrel, and he was busy with Mr. Cutter, the vegetable seller. A poor mermaid came in with a scrubbing sponge and a salve. She asked Mr. Cutter if he would let her do some cleaning for a bit of food. Mr. Cutter was in a hurry and said 'No', rather crossly. She was drifting away, all sad and hungry, when Mr. Laurence stabbed a big sea celery with his trident and held it out for her. He told her to 'float along and eat it', and she swam off hugging it, so happy! Wasn't it good of him? Oh, she did look so funny, hugging the big, slippery sea celery."

When they had laughed at Beth's story, they asked their mother for one. Mrs. Marsh smiled and began at once. She had told stories to this little audience for many years, and she knew how to please them.

"Once upon a time, there were four mermaid sisters. They had enough to eat and wear and keep their tails shined. They enjoyed many comforts and pleasures. They had kind friends and parents who loved them dearly. Yet they were not content." (Here the listeners stole sly looks at one another, and began to weave diligently.)

"These mergirls asked an old mermaid what spell they could use to make them happy. She said, 'When you feel discontented, think over your blessings. Be grateful for each one.'" (Here Jo looked up quickly, as if about to speak. She changed her mind and nestled back into her cushion, seeing that the story was not done yet.)

"Being sensible mergirls, they decided to try her advice. They were soon surprised to see how well off they were. One discovered that sand dollars couldn't keep shame and sorrow out of rich merpeople's houses. Another found that, though she was poor, she was a great deal happier than a certain fretful old merlady who couldn't enjoy her comforts. The third mergirl saw that, disagreeable as it was to help prepare dinner, it was harder still to go begging for it. The fourth, that even coral rings were not so valuable as good behavior."

"Now, Marmee, that is very cunning of you to turn our own stories against us, and give us a lesson instead of a romance," said Meg.

"I like that kind of lesson. It's the sort Father used to tell us," said Beth thoughtfully, putting the pins straight in Jo's weaving.

"I will be more careful than ever now. I've had warning from Sabrina's downfall," said Amy morally.

"We needed that lesson, and we won't forget it. If we do, just descend on us like the trench serpent in *Oyster Heaven*, 'Oooooo *oyssss*ters I'm going to *sssss*up upon you,'" added Jo in a spooky voice. She could not help but end a very long day in a laugh.

CHAPTER 7

Making Friends

"What in the Ocean are you swimming out to do now, Jo?" asked Meg one afternoon when the currents were particularly frigid. Jo had on her thickest cloak and long green gloves. She held a driftwood trident in one hand and a satchel in the other.

"Going out for exercise," answered Jo with a mischievous twinkle in her silver eyes.

"It's cold and dull out, and you should stay warm inside," said Meg with a shiver.

"Can't keep still all day, and not being a catfish, I don't like to nap on a deep sun crystal. I like adventures, and I'm going to find some."

Meg went back to resting on her tail and reading *The Fish Love*, and Jo swam outside with great energy. The waters were cold and heavy, but she resisted moving sluggishly. She took her trident and combed it through the plants that grew outside their cave. Tiny crustaceans fled out from the seaweed, scattering in every direction.

Crustaceans were sloppy things. When they outgrew

their limbs, they molted and just left their old skins lying about. They clotted up the plants around the Marsh's house, and made everything dirty. Jo found great amusement when she gathered the shelly bits. She pretended she was gathering treasure.

Now, the garden where Jo worked separated the Marshes' caves from that of Mr. Laurence. Both dwellings were on the edge of the great reef that made up their city. The edge was more country than city. The gardens between the dwellings were wide, and the waters quiet. A low coral hedge separated the two estates.

On one side of the hedge was a plain set of caves. This dwelling looked bare and even a bit shabby. Dull brown seaweed grew around the doors and windows.

On the other side of a hedge was a grand cave dwelling. The doors and window frames were mother-of-pearl, and the garden was full of colors imported from all over the Ocean. They had round stables for their seahorses, and a marble gazebo.

Yet it seemed a lonely, lifeless sort of cave dwelling. No merchildren frolicked in the garden waters. No motherly face ever smiled at the windows. Few merpeople swam in and out, except the old merman and his grandson.

To Jo's lively fancy, this fine cave dwelling seemed a kind of enchanted palace. She had long wanted to behold these hidden glories, and to know the Laurence merboy. He looked as if he would like to be friends, if he only knew how to begin. Since the party, she had been more eager than ever, and had planned many ways of making friends with him. But she hadn't seen him even once lately. Jo began to think he had swum away, and then she spied a brown face at an upper window. Laurie looked wistfully down into their garden, where she combed for shells.

"That merboy is suffering for society and fun," she said to herself. "His grandpa does not know what's good for him, and keeps him shut up all alone. He needs a party of jolly merchildren to play with. I've a great mind to dart over and tell the old merman so!"

The idea amused Jo, who liked to do daring things. Jo was always scandalizing Meg with her unusual actions.

When Jo saw Mr. Lawrence ride off on a seahorse, she decided to take her chances. She floated out to the hedge and took a survey. All was quiet, curtains pinned down at the lower windows. The household staff was out of sight. Not one merperson was visible except a curly black head leaning on a thin hand at the upper window.

When Laurie saw her at the hedge, his face gained a fresh sense of life. His big eyes brightened and his lips began to smile. Jo nodded and laughed, and flourished her stubby trident as she called out...

"How do you do? Are you sick?"

Laurie opened the window, and croaked out as hoarsely as an orca with a sore throat...

"Better, thank you. I've had a bad stomach, and been shut up a week."

"I'm sorry. What do you amuse yourself with?"

"Nothing. It's dull as tombs up here."

"Don't you read?"

"Read everything twice."

"Have someone swim over to visit you then."

"Don't know anyone."

"You know us," began Jo, then laughed and stopped.

"So I do! Will you swim over, please?" cried Laurie.

"I'll dart right over, if Mother will let me. I'll go ask her. Shut the window like a good merboy, and wait until I arrive." With that, Jo shouldered her trident and swished into the cave, wondering what they would all say to her.

Laurie was in a flutter of excitement at the idea of having company, and swam about to get ready. Just as Mrs. Marsh said, he was 'a decent little merman'. He honored the coming guest by brushing his curly hair and trying to tidy up the parlor. His parlor, in spite of half a dozen household staff, was anything but neat.

Presently the door shells rang out with a rattle. A determined voice asked for 'Mr. Laurie'. Then a surprised-looking housekeeper came swimming up to announce a young mermaid.

"All right, show her up. It's Miss Jo," said Laurie, swimming to the door of his little parlor. Jo appeared, looking rosy and quite at ease. She held a covered conch bowl in one hand and a delicate net with their catfish in the other. All sorts of nets existed in the Ocean. Some of them were comfortable for pets or even merpeople to ride in when they traveled.

"Here I am, net and nettage," she said briskly. "Mother sent her love, and was glad if I could do anything for you. Meg wanted me to bring some of her sea-cream puffs. She makes them very nicely. Beth thought her catfish would be comforting. I knew you'd laugh, but I couldn't refuse. She was so anxious to do something."

It so happened that Beth's funny loan was just the thing. In laughing over the catfish, Laurie forgot his bashfulness, and grew sociable at once.

"That looks too pretty to eat," he said, smiling with pleasure as Jo uncovered the conch bowl. The sea-cream puffs were surrounded by a garland of green nori leaves.

"It isn't anything, only they all felt kindly and wanted to show it. Tell your cook to feed it to you every meal until it is gone. It's so simple you can eat it, even with a bad stomach. What a cozy room this is!"

"What would you like to talk about?" asked Laurie, fluffing a seaweed cushion for his guest.

"Anything. I'll talk all day if you'll only set me going. Beth says I never know when to stop."

"Is Beth the blue-tailed one, who stays at home a good deal?" asked Laurie with interest.

"Yes, that's Beth. She's my mergirl, and a regular good one she is, too."

"The pretty one is Meg, and the golden-haired one is Amy, I believe?"

"How did you find that out?"

Laurie colored up, but answered frankly, "Why, you see I often hear you calling to one another. When I'm alone up here, I can't help looking over at your caves. You always seem to be having such good times. I beg your pardon for being so rude, but sometimes you forget to pin down the curtain at the kitchen window. Then I can see you all nestled around the table with your mother. Her face is right opposite, and it looks so sweet and matronly. I can't help watching it. I haven't got any mother, you know." And Laurie played with a rainbow shell to try to hide the little sobs he could not control.

The solitary, hungry look in his eyes went straight to Jo's warm heart. She had been so simply taught that there was no nonsense in her head. At fifteen she was as innocent and frank as any merchild. Her face was very friendly and her sharp voice unusually gentle as she said…

"I wish, instead of peeping, you'd swim over and see us. Mother is so splendid. She'd do you heaps of good, and Beth would sing to you if I begged her to, and Amy would dance. Meg and I would make you laugh over our funny stage plays, and we'd have jolly times. Wouldn't your grandpa let you?"

"I think he would, if your mother asked him. He's very kind, though he does not look so. He lets me do what I like, pretty much. Only he's afraid I might be a bother to strangers," began Laurie, brightening more and more.

"We are not strangers. We are neighbors, and you needn't think you'd be a bother."

"Do you like your school?" asked the merboy, changing the subject, after a little pause.

"I don't go to school, I'm a business mermaid—mergirl, I mean. I go to wait on my great-aunt, and a dear, cross old soul she is, too," answered Jo.

Laurie opened his mouth to ask another question. He remembered just in time that it was unmannerly to make too many inquiries into others' affairs. So he closed it again, and looked uncomfortable.

Jo quickly set him at ease. She didn't mind having a laugh at Aunt Marsh, so she gave him a lively description of the fidgety old merlady. Then she spoke of all about their theater plays and plans. She told him their hopes and fears for Father. She related the most interesting events of the little cave in which the sisters lived. Then they got to talking about scrolls, and to Jo's delight, she found that Laurie loved them as well as she did. He had read even more than herself.

"If you like them so much, swim on down and see ours. Grandfather is out, so you needn't be afraid," said Laurie, floating toward the door.

"I'm not afraid of anything," replied Jo, with a toss of her lavender hair.

"I don't believe you are!" exclaimed the merboy. He looked at her with much admiration. Although he privately thought she would have good reason to be a trifle afraid of the old merman. That is if she met him in some of his moods.

The decoration of the whole dwelling was as colorful as the Hot Season. Laurie led the way from room to room, letting Jo stop to examine whatever struck her fancy. And so, at last they came to the library.

"What richness!" sighed Jo, sinking into the depth of an exotically soft seaweed cushion. She gazed about her with intense satisfaction. "Theodore Laurence, you ought to be the happiest merboy in the Ocean," she added impressively.

"A fellow can't live on scrolls," said Laurie, shaking his head as he floated behind a table opposite.

Before he could say more, doors shells clattered together from the rooms below, and Jo rose up, exclaiming with alarm, "Mercy me! It's your grandpa!"

"Well, what if it is? You are not afraid of anything, you know," replied the merboy, looking mischievous.

"I think I am a little bit afraid of him, but I don't know why I should be. Marmee said I might swim over, and I don't think you're any the worse for it," said Jo. She composed herself, though she kept her eyes on the door.

"I'm a great deal better for it, and ever so much obliged," said Laurie gratefully.

The housekeeper popped her head back in and said, "The doctor to see you, sir." She beckoned as she spoke.

"Would you mind if I left you for a minute? I suppose I must see her," said Laurie.

"Don't mind me. I'm snug as a sea bug here," answered Jo.

Laurie swam away, and his guest amused herself in her own way. She was hovering in front of a fine portrait of the old merman when the door opened again. Without turning, she said decidedly, "I'm sure now that I shouldn't be afraid of him. He's got kind eyes, though his mouth is grim. He looks as if he has a tremendous will of his own. He isn't as handsome as my grandfather, but I like him."

"Thank you, ma'am," said a gruff voice behind her, and there, to her great dismay, floated old Mr. Laurence.

Poor Jo blushed until she couldn't blush any redder. For a minute a wild desire to swim away possessed her, but that was cowardly, and the mergirls would laugh at her. So she resolved to stay and get out of the scrape as best she could.

A second look showed her that the living eyes were kinder even than the painted ones. There was a sly twinkle in them, which lessened her fear a good deal. The gruff voice was gruffer than ever, as the old merman said abruptly, after the dreadful pause, "So you're not afraid of me, eh?"

"Not much, sir."

"And you don't think me as handsome as your grandfather?"

"Not quite, sir."

"And I've got a tremendous will, have I?"

"I only said I thought so."

"But you like me in spite of it?"

"Yes, I do, sir."

That answer pleased the old merman. He gave a short laugh and shook hands with her. Then he examined her face gravely, and said with a nod, "You've got your grandfather's spirit, if you haven't his face. He was a fine merman, my dear, but what is better, he was a brave and an honest one, and I was proud to be his friend."

"Thank you, sir," and Jo was quite comfortable after that, for it suited her exactly.

"What have you been doing to this merboy of mine, eh?" was the next question, sharply put.

"Only trying to be neighborly, sir." And Jo told how her visit came about.

"You think he needs cheering up a bit, do you?"

"Yes, sir, he seems a little lonely, and young merfolks would do him good perhaps. We should be glad to help if we could, for we don't forget the splendid Sea Queen's Day present you sent us," said Jo eagerly.

"Tut, tut, tut! That was the merboy's affair. How is the Hamfin merfamily?"

"Doing nicely, sir." Jo, talking very fast, told all about the poor, sick merfamily.

"I will glide over and see your mother some fine day. Tell her so," and with that the old merman glided out as silently as he had glided in. Jo sunk into a cushion, quite surprised that she had met the old merman and it went as well as it did. He was gruff, but not cross or fidgety like Aunt Marsh.

Laurie returned and would not let Jo swim home without a tour of the glass garden. A large glass parlor sat against the side of their caves. The water within was hot and sweet. It seemed quite enchanted as Jo swam up and down the aisles. Glowing vines sent drifting tendrils out to touch her face.

Her new friend picked the finest sea-flowers until his hands were full. Then he tied them up, saying, with the happy look Jo liked to see, "Please give these to your mother. Tell her I like the medicine she sent me very much."

"Thank you," said Jo, burying her nose in their sweet perfume.

"Would you like Mr. Brooke to escort you home, as I can't," added Laurie. He looked embarrassed that his stomach ache wouldn't let him continue with proper manners.

"No need of that. I am not a tiny merchild, and it's only two bits of a tail shake. Take care of yourself, won't you?"

"Yes, but you will swim back here again, I hope?"

"If you promise to swim over and see us after you are well."

"I will."

"Good night, Laurie!"

"Good night, Jo, good night!"

CHAPTER 8

Herringbone Harp

What good times the mergirls had after making friends with Laurie. Such theater plays with an extra player. Such water races and fish finding contests. Such pleasant evenings nestled into the seaweed cushions and sharing laughter. And every now and then, such merry little parties at the great cave dwelling.

Three of the mergirls were able to fully enjoy the new friendship. Meg could swim about in the glass garden whenever she liked, and Jo could borrow scrolls. Amy brought her inks over to paint pictures of their baubles.

Beth would not partake of these delights. Her shyness held her back from the joys at the Laurence's caves. She had sobbed for joy when she heard the Laurence merfamily had a herringbone harp. Then she sobbed again when she discovered she was too timid to cross the hedge and face the old merman. So she hovered at the kitchen window when her sisters swam over to read and garden and paint.

She hovered back, that is, until Mr. Laurence discovered her fear and set about mending matters. During one of the brief visits he made to the Marsh's cave, he artfully led the conversation to music. He talked about the dolphin choir he had seen, and the jingle shell drums he had heard. He told such charming anecdotes that Beth found it impossible to hide in her distant alcove. She drifted nearer and nearer, as if fascinated. A dolphin choir? Her imagination played their music in her ears. Taking no more notice of her than if she had been a sea bug, Mr. Laurence talked on about Laurie's lessons and teachers. And presently, as if the idea had just occurred to him, he said to Mrs. Marsh...

"The merboy neglects his music now, and the herring-bone harp suffers for want of use. Wouldn't some of your mergirls like to swim over, and practice on it now and then? Just to keep the strings limber, you know, ma'am?"

Beth floated forward, holding her arms at her side to keep from swaying in the water. This was an irresistible temptation. The thought of practicing on that splendid instrument quite made her tail tingle. Before Mrs. Marsh could reply, Mr. Laurence went on with an odd little nod and smile...

"They needn't see or speak to anyone, but just swim on in at any time. For I'm shut up in my study at the other end of the cave. Laurie is out a great deal, and the staff are never near the drawing room before evening."

Here he floated up, as if going, and Beth made up her mind to speak, for that last arrangement left nothing to be desired. "Please, tell the young mermaids what I say, and if they don't care to swim over, why, never mind." Here a little hand slipped into his, and Beth looked up at him with a face full of gratitude as she said, in her earnest yet timid way...

"Oh sir, they do care, very, very much!"

"Are you the musical mergirl?" he asked, without any startling "Eh!" as he looked down at her very kindly.

"I'm Beth. I love it dearly. I'll swim over to play, if you are quite sure nobody will hear me, and be disturbed," she added. She feared to be rude, and her tail trembled at her own boldness as she spoke.

"Not a creature, my dear. The cave is empty half the day, so swim over and strum away as much as you like. I will be obliged to you."

"How kind you are, sir!"

Beth blushed red as a crab under the friendly look he wore. She was not frightened now, and she gave his hand a grateful squeeze. She had no words to thank him for the precious gift he had given her. The old merman studied her face, and said, in a tone few merpeople ever heard...

"I had a little mergirl once, with a blue tail like yours. Bless you, my dear! Good day, madam." And away he swam, in a great hurry.

Beth had a rapture with her mother. Then she rushed up to impart the glorious news to her merfamily of dolls, as her sisters were not home. How blithely she sang that evening, and how they all laughed at her in the night. She pretended to play the harp as she slept, drifting her arms through the water as she dreamed.

The next day Beth watched at the window until both the old and young merman swam from the house. She bubbled up her courage and darted toward the hedge. After two or three retreats, she finally crossed it and reached the Laurence's side door. She slipped inside as noiselessly as the gentlest current.

She carefully swam to the drawing room, where the grand herringbone harp waited for her. Some pretty, easy music hung beside it on the wall. With trembling fingers, Beth at last touched the great instrument. She forgot her fear, herself, and everything else but the unspeakable delight of music. It was like the voice of a beloved friend.

She stayed until Mrs. Marsh floated over to call her home to dinner. But she had no appetite, and could only hover and smile upon everyone in a general state of beatitude.

After that, Beth's little blue tail slipped over the hedge nearly every day. The great drawing room was haunted by a tuneful spirit that came and went unseen. She never knew that Mr. Laurence opened his study door to hear the old-fashioned music he liked. She never saw Laurie mount guard in the hall to warn the staff away. She never suspected that the song scrolls she found pinned to the wall were there just for her. So she enjoyed herself heartily, and found that her granted wish was all she had hoped. Perhaps it was because she was so grateful for this blessing that a greater was given her. At any rate she deserved both.

"Mother, I'm going to weave Mr. Laurence an armlet. He is so kind to me, I must thank him, and I don't know any other way. Can I do it?" asked Beth, a few weeks after that eventful visit of his.

"Yes, dear. It will please him very much, and be a nice way of thanking him. The mergirls will help you weave it, and I will pay for the materials," replied Mrs. Marsh. She took peculiar pleasure in granting Beth's requests because she so seldom asked anything for herself.

After many serious discussions with Meg and Jo, the pattern was chosen. They decided on a school of sleek silver moon fish racing over a black background. She'd weave in slivers of clam shell cut to look like rocks on the ocean floor. So the materials were bought, and the armlet begun. Beth worked away early and late, with occasional help with the difficult parts. She was a nimble little weaver, and she finished the armlet before anyone grew tired of helping. Then she inked a short, simple note. With Laurie's help, she had it smuggled onto the study table one morning before the old merman was up.

When this excitement was over, Beth waited to see what would happen. All day passed and a part of the next before any acknowledgement arrived. She was beginning to fear she had offended her grumpy old merfriend. On the afternoon of the second day, she swam out to do an errand. She took poor Joanna, the doll with no tail, out for her daily exercise. As she returned to the cave dwelling, she saw three, yes, four heads peeking in and out of the parlor windows, and the moment they saw her, several hands were waved, and several joyful voices screamed...

"Here's a letter-in-a-bottle from the old merman! Come quick, and read it!"

"Oh, Beth, he's sent you..." began Amy, shaking her fins and curls about with unseemly excitement, but she got no further. Jo quenched her by snapping down the window.

Beth hurried on in a whirl of suspense. At the door her sisters seized and dragged her to the parlor in a triumphal procession. They all pointed and said at once, "Look there! Look there!" Beth did look, and turned pale with delight and surprise. There stood a shimmering, miniature harp with a letter-in-a-bottle tied to it with a golden string. A tag on the scroll read, "Miss Elizabeth Marsh."

"For me?" gasped Beth, holding onto Jo. She felt as if she should sink to the floor. It was such an overwhelming thing altogether.

"Yes, all for you, my precious! Isn't it splendid of him? Don't you think he's the dearest old merman in the Ocean? Do read the letter-in-a-bottle. We didn't uncork it, but we are dying to know what he says," cried Jo, hugging her sister and offering the glass container.

"You read it! I can't, I feel so strange in the head! Oh, it is too lovely!" and Beth hid her face in Jo's hair, quite upset by her present.

Jo opened the letter-in-a-bottle and began to laugh, for the first words she saw were...

"Miss Marsh: Dear Noble Mermaid—"

"How nice it sounds! I wish someone would write to me so!" said Amy, who thought the old-fashioned address very elegant.

"I have had many armlets about my arm in my life, but I never had any that suited me so well as yours," continued Jo. "Silver moon fish are my favorite creatures, and these will always remind me of the gentle giver. I like to pay my debts. So I know you will allow 'the old merman' to send you something which once belonged to the little grand-daughter he lost. With hearty thanks and best wishes, I remain 'Your grateful friend and humble servant, JAMES LAURENCE'."

"There, Beth, that's an honor to be proud of, I'm sure! Laurie told me how fond Mr. Laurence used to be of the merchild who died, and how he kept all her little things carefully. Just think, he's given you her harp. That comes of having a winsome blue tail and loving music," said Jo, trying to soothe Beth. The little mermaid trembled and looked more excited than she had ever been before.

"See the golden brackets to mount it to the floor so it doesn't float away. And the green sea-spider silk to cover it at night. Oh, and the little swirls and whorls carved so delicately into the bone!" Meg turned the instrument about, displaying its beauties.

"'Your humble servant, James Laurence'. Only think that he wrote that to you. I'll tell the mergirls. They'll think it's splendid," said Amy, much impressed by the note.

"Try it, sweetheart. Let's hear the sound of the miniature harp," said Nanna-pus, clinging to the ceiling with closed eyes, ready to be enraptured.

So Beth tried it, and everyone pronounced it the most remarkable harp ever heard. It had evidently been newly tuned and polished. Yet, perfect as it was, I think the real charm lay in the happiest of all happy faces which leaned over it. As Beth lovingly stroked the tender strings and kissed the soft carvings.

"You'll have to swim over and thank him," said Jo, by way of a joke. The idea of the merchild really swimming over never entered her head.

"Yes, I mean to. I guess I'll swim over now, before I get frightened thinking about it." And, to the utter amazement of the assembled merfamily, Beth swam straight out of their cave. Her little blue tail sailed straight over the coral hedge, and in through the Laurences' front door.

"Well, if that isn't the most surprising change of courage I've ever seen! The harp gave her the heart of a shark!" Nanna-pus pulled herself to the windowsill with five legs. The rest of the merfamily was rendered quite speechless by the miracle.

They would have been still more amazed if they had seen what Beth did once inside. She swam up and knocked at the study's door shells before she gave herself time to think, and when a gruff voice called out "come in!", she did.

She swam right up to Mr. Laurence, who looked quite taken aback. She held out her hand and said, with only a small quaver in her voice, "I came to thank you, sir, for..." But she didn't finish, for he looked so friendly that she forgot her speech. Only remembering that he had lost the little mergirl he loved, she put both arms round his neck and squeezed tightly.

If the roof of the cave had suddenly floated off, the old merman wouldn't have been more astonished. He was so touched and pleased by that firm little hug that all his crustiness vanished. He felt as if he had got his own little granddaughter back again.

Beth ceased to fear him from that moment, and talked to him as cozily as if she had known him all her life. For love casts out fear, and gratitude can conquer pride. When she swam home, he drifted along with her to her own gate. He shook hands cordially, and tapped his armlets as he glided back home again. The old merman looked very stately and erect, like a handsome, soldierly old merperson, as he was.

When the mergirls saw that performance, Jo somersaulted for joy. Amy nearly fell out of the window in her surprise, and Meg exclaimed, lifting her hands, "Well, I do believe the Ocean is coming to an end."

CHAPTER 9

Limed Sea Apples

"That merboy is a perfect hammerhead, isn't he?" said Amy one day, as Laurie galloped by on his seahorse, with a flourish of his trident as he passed their window.

"How dare you say so? He's got his eyes on the front of his head, not bulging off to the sides. And very handsome ones they are, too," cried Jo, who resented any slighting remarks about her friend.

"I didn't say anything about his eyes, and I don't see why you need to foam over when I admire his riding."

"Oh, my goodness! That little fish meant to say 'horse hand'. But she called him a hammerhead," exclaimed Jo, with a burst of laughter.

"You needn't be so rude, it's only a 'lapse of mind', as Teacher Wade says," retorted Amy. "I just wish I had a little of the sand dollar Laurie spends on that seahorse," she added. She spoke softly, as if to herself, yet hoping her sisters would hear.

"Why?" asked Meg kindly, for Jo had gone off in

another laugh by imagining Laurie as a hammerhead with his eyes bulging out to the sides.

"I need it so much. I'm dreadfully in debt, and it won't be my turn to have the sand dollar allowance for a month." Only one mergirl a month received the spare merfamily sand dollars. They took turns, one after another.

"In debt, Amy? What do you mean?" And Meg looked sober.

"Why, I owe at least a dozen limed sea apples. I can't pay them, you know, until I have sand dollars, for Marmee forbade me from going into debt at the sweet shop."

"Tell me all about it. Are sea apples the fashion now? It used to be nori wafers and chewing sponge." Meg tried to keep her countenance, because Amy looked so grave and important.

"Why, you see, the mergirls are always buying them, and unless you want to be thought rude, you must do it too. It's nothing but sea apples now. Everyone is sticking them in their desks during school time. We trade them at recess for ink pens, bead baubles, fish stamps, or something else. If one mergirl likes another, she gives her a sea apple. If she's mad with her, she eats one right in front of her without offering a taste. They take turns sharing with the class. I've had ever so many but haven't given them back. I ought to for they are debts of honor, you know."

"How much will pay them off and restore your credit?" asked Meg, taking out her satchel.

"A quarter sand dollar would more than do it, and leave a few bits over for a treat for you. Don't you like limed sea apples?"

"Not much. You may have my share. Here's the quarter. Make it last as long as you can, for it isn't very much, you know."

"Oh, thank you! It must be so nice to have spare sand dollars! I'll have a grand feast, for I haven't tasted a sea apple this week. I felt anxious about accepting any, as I didn't have any to share. I'm actually suffering for one."

Next day Amy was rather late at school. She could not resist the temptation of displaying, with pardonable pride, the package from the sweet shop. She left it out for only a moment before she consigned it to the inmost recesses of her desk. The rumor rippled quickly through the class. Amy Marsh had twenty-four delicious sea apples (she ate one on the way).

Her friends were sure that she was going to distribute them, and their attentions became quite overwhelming. Katiana Brown invited her to her next three parties on the spot. Maris Kingfish insisted on lending her her favorite ink pen until recess. Naia Suds, who often teased Amy for her lack of sea apples, promptly changed attitude. She floated over and offered to slip Amy answers to difficult questions. But Amy had not forgotten Naia Suds's cutting remarks about 'some merpersons whose tails are so dull, they blended right in with the cave walls.' So Amy instantly crushed 'that Suds girl's' hopes with a withering declaration. "You needn't be so polite all of a sudden. You won't get any."

A distinguished dolphin happened to visit the school that morning, and he praised Amy's beautifully inked maps. Amy was so delighted that she assumed the manner of a studious young pufferfish. But, alas, alas! Pride goes before a fall, and the honor Amy received rankled the soul of Naia Suds.

The vengeful Suds turned the tides with disastrous success. She took her revenge the moment the dolphin bowed out of the classroom. Under the pretense of asking an important question, Naia floated up to the teacher's desk. Once there, she informed Teacher Wade that Amy had limed sea apples in her desk.

Now Teacher Wade had declared limed sea apples a contraband article. He vowed to publicly shame the first student to smuggle them to school.

This was not the first law the crusty merman had laid upon his students. He vanquished chewing sponge after a long and stormy war. He shredded forbidden scrolls and fed the shreds to hungry crustaceans. He had done all that one merman could do to keep half a hundred rebellious merchildren in order. Merchildren are especially trying to nervous mermen with tyrannical tempers.

Teacher Wade was considered a fine teacher. This was only because manners, morals and feelings were not considered important. He knew everything except how to get along with other merfolk. This was his great weakness, and Naia knew it.

Teacher Wade had evidently rolled out on the wrong side of his night wrap this morning. There was a northeastern current, which always made his scales ache. And his students had not won him the praise which he felt he deserved from the distinguished dolphin. Therefore, to use the expressive, if not elegant, language of a merchild, "He was peeved as a piranha".

The word 'sea apples' sunk his mood to his tail tips. He

rapped on his desk with a passion which made Naia swim back to her seat with unusual rapidity.

"Young merchildren, attention, if you please!"

At the stern order, the friendly conversation ceased. Fifty pairs of blue, black, violet, brown, and yellow eyes fixed upon his awful countenance.

"Amy Marsh, swim up to the desk."

Amy began to rise with outward composure and secret fear. The sea apples weighed upon her conscience.

"Bring the sea apples you have in your desk," came the devastating command. Teacher Wade condemned her before she even reached the aisle.

"Don't take them all," whispered her neighbor, a young mermaid with great presence of mind.

Amy hid a half dozen in the back of her desk, and then swam the rest to Teacher Wade. She opened the package and shook the treats into the water under his nose. She knew their perfume would soften the heart of any good-hearted merperson. Unfortunately, not only did her teacher have a cruel heart, but he particularly detested the odor of limed sea fruit.

"Is that all?"

"Not quite," stammered Amy.

"Bring the rest immediately."

With a despairing glance at her lost sea apples, she obeyed.

"You are sure there are no more?"

"I never lie, sir."

"So I see. Now take these disgusting things two by two, and throw them out the window."

There was a simultaneous sigh, which created quite a

little current, as the last hope fled. Crab leg-red with shame and anger, Amy swam to and fro six dreadful times. Each trip she doomed a couple of sweet-smelling sea apples. They, looking oh, so plump and juicy, floated from her reluctant hands into the ocean waters. Outside the school cave, their perfume was much appreciated. Baby eels and trumpet fish snatched them right up. This—this was too much. All eyes flashed indignant or appealing glances at Teacher Wade. One passionate, limed sea apple lover burst into sobs.

As Amy returned from her last trip, Teacher Wade gave a portentous "Ahem!" and said, in his most impressive manner...

"Young mermaids, you remember what I said to you a week ago. I am sorry this has happened, but I never allow my rules to break. I never retreat from my word. Miss Marsh, hold out your hand."

She sent her teacher her most imploring look. A look she hoped would plead her case better than any words she could utter. She was rather a favorite with Teacher Wade, if his heart could know a favorite. It's my private belief that he would have broken his word if Naia Suds hadn't hissed just then. That hiss, faint as it was, irritated the irascible merman, and sealed the culprit's fate.

"Your hand, Miss Marsh!" was the only answer her mute appeal received. Too proud to sob or beg, Amy set her teeth, threw back her head defiantly, and bore without flinching several tingling blows on her little palm. They were neither many nor heavy, but that made no difference to her. For the first time in her life she had been struck, and the disgrace, in her eyes, was as deep as if he had bitten her.

"You will now float on the platform until recess," said Mr. Wade. He resolved to do the thing thoroughly, since he had begun it.

That was dreadful. It would have been bad enough to swim to her seat, and see the pitying faces of her friends. Or even to endure the satisfied ones of her few enemies. But to face the whole school, with that shame fresh upon her, seemed impossible. For a second she felt as if she could only sink down right where she was, and break her heart with sobbing. A bitter sense of wrong and the thought of Naia Suds helped her to bear it. So, taking the ignominious place, she fixed her eyes on the deep sun crystal above what now seemed a jumble of faces. She hovered there, so expression-less and pale that the mergirls found it hard to study. They couldn't bear the sad figure before them.

During the fifteen minutes that followed, the proud and sensitive little mergirl suffered a shame and pain which she never forgot. To others it might seem a ludicrous or trivial affair, but to her it was a hard experience. During the twelve years of her life she had been governed by love alone. A blow of that sort had never touched her before. The smart of her hand and the ache of her heart were forgotten in the sting of the thought, "I will have to tell them at home. They will be so disappointed in me!"

The fifteen minutes seemed an hour, but they came to an end at last. The word 'Recess!' had never seemed so welcome to her before.

"You can go, Miss Marsh," said Teacher Wade, looking, as he felt, uncomfortable.

He did not soon forget the reproachful glance Amy gave him. She swam past, without a word to anyone, leaving the place "forever," as she passionately declared to herself. She was in a sad state when she got home.

When the older mergirls arrived, some time later, an indignation meeting was held at once. Mrs. Marsh did not say much but looked disturbed. She comforted her afflicted little mergirl in her tenderest manner. Meg salved the insulted hand with their strongest lotion, made from pure sea lion's milk. Beth felt that even her beloved catfish would fail as a balm for griefs like this. Jo wrathfully proposed that Teacher Wade be arrested without delay. Nanna-pus balled all eight of her fists and spat black ink into the water for emphasis. Then she darted off to cook chondus cupcakes, for she felt a strong case of the grumps descending.

No notice was taken of Amy's escape from school, except by her friends. The sharpest-eyed mermaids noted that Mr. Wade made faltering efforts at kindness for the rest of the afternoon. He was also unusually nervous. Just before school closed, Jo appeared, wearing a grim expression. She floated up to the desk, pumping her tail with determination, to deliver a letter-in-a-bottle from her mother. Then she collected Amy's property and departed. She flicked Teacher Wade's cloak off its hook as she exited at the door. She wished she could thrash the whole school cave down with her tail.

"Yes, you can have a vacation from school, but I want you to study a little every day with Beth," said Mrs. Marsh that evening. "I don't approve of corporal punishment, especially for merchildren as young as you. I dislike Teacher Wade's manners entirely."

"That's good! I wish all the merchildren would swim off, and spoil his old school. It's perfectly maddening to think of those limed sea apples," sighed Amy, with the expression of a martyr.

"I am not sorry you lost them. You broke the rules, and deserved some consequence for disobedience," was the severe reply. This rather disappointed the young mermaid, who expected nothing but sympathy.

"Do you mean you are glad I was disgraced before the whole school?" cried Amy.

"I should not have handled the matter in such a despicable way," replied her mother. "It was horrid, and his fault is worse than yours. Yet you defied the class rules without a care.

"Life has many rules. Knowing which to break, which to bend, and which to keep takes much wisdom. Even grown merpeople never master this skill. In your case, I believe that you broke the rules solely because you felt that you were above them. You are getting to be rather arrogant, my dear, and it is quite time you set about correcting it. You have a good many little gifts and virtues, but there is no need of puffing around. Being delightful is not license to break life's rules willy nilly."

Amy fell quiet, pondering her mother's words. Laurie, however, was in a particularly lively humor, and sang delightfully for them that night. When he had swum home, Amy, who had been pensive all evening, said suddenly, as if struck by a new idea, "Is Laurie an accomplished merboy?"

"Yes, he has had an excellent education, and has much talent. He will make a fine merman, if not spoiled by vanity," replied her mother.

"And he isn't arrogant, is he?" asked Amy.

"Not in the least. That is why he is so charming and we all like him so much."

"I see. It's nice to have accomplishments and be elegant, but it's not proper to puff them about or use them to wheedle out of rules," said Amy thoughtfully.

"Any more than it's proper to wear all your vests and armlets all at once, that merfolks may know you've got them," added Jo. So the lecture ended in a hearty laugh.

CHAPTER 10

Seven Clamshells

"Sisters, where are you swimming off to?" asked Amy, floating into their room one Saturday afternoon. She spied them getting ready to swim out with a secrecy which excited her curiosity.

"Never mind. Little mergirls shouldn't ask questions," replied Jo sharply.

Now if there is anything mortifying to our feelings when we are young, it is to be told not to ask questions. To be bidden to "swim away, dear" is still more trying to us. Amy foamed over at this insult, and determined to find out the secret, even if she must get teased for an hour. Turning to Meg, who never refused her anything very long, she said coaxingly, "Do tell me! I should think you might let me swim along, too. Beth is fussing over her miniature harp, and I haven't got anything to do, and am so lonely."

"I can't, dear, because you aren't invited," began Meg, but Jo broke in impatiently, "Now, Meg, be quiet or you will spoil it all. You can't swim along with us, Amy, so don't be a merbaby and whine about it."

"You are swimming off somewhere with Laurie, I know you are. You were whispering and laughing together on the seaweed cushions last night. You stopped when I came in. Aren't you swimming off with him?"

"Yes, we are. Now do be still, and stop bothering."

Amy held her tongue, but used her eyes, and saw Meg slip a lorgnette into her satchel.

"I know! I know! You're swimming off to the theater to see *The Seven Clamshells!*" she cried. Then added resolutely, "And I will see it with you. Mother said I might see it, and I've got my sand dollar allowance. You are mean not to tell me in time."

"Just listen to me a minute, and be a good merchild," said Meg soothingly. "Mother doesn't wish you to swim along with us this week. Your eyes are not well enough yet to bear the splendor of this brilliant piece. Next week you can go with Beth and Nanna-pus, and have a nice time."

"I don't like that half as well as seeing it with you and Laurie. Please let me. I've been sick with this stomach cramp so long, and shut up, I'm dying for some fun. Do, Meg! I'll be ever so good," pleaded Amy, looking as pathetic as she could.

"Suppose we take her. I don't believe Mother would mind, if we bundle her up well," began Meg.

"If she goes I won't, and if I don't, Laurie won't like it, and it will be very rude, after he invited only us, to go and drag in Amy. I should think she'd hate to wiggle herself in where she isn't wanted," said Jo crossly. She disliked the trouble of overseeing a fidgety merchild when she wanted to enjoy herself.

Her tone and manner angered Amy, who began to put

her best shawl on, saying, in her most aggravating way, "I will go. Meg says I may. If I pay for myself, Laurie hasn't anything to do with it."

"You can't buy your own spot. Our places are reserved, and you mustn't nestle down somewhere alone with strangers. Laurie's good manners will force him to give you his place and take the one with strangers for himself. That will spoil our pleasure. It just isn't proper when you weren't asked. You will not see it with us. You may just sink down where you are and stay there," scolded Jo. She was crosser than ever, having just poked her finger with Meg's pearl comb in her hurry.

Sinking to the floor and hugging her tail, Amy began to sob. Meg tried to reason with her, when Laurie called from below. The two mergirls hurried down, leaving their sister wailing. For now and then she forgot her grown-up ways and acted like a spoiled merbaby. Just as the party was setting out, Amy called from the back of the cave in a threatening tone, "You'll be sorry for this, Jo Marsh. Just you wait until it's so."

"Fish sticks!" replied Jo, swishing out the front door.

They had a charming time, for *The Seven Clamshells Of The Pearl'd Grotto* was as brilliant and wonderful as the heart could wish. But in spite of the comical red lobsters, the sparkling, silver crusted-shrimp, and the drumming dolphins, Jo's pleasure had bitterness in it. The mermaid queen's yellow curls reminded her of Amy. Between the acts, she amused herself with wondering what her sister would do to make her 'sorry for it'.

She and Amy had had many lively skirmishes in the course of their lives. Both of them had quick tempers and were apt to be violent when fairly roused. Amy teased Jo, and Jo irritated Amy, and semi-occasional explosions occurred. Both of them were always much ashamed afterward. Although the oldest, Jo had the least self-control. She had hard times trying to curb the foamy spirit which continually led her into trouble. Her anger never lasted long. She quickly and humbly confessed her fault, and she sincerely repented and tried to do better. Poor Jo tried desperately to be good, but her anger was always ready to foam up and be hurtful. It took years of patient effort to find her balance.

When they got home, they found Amy reading in the parlor. She assumed an injured manner as they came in, never lifted her eyes from her scroll, or asked a single question. Perhaps curiosity might have conquered resentment, if Beth had not been there to do the asking. She offered dozens of questions and received a glowing description of the play.

When Jo swam upstairs to put away Meg's pearl comb, her first look was to the treasure chest beside her bed. In their last quarrel Amy had soothed her feelings by turning it upside down. Everything was in its place, and nothing was floating away. After a hasty glance into her various nets and satchels, Jo decided that Amy had forgiven and forgotten her wrongs.

There Jo was mistaken, for next day she made a discovery which produced a tempest. Meg, Beth, and Amy were nestled together, late in the afternoon, when Jo darted into the room. She looked excited and demanded sharply, "Has anyone taken my scroll?"

Meg and Beth said, "No," at once, and looked

surprised. Amy stared at the deep sun crystal and said nothing. Jo saw her color rise and was down upon her in a minute.

"Amy, you've got it!"

"No, I haven't."

"You know where it is, then!"

"No, I don't."

"That's a fib!" cried Jo, taking her by the shoulders. She looked fierce enough to frighten a much braver merchild than Amy.

"It isn't. I haven't got it, don't know where it is now, and don't care."

"You know something about it, and you'd better tell at once, or I'll make you." And Jo gave her a slight shake.

"Scold as much as you like, you'll never see your silly old scroll again," cried Amy, getting excited in her turn.

"Why not?"

"I fed it to the crustaceans."

"What! My little scroll I was so fond of, and worked over, and meant to finish before Father got home? Have you really fed it to those creatures?" said Jo, turning very pale, while her eyes glowed and her hands clutched Amy nervously.

"Yes, I did! I told you I'd make you pay for being so cross yesterday, and I have, so..."

Amy got no farther, for Jo's hot temper mastered her, and she shook Amy until her teeth chattered in her head, sobbing in a passion of grief and anger...

"You wicked, wicked mergirl! I never can write it again, and I'll never forgive you as long as I live."

Meg darted to rescue Amy, and Beth to pacify Jo, but Jo

was quite beside herself. With a parting slap on her sister's ear, she swam out of the room and up to the old seaweed cushion in the attic. There she finished her fight alone.

The storm cleared up below, for Mrs. Marsh swam home. Having heard the story, she soon brought Amy to a sense of the wrong she had done her sister. Jo's scroll was the pride of her heart, and was regarded by her merfamily as a literary sprout of great promise. It was only half a dozen little adventure tales, but Jo had worked over them patiently. She put her whole heart into her work, hoping to make something good enough to publish. Amy had fed the crustaceans the loving work of several years. It seemed a small loss to others, but to Jo it was a dreadful calamity, and she felt that it never could be made up to her. Beth mourned as for a departed catfish, and Meg refused to defend her little Amy. Mrs. Marsh looked grave and grieved. Amy felt that there would be no peace until she had asked pardon for the act which she now regretted more than any of them.

When they gathered to sing that evening, Jo appeared, looking so grim and unapproachable that it took all Amy's courage to say meekly...

"Please forgive me, Jo. I'm very, very sorry."

"I never will forgive you," was Jo's stern answer, and from that moment she ignored Amy entirely.

As Jo received her good-night kiss, Mrs. Marsh whispered gently, "My dear, speak with your sister. Understand each other. Forgive and begin again tomorrow."

Jo wanted to lay her head down on that motherly bosom, and sob her grief and anger all away. But she felt so deeply injured that she really couldn't quite forgive yet. So she tossed her lavender hair, and said gruffly because Amy was listening, "It was an abominable thing, and she doesn't deserve to be forgiven."

With that she swam off to bed, and there was no merry or confidential gossip that night.

The next day Amy was painting in the parlor when she heard Jo laugh outside the window. Amy looked out to see Jo and Laurie feeding the little Cold Season fish out of their hands.

"No!" Amy exclaimed, "Jo promised she would take me next time she went to feed the little fish. The school will soon migrate East. There won't be any more chances!"

"Now merchild, you were very naughty, and it is hard to forgive the loss of her precious little scroll. I think she might do it now, and I guess she will, if you bubble up the courage to ask again," said Meg. "Swim along and join her, and she'll be friends with you again with all her heart."

"I'll try," said Amy, for the advice suited her. After a flurry to gather more fish food, she swam after Jo and Laurie. The two older merchildren had already left the garden and were headed toward the gorge.

CHAPTER 11

At the Gorge

Jo and Laurie reached the gorge before Amy, and started calling in the little fish. A school quickly gathered about them, for Cold Season fish, although hardy, love to be doted upon. Jo saw Amy swimming toward them through the cloud of fish, and turned her back on her. Laurie did not see Amy, for he was carefully popping crumbs into dozens of little mouths.

"Look at all these colors. I've never seen orange fish in the Cold Season. Oh, and that one has squiggly green stripes!" Laurie said, as the colorful creatures nibbled at his thick black hair.

Jo turned to answer Laurie, but saw that Amy had almost reached them. So she zigzagged down deeper into the gorge. The fish were hungry down there, she told herself, but inwardly she knew the truth. Amy could not follow her where the currents were stronger. She would have to stay near the top with Laurie and be jealous. It would serve her right for destroying her scroll.

As Laurie noticed Jo's path, he shouted to her, "Be careful. The currents are too strong today." Jo heard, but she relished the tug of the water on her tail and hair. The gorge was dark and adventurous. Jo was just at the edge of safety from the lower rip tides.

For a minute Jo hovered still with a strange feeling in her heart. She resolved to go on, but some little whisper held her back.

The current surged just then, catching hundreds of little fish and whisking them down past Jo into the depths of the gorge. Orange, silver, pink—and a head of golden curls.

"Amy!" shouted Jo, reaching for her sister. Amy hovered, just out of reach, beating her tail as fast as she could to escape the current.

Jo tried to call Laurie, but the current caught her voice. She willed her tail to dive to Amy's rescue, but she was frozen in place. For a terrible second, she could only watch as her little sister disappeared.

Something aquamarine rushed swiftly past her, and Laurie's voice cried out, "Cut a long kelp. Quick, quick!"

How she did it, she never knew, but for the next few minutes she worked as if possessed. She pulled and tore and bit at a kelp vine, begging it to break from its stem.

At last it came free in her hands, and she dragged it with all her might down into the gorge. The current was awful, raging and resting in turns. She could only hope that Laurie was able to catch Amy before they were sucked to the bottom of the pit.

She looped one end of the kelp over an overhanging rock. Then she lowered herself down, inch by inch.

Moments seemed to stretch into years as Jo searched for her sister and friend.

She could never describe the joy when she heard two voices shouting her name. Arms were locked, tails joined in pumping, and the vine bore three desperate merchildren toward safety.

When at last they broke over the edge of the gorge, they could not rest. Little Amy was shivering badly. "We must swim her home as fast as we can," whispered Laurie so that Amy would not hear the concern in his voice.

Jo took off her cloak and swaddled her little sister. Shivering and sobbing, they carried Amy home.

Once in the warm and homey cave waters, Amy quickly fell asleep. Mother examined her and to everyone's relief, she said that Amy was only cold and frightened. So they rolled her up in a night wrap and tucked her in front of the sun crystal in the parlor.

"Are you sure she is safe?" whispered Jo, looking at the golden head, which might have been swept away forever into the gorge.

"Quite safe, dear. She is not hurt, and is already warm. You were so sensible in swaddling her and getting home quickly," replied her mother cheerfully.

"Laurie did it all. I only led her into danger." And Jo sank to the parlor floor in a passion of penitent sobs. She told all that had happened, bitterly condemning her hardness of heart. She sobbed out her gratitude for being spared the heavy punishment which might have come to pass.

"It's my dreadful temper! I try to cure it, I think I have, and then it foams up worse than ever. Oh, Mother, what will I do? What will I do?" cried poor Jo in despair.

"Never get tired of trying, dear. Never think it is impossible to grow and change," said Mrs. Marsh, drawing Jo's head to her shoulder. She kissed her cheek so tenderly that Jo sobbed even harder.

"You don't know, you can't guess how bad it is! It seems as if I could do anything when I'm in a passion. I get so savage, I could hurt anyone and enjoy it. I'm afraid I will do something dreadful some day, and spoil my life, and make everybody hate me. Oh, Mother, help me, do help me!"

"I will, my mergirl, I will. Remember this day, and resolve with all your soul that you will never know another like it. Jo, dear, we all have our temptations, some far greater than yours. You think your temper is the worst in the Ocean, but mine used to be just like it."

"Yours, Mother? Why, you are never angry!" And for the moment Jo forgot remorse in surprise.

"I am angry nearly every day of my life, Jo, but I have learned not to hurt others with it."

The patience and the humility of the face she loved so well was a better lesson to Jo than the wisest lecture, the sharpest reproof. She felt comforted at once by the sympathy and confidence given her. Her mother had a fault like hers, and tried to mend it.

"Mother, are you angry when you fold your lips tight together and swim out of the room sometimes? When Aunt Marsh scolds, or merpeople annoy you?" asked Jo, feeling nearer and dearer to her mother than ever before.

"Yes, I've learned to check the hasty words that foam to my lips. When I feel that they mean to pour out against my will, I just swim away for a minute. I close my eyes and count slowly," answered Mrs. Marsh with a sigh and a smile, as she smoothed and fastened up Jo's disheveled hair.

"How did you learn to keep still? That is what troubles me, for the sharp words foam out before I know what I'm doing. The more I say the worse I get, until it's a pleasure to hurt merpeople's feelings and say dreadful things. Tell me how you do it, Marmee dear."

"My good mother used to help me..."

"As you do us..." interrupted Jo, with a grateful kiss.

"Anger is a gift and a responsibility, Jo," continued Mrs. Marsh. "When we learn to love and accept every part of ourselves, we can learn to lead our passions. Otherwise our passions will lead us. You must not hate yourself for your anger, or you will only give it more strength to control you. We cannot overcome a desire to hurt other creatures with hatred for ourselves. Instead overcome hatred with love."

"Oh, Mother, if I'm ever half as good and loving as you, I will be satisfied," sobbed Jo.

"I hope you will be a great deal better, dear, but you must work at learning to live in peace with your feelings. You have had a warning. Remember it, and try with your heart and soul to not hurt others when you are angry."

"I will try, Mother, I truly will. But you must help me, remind me, and keep me from foaming over."

Mrs. Marsh wrapped her long and lanky merchild into her arms. Jo hugged her fiercely.

Mrs. Marsh whispered tenderly, "I will help you and love you forever, but know that you are a strong and brave little mermaid. You can overcome anything this Ocean pulls into your path. Love can never tire or change, and it can never be taken from you. You are love, my darling Jo.

Believe this heartily. Learn to treasure all your hopes, and feelings, and sorrows—even the uncomfortable ones."

Jo's only answer was to hold her mother close. In the silence which followed, she prayed without words the sincerest she had ever prayed. For in that sad yet happy hour, she had learned not only the bitterness of remorse and despair, but the sweetness of love and forgiveness.

Led by her mother's hand, she had drawn nearer to the love that surrounds and fills all Ocean creatures. The love stronger than that of any mother, tenderer than that of any sister. Love not only for her enemies, but for herself.

Amy stirred and sighed in her sleep. Jo looked at her with an expression on her face which it had never worn before.

"I wanted to hurt her. I wouldn't talk with her and learn to understand her heart, or teach her mine," said Jo, half aloud. She leaned over her sister, softly stroking the curls scattered in the water. "I love you, little sister."

As if she heard, Amy opened her eyes, and held out her arms, with a smile that swam straight to Jo's heart. Neither said a word, but they hugged one another close, in spite of the night wrap. Everything was forgiven and forgotten in one hearty kiss.

CHAPTER 12

Meg's Holiday

"Someone pinch my tail. I must be dreaming," swooned Meg one Warm Season day as she packed her travel net. All three of her sisters floated around her in the bedroom, as excited as walruses over clams.

"It is so nice of Ariel Moffin not to forget her promise to invite you for a holiday," said Jo. "A whole fortnight of fun will be regularly splendid." Jo's long arms packed Meg's neck ribbons and best armlets faster than marlins.

"And such lovely weather. I'm so glad of that," added Beth. She tidily sorted hair combs and jewel pins in her best satchel, lent for the great occasion.

"I wish I was swimming off to a holiday and could wear all these nice things," said Amy, petting Beth's catfish on its round belly.

"I wish you were all swimming along with me. Since you can't, I will remember all the adventures to tell you when I return. I'm sure it's the least I can do when you have been so kind. You've lent me so many things and helped me get ready," said Meg. She glanced round the room at the very simple set of travel nets, which seemed nearly perfect in their eyes.

The next day was fine, and Meg departed in style for a fortnight of novelty and pleasure.

The Moffins were very fashionable, and simple Meg was rather daunted at first. The splendor of their cave and the elegance of its occupants made her feel shy and colorless. But they were kindly merpeople, in spite of the frivolous life they led, and soon put their guest at ease. Perhaps Meg was able to feel that they were not particularly cultivated or intelligent merpeople. All their gilding could not quite conceal the ordinary material of which they were made.

It certainly was agreeable to float along with them in their bejeweled oyster sleigh. They kept it pulled by the finest set of black and silver seahorses. She ate sumptuously at every meal, and she could wear her best jewelry every day and do nothing but enjoy herself.

The three young mergirls became busily employed in 'having a good time'. They shopped, swam, rode in the sleigh, and called on friends all day. They swam to theaters and operas or danced at home in the evening. Ariel had many friends and knew how to entertain them. Her older sisters were very fine young mermaids. One sister was engaged, which was extremely interesting and romantic, Meg thought.

When the evening for the small party came, she found that her silk shawl wouldn't do at all. The other mergirls put on thin crepe, beaten from the most delicate of gold filigree. The fabric flowed over their shoulders and rippled in the water. It made them look very fine indeed.

So when Meg pulled out her shell corset, it looked older, duller, and shabbier than ever beside Sirena's ruby-studded top. Meg saw the mergirls glance at it and then at one another. Her cheeks began to redden, for with all her gentleness she was very proud. No one said a word about it, but in their silence, Meg felt only pity for her poverty.

Meg's tail felt very heavy as she hovered by herself, watching the other mergirls. Sirena and her friends laughed, chattered, and swam about like gauzy princesses. They had welcomed her into their cave, but were just as happy to leave her alone when she didn't interest them.

While a loneliness settled over Meg, a housekeeper swam in with a bouquet of sea-flowers. Before the house-keeper could speak, Ariel took them into her arms. All exclaimed at the lovely glow blooms, pearl trufts, and fin fronds within.

"It's for Belle, of course. Kai always sends her some, but these are altogether ravishing," cried Ariel with a great sniff.

"The delivery mermaid said they are for Miss Marsh. And here's the letter-in-the-bottle that came with them," added the housekeeper, holding it to Meg.

"What fun! Who are they from? Didn't know you had a lover," cried the mergirls, floating about Meg in a high state of curiosity and surprise.

"The letter-in-the-bottle is from Mother, and the sea-flowers from Laurie," said Meg simply, yet much gratified that he had not forgotten her.

"Oh, indeed!" said Ariel with a funny look.

Somehow the sea-flowers finished Meg's despondency. She tucked the glow blooms into her shell corset, and wove the fin fronds into her hair. Then she swam out and enjoyed herself, for she danced to her heart's content.

Meg had a very nice time, until she overheard a bit of conversation, which disturbed her extremely. She was perched just inside the glass garden, waiting for her partner to bring her a saltwater ice slush. She heard a voice ask on the other side of a towering sea-flower bush...

"How old is he?"

"Sixteen or seventeen, I should say," replied another voice.

"It would be a grand thing for one of those mergirls, wouldn't it? Sirena says they are very good friends now, and the old merman quite dotes on them."

"Mrs. Marsh has made her plans, I dare say, and will steer her little fishies well, early as it is. The mergirl evidently doesn't think of it yet," said Mrs. Moffin.

"She blushed like she did know when the sea-flowers arrived. Poor thing! She'd be so nice if she was only dressed in style. She has the perfectest paddle weed-green tail. Do you think she'd be offended if we offered to lend her a shell corset for Thursday?" asked another voice.

"She's proud, but I don't believe she'd mind, for that dowdy thing is all she has got."

Here Meg's partner appeared, finding her looking much flushed and rather agitated. She was proud, and her pride was useful just then. It helped her hide her mortification, anger, and disgust at what she had just heard. For, innocent and trusting as she was, she could not help understanding the gossip about Laurie.

She tried to forget it, but could not. The words kept somersaulting through her mind. "Mrs. Marsh has made her plans," "they are very good friends now," and "dowdy shell corset," until she was ready to swim home and sob.

She was glad when the dance ended. She retired as early as she could to the clam bed in the guest room. Here she could think and wonder and anger until her head ached.

Those foolish, yet well meant words had opened a new reality to Meg. Her innocent friendship with Laurie was spoiled by the silly speeches she had overheard. Her faith in her mother was shaken by the plans attributed to her by Mrs. Moffin, who judged others by herself. Her sense of distance from the other mergirls only grew wider.

Poor Meg had a restless night. She slipped out of her night wrap the next morning heavy-tailed and unhappy. She was half resentful toward her friends. The other half ashamed of herself for not speaking out frankly and setting everything right.

Everyone had a different energy at breakfast. Something in the manner of her friends struck Meg at once. They treated her with more respect, she thought. They took quite a tender interest in what she said. Somehow when they looked at her, their eyes betrayed curiosity. All this surprised and flattered her, though she did not understand it until Miss Belle looked up from her creamed dulse, and said, with a sentimental tone of voice...

"Meg, dear, I've sent an invitation to your friend, Mr. Laurence, for Thursday. We should like to know him, and it's only a proper compliment to you."

Meg colored, but a mischievous fancy to tease the mergirls made her reply demurely, "You are very kind, but I'm afraid he won't swim here."

"Why not, darling?" asked Miss Belle.

"He's too old."

"My merchild, what do you mean? What is his age? I beg to know!" cried Miss Clara.

"Nearly seventy, I believe," answered Meg, studying her conch bowl to hide the mischief in her eyes.

"You sly creature! Of course we meant the young merman," exclaimed Miss Belle, laughing.

"There isn't any. Laurie is only a little merboy." And Meg laughed also at the confused look which the sisters exchanged as she thus described her supposed lover.

"About your age," Nori said.

"Nearer my sister Jo's; I am seventeen in August," replied Meg, tossing her salmon-pink hair.

"It's very nice of him to send you sea-flowers, isn't it?" said Ariel, looking wise about nothing.

"Yes, he often does, to all of us, for their gardens are full, and we are so fond of them. My mother and old Mr. Laurence are friends, you know. So it is quite natural that we merchildren should play together," and Meg hoped that they would say no more.

Sirena dabbed a bit of jam from her lip and asked Meg, "What will you wear to Thursday's dance?"

"My shawl again," said Meg, trying to speak quite easily, but feeling very uncomfortable.

"I've got a sweet silk lace laid away, which I've outgrown, and you shall wear it to please me, won't you, dear?" Belle suggested.

"You are very kind," said Meg, imagining how beautiful the silk lace would be.

On Thursday evening, Belle and her maid, between the two of them, turned Meg into a fine merlady. They crimped and curled her hair. They polished her tail with fragrant salve, and then painted it with sea-flowers. They touched her lips with ground coralline to make them redder, and they laced her into a sparkling sapphire shell corset. A set of silver filigree jewelry was added, bracelets, armlets, and even a brooch to hang from her neck ribbon. The lacy silk shawl topped off the outfit, and it was even more beautiful than Meg had imagined.

"Come and show yourself," said Miss Belle, leading the way to the room where the others were waiting.

Her friends complimented Meg enthusiastically. For several minutes she floated among them, the center of new-found praise and recognition.

"You don't look a bit like yourself, but you are very nice. Belle has heaps of taste, and you're quite Coastline looking, I assure you," said Sirena. She tried not to care that Meg was prettier than herself.

Taking her friends in hand, Meg floated down to the lower levels. She swam into the drawing rooms, where the Moffins and a few early guests were assembled.

She very soon discovered that there is a charm about a fine outfit which attracts a certain class of merpeople and secures their respect. Several young merladies, who had taken no notice of her before, were very affectionate all of a sudden. Several young mermen, who had only stared at her at the other party, now not only stared, but asked to be introduced. They said all manner of foolish but agreeable things to her.

Meg was laughing at the feeble jokes of a young merman who tried to be witty, when she suddenly stopped laughing and looked confused. Just opposite, she saw Laurie.

"Silly creatures, to put such thoughts about Laurie into my head. I won't care for it, or let it change me a bit," thought Meg, and swam across the room to shake hands with her friend.

"I'm glad you swam here. I was afraid you wouldn't," she said, with her most grown-up manners.

"Jo wanted me to come and tell her how you looked. So I did," answered Laurie. "Would you like to dance?"

So Meg slipped her hands into Laurie's and they began to twirl toward the ceiling. To her complete dismay, everyone kept staring at her. She saw Belle nudge Ariel. Both glanced from her to Laurie, who, she noticed, looked unusually uncomfortable.

"Is something the matter?" Meg asked him.

"No, well—yes," said Laurie. "I don't know. Everybody is staring at us."

Meg felt absolutely mortified. She hoped the stares wouldn't make Laurie uncomfortable about their friendship. She squeezed Laurie's hand, and the two of them whirled off to a quiet alcove in a dining area.

"Why are they all staring at us?" Laurie asked.

"You know merfolk, they can be quite peculiar about things," was all that Meg would say. Meg was relieved that Laurie let the conversation drop, and like his usual jolly self, swam off to fetch them food.

When the holiday ended, Meg returned home and nested in the parlor with Jo and Mother. She told them how shabby and ignored she felt. Then, how they all swarmed around her with attention after the sea-flowers arrived. Finally, she bubbled up the courage to tell what she overheard about Laurie.

"Mother, do you have 'plans', as Mrs. Moffin said?" asked Meg bashfully.

"Yes, my dear, I have a great many, all mothers do, but

mine differ somewhat from Mrs. Moffin's, I suspect. I will tell you some of them."

"I want my merchildren to be happy. To be admired, loved, and respected. To lead useful, pleasant lives. All this with as little care and sorrow as possible."

"My dear mergirls, I am ambitious for you, but not to have you marry rich mermen merely because they are rich, or have splendid caves to live in. Wealth is a needful and precious thing, and even a noble thing when properly used. Yet I never want you to think sand dollars are the first or only prize to strive for.

"More than all else, I want you to find respect for who you are, not for who you marry."

"Oh, Mother, do you think that is what happened to me? That's why everyone paid attention to me after the sea-flowers?" asked Meg.

"Did the merpeople treat you differently from the first dance to the second?" Asked Jo, studiously.

"Yes," said Meg with a little sob. "And all that changed was that I was in fancy clothes and they thought I was going to marry Laurie. Won't anyone love me for me?"

"We'll never find mates," said Jo stoutly.

"Don't be troubled, my dear mergirls. Poverty seldom daunts a sincere lover. Some of the best and most honored mermaids I know were poor mergirls, but so true of spirit that they married happily. Leave these things to time.

"Remember this, marriage without respect is very trying indeed. Better to be happy without a mate than unhappily married. Respect yourselves, and only entertain friends who respect you," said Mrs. Marsh decidedly.

"Both your father and I hope and trust that our

mergirls, whether married or single, will be treasured. You are worth all the Ocean to us. Hold your worth in your hearts."

"We will, Marmee, we will!" cried both, with all their hearts, as she bade them good night.

CHAPTER 13

The Pickens Club

As Warm Season came on, a new set of amusements became the fashion. Gardening, leisurely swims and flower hunts employed the fine days. On cold days, they had indoor diversions, some old, some new, all more or less original. One of these was the 'P.C.'. Secret societies were popular among the distinguished. It was only proper for the mergirls to have one. Since all four of them admired the famed writer Pickens, they chose his name for their own. Their secret society became the Pickens Club.

With a few interruptions, they had kept this up for a year. They met every Saturday evening in the attic. The weekly ceremonies were as follows: Four seaweed cushions were arranged in a circle on the floor. Four white shells labeled the seats, with a big 'P.C.' in different colors on each. A news-scroll waited in the middle of the circle, the *Pickens Portfolio.* Each mergirl contributed something to the news, while Jo, who reveled in words and ink, was the editor.

At seven o'clock Saturday evening, the four members ascended to the clubroom. They pinned their badges onto their corsets, and then drifted to their seats with great solemnity. Meg, as the eldest, was Daisy Pickens. Jo, being of a literary turn, Anchovy Snodgrass. Beth, because she was blue and russet, Retta Bluefish. Amy, who was always trying to do what she couldn't, was Swordfish Pokes. Daisy Pickens, the president, read the news-scroll to the rest of the club. They delighted in the original tales, poetry, local news, and funny advertisements. They took hints, which reminded each other of their faults and shortcomings, with good nature. If a member wished to speak, she floated up out of her cushion into the water above it, and spoke down to the seated club.

On one occasion, Ms. Pickens put on a pair of spectacles without any glass. She floated up, holding the news-scroll and 'ah-hemmed'. She stared hard at Ms. Snodgrass, who draped her tail sloppily over the side of her cushion and onto the cave floor. When Snodgrass arranged herself properly, Pickens began to read:

"THE PICKENS PORTFOLIO"

WEEK 52
   POET'S CORNER
   ANNIVERSARY ODE

> *Again we meet to celebrate*
> *With badge and solemn rite,*
> *Our fifty-second anniversary,*
> *In Pickens Hall, tonight.*

We all are here in perfect health,
  None gone from our small band:
Again we see each well-known face,
  And press each friendly hand.

Our Pickens, always at her post,
  With reverence we greet,
As, spectacles on nose, she reads
  Our well-filled weekly sheet.

Old six-foot Snodgrass looms on high,
  With elephant seal grace,
And beams upon the company,
  Comic wisdom in her face.

Next our peaceful Bluefish comes,
  So rosy, plump, and sweet,
Who chokes with laughter at the puns,
  And tangles up her seat.

Prim little Pokes too is here,
  With every hair in place,
A model of propriety,
  Though she hates to scrub her face.

The year is gone, we still unite
  To joke and laugh and read,
And glide the path of literature
  That does to glory lead.
Long may our scroll read on well,
  Our club unbroken be,

*And coming years bless in full
Society: 'P. C.'.*

By A. Snodgrass

THE HISTORY OF A SEA APPLE

Once upon a time, a farmer planted a juicy sea apple plant in his garden. Now some merfolks think the sea apple is a friendly animal who grows fruit on its head for the good of all. Others say it is a plant who doesn't know what it is doing. Truth is, we'll never know—except that it tastes good.

After a while the sea apple, plant or animal, started sprouting fruit atop its oval body. When they were ripe, the farmer plucked one and took it to market. A grocer bought it and put it in her shop.

That same morning, a little mergirl with golden curls and crystal-white eyes, went and bought it for her mother. She lugged it home, cut it up, and her friend the octopus taught her how to lime it.

Two weeks later, it was eaten by a merfamily named Marsh.

By R. Bluefish

Ms. Pickens, *Ma'am:*—

I address you upon the subgect of a mermaid named Pokes who makes trouble in this club. She apologizes for laughing and interripting things. I hope you will pardone her trouble and let her submit a Coastline fable.

She has one in her head that is just waiting to get out. If only she didn't have so much sckool work.

Yours respectibly,
S. POKES

[The above is a handsome acknowledgment of past misdemeanors. If our young friend studied spelling, it would be well.]

THE PUBLIC BEREAVEMENT

It is our painful duty to record the sudden and mysterious disappearance of our cherished friend, Mrs. Snowfin Paw Paw. This lovely and beloved catfish was the pet of a large circle of warm and admiring friends. Her beauty attracted all eyes, and her graces and virtues endeared her to all hearts. Her loss is deeply felt by the whole community.

She was last seen near the thoroughfare, watching the grocer's sleigh with great longing. It is feared that some villain, tempted by her charms, basely stole her. Weeks have passed, but no trace of her has been discovered. We relinquish all hope, and weep for her as one lost to us forever.

Our sympathizing Anchovy sends the following gem:

A LAMENT
FOR SNOWFIN PAW PAW

> *We mourn the loss of our little fish,*
> *And sigh o'er her hapless fate,*
> *She'll nevermore swim or swish,*
> *Our loss is ever so great.*
> *Another catfish takes up her place*
> *A catfish who is not she*
> *We'll miss Snowfin's fishy grace*
> *For'ere in this deep blue sea.*

Bereavement by Daisy P., Poem Anchovy S.

ADVERTISEMENTS

MISS URSULA BALEEN, the accomplished strong-minded lecturer, will deliver her famous lecture on "WHALES IN THE SOCIAL ORDER" at Pickens Hall, next Saturday Evening, after the usual performances.

A WEEKLY MEETING will be held at Kitchen Place, to teach young merchildren how to cook. Nesmeralda Nanagoona Nettles will preside, and all are invited to attend.

THE SCRUBBING SOCIETY will meet on Wednesday next, and parade through the full length of the attic. All members to appear in uniform and present their sponges at nine precisely.

MRS. JOANNA BETH will open her new assortment of Doll's Millinery next week. The latest Coastline fashions have arrived, and orders are respectfully solicited.

A NEW PLAY will appear at the Attic Theater, in the course of a few weeks. It will surpass anything ever seen on the Deep Ocean stage. "TRITON AVENGES," is the name of this thrilling drama!!!

HINTS

If D.P. didn't use so much suds on her hands, she wouldn't always be late at breakfast. A.S. is requested not to whistle when others are trying to sleep. R.B. please don't forget Amy's armlet. S.P. must not fret because her tail polish is not a Coastline recipe.

WEEKLY REPORT

- Meg—Good.
- Jo—Bad.
- Beth—Very Good.
- Amy—Middling.

When the President finished reading the scroll, a round of applause broke out. Then Ms. Snodgrass floated up from her cushion to make a proposition.

"Ms. President and distinguished mermaids," she began, assuming a parliamentary attitude and tone. "I wish to propose the admission of a new member—one who highly deserves the honor, and would be deeply grateful for it. This addition would add immensely to the spirit of the club, and the literary value of the news-scroll. This member would be no end of jolly and nice. I propose Mr. Theodore Laurence as an honorary member of the Pickens Club. Please now, do accept him."

Jo's sudden change of tone made the mergirls laugh, but all looked rather anxious. No one said a word as Snodgrass sank back into her cushion.

"We'll put it to a vote," said the President, rising. "All in favor of this motion, please say, 'Aye'."

A loud response from Snodgrass, followed, to everybody's surprise, by a timid one from Beth.

"Contrary-minded say, 'No'."

Meg and Amy were contrary-minded, and Ms. Pokes rose to say with great elegance, "We don't wish any merboys. They only joke and tell our secrets. This is a mermaid's club, and we wish to be private and proper."

"It's true. I'm afraid he'll laugh at our scroll, and make fun of us afterward," observed Pickens. She pulled at the little salmon-pink curl on her forehead, as she always did when doubtful.

Up floated Snodgrass, very much in earnest. "Ma'am, I give you my word as a distinguished literary mermaid. Laurie won't do anything of the sort. He likes to write, and he'll give a tone to our contributions and keep us from being sentimental, don't you see? We can do so little for him, and he does so much for us. I think the least we can do is to offer him a place here, and make him welcome."

This artful allusion to benefits conferred caused Blue-fish to rise into the water. She spoke as if she had quite made up her mind, "Yes. We ought to do it, even if we are afraid. I say he may join, and his grandpa, too, if he likes."

This spirited burst from Beth jolted the club, and Jo floated over to tap tail fins approvingly. "Now then, vote again. Everybody remember it's our Laurie, and say, 'Aye!'" she cried in her Snodgrass voice excitedly.

"Aye! Aye! Aye!" replied three voices at once.

"Good! Bless you! Now, as there's nothing like the present, our new member!" To the dismay of the rest of the club, Jo threw open a large driftwood chest and displayed Laurie curled up inside it. The merboy flushed and twinkled with suppressed laughter.

"You rogue! You traitor! Jo, how could you?" cried the three mergirls, as Snodgrass helped her friend unfold himself from the tiny space. Producing both a cushion and a shell badge, she inducted him in a jiffy.

"The nerve of you two rascals is amazing," began Daisy Pickens. She tried to muster an awful frown, but only succeeded in producing an amiable smile.

The new member was equal to the occasion. He rose into the water with a grateful salutation to the Chair. Then he spoke in the most engaging manner, "Ms. President and distinguished mermaids, allow me to introduce myself as Seabug Wells. I am the very humble servant of the club."

"Good! Good!" cried Jo, grabbing her driftwood trident and waving it affirmingly.

"My faithful friend and noble patron," continued Laurie with a wave of the hand, "has presented me so flatteringly. She must not be blamed for the base stratagem of tonight. I planned it, and she only gave in after lots of teasing."

"Come now, don't lay it all on yourself. You know I proposed the driftwood chest," broke in Snodgrass, who was enjoying the joke amazingly.

"Never mind what she says. I'm the bottom-feeder that did it, ma'am," said the new member, with a nod to Daisy Pickens. "But on my honor, I never will do so again. I henceforth devote myself to the interest of this immortal club."

"Hear! Hear!" cried Jo, pounding the base of her trident on the driftwood chest.

"Continue, continue!" added Pokes and Bluefish, while the President bowed benignly.

"I merely wish to say that I have made you a token of my gratitude for the honor done to me. I intend to promote friendly relations between adjoining nations. I have set up a post office in the hedge in the lower corner of the garden. It's an old grocer's chest, so it will hold all sorts of things, and save us valuable time. Letters-in-bottles, scrolls, and satchels can be passed in there. As each nation has a key, it will be uncommonly secure, I fancy. Allow me to present the club key with many thanks for your favor."

Great applause erupted as Mr. Wells deposited a little key in Meg's hand and subsided. Jo's trident thunked wildly. It was some time before order could be restored. A long discussion followed. It was such an unusually lively meeting, that it did not adjourn until a late hour. They swam out of the attic with three merry cheers for the new member.

No one ever regretted the admittance of Seabug Wells. A more devoted, well-behaved, and jovial member no club could have. He certainly did add 'spirit' to the meetings, and 'a tone' to the news-scroll. His orations convulsed his hearers and his contributions were excellent. He was patriotic, classical, comical, or dramatic, but never sentimental. Jo regarded him with great respect, and challenged herself to bring her own composition to a higher standard.

The post office was a capital little institution and flourished wonderfully. Nearly as many strange things passed through it as through the real Ocean Post. Tragedies and neck ribbons. Poetry and hairpins. Garden seeds and squid ink. Music and ginger-kelp crisp, invitations, scoldings, and kittenfish. Old merman Laurence liked the fun, and amused himself by sending odd bundles, mysterious messages, and funny telegrams. His gardener, who was smitten with Nanna-pus' charms, actually sent a declaration of love into Jo's care. How they laughed when the secret came out. They never dreamed how many love letters that little post office would hold in the years to come.

CHAPTER 14

Laurie's Picnic

One fine morning a little letter-in-a-bottle arrived from Laurie. He inked in a big, dashing hand...

Dear Jo, What ho!

Some Coastline mergirls and merboys are swimming over to see me tomorrow and I want to have a jolly time. If the currents agree, I'm going to sleigh the whole crew to Longweeden Field to lunch and waterball. We'll cook in the wild, make messes, and host all sorts of adventures. They are nice merpeople, and like such things. I want you all to ride along with us. We can't let Beth stay back at the cave at any price, and nobody will worry her. Don't bother about rations, I'll see to that and everything else, only do ride along!

In a tailspin of hurry, Yours ever, Laurie.

"Here's richness!" cried Jo, floating in to tell the news to Meg.

"Of course we can ride to Longweeden, Mother? It will be such a help to Laurie, for I can host adventures, and Meg see to the lunch, and the merchildren be useful in some way."

"I hope the Waverlys are not fine grown-up merpeople. Do you know anything about them, Jo?" asked Meg.

"Only that there are four of them. Kayla is older than you, Fred and Frank (twins) about my age, and a little mergirl (Grace), who is nine or ten. Laurie knew them abroad, and liked the merboys. I fancied, from the way he soured up his mouth in speaking of her, that he didn't admire Kayla much."

"I'm so glad my Coastline style neck ribbon is clean, it's just the thing and so becoming!" observed Meg complacently. "Have you anything decent, Jo?"

"Rugged kelp armlets and a thick-shelled corset are good enough for me. I will sleigh and swim about, so I don't want any delicate baubles to think of. You'll come, Beth?"

"If you won't let any merboys talk to me."

"Not a merboy!"

"I like Laurie, and I'm not afraid of Mr. Brooke, he is so kind. But I don't want to play, or sing, or say anything. I'll work hard and not trouble anyone, and you'll take care of me, Jo, so I'll swim along."

"That's my good mergirl. Now let's dash about, and do double duty today. Tomorrow we can play with free minds," said Jo, taking the night wrap comb in hand.

The next day, Laurie swam over to present his friends to the Marsh mergirls in the most cordial manner. There was a mermaid, a little mergirl, and twin merboys. They all dressed in the latest Coastline fashions, and one of the merboys had his arm in a sling. The garden was the reception room, and for several minutes a lively scene was enacted there.

Meg was curious why Kenn Moffin joined the group, but Kayla, the new mermaid, said he came to see her. Jo understood why Laurie 'soured up his mouth' when speaking of Kayla. That young merlady had a standoff-don't-touch-me attitude. Beth observed the new merboys and decided that even though they were twins, they were nothing alike. She felt that the injured one was not 'dreadful', but gentle and sweet. She would be kind to him on that account. The other one seemed quite riotous, and she would do her best to avoid him.

Amy found Grace a well-mannered, merry, little merperson. After staring shyly at one another for a few minutes, they suddenly became very good friends.

The tents, lunch, and waterball utensils were already sent to the picnic site, so the party soon embarked. The two oyster sleighs pushed off together, leaving Mr. Laurence waving behind them. Laurie and Jo guided one sleigh. Mr. Brooke and Kenn guided the other. Fred Waverly, the riotous twin, did his best to upset both by flipping his tail around.

Meg, in the other sleigh, was delightfully situated. She rode face to face with the mermen, who both loved to be admired. So they held their seahorse reigns with uncommon 'skill and dexterity'.

Mr. Brooke was a grave, silent young merman, with handsome brown eyes and a pleasant voice. Meg liked his quiet manners and considered him an encyclopedia of useful knowledge. He never talked to her much, but he looked at her a good deal, and she felt sure that he did not regard her with aversion.

They sailed a good ways from their city in the coral reef, to wide open fields of ocean seagrass. The grass was long as a full-grown mermaid. It waved in the currents and smelled salty and wild. It was just the length to make waterball challenging, but not impossible.

"Welcome to Picnic Laurence!" said the young host, as they disembarked with exclamations of delight. "Isn't it grand?"

"This granite slab here is our kitchen. That elkhorn coral on the edge of the seagrass is our gathering place. Now, let's have a game before it gets hot, and then we'll see about dinner."

They quickly pitched the tent and assembled the waterball equipment. Frank, Beth, Amy, and Grace nestled on the branches of the elkhorn coral to watch the game played by the other six. Most of the wickets were posted on stakes that held them above the seagrass for easy observation. The few that were assembled on the ocean floor made for great suspense and cheering. The players dove into the thick seagrass to make their shots. The audience hovered anxiously, peering into the thicket for any sign of progress. When the player's head poked out from the grass with a "yeah" or a "nay", the audience cheered and somersaulted.

The teams for the first game of Camp Laurence divided as follows. Mr. Brooke chose Meg and Fred. Laurie took Kayla and Jo and Kenn. They all choose to play with zest and passion.

Jo and Fred had several skirmishes and once narrowly escaped fighting words. Jo was through the last wicket and had missed the stroke, which failure foamed her up a good deal. Fred was close behind her and his turn came before hers. He gave a stroke, his ball hit the wicket, and floated an inch on the wrong side. No one was very near, and swimming up to examine, he gave the ball a sly nudge with the tip of his tail. It responded to his tap, and floated just through the wicket, giving him the score.

"I'm through! Now, Miss Jo, I'll show you how to win," cried the young merman, swinging his mallet through the water for another blow.

"You pushed it with your tail. I saw you. It's my turn now," said Jo sharply.

"Upon my word, I didn't move it. It drifted a bit, perhaps, but that is allowed. So, float off please, and let me have a go at the victory stake."

"We don't play tricks like that in my merfamily, but you can, if you choose," said Jo angrily.

"You seem tricky enough to me. There you go!" replied Fred, batting her ball far away.

Jo opened her lips to say something rude, but restrained herself in time. She colored up to her forehead and hovered a minute, hammering down a wicket with all her might. Fred hit the stake and declared a point for his team with much exultation.

She swam off to get her ball, and was a long time finding it among the seagrass. But when she replied, she looked cool and quiet, and waited her turn patiently. It took several strokes to regain the place she had lost, and when she got there, the other side had nearly won.

"My merfamily does have a trick. Our trick is being generous to our enemies," said Jo, with a look that made the merboy redden. "Especially when we beat them," she added, as she won the game with a clever stroke.

Laurie began a backflip, then remembered that it wouldn't do to exult over the defeat of his guests. So he stopped in the middle of the cheer to whisper to his friend, "Good for you, Jo! He did cheat. I saw him. We can't tell him so, but he won't do it again, take my word for it."

Meg drew her aside, under pretense of pinning up a loose braid. She said approvingly to her sister, "It was dreadfully provoking, but you used your anger just perfectly, and I'm so glad, Jo."

"Don't praise me, Meg, for I could pull his tail this minute. I should certainly have foamed over if I hadn't stayed among the seagrass until I got my rage under control enough to keep my tail from thrashing him. It's still thrashing a bit now. So I hope he'll keep out of my way," replied Jo, biting her lips as she glowered at Fred from across the swaying seaweeds.

"Time for lunch," said Mr. Brooke, his stomach rumbling audibly. "Who can make sandwiches?"

"Jo can," said Meg, glad to recommend her sister. So Jo, feeling that her recent lessons in cookery were to do her honor, swam over to preside over the sandwich making. The smallest merchildren gathered pretty pebbles to decorate the outdoor table. Miss Kayla sketched the picnic scene on a small art board, while Beth wove seagrass placemats.

The merchildren soon set the granite slab with an inviting array of eatables. They arranged the pink, blue and silver pebbles they'd found on it with pride. Jo announced that the sandwiches were ready. Everyone nestled in for a hearty meal. Their exercise had given them wholesome appetites. A very merry lunch it was, for everything seemed fresh and funny. Frequent peals of laughter startled a venerable walrus who gathered clams nearby. There was a pleasing unevenness to the stone table, and the slope produced many mishaps to bowls and baubles. Sand mixed with their sandwiches. Sea bugs slipped into the jam. Tiny Hot Season fish nibbled at the merchildren's ears, begging for food. Three wide-headed dolphins peeped over a hedge of pink coral, and a catfish swam off with a cake.

"There's seasoning here," said Laurie, as he handed Jo a saucer of brown dulse.

"Thank you, I prefer sea bugs," she replied, fishing up two unwary little ones who had nestled in the brown leaf.

"What will we do when we can't eat anymore?" asked Laurie, as they both laughed and ate out of one bowl, like regular soldiers.

"Have games until the cool evening current rolls in. I brought Authors, and I dare say Miss Kayla knows something new and nice. Swim over and ask her. She's company, and you ought to visit with her more."

"Aren't you company too? I thought she'd suit Brooke, but he keeps talking to Meg. Kayla just stares at them and fidgets that extravagantly painted tail of hers. I'll swim off to them, so you needn't try to preach propriety, for you can't do it, Jo."

Miss Kayla did know several new games. She explained to them the rules of Rigmarole.

"One merperson begins a story, any nonsense you like, and tells as long as he or she pleases. The only rule is to stop at some exciting point, when the next takes it up and does the same. It's very funny when well done, and makes a perfect jumble of tragical comical stuff to laugh over."

This struck the group as delightful. As the merchildren could not eat anymore, they all gathered at the base of the elkhorn coral to play at once.

CHAPTER 15

Rigmarole

Floating on the green algae at the foot of the elkhorn coral, Mr. Brooke obediently began the story. He softly swished his tail as he spoke, his handsome brown eyes fixed upon the blue Ocean above them.

"Once upon a time, a warrior octopus went out into the Ocean to seek his fortune. He was a poor chap, with only four stubby swords and two dented shields. He'd fight with four arms, you see. He'd use two others to hold up the shields and the remaining two to propel him.

"He traveled a long while, nearly eight-and-twenty years. He had a hard time winning anything, until he came to the palace of a good old Sea King. The Sea King offered a reward to anyone who could tame and train a fine but wild seahorse colt, of which he was very fond. The warrior octopus agreed to try, and got on slowly but surely. The colt was gallant and soon learned to love his eight-armed rider, though he was skittish and wild.

"Every day, the warrior octopus rode the seahorse colt

through the city reef. As he rode, he looked everywhere for a face which he had seen many times in his dreams, but never found.

"One day, as he went bobbing along a quiet thorough-fare, he saw the face in the window of a ruinous cavern. He was delighted, until he discovered she was one of several captive princesses kept there by a spell.

"The warrior octopus wished intensely that he could free them. He swam to the cavern to ask how he could help. He knocked at the door with all eight arms. The door creaked open, and he beheld..."

"A ravishingly lovely mermaid, who exclaimed, with a sob of rapture, 'At last! At last!'" continued Kayla, who had read Coastline novels, and admired the style. "'Tis she!' cried the warrior octopus, and sank before her in an ecstasy of joy. 'Oh, rise!' she said. 'Never! Until you tell me how I may rescue you,' swore the octopus, still kneeling on three of his appendages. 'Go to my captor in the coral kitchen, brave heart, and save me from despair.' After these words from the mermaid, the octopus darted down the corridor. He flung open the door to the coral kitchen. He was about to enter, when he received..."

"A stunning whack from a heavy dictionary scroll—which an old dolphin in a black gown had swung at him," said Frank. "He had entered the library by mistake! Instantly, Sir Octopus recovered himself, apologized to the dolphin, and turned to find the coral kitchen.

"In a fine display of bravery, he smashed in the kitchen door. At the back of the room was a sight that made him spit ink..."

"A long figure, all in white, with a veil over its face,"

went on Meg. "The figure hovered, assembling deathly sandwiches. Sensing the octopus, it turned and beckoned. The octopus raised his two shields in front of him, but the specter laughed and waved threateningly before him a..."

"Satchel of limed sea apples," said Jo, in a sepulchral tone, which convulsed the audience. "'Thankee,' said the warrior politely. He took a bite and sneezed seven times so violently that his head fell off. The ghost laughed and packed the Octopus in the pantry, with eleven other warriors who had sought to rescue the princesses.

"But, the octopus wasn't dead! He hid his head within his many arms. When the pantry door closed, he popped his head back on, gave it a good twist, and..."

"Oh, gracious! What will I say?" cried Amy, as Jo ended her rigmarole, with the brave octopus freshly resurrected.

"Well, he broke out of the pantry, and the nice mermaid princess welcomed him. Then the octopus and the princess took pity on the other headless warriors. They promised the bodies that they would return someday with new heads. So they very quietly opened the castle door and..."

"The seahorse colt!" continued Laurie promptly. "Just then the colt proved how much it loved the octopus. It charged in and trampled the ghost to death.

"They rode the colt the whole way back to the Sea King. The octopus had to hold his head on since it was still loose. When they got there, the King gave them the biggest reward. What he gave them, I will let Frank tell you."

"I can't. I'm not playing, I never do," said Frank. He was dismayed that he'd have to think up a reward worthy of the absurd couple. Beth had disappeared behind Jo, and Grace was asleep.

"So the poor warrior octopus is to be left with no reward, is he?" asked Mr. Brooke, still gazing into the Ocean, and playing with the green algae beneath him.

"I guess the princess gave him a kiss, and the King paid him for training his colt," said Laurie, smiling knowingly, as he threw pebbles at his tutor.

"What a piece of nonsense we have made! With practice we might do something quite clever," said Jo. "We could even publish and make our fortunes!"

All the merchildren laughed at this, and the game was finished. Some of them nestled down and chatted. Others romped around playing tag among the elkhorn branches.

Beth noticed that Frank had drifted away from the group, and was nestled down watching them from afar. Slipping over to him, she said, in her shy yet friendly way, "I'm afraid you are tired. Can I do anything for you?"

"Talk to me, please. It's dull, drifting around by myself," answered Frank, who had taken his arm out of its sling and was testing its strength in the waters.

If he asked her to deliver a Coastline opera, it would not have seemed a more impossible task to bashful Beth. There was no Jo to hide behind now. The poor boy looked so wistfully at her that she bravely resolved to try.

"What do you like to talk about?" asked Beth, softly.

"Well, I like to hear about sea monsters and whirlpools and politics," said Frank.

My heart! What will I do? I don't know anything about them, thought Beth. Forgetting the merboy's misfortune in her flurry, she said, hoping to make him talk, "I never saw any sea monsters, but I suppose you know all about them."

"I saw a monster once, but I can never see one again.

For the specimen we had in our zoo died of barnacles. And I'll never swim out so far in the wild to see a sea monster for myself. A shark caught my arm last time I swam off on an adventure. See the scars?" Frank held his arm up and continued to the now blanched little mermaid, "So I can't swim too long without tiring anymore." He heaved a sigh that made Beth hate herself for her innocent blunder.

Yet speaking of sea monsters proved soothing and satisfactory to Frank. He uncurled his tail and actually smiled.

In her eagerness to amuse another, Beth forgot herself and was quite unconscious of her sisters. The sisters watched, surprised and delighted at the spectacle of Beth talking away. And not just talking to anyone, but to one of the dreadful merboys, against whom she had begged protection.

"Bless her heart! She cares for him, so she is good to him," said Jo, beaming at her from the elkhorn branches.

"I always said she was a little angelfish," added Laurie, as if there could be no further doubt of it.

"I haven't heard Frank laugh so much for ever so long," said Grace to Amy, as they sat discussing dolls.

"My sister Beth is a very fastidious mergirl, when she likes to be," said Amy, well pleased at Beth's success. She meant 'fascinating', but as Grace didn't know the exact meaning of either word, fastidious sounded well and made a good impression.

While this went on, the three elders hovered apart, talking. Miss Kayla took out her sketch again, and Meg watched her. Mr. Brooke lay on the algae with a scroll, which he did not read.

"How beautifully you do it! I wish I could draw," said Meg, with mingled admiration and regret in her voice.

"Why don't you learn? I should think you had taste and talent for it," replied Miss Kayla graciously.

"I haven't time."

"Your mamma prefers other accomplishments, I fancy. So did mine, but I proved to her that I had talent by taking a few lessons with my governess. Then she was quite willing I should continue painting. Can't you do the same with your governess?"

"I have none."

"I forgot merfolk in the Deep Ocean go to community school more than we do at the Coastline. Very fine schools they are, too, Papa says. You go to a private one, I suppose?"

"I don't go at all. I am a governess myself."

"Oh, indeed!" said Miss Kayla, but she might as well have said, "Dear me, how dreadful!" for her tone implied it, and something in her face made Meg color, and wish she had not been so frank.

Mr. Brooke looked up and said quickly, "Young merfolk in the Deep Ocean love independence as much as their ancestors did. They are admired and respected for supporting themselves."

"Oh, yes, of course it's very nice and proper for them to do so. We have many most respectable and worthy young merfolk who do the same and are employed by the nobility. There is suitable work for the well-bred and accomplished, you know," said Miss Kayla. Her patronizing tone hurt Meg's pride, and made her work seem not only more distasteful, but degrading.

Mr. Brooke broke the awkward pause that followed.

"Did you enjoy the Coastline poem-in-a-bottle that came in the post last week, Miss Marsh?"

"Oh, yes! It was very sweet, and I'm much obliged to whoever translated it for me." Meg's downcast face brightened as she spoke.

"Don't you read Coastline?" asked Miss Kayla with a look of surprise.

"Not very well. My father, who taught me, is away. I don't get on very well alone, for I've no one to correct my pronunciation."

"Try a little now. Here is Schillfins's *Marina Seaworth* and a tutor who loves to teach." And Mr. Brooke passed her the scroll he was reading.

"It's so hard I'm afraid to try," said Meg. She was grateful, but bashful in the presence of the accomplished young mermaid beside her.

"I'll read a bit to encourage you," and Miss Kayla read one of the most beautiful passages in a perfectly correct but perfectly expressionless manner.

Mr. Brooke made no comment as she returned the scroll to Meg, who said innocently, "I thought it was poetry."

"Some of it is. Try this passage."

There was an odd smile about Mr. Brooke's mouth as he opened the scroll to Marina Seaworth's lament.

Meg obediently followed the tutor's finger, which he used to point with. She read slowly and timidly, unconsciously making poetry of the hard words by the soft intonation of her musical voice. Down the page went the finger guide. Forgetting her listener in the beauty of the sad scene, Meg read as if alone. She gave a little touch of tragedy to the words of the unhappy Seaworth. If she had seen Mr. Brooke's brown eyes then, she would have stopped short. But she never looked up, and the lesson was not spoiled for her.

"Very well indeed!" said Mr. Brooke, as she paused. He quite ignored her many mistakes, and looked as if he did indeed love to teach.

Miss Kayla bundled up her art board, saying with condescension, "You've a nice accent and in time will be a clever reader. I advise you to learn, for Coastline is a valuable accomplishment to teachers. I must look after Grace. She is romping." And Miss Kayla swam away, adding to herself with a shrug, "I didn't come to chaperone a governess, though she is young and pretty. How odd these Deep Ocean merpeople are. I'm afraid Laurie will be quite spoiled among them."

"I forgot that Coastline merpeople rather turn up their noses at governesses and don't treat them as we do," said Meg. She watched the retreating figure with an annoyed expression.

"Tutors do have rather a hard time of it there, as I know to my sorrow. There's no place like the Deep Ocean for us teachers, Miss Margaret." And Mr. Brooke looked so content and cheerful that Meg was ashamed to lament her hard lot.

"I'm glad I live here then. I don't like my work, but I get a good deal of satisfaction out of it after all. So I won't complain. I only wished I liked teaching as you do."

"I think you would if you had Laurie for a pupil. I will be very sorry to lose him next year," said Mr. Brooke, busily punching holes in the turf.

"He's swimming off to college, I suppose?" Meg's lips asked the question, but her violet eyes added, "And what becomes of you?"

"Yes, it's high time he did so, because he is ready. As soon as he is off, I will turn soldier. I am needed."

"I am glad of that!" exclaimed Meg. "I should think every young merperson would want to help. Though it is hard for the merfamily who stays home," she added sorrowfully.

"I have no merfamily, and very few friends to care whether I live or die," said Mr. Brooke rather bitterly. He absently put a dead glow bloom in the hole he had made and covered it up, like a little grave.

"Laurie and his grandfather would care a great deal, and we should all be very sorry to have any harm happen to you," said Meg heartily.

"Thank you, that sounds pleasant," began Mr. Brooke, looking cheerful again. Before he could finish his speech, Laurie struck together two shells and called the group to pack for home.

After a flurry of activity and a ride full of laughter, the seahorses drew their sleighs up to the Lawrence cave dwelling. The merfolk slipped out of the oyster shell, and all said goodbye and goodnight.

As the four sisters swam home through the garden, Miss Kayla watched them. She said, without the patronizing tone in her voice, "In spite of their manners, Deep Ocean mergirls are very nice when one knows them."

"I quite agree with you," said Mr. Brooke.

CHAPTER 16

Writing and Secrets

Jo was very busy in the attic, for the Cool Season days began to grow chilly, and the currents ran faster at night. For two or three hours, warm waters still slipped slowly past the heart-shaped window. Jo rested behind the glass, nestled into the old seaweed cushion. She inked busily, with squid ink staining her hands and hair. Scrabble, the attic goldfish, promenaded the beams overhead. He was accompanied by his oldest son, a fine young fellow, who was very proud of his butterscotch coloring. Quite absorbed in her work, Jo scribbled away until the last page was filled, when she signed her name with a flourish and twirled her pen off into the water, exclaiming...

"There, I've done my best! If this won't suit, I will have to wait until I can do better." Nestling back deeper into the cushion, she read the scroll carefully through. She made dashes here and there, and added many exclamation marks, which looked like little bubbles. Then she rolled it up and fastened it off with a smart red ribbon.

She hovered a minute, looking at it with a sober

expression. Her wistful eyes plainly showed how earnest her work had been. She blinked, came back to action and stashed her ink, pens and scrolls in her desk.

Jo's desk up here was an old oven which leaned against the wall. It hadn't any heat source, but that was just as well for Jo. Scrabble, who, being likewise of a literary turn, was fond of unrolling scrolls and eating their edges. So the oven served for taking food instead of giving, a protector of her scrolls.

From this old receptacle, Jo produced another completed scroll. Scrabble and son looked disappointed when she closed the oven up tightly. They bumped their noses against the side of the oven, begging to eat her work, but Jo had other readership in mind. Putting both scrolls in her satchel, she swam quietly to the lower rooms.

She put on her cloak as noiselessly as possible. She did not swim to the front door, but glided to the back entry window, and squirmed through it. After a bit of wriggling and wrangling, she slipped outside and swam off unnoticed. She darted in and out of the garden corals until she reached the thoroughfare. Once there, she composed herself and swam into the reef city, looking very merry and mysterious.

If anyone had been watching her, they would have thought her movements decidedly peculiar. For she swam at a great pace until she reached a certain cave along a certain busy thoroughfare. This thoroughfare was lined with many shops and much commerce. Colorful signs called out over every door. Our Jo paused in front of a large sign that read, "Dr. Hydra, Dentist." Underneath it, in smaller letters, "And The Rockfish Rambler and Gilly's Custom Armlets."

She slipped into the doorway and hovered just inside, staring down a long tunnel. Then she flipped over and darted back to the thoroughfare. This maneuver she repeated several times, to the great amusement of a mermaid cleaning the windows of a building opposite. On returning for the third time, Jo shook out her tail, pulled her cloak in tightly, and swam down the corridor. She grimaced as if she was going to have to pull three teeth.

She did not notice the young merman who bobbed down the thoroughfare at that very moment, but the young merman saw her. He floated in the thoroughfare outside the building, thinking, "It's like her to swim here alone, but if she has a bad time, she'll need someone to help her home."

In ten minutes, Jo came swimming back out at top speed. She had a very red face and the general appearance of a merperson who had just passed through a trying ordeal. When she saw the young merman, she looked anything but pleased, and passed him with a nod. But he followed, asking with great sympathy, "Did you have a bad time?"

"Not very."

"You got through quickly."

"Yes, thank goodness!"

"Why did you swim there alone?"

"Didn't want anyone to know."

"You're the oddest mermaid I ever saw."

Jo looked at her friend as if she did not understand him, then began to laugh as if mightily amused at something.

"There are two which I want to have come out, but I must wait a week."

"What are you laughing at? You are up to some mischief, Jo," said Laurie, looking mystified.

"So are you. What were you doing, sir, up in that billiard saloon?"

"Begging your pardon, ma'am, it wasn't a billiard saloon, but a gymnasium, and I was taking a lesson in trident fighting."

"I'm glad of that."

"Why?"

"You can teach me. Then when we perform in our attic theater, we'll make a realistic show of the battle scenes."

Laurie burst out with a hearty laugh, which made several passing walruses smile in spite of themselves.

"I'll teach you whether we have realistic theater fights or not. It's grand fun and will straighten you up capitally. But I don't believe that was your only reason for saying 'I'm glad' in that decided way, was it now?"

"No, I was glad that you were not in the saloon, because I hope you never go to such places. Do you?"

"Not often."

"I wish you wouldn't."

"It's no harm, Jo. I have billiards at home, but it's no fun unless you have good players. So, as I'm fond of it, I come sometimes and have a game with Kenn Moffin or some of the other fellows."

"Oh, dear, I'm so sorry, for you'll get to liking it better and better. You will waste time and sand dollars, and grow like those dreadful merboys. I did hope you'd stay respectable and be a satisfaction to your friends," said Jo, shaking her head.

"Can't a fellow take a little innocent amusement now and then without losing his respectability?" asked Laurie, looking annoyed.

"That depends upon how and where he takes it. I don't like Kenn and his set, and wish you'd keep out of it. Mother won't let us have him at our cave, though he wants to visit us. And if you grow like him, she won't be willing to have us frolic together as we do now."

"Won't she?" asked Laurie anxiously.

"No, she can't bear dissipated young mermen. She'd net

us and hang us on the wall rather than have us associate with them."

"Well, she needn't haul out her net yet. I'm not a dissipated creature and don't mean to be, but I do like harmless adventures now and then, don't you?"

"Yes, nobody minds them, so adventure away, but don't get wild, will you? Or there will be an end to all our good times."

"I'll be a perfectly polished angelfish."

"I can't bear angelfish. Just be a simple, honest, respectable merboy, and we'll never desert you. I don't know what I should do if you acted like Mr. Kingfish's son. He had plenty of sand dollars, but didn't know how to spend it. He got tipsy and gambled, and swam away, and forged his father's name, I believe, and was altogether horrid."

"You think I'm likely to do the same? Much obliged."

"No, I don't—oh, dear, no!—but I hear merpeople talking about sand dollars being such a temptation, and I sometimes wish you were poor. I shouldn't worry then."

"Do you worry about me, Jo?"

"A little, when you look moody and discontented, as you sometimes do. For you've got such a strong will, if you once get started wrong, I'm afraid it would be hard to stop you."

Laurie hovered in silence a few moments, and Jo watched him, wishing she had chosen better words. His eyes looked angry, though his lips smiled as if at her warnings.

"Are you going to deliver lectures all the way home?" he asked presently.

"Of course not. Why?"

"Because if you are, I'll return home alone. If you're not, I'd like you to ride my seahorse with me. I'll tell you something very interesting."

"I won't preach any more, and I'd like to hear the news immensely."

"Very well, then, grab onto my back. It's a secret, and if I tell you, you must tell me yours."

"I haven't got any," began Jo, but stopped suddenly, remembering that she had.

"You know you have—you can't hide anything, so up and 'fess, or I won't tell," cried Laurie, bobbing the seahorse out into the busy thoroughfare.

"Is your secret a nice one?" asked Jo.

"Oh, isn't it! All about merpeople you know, and such fun! You ought to hear it, and I've been aching to tell it this long time. Come, you begin."

"You'll not say anything about it at our cave, will you?"

"Not a word."

"And you won't tease me in private?"

"I never tease."

"Yes, you do. You get everything you want out of merpeople. I don't know how you do it, but you are a born wheedler."

"Thank you. Now confess."

"Well, I've left two story scrolls with a magazine called *The Rockfish Rambler*. The editor is to give his answer next week," whispered Jo, in her confidant's ear.

"Hurrah for Miss Marsh, the most celebrated inker in the Ocean!" cried Laurie, steering the seahorse into a prancing whirl, to the great delight of two merchildren, four catfish, and half a dozen lobsters.

"Hush! It won't come to anything, I dare say, but I couldn't rest until I had tried. I said nothing about it because I didn't want anyone else to be disappointed."

"It won't fail. Why, Jo, your stories are works of fine literature compared to half the rubbish that is published every day. Won't it be fun to see them in print, and shan't we feel proud of our story-weaver?"

Jo's eyes sparkled, for it is pleasant to be believed in. A friend's praise is always sweeter than a limed sea apple.

"Where's your secret? Play fair, Laurie, or I'll never believe you again," she said, still enjoying the hope bubbling over the word of encouragement.

"I may get into a scrape for telling, but I didn't promise not to tell. So I will, for I never feel easy in my mind until I've told you any delicious bit of news I get. I know where Meg's glove is."

"Is that all?" said Jo, looking disappointed, as Laurie nodded and twinkled with a face full of mysterious intelligence.

"It's quite enough for a delicious secret, as you'll agree when I tell you where it is."

"Tell, then."

Laurie turned his head, and whispered three words back toward his passenger. They produced an immediate, comical change. Her entire face scrunched up, looking both surprised and displeased. Rubbing the scrunch out with the palm of one hand, she said sharply, "How do you know?"

"Saw it."

"Where?"

"Satchel."

"All this time?"

"Yes, isn't that romantic?"

"No, it's horrid."

"Don't you like it?"

"Of course I don't. It's ridiculous. It won't be allowed. My patience! What would Meg say?"

Laurie winced and the seahorse startled. "You are not to tell anyone. Mind that."

"I didn't promise," said Jo, holding on more tightly.

"That was understood, and I trusted you," said Laurie, patting the seahorse on the neck.

"Well, I won't for the present, anyway, but I'm disgusted, and wish you hadn't told me."

"I thought you'd be pleased."

"At the idea of anybody harpooning Meg away? No, thank you."

"You'll feel better about it when somebody harpoons you away."

"I'd like to see anyone try it," cried Jo fiercely.

"So should I!" and Laurie chuckled at the idea.

"I don't think secrets agree with me. I feel rumpled up in my mind since you told me that," said Jo rather ungratefully.

"Come now, let's gallop home as fast as we can, and see if we can unrumple you," suggested Laurie. Jo hung on tightly as the seahorse bobbed at full speed, but even the strong current in her hair couldn't ease the sad feeling in her heart.

CHAPTER 17

Express Bottle

"The beginning of the Cold Season is the most disagreeable part of the whole year," said Meg. She hovered at the window one dull afternoon, looking out at the garden. The Cool Season flowers had fallen, and the cold blooms were still baby buds, not yet open.

"That's the reason I was born in it," observed Jo pensively, quite unconscious of the ink blot on her nose.

"If something very pleasant should happen now, we should think it a delightful time," said Beth. She took a hopeful view of everything, even the first days of Cold Season.

Meg sighed, and turned to the colorless garden again. Jo groaned and floated on her back in a despondent attitude. Amy painted away at a landscape of dead coral. Beth, who floated at the other window, said, smiling, "Two pleasant things are going to happen right away. Marmee is swimming down the thoroughfare, and Laurie is bobbing through the garden as if he had something nice to tell."

In they both swam, Mrs. Marsh with her usual question, "Any letter-in-a-bottle from Father, mergirls?" and Laurie to say in his persuasive way, "Won't some of you swim out for a ride? I've been working away at mathematics until my head is in a muddle, and I'm going to freshen my wits by a brisk gallop. It's a dull day, but I'm taking Brooke home to his merry cave. It will be happy weather in our hearts, if it isn't in the Ocean. Ride with us, Jo, you and Beth will too, won't you?"

A sharp clack of the door shell interrupted the answer, and a moment later Nanna-pus floated in with a tiny cylinder.

"It's one of those horrid express bottle things," she said, dangling it at the extremity of one appendage, as if she was afraid it would explode.

At the word 'express bottle', Mrs. Marsh snatched it, and read the two lines it contained. She crumpled back into her seaweed cushion as white as if the little scroll had sent a javelin through her heart. Laurie dashed to grab her a soft shawl, while Meg and Nanna-pus supported her, and Jo read aloud, in a frightened voice...

Mrs. Marsh:
> Your husband is very ill. Come at once.
> S. HALE
> Plankton Hospital, Pink City.

How still the room was now, how strangely the waters darkened outside, and how suddenly the whole Ocean seemed to change. The mergirls gathered about their mother. They felt as if all the happiness and support of their lives was about to drift away from them.

Mrs. Marsh was soon herself again, and read the message a third time. Then she stretched out her arms to her daughters, saying, in a tone they never forgot, "I will swim there at once, but it may be too late. Oh, merchildren, merchildren, help me to bear it!"

For several minutes there was nothing but the sound of sobbing in the room, mingled with broken words of comfort. They mixed in tender assurances of help, and hopeful whispers that died away in frowns.

Poor Nanna-pus was the first to recover. "Let me help you get your nets packed," she said heartily, then she darted to the upper rooms with the determination of an army of mermaids in one tiny octopus.

"She's right, there's no time for tears now. Be calm, mergirls, and let me think."

They tried to be calm, poor things, as their mother rose up, looking pale but balanced. She put away her grief to think and plan for them.

"Where's Laurie?" she asked presently, when she had collected her thoughts and decided on the first duties to be done.

"Here, ma'am. Oh, let me do something!" cried the merboy. He swam back in from the next room. He'd withdrawn to be polite, feeling that their first sorrow was too sacred for even his friendly eyes to see.

"Send an express bottle saying I will be there at once. The next caravan goes early in the morning. I'll take that."

"What else? The seahorses are ready. I can swim

anywhere, do anything," he said, looking ready to gallop to the ends of the Ocean.

"You can deliver a letter-in-a-bottle to Aunt Marsh. Jo, give me that pen and an empty scroll."

Tearing off the bottom of one of her longer scrolls, Jo passed it to her mother. She fetched her a slate tablet as well, to help her write from the comfort of her seaweed cushion. The words her mother would ink would not be easy. Jo knew that they would have to borrow the sand dollars for the long, sad journey. She wished and wished there could be anything to add a little to the sand dollars for her father.

"Now swim along, Laurie dear, but don't kill yourself bobbing those seahorses at a desperate pace. There is no need of that."

Mrs. Marsh's warning was evidently thrown away. Not five minutes later Laurie galloped by the window on his seahorse, bobbing as if for his life.

"Jo, swim into the city, and tell Mrs. Kingfish that I can't come. On the way buy these things. I'll make a list. They'll be needed and I must arrive prepared for nursing. Hospital supplies are not always good. Beth, swim over and ask Mr. Laurence for a couple of jars of Coastline salve. I'm not too proud to beg for Father. He will have the best of everything. Amy, ask Nanna-pus to get down the big driftwood chest. Meg, float over and help me find my things, for I'm half bewildered."

Writing, thinking, and directing all at once might well bewilder the poor merlady. So Meg begged her mother to nestle down quietly in her room for a little while, and let them work. Everyone scattered like crustaceans before a sand shark. The quiet, happy household was broken up as suddenly as if the express bottle had been an evil spell.

Mr. Laurence hurried back with Beth. He brought every comfort the kind old merman could think of for the sick. He promised to watch after the mergirls as a dear friend during their mother's absence. This comforted Mrs. Marsh very much. There was nothing he didn't offer, from his own night wrap to himself as escort. But the last was impossible. Mrs. Marsh would not hear of the old merman undertaking the long journey. Yet he saw the look of longing for a companion on her face. Traveling alone in times of uncertainty can create much anxiety. So he scrunched his heavy eyebrows, rubbed his hands, and swished abruptly away, saying he'd be back directly. No one had time to think of him again until, as Meg swam through the entry, with a comb in one hand and a cake for mother in the other, she came suddenly upon Mr. Brooke.

"I'm very sorry to hear of your father, Miss Marsh," he said. His kind, quiet tone sounded very pleasant to her perturbed spirit. "I swam over to offer myself as an escort to your mother. Mr. Laurence has errands for me in Pink City. It will give me real satisfaction to be of service to her there."

The comb drifted out of Meg's hand, and the cake was very near following. Her face was so full of gratitude. Mr. Brooke felt repaid for a sacrifice even greater than the small one he was about to undertake.

"How kind you all are! Mother will accept, I'm sure, and it will be such a relief to know that she has someone to take care of her. Thank you very, very much!"

Meg spoke earnestly, and forgot herself entirely until something in the brown eyes looking down at her made her remember the cake. She swam quickly into the parlor, saying she would call her mother.

Everything was arranged by the time Laurie returned with a satchel from Aunt Marsh. She'd sent the desired sand dollars, and a letter-in-a-bottle repeating what she had often said before. She had always told them it was absurd for Mr. Marsh to swim out with the army, and always predicted that no good would come of it. She hoped they would take her advice the next time. Mrs. Marsh fed the letter to the crustaceans just outside the door, put the sand dollars in her satchel, and went on with her preparations. She pressed her lips tightly together in a way which Jo would have understood if she had been there.

The short afternoon wore away. All other errands were done, and Meg and her mother were busy at some necessary weaving. Nanna-pus prepared to spend the night with the Marsh's, unwilling to let her friends sleep alone. Beth and Amy nibbled at cakes between sobs. Jo still did not swim home. They began to get anxious, and Laurie swam off to find her, for no one knew what scheme Jo might take into her head. He missed her, however, and she came swimming in with a very strange expression. It was a mixture of fun and fear, satisfaction and regret in it. This puzzled the merfamily as much as did the stack of sand dollars she put into her mother's hands. Jo spoke with a little choke in her voice, "That's my contribution toward making Father comfortable and bringing him home!"

"My dear, where did you get it? Twenty-five sand dollars! Jo, I hope you haven't done anything rash?"

"No, it's mine honestly. I didn't beg, borrow, or steal it.

I earned it, and I don't think you'll blame me, for I only sold what was my own."

As she spoke, Jo pulled the hood of her cloak off of her head. A general outcry arose, for all her lavender hair was cut short.

"Your hair! Your beautiful hair!" "Oh, Jo, how could you? Your one beauty." "My dear mergirl, there was no need of this." "She doesn't look like my Jo any more, but I love her dearly for it!"

As everyone exclaimed, Beth hugged the cropped head tenderly. Jo assumed an indifferent manner, which did not deceive anyone a particle. She said, running a comb through the short tufts and trying to look as if she liked it, "It doesn't affect the fate of the Ocean. So don't wail, Beth. It will do my brains good to have that weight taken off. My head feels deliciously light and cool. The barber said I could soon have a curly crop, which will be youthful, becoming, and easy to keep in order. I'm satisfied, so please take the sand dollars and let's have supper."

"Tell me all about it, Jo. I am not quite satisfied, but I can't blame you. I know how willingly you sacrificed your vanity, as you call it, to your love. But, my dear little fish, I'm afraid you'll regret it," said Mrs. Marsh.

"No, I won't!" replied Jo stoutly, feeling much relieved that her efforts were not entirely condemned.

"What made you do it?" asked Amy, who would have thought of cutting off her head before her pretty curls.

"Well, I was wild to do something for Father," replied Jo, as they gathered about the table. For healthy merpeople can eat even in the midst of trouble. "I hate to borrow as much as Mother does. I knew Aunt Marsh would complain, she always does, if you ask for a half a sand dollar. Meg gave all her quarterly salary toward the rent. I only got some shell corsets with mine, so I felt bad. I had to contribute some sand dollars, if I sold the scales off my tail to get them."

"You needn't feel bad, my darling merchild! You had no Cold Season outfits and got the simplest with your own hard earnings," said Mrs. Marsh with a look that warmed Jo's heart.

"I hadn't the least idea of selling my hair at first, but as I swam along, I kept thinking about what I could do. In a barber's window I saw braids of hair with the prices marked. One bright red braid, not so thick as mine, was forty sand dollars. It came to me all of a sudden that I had one way to make sand dollars honestly. Without stopping to think, I swam in, asked if they bought hair, and what they would give for mine."

"I don't see how you dared to do it," said Beth in a tone of awe.

"Oh, the barber was a grim walrus who looked as if he merely lived to oil his mustache. He rather stared at first, as if he wasn't used to having mergirls bounce into his shop and ask him to buy their hair. He said he didn't care about mine, lavender wasn't the fashionable color, and he never paid much for it in the first place. The work put into it made it dear, and so on. It was getting late, and I was afraid if it wasn't done right away that I shouldn't have it done at all. You know when I start to do a thing, I hate to give it up. So I begged him to take it, and told him why I was in such a hurry. It was silly, I dare say, but it changed his mind. I got rather excited, and told the story in my topsy-turvy way. His wife, a lady walrus, heard, and said so kindly, 'Take it, Thomas, and oblige the young merlady. I'd do as much for our Jimmy any day if I wasn't bald as a rock."

"Who was Jimmy?" asked Amy, who liked to have things explained in the middle of stories.

"Her son, she said, who was fighting at the Abysmal Trench. How friendly such things make strangers feel, don't they? She talked away all the time the walrus clipped, and diverted my mind nicely."

"Didn't you feel dreadful when the first cut came?" asked Meg, with a shiver.

"I took a last look at my hair while the walrus pulled out his knife, and that was the end of it. I never snivel over trifles like that. I will confess, though, I felt strange when I saw the dear old hair float off in the water. Now my head feels rough and short as algae. It almost seemed as if I'd cut off an arm or a tail fin. The lady walrus picked out a long lock for me to keep. I'll give it to you, Marmee, just to remember past glories by. Short hair is so comfortable I don't think I will wear it long again."

Mrs. Marsh folded the wavy lavender lock, and laid it away with a short gray one in her desk. She only said, "Thank you, deary," but something in her face made the mergirls change the subject. They spoke as cheerfully as they could about Mr. Brooke's kindness. There was a good prospect of a fine day tomorrow. And they'd have happy times when Father returned home to be nursed.

No one wanted to tuck into their night wraps when at ten o'clock Mrs. Marsh put away her work, and said, "Come mergirls." Beth swam to the harp and played their father's favorite song. All began to sing bravely, but broke down in sobs one by one. Soon Beth was left alone, singing with all her heart, because music was more comforting to her than sobbing.

"Swim off to bed and don't talk late. We must be up early and will need all the sleep we can get. Good night, my darlings," said Mrs. Marsh after the song finished. No one had the heart to try to sing another.

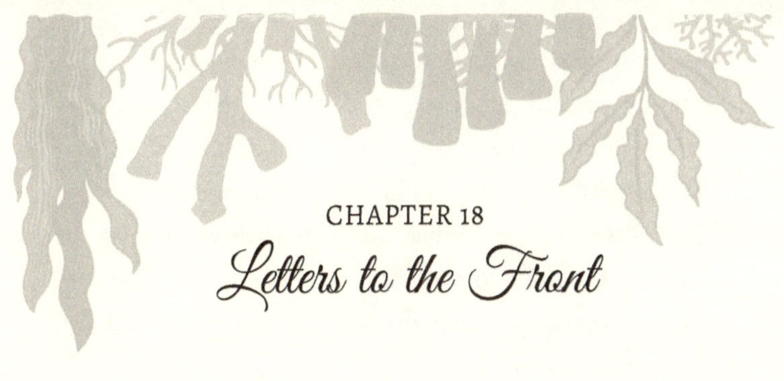

CHAPTER 18

Letters to the Front

News from their father comforted the mergirls very much. Though dangerously ill, the presence of the best and tenderest of nurses had already done him good. Mr. Brooke sent a letter-in-a-bottle every day, and as the oldest, Meg insisted on reading them aloud. The news grew more cheerful as the weeks passed. At first, everyone was eager to write. Plump scrolls were carefully corked into bottles by one or two sisters a day. The mergirls felt rather important with their Pink City correspondence.

The contents of one such bottle to Pink City read as follows:

My dearest Mother,

It is impossible to tell you how happy your last letter-in-a-bottle made us. The news was so good we couldn't help laughing and sobbing over it. How very kind Mr. Brooke is, and how fortunate he can be with you for so long. He must be so useful to you and Father. The mergirls are all as good as gold. Jo helps me with the weaving, and insists on doing all sorts of hard jobs. I should be afraid she might overdo, if I didn't know that her love for adventure would keep her from overwork. Beth is as regular about her tasks as the tides, and never forgets what you told her. She grieves about Father, and looks sober except when she is at her miniature harp. Amy minds me nicely, and I take great care of her. She does her own hair, and I am teaching her to string beads and mend her own armlets. She tries very hard, and I know you will be pleased with her improvement when you return. Mr. Laurence watches over us like a motherly old whale, as Jo says, and Laurie is very kind and neighborly. He and Jo keep us merry, for we get pretty sad sometimes, and feel like orphans, with you so far away. Nanna-pus is a perfect angelfish. She is always there for hugs when we need them. We are all well and busy, but we long, day and night, to have you back. Give my dearest love to Father, and believe me, ever your own...

MEG

This note, prettily written on a scented scroll, was a great contrast to the next. This letter-in-a-bottle was scribbled on a large sheet of pressed kelp paper. Then it was ornamented with blots and all manner of flourishes and curly-tailed letters.

My precious Marmee:

Three cheers for dear Father! Brooke was an angelfish to send an express bottle right off, and let us know the minute he was better. I rushed right up to the attic when the express-bottle arrived. I tried to compose a fine poem, but I could only sob, and say, "I'm glad! I'm glad!" Did that do as well as a poem—or as well as a prayer? For I felt a great many in my heart. We have such funny times, and now I can enjoy them. Everyone is so desperate to be good, it's like living in a school of blanched sardines. You'd laugh to see Meg head the table and try to be motherish. She gets prettier every day, and I'm in love with her sometimes. The merchildren are regular darlings, and I—well, I'm Jo, and never will be anything else.

Oh, I must tell you that I had a quarrel with Laurie. I shared my mind about a silly little thing, and he was offended. I was right, but I didn't use the polite language that I should have. He swam home, saying he wouldn't see me again until I begged forgiveness. I declared I wouldn't and got mad. It lasted all day. I felt horrible and wanted you very much.

Laurie and I are both so proud that it's hard to admit our wrongs. I thought he'd swim back and apologize eventually, but he didn't. That evening I remembered what you said when Amy fell into the gorge. I resolved not to hurt others needlessly in my anger, and swam over to tell Laurie I was sorry. I met him at the hedge, swimming to me for the same purpose. We both laughed, begged each other's forgiveness, and felt all good and comfortable again.

I inked a silly poem yesterday, when I was helping Nanna-pus scrub. Because Father likes my silly little things, I put it in to amuse him. I intended to write a lyrical dedication to his health. But, knowing me, this is what you get. Give him my lovingest hug that ever was, and kiss yourself a dozen times from your...

TOPSY-TURVY JO

A SONG FROM THE SCRUB

Queen of the scrub, I merrily sing,
With sponge and froth and foam,
Rub-dub-dub *the conch bowls clean,*
And put to their nooks for home.
I wish we could scrub from our hearts 'n
    scales,
Our sobs and sorrows away,
And sponge and foam and dub-rub-rub,
Ourselves as clean as they.
Then in the Ocean we'd enjoy,
A scrubbing bubbling day!

Dear Mother,

There is only room for me to send my love, and some glow blooms I keep safely potted in the cave for Father to see. I read every morning, try to be good all day, and sing myself to sleep. I can't sing Father's favorite, the 'Land of the Seals' anymore. It makes me sob. Everyone is very kind, and we are as happy as we can be without you. Amy wants to share this scroll with me. So I must stop so she has enough room too.

Kiss dear Father on the cheek he calls mine. Oh, do swim home soon to your loving...

LITTLE BETH

My Dear Mamma,

We are all well. I do my lessons always and never corroberate the mergirls—Meg says I mean contradick. So I put in both words and you can take the properest. Meg is a great comfort to me and lets me have jam every afternoon cake time. It's so good for me—Jo says— because it keeps me sweet tempered. Laurie is not as respeckful as he ought to be now that I am almost in my teens. He calls me Guppy and hurts my feelings by talking Coastline to me very fast when I say *Danqooo* or *Quaq noma* as Hera Kingfish does. The armlets that match my blue vest were all worn out. Meg wove in some new fibers, but they ended up different sizes. So my left arm is more covered than my right. I felt bad but did not fret. I bear my troubles well but I do wish Nanna-pus wouldn't insist on sleeping over at our cave every night. Can she stay at her own cave? Didn't I make that interrigation point nice? Meg says my punchtuation and spelling are disgraceful. I am mortyfied but dear me I have so many things to do, I can't stop. Fare-thee-well, I send heaps of love to Papa. Your affectionate daughter...
AMY CURTIS MARSH

My dearest friend,

I'll just drop a couple of lines to let you know we are doing well. The mergirls are clever and hardworking. Meg is turning into a good cook. I think she likes it more than she lets on. She picks up new skills surprisingly fast. Jo, however, is heart but no calculation. She dives in to help, but then makes a mess. She was chasing crustaceans through the parlor the other day with a hair comb. A hair comb! Beth is the best of little creatures. She tries to learn everything, and seems beyond her years. I'm teaching her accounting as she has a head for numbers. She's helping me pinch the sand dollars and we are making it. I don't let the mergirls have limed sea apples more than once a week, according to your wishes. I try to keep their diets healthy. Solid kelp and dulse and algae for vitamins. It's hard to do since Mr. Lawrence keeps delivering care satchels. He means well, but your mergirls would be so limed up if they eat all those sea-fruits—their tails would calcify. My kelp crisp is ready to pop into the oven, so no more at this time. I send my regards to Mr. Marsh, and hope he's seen the last of his sickness.

Yours respectfully,

NESMERALDA NANAGOONA NETTLES

Head Nurse of Ward No. 2,

All serene at the home caves. Troops in fine condition. Commissary department well-conducted. The Trident Guard under Colonel Laurie always on duty. Commander in Chief General Laurence reviews the army daily. Quartermaster Mollusk keeps order in camp, and Major Sea Lion does picket duty at night. A salute of twenty-four tridents was raised on receipt of good news from Pink City. Commander in Chief sends best wishes, in which he is heartily joined by...

COLONEL LAURIE

Dear Madam:

The little mergirls are all well. Beth and my merboy report daily. Nesmeralda is a model friend, and guards your cave dwelling like a shark. Glad the fine weather holds. Pray make Brooke useful, and draw on me for sand dollars if expenses exceed your estimate. Don't let your husband want anything.

Your sincere friend and servant, JAMES LAURENCE

CHAPTER 19

Faithful Beth

For a week everyone seemed in a disciplined frame of mind, and self-denial was all the fashion. Soon enough, after much tremendous exertion, they felt they deserved a holiday, and they took a good many.

Jo caught a head cold, and Aunt Marsh ordered her to remain far away from her until she felt better. She didn't like to hear merpeople read with sick voices.

Jo liked this, and she energetically rummaged through all the nooks in the Marsh cave dwelling. Then she nestled in to medicate with unread scrolls.

Amy found that housework and art did not go well together, and returned to her painting.

Meg swam off daily to her pupils. She returned home to weave, or thought she did. She spent more time than she realized writing long letters-in-bottles to her mother, or reading the Pink City dispatches over and over.

Beth kept on, with only slight relapses into wistfulness or grieving. All of Beth's little duties were faithfully done each day, and many of her sisters' also. When her heart grew heavy with longings for Mother or fears for Father, she nestled into a certain alcove and hugged her tail. She made little moans and prayed her little prayers quietly by herself. Nobody knew this is what cheered her up after a somber fit. Yet everyone felt how sweet and helpful Beth was. They fell into a habit of swimming to her for comfort or advice in their small affairs.

"Meg, I wish you'd go and see the Hamfin's. You know Mother told us not to forget them," said Beth, ten days after Mrs. Marsh's departure.

"I'm too tired to go this afternoon," replied Meg, nestling comfortably as she wove.

"Can't you, Jo?" asked Beth.

"The currents are too fierce for me with my head cold."

"I thought it was almost well."

"It's well enough for me to go out with Laurie, but not well enough to go to the Hamfin's," said Jo, laughing. She looked a little ashamed of her inconsistency.

"Why don't you swim over yourself?" asked Meg.

"I have been every day, but the merbaby is sick, and I don't know what to do for it. Mrs. Hamfin goes away to work, and Lara takes care of it. But it gets sicker and sicker, and I think you or Nanna-pus ought to go."

Beth spoke earnestly, and Meg promised she would visit them tomorrow.

"Ask Nanna-pus for some food fit for a merbaby and take it to them, Beth. The swim will do you good," said Jo, adding apologetically, "I'd help but I want to finish my inking."

"My head aches and I'm tired, so I thought maybe some of you would swim it over," said Beth.

"Amy will be home soon. She could swim over for us," suggested Meg.

So Beth curled up on her favorite seaweed cushion, the others returned to their work, and the Hamfins were forgotten. An hour passed. Amy did not come home, and Meg floated off to her room to polish her jewelry. Jo was absorbed in her story, and Nanna-pus was gliding about in the yard on her pet turtle. So nobody noticed when Beth quietly filled a net with odds and ends for the poor merchildren. She put on her cloak and swam out into the chilly waters with a heavy tail and a grieved look in her patient eyes.

It was late when she swam back home. No one saw her drift up the tunnel and shut herself into her mother's room. Half an hour after, Jo swam to 'Mother's treasure chest' for something. There she found little Beth floating before the medicine nook. She looked very grave, with red eyes and a shell of salve in her hand.

"Mackerels and mayhem! What's the matter?" cried Jo, as Beth put out her hand as if to warn her off, and asked quickly...

"You've had scale-breaker fever, haven't you?"

"Years ago, when Meg did. Why?"

"Then I'll tell you. Oh, Jo, the merbaby's dead!"

"What merbaby?"

"Mrs. Hamfin's. It died in my arms before she swam home," cried Beth with a sob.

"My poor dear, how dreadful for you! I ought to have swam over myself," said Jo. She took her sister into her arms and carried her over to Mother's big clam bed. She nestled Beth in with a remorseful face.

"It wasn't dreadful, Jo, only so sad! I saw in a minute it was sicker, but Lara said her mother had swum out for a doctor. So I took Baby and let Lara rest. It seemed asleep, but all of a sudden it gave a little sob and trembled, and then lay very still. I tried to warm its tail fins, and Lara gave it some dulse pudding, but it didn't stir, and I knew it was dead."

"Oh my poor dear! What did you do?"

"I just nestled down and held it softly until Mrs. Hamfin swam home with the doctor. The doctor said it was dead. Then she looked at Mernon and Minna, who have sore throats. 'Scale-breaker fever, ma'am. Ought to have called me before,' she said crossly. Mrs. Hamfin told her she was poor, and had tried to cure the merbaby herself. Now that it was too late, she could only ask her to help the others and trust charity for her pay. She smiled then, and was kinder, but it was very sad. I sobbed with them until the doctor turned round all of a sudden and saw me. She told me to swim home and take waterroot right away, or I'd have the fever."

"No, you won't!" cried Jo, hugging her close, with a frightened look. "Oh, Beth, if you should be sick, I never could forgive myself! What will we do?"

"Don't be frightened, I guess I shan't have it badly. I looked in Mother's scroll, and saw that it begins with headache, sore throat, and odd feelings like mine. So I did take some waterroot and I feel better," said Beth. She pressed her cold hands on her hot forehead and tried to look well.

"If Mother was only at home!" exclaimed Jo, seizing the scroll, and feeling that Pink City was an immense way off.

She read a bit, then examined Beth. She felt her head, peeped into her throat, and then said gravely, "You've been over to the merbaby every day for more than a week. I'm afraid you are going to have it, Beth. I'll call Nanna-pus. She knows all about sickness."

"Don't let Amy come. She never had it, and I should hate to give it to her. Can't you and Meg have it over again?" asked Beth anxiously.

"I guess not. Don't care if I do. Serves me right, selfish blubber that I am, to let you go, and stay inking rubbish myself!" muttered Jo, as she went to consult Nanna-pus.

Their friend the octopus took the lead at once. She assured them that there was no need to worry; everyone caught scale-breaker fever at some point. If rightly treated, nobody died. Jo believed this, and felt much relieved as they swam up to call Meg.

"Now I'll tell you what we'll do," said Nanna-pus, when she had examined and questioned Beth, "we will have Dr. Bangs, just to take a look at you, dear. She'll make sure we treat you right. Then we'll send Amy off to Aunt Marsh's for several days, to keep her out of harm's way. One of you older mergirls can stay at home at the cave and amuse Beth for a day or two."

"I will stay, of course, I'm the oldest," began Meg, looking anxious and self-reproachful.

"I will, because it's my fault she is sick. I told Mother I'd do the errands, and I haven't," said Jo decidedly.

"Which will you have, Beth?" asked Nanna-pus.

"Jo, please," and Beth leaned her head against her sister with a contented look, which effectually settled that point.

"I'll swim down and tell Amy," said Meg, feeling a little

hurt, yet rather relieved on the whole, for she did not like nursing, and Jo did.

Amy rebelled outright. She passionately declared that she would rather have the fever than visit Aunt Marsh. Meg reasoned, pleaded, and commanded—all in vain. Amy protested that she would not go, and Meg swam away from her in despair to ask Nanna-pus what to do.

Before Meg came back, Laurie drifted into the parlor to find Amy sobbing, with her head in a cushion. She told her story, expecting to be consoled, but Laurie only put his hands through his hair and glided about the room. He whistled softly, as he knit his brows in deep thought. Presently he nestled down beside her, and said, in his most wheedlesome tone, "Now be a sensible little merperson, and do as they say. No, don't sob, but hear what a jolly plan I've got. You stay with Aunt Marsh, and I'll swim over and take you out every day, riding or swimming. We'll have capital times. Won't that be better than moping here?"

"I don't wish to be sent off as if I was in the way," began Amy, in an injured voice.

"Bless your heart, Amy, it's to keep you well. You don't want to be sick, do you?"

"No, I'm sure I don't, but I dare say I will be, for I've been with Beth all the time."

"That's the very reason you ought to swim away at once, so that you may escape it. Change of water will keep you well, I dare say, or if it does not entirely, you will have the fever more lightly. I advise you to be off as soon as you can. Scale-breaker fever is no joke, miss."

"But it's dull at Aunt Marsh's, and she is so cross," said Amy, looking rather frightened.

"It won't be dull with me bubbling in every day to tell you how Beth is, and take you out gallivanting. The old merlady likes me, and I'll be as sweet as possible to her, so she won't nibble at us, whatever we do."

"Will you take me out in the oyster sleigh with the pink seahorse?"

"On my honor as a merman."

"And come every single day?"

"See if I don't!"

"And bring me back the minute Beth is well?"

"The identical minute."

"And go to the theater, truly?"

"A dozen theaters, if we may."

"Well—I guess I will," said Amy slowly.

"Good mergirl! Call Meg, and tell her you'll give in," said Laurie, with an approving pat, which annoyed Amy more than the 'giving in'.

Meg and Jo came swimming down to behold the miracle which had been wrought by Laurie. Amy, feeling very precious and self-sacrificing, promised to go, if the doctor said Beth was going to be ill.

"How is the little dear?" asked Laurie, for Beth was his special pet, and he felt more anxious about her than he liked to show.

"We've tucked her into Mother's night wrap, and she feels better. The merbaby's death troubled her, but I dare say she has only got a head cold. Nanna-pus says she thinks so, but she looks worried, and that makes me fidgety," answered Meg.

"What a trying Ocean it is!" said Jo, rumpling her short hair in a fretful way. "No sooner do we get out of one trouble than down comes another. There doesn't seem to be anything to hold on to when Mother's gone. I'm adrift in gorge water."

"Well, don't scratch your head so," complained Laurie, who never had been reconciled to the loss of his friend's one beauty. "You look like a bald walrus rubbing on a rock—"

"All walruses are bald," Jo interrupted.

Laurie sighed and continued, "Tell me if I must send an express bottle to your mother, or do anything?"

"That is what troubles me," said Meg. "I think we ought to tell her if Beth is really ill, but Nanna-pus says we mustn't. She says that Mother can't leave Father, and it will only make them anxious. Beth won't be sick long, and Nanna-pus knows just what to do. Mother said we were to mind her, so I suppose we must, but it doesn't seem quite right to me."

"Hum, well, I can't say. Suppose you ask Grandfather after the doctor has been here."

"We will. Jo, swim off and get Dr. Bangs at once," commanded Meg. "We can't decide anything until she has been here."

"Stay where you are, Jo. I'm the errand merman to this establishment," said Laurie, taking up his satchel.

"I'm afraid you are busy," began Meg.

"No, I've done my lessons for the day."

"Do you study in vacation time?" asked Jo.

"I follow the good example my neighbors set me," was Laurie's answer, as he propelled himself out of the room.

"I have great hopes for that merboy," observed Jo, watching him swim over the hedge with an approving smile.

"He does very well, for a merchild," was Meg's somewhat ungracious answer, for the subject did not interest her.

Dr. Bangs came and said Beth had symptoms of the fever. She thought she would have it lightly, though she looked sober over the Hamfin story.

Amy was ordered off at once. Provided with salves to ward off danger, she departed in great fanfare, with Jo and Laurie as escort.

Aunt Marsh received them with her usual hospitality.

"What do you want now?" she asked, looking sharply over her trident, while the parrotfish, floating behind her, called out...

"Go away. Go away."

Laurie drifted over to the window, and Jo told her story.

"No more than I expected, if you are allowed to go swishing about among poor sea creatures. Amy can stay and make herself useful if she isn't sick, which I've no doubt she will be. She looks like it now. Don't sob. It worries me to hear merfolks sniff."

Amy was on the point of sobbing, but Laurie slyly tickled the parrotfish's tail. This caused Polly to utter an astonished croak and call out, "Dunk my dorsals!" in such a funny way, that she laughed instead.

"What do you hear from your mother?" asked the old merlady gruffly.

"Father is much better," replied Jo, trying to keep sober.

"Oh, is he? Well, that won't last long, I fancy. Marsh never had any stamina," was the cheerful reply.

"Ha, ha! Goodbye, goodbye!" squalled Polly, swimming on his back and biting at the old merlady's hair comb.

"Silence, Polly! And, Jo, you'd better swim off at once. It isn't proper to be gadding about so late with a rattle-pated merboy like—"

"Silence, silence!" cried Polly, somersaulting away from his owner. He bobbed over to nibble at the 'rattle-pated' merboy, who was shaking with laughter at the parrotfish's antics.

"I don't think I can bear it, but I'll try," thought Amy, as she was left alone with Aunt Marsh.

"Bear it! Bear it!" screamed Polly. At this proclamation, Amy could not restrain a sob.

CHAPTER 20
Heavy Hours

Beth did have scale-breaker fever, and was much sicker than anyone but Nanna-pus and the doctor suspected. The mergirls knew nothing about illness, and Mr. Laurence was not allowed to see her. So Nanna-pus had everything her own way, and busy Dr. Bangs did her best, but left a good deal to the excellent nurse. Meg stayed at home, lest she should infect the King-fish's. She kept house, feeling very anxious and a little guilty when she inked letters-in-bottles in which no mention was made of Beth's illness. She could not think it right to deceive her mother, but she had been bidden to mind Nanna-pus, who wouldn't hear of worrying her parents.

Jo devoted every hour to Beth. This was not a hard task, for Beth was very patient. She bore her pain uncomplainingly as long as she could control herself. But there came a time when during the fever fits, she began to talk in a hoarse, broken voice. Or to try to play the rim of Mother's clam bed like her miniature harp. She tried to sing with a throat so swollen that there was no music left. Then a time came when she did not know the familiar faces around her, but addressed them by wrong names. She called imploringly for her mother night and day. Then Jo grew frightened, Meg begged to be allowed to ink the truth. Nanna-pus said she 'would think of it, though there was no danger yet'. A letter-in-a-bottle from Pink City added to their trouble. Mr. Marsh had had a relapse, and could not think of traveling home for a long while.

How heavy the hours seemed now. How quiet and lonely the cave. How sad were the hearts of the sisters as they worked and waited. The specter of death hovered over the once happy dwelling.

Then it was that Meg, sitting alone at her work, felt how rich she had been in things more precious than sand dollars could buy. She was rich in love, protection, peace, and health, the real blessings of life. Then it was that Jo learned too, living in that lonely room, with that suffering little sister always before her eyes. She fully saw and understood the beauty and the sweetness of Beth's nature. She felt how deep and tender a place she filled in all hearts. The worth of Beth's unselfish ambition to live for others settled into Jo. Beth had made their cave happy by the exercise of simple virtues. The virtues that all should love and value more than talent, wealth, or beauty. And Amy, in her exile, longed eagerly to be at home, that she might work for Beth. She felt now that no service would be hard or irksome. She remembered with regretful grief, how many neglected tasks Beth's willing hands had done for her.

Laurie haunted the caves like a restless ghost, and Mr. Laurence locked away the herringbone harp. He could not bear to be reminded of the young neighbor who used to make pleasant music for him.

Everyone missed Beth. The tinker, grocer and sweet shop owner inquired how she did, poor Mrs. Hamfin came to beg pardon for her thoughtlessness. The neighbors sent all sorts of comforts and good wishes. Even those who knew her best were surprised to find how many friends shy little Beth had made.

Meanwhile she lay on her bed with her doll Joanna at her side, for even in her wanderings she did not forget her forlorn protege.

She longed for her catfish, but would not have it

brought, lest it should get sick. In her quiet hours she was full of anxiety about Jo, who nursed her closely. She sent loving letters-in-bottles to Amy, and bade them tell their mother that she would write soon. She often begged for pen and scroll to try to ink a word to Father, that he might not think she had neglected him. But soon even these intervals of consciousness ended. She lay hour after hour, tossing to and fro, with incoherent words on her lips. Or she sank into a heavy sleep which brought her no refreshment. Dr. Bangs visited twice a day, and Nanna-pus watched her all night. Meg kept an express bottle in her desk all ready to send off at any minute, and Jo never stirred from Beth's side.

The middle of Cold Season was frigid indeed, for a bitter current rumbled in and battered the cave walls. It froze to death three corals outside their door, and seemed prepared to destroy even more. When Dr. Bangs came that morning, she looked long at Beth. She held the hot hand in both her own for a minute. Then she laid it gently down, saying, in a low voice to Nanna-pus, "If Mrs. Marsh can leave her husband, she'd better be sent for."

Nanna-pus nodded without speaking. Her many appendages twitched nervously. Meg sunk down to the floor. The strength fled from her tail at the sound of the doctor's words. Jo, hovering with a pale face for a minute, swam to the parlor and snatched up the express bottle. Throwing on her warmest cloak, she pushed herself out into the harsh currents.

* * *

Before long, Jo returned to the cave and noiselessly slipped off her cloak. Laurie glided in with a letter-in-a-bottle, saying that Mr. Marsh was mending again. Jo read it thankfully, but the heavy weight did not seem lifted off her heart. Her face was so full of misery that Laurie asked quickly, "What is it? Is Beth worse?"

"I've sent for Mother," said Jo, massaging the cold out of her tail with a tragic expression.

"Good for you, Jo! Did you do it on your own responsibility?" asked Laurie, as he rubbed her tail fin between his hands, seeing how her own hands shook.

"No. The doctor told us to."

"Oh, Jo, it's not so bad as that?" cried Laurie, with a startled face.

"Yes, it is. She doesn't know us. She doesn't look like my Beth, and there's nobody to help us bear it. Mother and Father both gone. Love seems so far away, it breaks my heart."

As sobs heaved Jo's chest, she stretched out her hand in a helpless sort of way, as if groping in the dark. Laurie took it in his, whispering as well as he could with a lump in his throat, "I'm here. Hold on to me, Jo, dear!"

She could not speak, but she did 'hold on', and the warm grasp of the friendly hand over hers comforted her sore heart.

Laurie longed to say something tender and comforting, but no fitting words came to him. So he hovered beside her silently, gently stroking her bent head as her mother used to do. It was the best thing he could have done, far more soothing than the most eloquent words. For Jo felt the unspoken sympathy, and in the silence learned the sweet solace which affection administers to sorrow. Soon she released her grip on his hand, and looked up with a grateful face.

"Thank you, Laurie, I'm better now. I don't feel so forlorn, and will try to bear the worst if it happens."

"Keep hoping for the best. Soon your mother will be here, Jo, and then everything will be all right."

"I'm so glad Father is feeling better. Now she won't feel so bad about leaving him. Oh, me! It does seem as if all the troubles attacked us at once, and I'm spearing the biggest shark alone," sighed Jo, smoothing her vest, which had become quite rumpled.

"Doesn't Meg do her fair share?" asked Laurie, looking indignant.

"Oh, yes, she tries to, but she can't love Bethy as I do, and she won't miss her as I will. Beth is my conscience, and I can't give her up. I can't! I can't!"

Down went Jo's face into her hands, and she sobbed despairingly. Laurie could not speak until he had subdued the choky feeling in his throat and steadied his lips. Presently, as Jo's sobs quieted, he said hopefully, "I don't think she will die. She's so good and I can't imagine the Ocean without her."

"The good and dear merpeople always do die," groaned Jo. She stopped sobbing, for her friend's words cheered her up in spite of her own doubts and fears.

"Poor mergirl, you're worn out. Rest here a bit. I'll hearten you up in a jiffy."

Laurie darted up the tunnel with a few powerful strokes of his tail. Jo laid her wearied head down on Beth's little brown cloak, which no one had thought of moving from the table where she left it. It must have possessed some magic, for the quiet spirit of its gentle owner seemed to enter into Jo. When Laurie came swimming back again with a Coastline coconut cupcake, she took it with a smile. She said bravely, "You are a good doctor, Laurie, and such a comfortable friend. How can I ever repay you?" she added, as the cupcake refreshed her body, as the kind words had done her troubled mind.

"I'll send my bill, by-and-by. Tonight I'll give you something that will warm the cockles of your heart better than cupcakes," said Laurie. He beamed at her with a face of suppressed satisfaction at something.

"What is it?" cried Jo, forgetting her woes for a minute in her wonder.

"I sent an express bottle to your mother yesterday, and Brooke answered she'd return home at once. She'll be here tonight, and everything will be all right. Aren't you glad I did it?"

Laurie spoke very fast, and turned red and excited all in a minute. He had kept his plot a secret, for fear of disappointing the mergirls or harming Beth. Jo grew quite white and rose up off the floor. The moment he stopped speaking, she astonished him by throwing her arms round his neck. She sobbed out, with a joyful sob, "Oh, Laurie! Oh, Mother! I am so glad!" She did not sob again, but laughed and trembled and clung to her friend as if she was a little bewildered by the sudden news.

Laurie, though decidedly amazed, behaved with great presence of mind. He patted her back soothingly. Finding that she was recovering, he followed it up by a bashful kiss or two on the cheek, which brought Jo round at once.

Holding on to the wall, she pushed him gently away, saying hoarsely, "Oh, don't! I didn't mean to, it was dreadful of me, but you were such a dear to go and do it in spite of Nanna-pus. I couldn't help hugging you. Tell me all about it, and don't give me coconut cupcakes again. They make my head spin."

"I don't mind," laughed Laurie, as he adjusted his armlet. "Why, you see I got fidgety, and so did Grandpa. We thought Nanna-pus was overdoing the authority business, and your mother ought to know. She'd never forgive us if Beth... Well, if anything happened, you know. So I got Grandpa to say it was high time we did something. I swam off to the office yesterday, for the doctor looked sober. Nanna-pus almost twisted my head off when I proposed an express bottle. I never can bear to be 'lorded over', so that settled my mind, and I did it.

"Your mother will be here soon, I know. The last caravan is in late tonight. I will swim out to get her. You've only got to bottle up your rapture, and keep Beth quiet until that blessed merlady gets here."

"Laurie, you're an angelfish! How will I ever thank you?"

"Hug me again. I rather liked it," said Laurie, looking mischievous, a thing he had not done for a fortnight.

"No, thank you, but I'll tell your grandpa that you deserve a hearty embrace. You can collect your hug from him tonight. Now swim home and rest. You'll be up very late. Bless you, Laurie, bless you!"

Jo had backed into an alcove as she finished her speech. Then she vanished into the kitchen. She plucked up the catfish and told it she was "happy, oh, so happy!" while

Laurie departed, feeling that he had made a rather neat thing of it.

"That's the interferingest merchild I ever saw. But I forgive him and do hope Mrs. Marsh is arriving right away," said Nanna-pus, with relief when Jo told her the good news.

The night wore on, and Nanna-pus, quite worn out, curled up atop Mother's trunk and snored loudly. Mr. Laurence swam to and fro in the parlor. Laurie nestled into a seaweed cushion, pretending to rest. He stared at the sun crystal thoughtfully. The warm glow made his black eyes beautifully soft and clear.

The mergirls never forgot that night, for no sleep came to them as they kept their watch. They felt that dreadful sense of powerlessness which visits us in hours like those.

"If Beth survives, I never will complain again," whispered Meg earnestly.

"If Beth survives, I'll try to love and be good all my life," added Jo with equal fervor.

"I wish I had no heart, it aches so," sighed Meg, after a pause.

"If life is often as hard as this, I don't see how we ever will get through it," added her sister despondently.

Here the tempest slapped against the windows and subsided. They both forgot themselves in watching Beth, for they fancied a change passed over her wan face. The cave was still as death, and nothing but the clattering of the current broke the deep hush. Weary Nanna-pus slept on, and no one but the sisters saw the pale specter which seemed to fall upon the little clam shell bed. An hour went by, and nothing happened except Laurie's quiet departure for the station. Another hour, still no one returned. Anxious fears of delay in the stormy waters, or accidents by the way, haunted the mergirls.

It was deep in the night, when Jo, who hovered at the window thinking how unfriendly the Ocean looked under the cold waters, heard a movement by the bed. Turning quickly, she saw Meg floating with her face hidden in her hands. A dreadful fear passed coldly over Jo, as she thought, *Beth is dead, and Meg is afraid to tell me.*

She darted back her post in an instant, and to her excited eyes a great change seemed to have taken place. The fever flush and the look of pain were gone. The beloved little face looked so pale and peaceful in its utter repose that Jo felt no desire to sob or to lament. Leaning low over this dearest of her sisters, she kissed the forehead with her heart on her lips. She softly whispered, "Good-bye, my Beth. Good-bye!"

As if awakened by the storm, Nanna-pus sprang from her repose on the trunk. She looked at Beth, felt her hands, and listened at her lips. Then, waving all eight appendages for joy, exclaimed, "The fever's turned. She's sleeping naturally, and she breathes easy. Praise be given! Oh, my goodness me!"

Before the mergirls could believe the happy truth, the doctor came to confirm it. She was a homely mermaid, but they thought her face quite heavenly. She smiled and said, with a doctorly look at them, "Yes, my dears, I think the little mergirl will pull through this time. Keep the caves quiet, let her sleep, and when she wakes, give her..."

What they were to give, neither heard. The sisters held hands and twirled about the room, rejoicing with hearts too full for words. When they swam back to be kissed and cuddled by Nanna-pus' many arms, they found Beth nestled peacefully. Her cheek rested on her hand, the dreadful pallor gone, and breathing quietly, as if just fallen asleep.

"If Mother would only come now!" said Jo, as the Cold Season night began to wane.

"See," said Meg, floating up with a white, half-opened sea-flower. "I thought this would hardly be ready to lay in Beth's hand tomorrow if she—she slipped away from us. But it has blossomed in the night, and now I mean to put it in my vase here. When the darling wakes, the first thing she sees will be the little sea-flower, and Mother's face."

Never had the day started so beautifully. Never had the Ocean seemed so lovely as it did to the heavy eyes of Meg and Jo, when their long, sad vigil was done.

"It looks like a dream Ocean," said Meg, smiling to herself.

"Hark!" cried Jo, rising quickly.

Yes, there was a sound of shells clanging at the door below. A sob from Nanna-pus, and then Laurie's voice saying in a joyful whisper, "Mergirls, she's here! She's here!"

CHAPTER 21
Amy's Last Wish

While these things were happening at home, Amy was having hard times at Aunt Marsh's. She felt her exile deeply, and for the first time in her life, realized how much she was beloved and cared in her own home cave. Aunt Marsh never doted on anyone. She did not approve of spoiling merchildren, but she meant to be kind. In fact, the well-behaved little mergirl pleased her very much.

Aunt Marsh had a soft place in her old heart for her nephew's merchildren, though she didn't think it proper to confess it. She really did her best to make Amy happy, but, dear me, what mistakes she made. Some older merfolk keep young at heart in spite of brittle scales and gray hairs. They can sympathize with merchildren's little cares and joys, and can make them feel always welcome. They can hide wisdom in pleasant games, and give and receive friendship in the sweetest way. But Aunt Marsh had not this gift. She worried Amy very much with her rules and orders, her prim ways, and long, prosy talks.

The old mermaid found this merchild more docile and amiable than her sister. So she felt it her duty to try and counteract, as far as possible, the bad effects of freedom and indulgence. She took Amy tail to tail, and taught her as she herself had been taught sixty years ago. This process carried dismay to Amy's soul, and made her feel like a guppy hunted by a very proper eel.

She had to scrub the bowls every day, and polish up the old-fashioned forks. They were fashioned like tiny, three-pronged tridents. Elegant, but made of very old coral, which grew brittle quickly. Then she must comb the crustaceans and sea bugs from each room, and what a trying job that was. Not an outgrown shell or discarded leg escaped Aunt Marsh's eye. A thick, opulent algae carpet covered the floor, giving the tiny creatures plenty of places to molt. Then Polly had to be fed, and his debris scraped from the sun crystal, where he liked to nest. It took a dozen swims up and down the tunnels to get things or deliver orders for Aunt Marsh. The old merlady's tail was very stiff and she seldom left her favorite cushion. After these tiresome labors, Amy did her lessons. These proved a daily trial of every virtue she possessed. Then she was allowed one hour for exercise or play, and didn't she enjoy it?

Laurie came every day, and wheedled Aunt Marsh until Amy was allowed to go out with him. They swam and galloped and had capital times.

After dinner, Amy had to read aloud to her Aunt, and stay still while the old merlady slept. Aunt Marsh usually slept for an hour, as she nodded off near the beginning of the scroll. Then weaving practice appeared, and Amy worked with outward meekness and inward rebellion.

Then, she was allowed to amuse herself as she liked until afternoon cakes.

The evenings were the worst of all, because Aunt Marsh nestled down to tell long stories about her youth. These were so unutterably dull that Amy was always ready to escape to bed. Each night she curled up in her clam shell, intending to sob herself to sleep. Yet she usually fell to sleep too quickly to properly mourn over the difficulty of her life.

If it had not been for Laurie, and Emeraldina, the housekeeper, she felt that she never could have got through that dreadful time. Emeraldina was a Coastline mermaid, who had lived with 'Madame', as she called her employer, for many years. The old merlady could not get along without her.

Emeraldina took a fancy to Amy, and amused her very much with odd stories of her life at the Coastline. She also allowed Amy to swim around the great cave dwelling, exploring the curious and pretty things stored away in the ancient chests.

Aunt Marsh piled up many a treasure in her long life. Amy's chief delight was a Coastline cabinet, full of odd-sized drawers and secret places. They were all stuffed with ornaments, some precious, some merely curious, all more or less antique.

Examining and arranging these things gave Amy great satisfaction. She especially adored the jewel cases. They were made of delicate dove shells, covered in mother-of-pearl. Inside them, on velvet cushions, reposed the ornaments which had adorned her Aunt forty years ago. There was the garnet set which Aunt Marsh wore when she came out, and the pearls her father gave her on her wedding day. Her lover's obsidian hair combs, the jet mourning shawls, and the merbaby ribbons her one little daughter had worn. In a shell case all by itself lay Aunt Marsh's wedding ring. It was too small now for her fat finger, but put carefully away like the most precious jewel of them all.

"I wish I knew where all these pretty things would go when Aunt Marsh dies," Amy said to Emeraldina, as she shut the jewel cases one by one.

"To you and your sisters. I know it. Madame confides in me. I witnessed her will, and it is to be so," whispered Emeraldina, smiling.

"How nice! But I wish she'd let us have them now. Procrastination is not agreeable," observed Amy, taking a last look at the luxurious, obsidian combs.

"It is too soon yet. You mermaids are too young yet to wear these things. The first one who engages to be married will have the pearls. Madame has said it, and I have a fancy that the little turquoise ring will be given to you when you return home from here. Madame approves of your good behavior and charming manners."

"Do you think so? Oh, I'll be an angelfish, if I can only have that lovely ring! It's ever so much prettier than Charisma Currente's. I do like Aunt Marsh after all." And Amy tried on the turquoise ring with a delighted face and a firm resolve to earn it.

In her first effort at being very, very good, she decided to make her will, as Aunt Marsh had done. This way, if she did fall ill and die, her possessions might be justly and generously divided.

During one of her play hours she inked out the important document as well as she could. Emeraldina helped with certain legal terms. When the good-natured Coastline mermaid had signed her name, Amy felt relieved. She laid it aside to show Laurie, whom she wanted as a second witness. Because the currents were too strong to play outside today, she swam up to amuse herself in one of the large chambers.

In this room there was a chest full of old-fashioned costumes with which Emeraldina allowed her to play. It was her favorite amusement to array herself in the faded brocades. Then she'd parade up and down before the long mirror.

So busy was she on this day that she did not hear Laurie clatter the doors shells. Nor did she see his face peeping in at her as she gravely promenaded to and fro, twirling her trident and tossing her head. She wore a great pink turban, contrasting oddly with her blue brocade vest and yellow gloves. She was obliged to swim carefully, for she had fin jewels, which pinched at her tail if she swung it too quickly. As Laurie told Jo afterward, it was a comical sight to see her float along like a Sea Queen in her glory.

Laurie restrained an explosion of merriment, lest it should offend her majesty, and entered. He was graciously received.

"Nestle down and rest while I put these things away. Then I want to consult you about a very serious matter," said Amy. She removed the pink mountain from her head, and Laurie sunk into a springy seaweed cushion.

"Now I'm ready," said Amy, shutting the chest and lifting her scroll. "I want you to read this, please, and tell me if it is legal and right. I felt I ought to do it. Life is uncertain, and I don't want any ill feeling over my grave."

Laurie bit his lip, turning a little from the pensive speaker. He read the following document, with praise-worthy gravity, considering the spelling:

MY LAST WILL AND TESTIMENT

I, Amy Curtis Marsh, being in my sane mind, go give and bequeethe all my earthly property—viz. to wit:—namely

To my father, my best picktures, sketches, maps, and works of art, including frames. Also my sand dollars, to do what he likes with.

To my mother, all my outfits, except the blue vest with pink brocade—also my portrait, and my dove shell, with much love.

To my dear sister Margaret, I give my turkquoise ring (if I get it). Also my driftwood chest with the etched fish.

Also my favorite neck ribon (the silky one), and my sketch of her as a memorial of her 'little mergirl'.

To Jo, I leave my best comb, the one with the pearls replaced. Also my squid ink holders —she lost the covers —and my most precious marble mermaid statue, because I am sorry I fed her story to the crustaceans.

To Beth, (if she lives after me) I give my dolls and their extra outfits. And I herewith also leave her my regret that I ever made fun of tailless Joanna.

To my friend and neighbor Theodore Laurence, I bequeethe my artistick supplies, my clay model of a seahorse—though he did say it hadn't any neck. Also in return for his great kindness in the hour of affliction, any one of my artistick works he likes (*Pink City Tempest* is the best).

To our venerable benefactor Mr. Laurence, I leave my purple shell case with a looking glass in the cover. It will be nice for his pens and remind him of the departed mergirl who thanks him for his favors to her merfamily, especially Beth.

I wish my favorite playmate Charisma Currente to have the blue vest with pink brocade and my gold-bead ring with a kiss.

To Nanna-pus I give also a piece of art as she chooses, so that she 'will remember me, when it you see'.

And now having disposed of my most valuable property I hope all will be satisfied and not blame the dead. I forgive everyone, and trust we may all meet in the hereafter. So be it.

To this will and testament I set my hand and seal on this day.

Amy Curtis Marsh
Witnesses:
Emeraldina Valor, Theodore Laurence.

The last name was inked very lightly in gray. Amy explained that he was to rewrite it in black and seal it up for her properly.

"What put it into your head? Did anyone tell you about Beth's giving away her things?" asked Laurie soberly, as Amy set the black squid ink before him.

She asked anxiously, "What about Beth?"

"I'm sorry I spoke, but because I did, I'll tell you. She felt so ill one day that she told Jo that she wanted to give her harp to Meg, her catfish to you, and the poor old doll to Jo, who would love it for her sake. She was sorry she had so little to give. So she left locks of hair to the rest of us, and her best love to Grandpa. She never thought of a will."

Laurie was signing and sealing as he spoke, and did not look up when he heard a little sob. Amy's face was full of trouble, but she only said, "Don't merpeople put sort of postscripts to their wills, sometimes?"

"Yes, 'codicils', they call them."

"Put one in mine then, that I wish all my curls cut off, and given round to my friends. I forgot it, but I want it done though it will spoil my looks."

Laurie added it, smiling at Amy's last and greatest sacrifice. Then he amused her for an hour, and was much interested in all her trials. When he rose to leave, Amy held him back to whisper with trembling lips, "Is there really any danger about Beth?"

"I'm afraid there is, but we can still hope for the best."

Laurie put his arm about her with a brotherly gesture which was very comforting.

When he had gone, she swam to her little clam shell bed. She sank to the floor beside it and prayed for Beth, with sobs and an aching heart. She felt that a million turquoise rings would not console her for the loss of her gentle little sister.

Amy made a solemn promise, deep in her heart. If Aunt Marsh gave her the turquoise ring, she would wear it in tribute to Beth. The ring would remind her to be unselfish, to love others, and to treasure every moment of her life.

CHAPTER 22
Mother Marsh

I don't think I have any words in which to tell the meeting of the mother and mergirls. Such hours are beautiful to live, but very hard to describe. So I will leave it to the imagination of my readers, merely saying that the cave was full of genuine happiness.

Meg's tender hope happened just as she'd wished. When Beth woke from that long, healing sleep, the first objects she saw were the white sea-flower and Mother's face. Too weak to wonder at anything, she only smiled and nestled close in the strong arms about her. She felt all her longings for love satisfied at last. Then she slept again, and the mergirls waited upon their mother. Mrs. Marsh would not let go of Beth's thin hand which clung to hers even in sleep.

Nanna-Pus had 'dished up' an astonishing breakfast for the traveler. The friendly octopus knew of no better way to express her excitement than to cook up a whirlpool's worth.

Meg and Jo served their mother, while they listened to her whispered account of Father's health. Mr. Brooke had promised to stay and nurse him to her great relief. She shivered at the account of the delays which the fierce cold currents had made on her travel home. She smiled as she spoke of the unspeakable comfort Laurie's hopeful face had given her when she arrived. He strengthened her, who had been so worn out with fatigue, anxiety, and cold.

What a strange yet pleasant day that was. So clear and joyful without, for all the Ocean seemed to sway in the crisp, cold currents. So quiet and reposeful within, for everyone slept with relief. A stillness reigned through the caves, hard won and well savored.

With a blissful sense of burdens lifted off, Meg and Jo closed their weary eyes. They curled up at rest, like sea slugs in new-fitted shells. Mrs. Marsh would not leave Beth's side, but nestled down beside her in the big clam bed. She brooded over her like she was a lost pearl, finally returned to its berth.

Laurie meanwhile swam off to comfort Amy. He told his story so well that Aunt Marsh actually 'sniffed' and never once said "I told you so". Amy restrained her impatience to see her mother, and never even thought of the turquoise ring.

Even the old merlady heartily agreed with Laurie's opinion of Amy. She behaved 'like a capital little mermaid'. Polly also seemed impressed. He called her a good mergirl, and begged, "Take me swim? Take me swim?" in his most affable tone. She would very gladly have swum out to enjoy the bright cold waters with the parrotfish, but she noticed that Laurie was sinking with sleepiness. So she persuaded him to rest, leading him to a particularly deep seaweed cushion. She floated off for a few moments, and when she returned, he was hugging his tail, sound asleep. Aunt Marsh had pulled down the curtains and rested too, in an unusual fit of peacefulness.

After a while, they began to think Laurie was not going to wake up until night. This might have proved true, had he not been effectually roused by Amy's cry of joy at the sight of her mother.

There probably were a good many happy little mermaids in and about the city reef that day. It is my private opinion that Amy was the happiest of all, when she nestled in her mother's arms and told her trials. Her mother consoled and compensated with approving smiles and fond caresses. When Amy swam home from Aunt Marsh's, she did so with one hand in her mother's and the other wearing the turquoise ring.

* * *

That evening while Meg was writing to her father to report Mother's safe arrival, Jo swam up into Beth's room. Finding her mother in her usual place, Jo hovered a minute. She twisted her fingers in her algae-short hair, with a worried gesture and an undecided look.

"What is it, deary?" asked Mrs. Marsh, holding out her hand, with a face which invited confidence.

"I want to tell you something, Mother."

"About Meg?"

"How quickly you guessed! Yes, it's about her, and though it's a little thing, it twitches my tail."

"Beth is asleep. Speak low, and tell me all about it. That

Kenn Moffin hasn't been here, I hope?" asked Mrs. Marsh rather sharply.

"No. I should have shut the door in his face if he had," said Jo, floating down upon the floor at her mother's tail fin. "Last Hot Season Meg left a pair of gloves over at the Laurences' and only one was returned. We forgot about it, until Laurie told me that Mr. Brooke confessed he had it and that he liked Meg. Only he didn't dare say so, since she was so young and he so poor. Now, isn't it a dreadful state of things?"

"Do you think Meg cares for him?" asked Mrs. Marsh with an anxious look.

"Mackerel me! I don't know anything about love and such nonsense!" cried Jo, with a funny mixture of interest and contempt. "In scroll-stories, the mergirls show it by starting and blushing. Or they faint away, grow thin, and act like fools. Now Meg does not do anything of the sort. She eats and sleeps like a sensible creature. She looks straight in my face when I talk about that merman. She only blushes a little bit when Laurie jokes about lovers. I forbade him to do it, but he doesn't mind me as he ought."

"Then you fancy that Meg is not interested in John?"

"Who?" cried Jo, staring.

"Mr. Brooke. I call him 'John' now. We fell into the way of doing so at the hospital, and he likes it."

"Oh, dear! I know you'll take his side. He's been good to Father, and you won't send him away, but let Meg marry him, if she wants to. Scheming thing! To go nursing Papa and helping you, just to wheedle you into liking him." And Jo pulled her hair again with a wrathful tweak.

"My dear, don't get angry about it, and I will tell you how it happened. John traveled with me at Mr. Laurence's request, and was so devoted to poor Father that we couldn't help growing fond of him. He was perfectly open and honorable about Meg. He told us he loved her, but would wait until the time was right before he asked her to marry him. He only wanted our blessing to love her and work for her, and the right to make her love him if he could. He is a truly excellent young merman. We could not refuse to listen to him, but I will not consent to Meg's engaging herself so young."

"Of course not. It would be idiotic! I knew there was mischief afloat. I felt it, and now it's worse than I imagined. I just wish I could marry Meg myself, and keep her safe in the merfamily."

This odd plan to protect Meg made Mrs. Marsh smile. Yet she said gravely, "Jo, I confide in you and don't wish you to say anything to Meg yet. When John returns, and I see them together, I can judge better her feelings toward him."

"She'll see those handsome eyes that she talks about, and then it will be all up with her. She's got such a sticky heart. It's stickier even than a barnacle. She'll attach to anyone who looks sentimentally at her. She read the short reports he sent more than she did your letters-in-bottles. She pinched me when I spoke of it. She likes brown eyes, and doesn't think John an ugly name. She'll go and sink into love, and there's an end of peace and fun, and cozy times together. I see it all! They'll go lovering around the cave, and we will have to dodge them. Meg will be absorbed and no good to me any more. Brooke will scratch up a fortune somehow, swim off with her, and make a hole in the merfamily. I will break my heart, and everything will be abominably uncomfortable. Oh, dear me! Why weren't we all committed to staying home forever?"

Jo leaned her chin on her hand in a disconsolate attitude and shook her fist at the reprehensible John. Mrs. Marsh sighed, and Jo looked up with hope in her eyes.

"You don't like it, Mother? I'm glad of it. Let's send him swimming away, and not tell Meg a word of it, but all be happy together as we always have been."

"I did wrong to sigh, Jo. It is natural and right you should all make cave dwellings of your own in time. I do want to keep my mergirls as long as I can, and I am sorry that this happened so soon. Meg is only seventeen and it will be some years before she and John can start a cave of their own. Your father and I have agreed that she will not bind herself in any way, nor be married, before twenty. If she and John love one another, they can wait, and test the love by doing so. She is conscientious, and I have no fear of her treating him unkindly. My pretty, tender-hearted mergirl! I hope things will go happily with her."

"Hadn't you rather have her marry a rich merperson?" asked Jo, as her mother's voice faltered a little over the last words.

"Sand dollars are a good and useful thing, Jo, and I hope my mergirls will never feel the need of it too bitterly. Or be tempted by them too much. I should like to know that John and Meg were firmly established in some good business. Something which would give them an income large enough to keep free from debt and be comfortable. I'm not ambitious for a splendid fortune, a fashionable position, or a great name for my mergirls. If status and sand dollars come with love and virtue, also, I should accept them gratefully. I know, by experience, how much genuine happiness can be had in a plain little cave. The daily kelp crisp is earned, and some privations give sweetness to the few pleasures. I am content to see Meg begin humbly, for if I am not mistaken, she will be rich in the possession of a good merman's heart. This is better than a trench-full of sand dollars."

"I understand, Mother, and quite agree, but I'm disappointed about Meg. I'd planned to have her marry Laurie by-and-by and rest in the lap of luxury all her days. Wouldn't it be nice?" asked Jo, looking up with a brighter face.

"He is younger than she, you know," began Mrs. Marsh, but Jo broke in...

"Only a little, he's old for his age, and long and strong, and can be quite grown-up in his manners if he likes. Then he's rich and generous and good, and loves us all, and I say it's a pity my plan is spoiled."

"I'm afraid Laurie is hardly grown-up enough for Meg. He's altogether too much of a prankster just now for anyone to depend on. Don't make plans, Jo, but let time and their own hearts marry those you love. We can't meddle safely in such matters. We had better not get 'romantic rubbish' as you call it, into our heads, lest it spoil our friendships."

"Well, I won't, but I hate to see things going all criss-cross and getting snarled up. Especially when a pull here and a snip there would straighten it out. I wish we could keep us from growing up. But calves will be whales, and kittenfish grow into catfish, more's the pity!"

"What's that about calves and catfish?" asked Meg, as

she floated into the room with the finished letter-in-a-bottle in her hand.

"Only one of my stupid speeches. I'm going to bed. Come, Meggy," said Jo, unfurling herself like an animated puzzle.

"Quite right, and beautifully written. Please add that I send my love to John," said Mrs. Marsh, as she glanced over the letter-in-a-bottle and gave it back.

"Do you call him 'John'?" asked Meg, smiling, with her innocent eyes looking down into her mother's.

"Yes, he has been like a son to us, and we are very fond of him," replied Mrs. Marsh, returning the look with a keen one.

"I'm glad of that, he is so lonely. Good night, Mother dear. It is so inexpressibly comfortable to have you here," was Meg's answer.

The kiss her mother gave her was a very tender one. As Meg swam away, Mrs. Marsh said, with a mixture of satisfaction and regret, "She does not love John yet, but will soon learn to."

CHAPTER 23

Father Marsh

Like soft sea-flowers peeking open after a tempest, were the peaceful weeks which followed. The sick ones improved rapidly, and Mr. Marsh began to talk of returning early in the new year. Beth was soon able to nestle into a parlor cushion all day, amusing herself with the well-beloved catfish. In time her little hands were strong enough to weave doll clothes, in which she had fallen sadly behind. Her once active tail was so stiff and feeble that Jo took her for daily swims about the cave, guiding her gently in arm. Meg cheerfully burned her fingers at the oven to cook delicate meals for 'the dear angelfish'. Amy, loyal to her ring-promise, celebrated her return by giving away as many of her treasures as she could prevail on her sisters to accept.

As Sea Queen's Day approached, the usual scheming began to haunt the house. Jo frequently convulsed the merfamily by proposing utterly impossible or magnificently absurd ceremonies. She insisted they honor this unusually happy Sea Queen's Day with vim and vigor. Laurie was equally impracticable. He suggested Coastline waltzes, squid races, and painting letters on the backs of ten turtles. He proposed training them to do acrobatics which spelled O-C-E-A-N-Q-U-E-E-N as their finale. After many skirmishes and snubbings, the merfamily quenched these wild plans. Jo and Laurie drifted about with forlorn faces, which were rather belied by explosions of laughter when the two got together.

Several days of unusually mild weather fitly ushered in a splendid Sea Queen's Day. Nanna-pus 'felt in her arms' that it was going to be an unusually happy holiday. She proved herself a true oracle, for everybody and everything seemed bound to produce a grand success. To begin with, Mr. Marsh inked that he should soon be with them. Then Beth felt uncommonly well that morning. They dressed her in her mother's gift, a soft crimson, twill weave vest. Then they carried her to the parlor window in high triumph to behold the offering of Jo and Laurie. The Holiday Schemers strove to live up to their name. They had worked by night and conjured up a comical surprise. Out in the garden stood a stately stone mermaid statue, made with piled up rocks and crowned with vines and kelp. She held a net of limed sea fruits and flowers in one hand, and a great scroll of music in the other. They'd attached two halves of a broken rainbow shell for her eyes, and a white cone shell as her nose. Out of her mouth fluttered a narrow kelp-paper scroll, like a long, lolling tongue in the open waters.

The message was a holiday song, which read...

THE STONE MERMAID TO BETH

Ocean hold you, dear Queen Bess!
May nothing you dismay,
But health and peace and happiness
Float to you, this Sea Queen's Day.

Here's sea-fruit for our angelfish,
Glow blooms for her vest.
Here's a jolly New Year's wish,
May this one be the best,

A portrait of our merfamily, see,
by our Amy just for you,
Who labored with great industry,
To make it fair and true.

Accept a ribbon red, we beg,
For your blessed catfish's tail,
And sweet dulse by our lovely Meg,
Whose desserts will never fail.

Their dearest love my makers laid,
Head above to tail below,
Accept me then, the stone mermaid,
From Laurie and from Jo.

How Beth laughed when she saw it, and how Laurie swam back and forth to bring in the gifts. More than all, what ridiculous speeches Jo made as she presented them.

"I'm so full of happiness, that if Father was only here, I

couldn't hold one drop more," said Beth. She quite hummed with contentment as Jo nestled her back into the cushions to rest after the excitement. Beth refreshed herself with some of the delicious sweet dulse the 'stone mermaid' had sent her.

"So am I," added Jo, somersaulting so joyfully over her long-awaited copy of *Whales and Mantas,* that the catfish fled from the room.

"I'm sure I am," echoed Amy, studying the painting of *The Dance of the Manatee Mermaid,* which her mother had given her in a pretty, driftwood frame.

"Of course I am!" cried Meg, smoothing the gossamer folds of her first gold filigree shawl, for Mr. Laurence had insisted on giving it. "How can I be otherwise?" said Mrs. Marsh gratefully, as her eyes went from her husband's letter to Beth's smiling face. Her hand caressed the brooch made of hair, gray and golden, lavender, russet and salmon pink. The mergirls had presented this keepsake to her with great affection.

Now and then, in this Ocean, things do happen in the delightful story-scroll fashion, and what a comfort it is. Half an hour after everyone had said they were so happy they could not hold one drop more, the drop came. Laurie opened the parlor door and tried to peep in very quietly. He might just as well have done a backflip and bellowed like a whale. His face was so full of suppressed excitement and his voice so treacherously joyful that he startled everyone. He only said, in an odd, breathless voice, "Here's another holiday present for the Marsh merfamily."

Before the words were well out of his mouth, he was whisked away somehow. In his place appeared a long merman, cloaked to the eyes, leaning on the arm of another long merman, who tried to say something and couldn't. Of course there erupted a wild whirl of arms and tails. For several minutes everybody seemed to lose their wits. The strangest things were done, and no one said a word.

Mr. Marsh became invisible in the embrace of four pairs of loving arms. Jo disgraced herself by nearly fainting away, and had to be nursed by Laurie after sinking to the floor. Mr. Brooke kissed Meg entirely by mistake, as he somewhat incoherently explained. And Amy, the dignified, tangled in the seaweed of her cushion, dragged it across the cave by her tail to her father. She hugged and sobbed over him in the most touching manner. Mrs. Marsh was the first to recover herself, and held up her hand with a warning, "Hush! Remember Beth."

But it was too late. The parlor door flew open, the crimson vest and blue tail appeared on the threshold. Beth, strengthened by joy, darted straight into her father's arms. Never mind what happened just after that, for the full hearts bubbled over with joy. The bitterness of the past dissolved away and left only the sweetness of the present.

It was not at all the dignified reunion of story-scrolls, but they laughed long and heartily. Soon Nanna-pus burst in, sobbing into the kelp salad, which she had forgotten to put down when she darted from the kitchen. This made the merfamily laugh until they sobbed. Soon they fell to nibbling on the kelp that had escaped Nanna-pus' bowl and floated in the parlor around them. Mrs. Marsh began to thank Mr. Brooke for his faithful care of her husband, at which Mr. Brooke suddenly remembered that Mr. Marsh needed rest. Seizing Laurie by the armlets, he precipitately retired. Then the two sick Marsh's were ordered to repose. They did so by nestling down on cushions and talking as fast as their words could spill.

Mr. Marsh told how he had longed to surprise them. When an unexpected warm current came, he had been allowed by his doctor to take advantage of it. He told how devoted Brooke had been, and how he was altogether a most estimable and upright young merman. Mr. Marsh paused a minute just there. After a glance at Meg, who was violently polishing the sun crystal, he looked at his wife with an inquiring lift of the eyebrows. Mrs. Marsh mysteriously nodded her head and asked, rather abruptly, if he wouldn't like another bite of kelp salad. Jo saw and understood the look, and she swam grimly away to get limed fruit and nori wafers. She muttered to herself as she slammed the door, "I hate estimable young mermen with brown eyes!"

There never was such a Sea Queen's Day dinner as they had that day. The algae roast was a sight to behold, when Nanna-pus settled it on the slate table, garnished and glazed with edible sea-flowers. So was the saltwater ice slush, which melted in one's mouth. Likewise the sweet dulse, in which Amy reveled like a sardine in an anemone. Everything turned out well, which was a mercy, Nanna-pus said, "My mind was so flustered, it's a miracle that I didn't lose any of my arms!" She grinned her round, octopus-sort of smile under the praise of her friends. Having no merfamily near of her own, she relished the chance to have such a dear Sea Queen's Day. She would have hugged them all tight, but even a creature such as she couldn't hold that many merfolk at once.

Mr. Laurence and his grandson dined with them, also

Mr. Brooke. Jo glowered at him darkly, to Laurie's infinite amusement. Beth and Father shared the head of the table, feasting modestly on kelp and a little limed fruit. They told stories, sang songs, 'reminisced', as the old merfolks say, and had a thoroughly good time. An oyster sleigh ride had been planned, but the mergirls would not leave their father. So the guests departed early, and the happy merfamily nestled together near the warm sun crystals.

"Just a year ago we were groaning over the dismal holiday we expected to have. Do you remember?" asked Jo, breaking a short pause which had followed a long conversation about many things.

"Rather a pleasant year on the whole!" said Meg, smiling at the crystal. She privately congratulated herself on having treated Mr. Brooke with dignity.

"I think it's been a pretty hard one," observed Amy, watching the light twinkle on her ring with thoughtful eyes.

"I'm glad it's over, because we've got you back," whispered Beth, who leaned on her father's shoulder.

"This year was a difficult one for you, but I think you have borne it bravely and grown from it," said Mr. Marsh. He looked with fatherly satisfaction at the four young faces gathered round him.

"How do you know we've been good? Did Mother tell you?" asked Jo.

"Not much. The seafloor shows the way the currents run, I suppose. I've made several discoveries today."

"Oh, tell us what they are!" cried Meg, who nestled beside him.

"Here is one," he said, taking up the hand of his eldest mergirl. He pointed to the roughened forefinger, a burn on the knuckle, and two or three little hard spots on the palm. "I remember a time when this hand was white and smooth, and your first care was to keep it so. It was very pretty then, but to me it is much prettier now, for in these seeming blemishes I read a little history. This hardened palm has earned something better than blisters. I'm sure the weaving done by these pricked fingers will last a long time, so much goodwill went into the stitches. Meg, my dear, I value the skill which loves with action more than the perfect hands of those who love only in word. I'm proud to shake this good, industrious little hand, and hope I will not too soon see it clasped in marriage."

If Meg had wanted a reward for hours of patient labor, she received it in a father's handshake and approving smile.

"What about Jo? Please say something nice, for she has tried so hard and been so very, very good to me," said Beth in her father's ear.

He laughed and looked at the long mergirl who sat opposite, with an unusually mild expression on her face.

"In spite of the merbaby-short hair, I don't see the Jo who is scared of growing up, whom I left a year ago," said Mr. Marsh. "I see a young merlady who has accepted growing older with the responsibilities it brings. A mermaid who is willing to consider others, and not just the pranks and adventures of youth. She balances fun with fate. Uses the fierceness of her personality for good, not ill. Her face is rather thin and pale just now, with watching and anxiety, but I like how it has changed underneath. Jo has grown, and her voice is smoother. I rather miss my wild merbaby, but if I get a strong, soulful, shark-hearted mermaid in her place, I will feel quite satisfied. I don't know whether cutting your hair released you from clinging to your youth. I do know that in all Pink City I couldn't find anything beautiful enough to be bought with the five-and-twenty sand dollars my good mergirl sent me."

Jo's thin face grew rosy in the crystal light as she received her father's praise. She felt that she did deserve at least a bit of it.

"Now, Beth," said Amy, longing for her turn, but ready to wait.

"I'm afraid to compliment Beth too loudly, for fear she will swim off and hide. Though she is not so shy as she used to be," began their father cheerfully. But recollecting how nearly he had lost her, he held her close, saying tenderly, "I've got you safe, my Beth, and I'll keep you so. You deserve all the praise and love in the Ocean."

After a minute's silence, he looked down at Amy, who nestled into a cushion near him...

"I observed that Amy took modest portions at dinner, and swam to and fro on errands for her mother all the afternoon. She gave Meg her place tonight, and has waited on every one with patience and good humor. I also observe that she does not fret much, nor has she flaunted a very pretty ring which she wears. So I conclude that she has learned to think of other merpeople more and of herself less. She has decided to try and beautify her character as carefully as she paints her pictures. I am glad of this. I would be very proud of a picture painted by her. And I will be infinitely prouder of a daughter with a talent for making life beautiful for herself and others."

"What are you thinking of, Beth?" asked Jo, when Amy had thanked her father and told about her ring.

"I was thinking of how hard the year was, but how many lovely things were in it," answered Beth. Then she slipped from her cushion and swam to her miniature harp. "It's singing time now, and I want to be in my old place. I composed the music for Father, because he likes the verses."

So, sitting at the dear harp, Beth softly touched the strings. In a sweet voice the merfamily had feared never to hear again, she sang to them. She'd composed her own music to go with the ancient poem, which was a singularly fitting song for her.

> *She that is down needn't fear the tide,*
> *She that is low no squall.*
> *If she is loving, if she is true,*
> *She'll float again and again.*
>
> *I am content with what I have,*
> *My path is a beautiful swim.*
> *Come travel with me! Toss me your tail!*
> *We'll float again and again.*

CHAPTER 24

Questions

Like guppies burrowed into the silty Ocean floor, mother and mergirls clung to Mr. Marsh the next day. They neglected everything to look at, wait upon, and listen to the new patient at the merfamily hospital. He rested in the parlor, propped up on a lumpy seaweed cushion. Father insisted that Beth continue to use the best cushion for herself. There were plenty of supplies for two patients, the merfamily assured him. Nothing seemed needed to complete their happiness.

But something was needed, and the elder ones felt it, though none confessed the fact. Mr. and Mrs. Marsh looked at one another with an anxious expression, as their eyes followed Meg. Jo had sudden fits of sobriety, and was seen to shake her tail at Mr. Brooke's cloak, which had been left in the hall. Meg was absent-minded, shy, and silent. She twitched when the door shells clattered, and colored when John's name was mentioned. Amy said, "Everyone seems like they're waiting for something, and can't settle down. Isn't it strange since we have Father already safe at home?"

Beth innocently wondered why their neighbors didn't swim over as usual.

Laurie bobbed by in the afternoon. Noticing Meg at the window, he seemed suddenly possessed with a melodramatic fit. He pulled his seahorse to a stop, and writhed off it, sinking to the Ocean floor. He tore at his hair, and clasped his hands imploringly, as if begging some boon. When Meg told him to behave himself and swim away, he heaved imaginary sobs. Then he wobbled back onto his seahorse while feigning utter despair.

"What does the goosefish mean?" said Meg, laughing and trying to look unconscious.

"He's showing you how your John will go on without you. Touching, isn't it?" answered Jo scornfully.

"Don't say my John. It isn't proper or true," but Meg's voice lingered over the words as if they sounded pleasant to her. "Please don't plague me, Jo. I've told you I don't care much about him. There isn't anything to be said, but we are all to be friendly, and continue as before."

"We can't, for something has been said. You are not like your old self a bit, and seem ever so far away from me. I don't mean to plague you and will bear it like a grown merperson, but I do wish it was all settled. I hate to wait, so if you mean ever to do it, make haste and have it over quickly," said Jo pettishly.

"I can't say anything until he speaks, and he won't, because Father said I was too young," said Meg. She hovered over her weaving with a mysterious smile, which suggested that she did not quite agree with her father on that point.

"If he did speak, you wouldn't know what to say. You'd

sob or blush, or let him have his own way, instead of giving a good, decided no."

"I'm not so silly and weak as you think. I know just what I should say, for I've planned it all, so I needn't be taken unawares. There's no knowing what may happen, and I wish to be prepared."

Jo couldn't help smiling at the important attitude which Meg had unconsciously assumed. Her confidence was as becoming as the pretty pink color rising in her cheeks.

"Would you mind telling me what you'd say?" asked Jo more respectfully.

"I'd be happy to. You are sixteen now, quite old enough to be my confidant. My experience will be useful to you by-and-by, perhaps, in your own affairs of this sort."

"I don't mean to have any affairs of this sort. It's fun to watch other merpeople turn fools for love, but I should feel very much like avoiding it myself," said Jo, looking alarmed at the thought.

"I think not, if you liked anyone very much, and he liked you," Meg spoke as if to herself. She glanced out at the thoroughfare where she had often seen lovers swimming together in the Hot Season.

"I thought you were going to tell me your speech to that merman," said Jo, rudely shortening her sister's reverie.

"Oh, I should merely say, quite calmly and decidedly, 'Thank you, Mr. Brooke. You are very kind, but I agree with Father that I am too young to enter into any engagement at present. So please say no more, but let us be friends as we were.'"

"Hum, that's stiff and cool enough! I don't believe

you'll ever say it, and I know he won't be satisfied if you do. If he goes on like the rejected lovers in scrolls, you'll give in, rather than hurt his feelings."

"No, I won't. I will tell him I've made up my mind, and will glide out of the room with dignity."

Meg floated up as she spoke. She was going to rehearse the dignified exit when a noise in the corridor scared her back into her cushion. She weaved as fast as if her life depended on finishing that particular twist in a given time. Jo smothered a laugh at the sudden change. Then someone opened the door with a grim aspect which was anything but hospitable.

"Good afternoon. I swam over to get my cloak. That is, to see how your father finds himself today," said Mr. Brooke, getting a trifle confused as his eyes went from one telltale face to the other.

"It's very well, he's hanging just there. I'll get him, and tell it you are here." And having jumbled her father and the cloak well together in her reply, Jo swam out of the room. She was considerate enough to give Meg a chance to make her speech with dignity. But the instant she vanished, Meg began to swim toward the door, murmuring...

"Mother will like to see you. Please take a seaweed cushion. I'll call her."

"Don't swim away. Are you afraid of me, Margaret?" Mr. Brooke looked so hurt that Meg thought she must have done something very rude. She blushed up to the salmon-pink curl on her forehead. He had never called her Margaret before. She was surprised to find how natural and sweet it seemed to hear him say it. Anxious to appear friendly and at ease, she put out her hand with a confiding gesture, and said gratefully...

"How can I be afraid when you have been so kind to Father? I only wish I could thank you for it."

"Should I tell you how?" asked Mr. Brooke, holding the small hand fast in both of his own. He looked down at Meg with so much love in the brown eyes that her heart began to flutter. She both longed to run away and to stop and listen.

"I won't trouble you. I only want to know if you care for me a little, Meg. I love you so much, dear," added Mr. Brooke tenderly.

This was the moment for the calm, proper speech, but Meg didn't make it. She forgot every word of it, hung her head, and answered, "I don't know," so softly that John had to stoop down to catch the reply.

He seemed to think it was worth the trouble, for he smiled to himself as if quite satisfied. He pressed the plump hand gratefully, and said in his most persuasive tone, "Will you try and find out? I want to know so much, for I can't work with any heart until I learn whether I am to have my reward in the end or not."

"I'm too young," faltered Meg, wondering why she was so flustered, yet rather enjoying it.

"I'll wait, and in the meantime, you could be learning to like me. Would it be a very hard lesson, dear?"

"Not if I chose to learn it, but..."

"Please choose to learn, Meg. I love to teach, and this is easier than Coastline," broke in John, gaining possession of her other hand. She had no way of hiding her face as he bent to look into it.

His tone was properly beseeching, but stealing a shy

look at him, Meg saw that his eyes were merry as well as tender. He wore the satisfied smile of one who had no doubt of his success. This netted her. Ariel Moffin's foolish lessons in coquetry came into her mind. The love of flirting woke up all of a sudden and took possession of her. She felt excited and strange, and not knowing what else to do, followed a capricious impulse. She withdrew her hands, and said petulantly, "I don't choose. Please swim away and let me be!"

Poor Mr. Brooke looked as if his dreams were sinking. He had never seen Meg in such a mood before, and it rather bewildered him.

"Do you really mean that?" he asked anxiously, following her as she swam away.

"Yes, I do. I don't want to be worried about such things. It's too soon and I'd rather not."

"May I hope you'll change your mind by-and-by? I'll wait and say nothing until you have had more time. Don't play with me, Meg. I didn't think that of you."

"Don't think of me at all. I'd rather you wouldn't," said Meg, taking a naughty satisfaction in trying her lover's patience.

He was grave and pale now, and looked decidedly more like the scroll-stories heroes whom she admired. But he neither slapped his forehead nor beat his tail like they do. He just floated there, looking at her so wistfully, so tenderly. She found her heart relenting in spite of herself. What would have happened next I cannot say, if Aunt Marsh had not come swimming in at this interesting minute.

The old merlady couldn't resist her longing to see her nephew. She had met Laurie as he rode past her grand cave dwelling. Hearing of Mr. Marsh's arrival, she ordered her groom to ready her sleigh immediately.

The Marsh's were all busy in the back part of the caves. So she glided quietly in, hoping to surprise them. She did surprise two of them so much that Meg startled as if she had seen a shark, and Mr. Brooke vanished into the study.

"Bless me, what's all this?" cried the old merlady with a rap of her trident on the floor. She glanced from the disappearing young merman to the scarlet young merlady.

"It's Father's friend. I'm so surprised to see you!" stammered Meg, feeling that she was in for a lecture now.

"That's evident," answered Aunt Marsh. She sunk into a seaweed cushion without loosening her grip on her trident. "But what is Father's friend saying to make you look as red as a crab? There's mischief afloat, and I insist upon knowing what it is." She rapped her trident on the floor again.

"We were only talking. Mr. Brooke swam here for his cloak," began Meg, wishing that Mr. Brooke and his cloak were safely out of the cave.

"Brooke? That merboy's tutor? Ah! I understand now. I know all about it. Jo blundered into a wrong message in one of your Father's letters-in-bottles, and I made her tell me. You haven't gone and accepted him, merchild?" cried Aunt Marsh, looking scandalized.

"Hush! He'll hear. Shan't I call Mother?" said Meg, much troubled.

"Not yet. I've something to say to you, and I must free my mind at once. Tell me, do you mean to marry this tutor? If you do, not one sand dollar of my treasure ever goes to you. Remember that, and be a sensible mergirl," said the old merlady impressively.

Now Aunt Marsh perfected the art of rousing the spirit of opposition in the gentlest of merpeople. She enjoyed doing it. The best of us have a ripple of resistance in us, especially when we are young and in love. If Aunt Marsh had begged Meg to accept John Brooke, she would probably have declared she couldn't think of it. Now that she was ordered not to like him, she immediately made up her mind that she would. Inclination as well as resistance made the decision easy. Being already much excited, Meg opposed the old merlady with unusual spirit.

CHAPTER 25

Answers

"I will marry whom I please, Aunt Marsh. You can leave your sand dollars to anyone you like," Meg said, nodding her head in a resolute manner.

"Floaty-toaty! Is that the way you take my advice, Meg? You'll be sorry for it by-and-by, when you've tried love in a shrimpy cave and found it a failure."

"It can't be a worse life than some merpeople find in grand dwellings," retorted Meg.

Aunt Marsh peered over her trident and took a look at the mergirl, for she did not know her in this new mood. Meg hardly knew herself, she felt so brave and independent. She was glad to defend John and assert her right to love him. Aunt Marsh saw that she had begun wrong, and after a little pause, made a fresh start. She spoke as mildly as she could, "Now, Meg, my dear, be reasonable and take my advice. I mean it kindly, and don't want you to spoil your whole life by making a mistake at the beginning. You ought to marry well and help your merfamily. It's your duty to make a rich match and it ought to be impressed upon you."

"Father and Mother don't think so. They like John though he is poor."

"Your parents, my dear, have no more material wisdom than a pair of merbabies."

"I'm glad of it," cried Meg stoutly.

Aunt Marsh took no notice, but went on with her lecture. "This merboy is poor and hasn't got any rich relations, has he?"

"No, but he has many warm friends."

"You can't live on the warmth of friends. Try it and see how cool they'll grow. He hasn't any business, has he?"

"Not yet. Mr. Laurence is going to help him."

"That won't last long. James Laurence is a crotchety old merman and not to be depended on. So you intend to marry a merman without sand dollars, position, or business when you have none of those yourself? You would work harder than you do now, when you might be comfortable all your days by minding me and doing better? I thought you had more sense, Meg."

"I couldn't do better if I waited half my life! John is good and wise. He's got heaps of talent. We are both willing to work and sure to be able to support ourselves. He's so energetic and brave. Everyone likes and respects him, and I'm proud to think he cares for me," said Meg, looking prettier than ever in her earnest confidence.

"He knows you have got rich relations, merchild. That's the secret of his liking, I suspect."

"Aunt Marsh, how dare you say such a thing? John is above such scheming. I won't listen to you a minute if you talk so," cried Meg indignantly. She forgot everything but the injustice of the old merlady's suspicions. "My John wouldn't marry for sand dollars, any more than I would. We are willing to work and we mean to wait. I'm not afraid of being poor, for I've been happy so far, and I know I shall be with him because he loves me, and I…"

Meg stopped there, remembering all of a sudden that she hadn't made up her mind. She had even told 'her John' to swim off, and that he might be overhearing her inconsistent remarks.

Aunt Marsh was very angry, for she had set her heart on having her pretty niece make a fine match. Something in the mergirl's happy young face made the lonely old mermaid feel both sad and sour.

"Well, I scrub my hands of the whole affair! You are a willful merchild, and you've lost more than you know by this piece of folly. No, I won't stop. I'm disappointed in you, and haven't the spirit to see your father now. Don't expect anything from me when you are married. Your Mr. Brooke's friends must take care of you. I'm done with you forever."

And slamming the door in Meg's face, Aunt Marsh swam off in sour spirits. She seemed to take all the mergirl's courage with her. When left alone, Meg hovered for a moment, undecided whether to laugh or sob. Before she could make up her mind, Mr. Brooke appeared, saying all in a tumble, "I couldn't help hearing, Meg. Thank you for defending me, and Aunt Marsh for proving that you do care for me a little bit."

"I didn't know how much until she insulted you," began Meg.

"And I needn't swim off forever, but may stay and be happy, may I, dear?"

Here was another fine chance to make the crushing speech and the stately exit, but Meg never thought of doing either. She disgraced herself forever in Jo's eyes by meekly whispering, "Yes, John," and hiding her face in Mr. Brooke's vest.

Fifteen minutes after Aunt Marsh's departure, Jo swam softly down the corridor. She paused an instant at the parlor door. Hearing no sound within, she nodded and smiled with a satisfied expression. She said to herself, "She has sent him swimming away as we planned, and that affair is settled. I'll go and hear the fun, and have a good laugh over it."

But poor Jo never got her laugh. She was transfixed upon the threshold by a spectacle which held her there. Her mouth stretched nearly as wide open as her eyes. She expected to exult over a fallen enemy. She intended to praise a strong-minded sister for banishing an objectionable lover. It certainly was a shock to behold the aforesaid enemy serenely nestled into a cushion. And worse—the strong-minded sister cuddled beside him! Jo gave a sort of gasp, as if a frigid current had suddenly slapped her. Such an unexpected turning of the tides actually made her scales tingle. The lovers turned and saw her. Meg rose up, looking both proud and shy, but 'that merman', as Jo called him, actually laughed. He called warmly to the astonished newcomer, "Sister Jo, congratulate us!"

That was adding insult to injury, and was altogether too much. Making some wild demonstration with her tail, Jo vanished without a word. Hurling herself up to the bedrooms, she startled her parents by exclaiming tragically as she burst in, "Oh, do somebody go down quick! John Brooke is acting dreadfully, and Meg likes it!"

Mr. and Mrs. Marsh darted from the room with speed. Casting herself upon the clam shell bed, Jo sobbed and scolded tempestuously, as she told the awful news to Beth and Amy. The little mergirls, however, considered it a most agreeable and interesting event. Jo got little comfort from them. So she swam up to her refuge in the attic, and confided her troubles to the goldfish.

Nobody ever knew what went on in the parlor that afternoon, but a great deal of talking was done. Quiet Mr. Brooke astonished his friends. He mustered eloquence and spirit to plead his case and persuade them to accept his suit.

The time for afternoon cakes arrived before he had finished describing the paradise which he meant to build with Meg. He proudly escorted her to the slate table, both looking so happy that Jo hadn't the heart to be jealous or dismal. Amy was very much impressed by John's devotion and Meg's dignity. Beth beamed at them from a distance. Mr. and Mrs. Marsh surveyed the young couple with tender satisfaction. It was perfectly evident Aunt Marsh was right in calling them as 'materially wise as a pair of merbabies'. No one ate much, but everyone looked very happy. The old room seemed to brighten up amazingly when the first romance of the merfamily began there.

"You can't say nothing pleasant ever happens now, can you, Meg?" said Amy, trying to decide how she would pose the lovers in a portrait she was planning to make.

"No, I'm sure I can't. How much has happened since I said that! It seems a year ago," answered Meg, who was in a blissful dream, floating far above such common things as cakes and jam.

"The joys come close upon the sorrows this time, and I rather think the changes have begun," said Mrs. Marsh. "In most families there comes, now and then, a year full of events. This has been such a one, but it ends well, after all."

"Hope the next will end better," muttered Jo, who found it very hard to see Meg absorbed in a stranger before her face. Jo loved a few merpersons very dearly and dreaded to have their affection lost or lessened in any way.

"I hope the third year from this will end better. I mean it will, if I live to work out my plans," said Mr. Brooke, smiling at Meg, as if everything had become possible to him now.

"Doesn't it seem very long to wait?" asked Amy, who was in a hurry for the wedding.

"I've got so much to learn before I will be ready. Three years seems a short time to me," answered Meg, with a sweet gravity in her face never seen there before.

"We will learn together, my dear mermaid," said John with an expression which caused Jo to shake her head. She felt relief at the sound of the front door, and said to herself, "Here comes Laurie. Now we will have some sensible conversation."

But Jo was mistaken, for Laurie came bubbling in, overflowing with good spirits. He bore a great bridal-looking bouquet for 'Mrs. John Brooke'. He evidently held the delusion that the whole affair had been brought about by his excellent management.

"I knew Brooke would have it all his own way, he always does. When he makes up his mind to accomplish anything, he does it. Regardless of the tides," said Laurie, presenting his offering and his congratulations.

"Much obliged for that recommendation. I take it as a good omen for the future, and invite you to our wedding on the spot," answered Mr. Brooke. He felt at peace with all merfolk, even his mischievous pupil.

"I'll swim to it even if it is at the edge of the Ocean. The sight of Jo's face alone on that occasion would be worth a long journey. You don't look festive, ma'am, what's the matter?" asked Laurie, following her into an alcove in the parlor, where all had adjourned to greet Mr. Laurence.

"I don't approve of the match, but I've made up my mind to bear it, and will not say a word against it," said Jo solemnly. "You can't know how hard it is for me to give up Meg," she continued with a little quiver in her voice.

"You don't give her up. You only go halves," said Laurie consolingly.

"It can never be the same again. I've lost my dearest friend," sighed Jo.

"You've got me, anyhow. I'm not good for much, I know, but I'll be your friend, Jo, all the days of my life. Upon my word I will!" and Laurie meant what he said.

"I know you will, and I'm ever so much obliged. You are always a great comfort to me, Laurie," answered Jo, gratefully tapping her tail fin to his.

"Well, now, don't be dismal. It's all right, you'll see. Meg is happy, and Brooke will swim around and get settled immediately. Grandpa will attend to them, and it will be very jolly to see Meg in her own little cave. We'll have capital times after she is wed. I will be through college before long, and then we'll swim abroad on some nice trip or other. Wouldn't that console you?"

"I rather think it would, but there's no knowing what may happen in three years," said Jo thoughtfully.

"That's true. Don't you wish you could take a look forward and see where we will all be then? I do," replied Laurie.

"I think not, for I might see something sad. Everyone looks so happy now, I don't believe they could be much improved." And Jo's eyes went slowly round the room, brightening as they looked, for the prospect was a pleasant one.

Father and Mother nestled together, quietly reliving the first chapter of the romance which for them began some twenty years ago. Amy was painting the lovers, who floated apart in a beautiful Ocean of their own. Happiness touched their faces with a grace the little artist could not capture in squid ink. Beth nestled on her favorite cushion, talking cheerily with her friend, the Old Mr. Laurence. He held her little hand as if it possessed the power to lead him to the same peace she held in her heart. Jo lounged in her favorite spot in the parlor, with the grave, quiet look which best became her. Laurie, hovering with his chin on a level with her lavender head, smiled in his friendliest way. He nodded at her in the long mirror which reflected them both.

So the curtain falls upon the most eventful year for Meg, Jo, Beth, and Amy.

PART TWO

Three Years Later

CHAPTER 26

First Wedding

The little fish outside the cave were bright and early on the first morning of Hot Season. They rejoiced with all their hearts in the clear, warm water. They spied the feast behind the kitchen window, and bumped their noses against the glass. Some peeped in the upstairs windows, where the sisters dressed the bride. Others nibbled at the merfolk who performed various errands in garden, porch, and hall. All, from the rosiest beta, to the palest anchovy, dipped and darted in joy.

Meg looked very joyful herself. All that was best and sweetest in her heart and soul seemed to swim up into her face. She was fair and tender, with a charm more beautiful than beauty. She would not wear a gold filigree veil over her face. Nor would she paint her tail wedding-white. "I don't want a fashionable wedding, but only those about me whom I love. I wish to look to them like my familiar self."

So she made her wedding vest herself. She wove into it the tender hopes and innocent romances of a mergirlish heart. Her sisters did up her pretty hair. The only ornaments she wore were turquoise flowers, the blooms from the heart-of-the-seas. 'Her John' liked them best of all the sea-flowers that grew.

"You do look just like our own dear Meg. You are so very sweet and lovely, that I should hug you if it wouldn't rumple your hair," said Amy. She surveyed her sister with delight when all was done.

"Then I am satisfied. But please hug and kiss me, every-one, and don't mind my hair. I want a great many rumples of this sort put into it today," and Meg opened her arms to her sisters. They held each other for a long minute, feeling that the new love had not changed the old.

"Now I'm going to bind John's armlets for him. Then I'll stay a few minutes with Father quietly in the study," and Meg swam down to perform these little ceremonies. After-wards she followed her mother wherever she went. Meg sensed that in spite of the smiles on the motherly face, a secret sorrow hid in the motherly heart. Today was the first wedding in their little merfamily.

The merfamily was growing and changing, for the tides do not stand still and three years have passed.

Jo's angles have softened much. She has learned to carry herself with ease, if not grace. Her crop of algae-short hair has lengthened into a thick coil. There was a fresh color in her cheeks, and a soft shine in her silver eyes.

The news-scroll ordered Jo's stories regularly, and paid her a sand dollar a column. She diligently inked out stirring adventure after adventure. Great plans fermented in her busy brain and ambitious mind, and as long as the sand dollars kept rolling in, she felt herself a mermaid of means.

Beth has grown slender, pale, and more quiet than ever.

The beautiful, kind blue eyes seem larger too. They hold an expression that saddens one, although it is not sad itself. She never fully recovered her strength from her long sickness. Beth seldom complains and always speaks hopefully of 'being better soon'. She loves and dotes on her merfamily, who loves her dearly and cares for her.

Amy is with truth considered 'the sea-flower of the merfamily'. At sixteen she has the manners and bearing of a full-grown mermaid. She has taken Jo's place as Aunt Marsh's companion, and Aunt Marsh likes to take credit for teaching Amy graces beyond her years. One saw charm in the lines of Amy's figure, the make and motion of her hands, the flow of her tail. Amy's dull green tail still afflicted her, for it never would shine as much as she'd like it to. Her golden curls were fuller and curlier than ever.

All three mergirls looked just what they were, fresh-faced, happy-hearted mergirls. And, at this moment in their busy lives, they paused to celebrate love. All three wore vests of sparkling silver thread. They wore white sea-flowers in their hair, and sapphire ribbons at their neck. Their faces were alight with so much happiness for Meg and her merman.

According to Meg's wishes, there were to be no ceremonious performances. Everything was to be as natural and homelike as possible. When Aunt Marsh arrived, she was scandalized to find the bridegroom and the father-of-the-bride setting tables. When the bride swam up to welcome her personally, she nearly fainted.

"Upon my word, here's a state of things!" complained the old merlady, nestling into the cushion of honor prepared for her. She smoothed the folds out of her saffron vest. "You ought not to be seen until the last minute, Margaret."

"I'm not a show, Aunty, and no one is coming to stare at me, to criticize my hair, or count the cost of my luncheon. I'm too happy to care what anyone says or thinks, and I'm going to have my little wedding just as I like it. John, dear, here are the forks." And away went Meg to help the bridegroom in his highly improper employment.

Mr. Brooke didn't even say, "Thank you." Instead he kissed his little bride, with a look that made Aunt Marsh swallow a sudden sob.

There was no bridal procession. A sudden silence fell spread through the water as Mr. Marsh and the young couple took their places in the garden. Mother and sisters gathered close, as if loath to give Meg up. The fatherly voice broke more than once, which only seemed to make the service more beautiful and solemn. The bridegroom's tail trembled visibly, and no one heard his replies. But Meg looked straight up in her husband's eyes, and said, "I do!" with such tender trust in her own voice that her mother's heart rejoiced and Aunt Marsh sniffed audibly.

Jo did not sob, though she was very near it once. She was only saved by the consciousness that Laurie was staring at her. He held a comical mixture of merriment and emotion in his large black eyes. Beth kept her face hidden on her mother's shoulder. Amy hovered like a graceful statue, with most becoming swishes of her tail.

It wasn't in style or proper in the least, but the minute she married, Meg shouted, "The first kiss for Marmee!" and turning, gave it with her heart on her mother's surprised cheek. Only then did she let John kiss the bride.

During the next fifteen minutes Meg looked more like an angelfish than ever in her life. Everyone hugged and congratulated her to the fullest, from Mr. Laurence to Nanna-pus. The familial octopus gave her a small statue of two octopi hugging each other with sixteen legs. "For good luck," she said. "Bless you, deary, a hundred times!”

Everybody tried to bless the couple with some brilliant words, or nearly so. Nearly brilliant words did just as well, for laughter is ready when hearts are light. There was no display of gifts, for they were already in Meg and John’s little cave. Nor was there an elaborate feast, but a plentiful lunch of cake and jam, garnished with dulse and nori wafers.

After lunch, merpeople floated about, by twos and threes, through the cave and garden. Meg and John were nestled together on a mushroom coral bench, when Laurie was seized with an inspiration. This inspiration would put the finishing touch on this unfashionable wedding.

“All the married merpeople take hands and dance round the new-made couple, as the Coastlines do. While we bachelors and bachelorettes twirl in circles around you all!” cried Laurie, swimming toward Meg and John with such infectious spirit that everyone followed without a murmur. Mr. and Mrs. Marsh, Aunt and Uncle Caldwell began it, others rapidly joined in. Even Sirena Moffin, after a moment’s hesitation, tossed her hair over her arm and whisked Kenn into the ring. But the crowning joke was Mr. Laurence and Aunt Marsh. When the stately old merman glided up to the old merlady, she tucked her trident under her arm, and swam away. He was faster than she was, and managed to propel himself in front of her. He formally asked her to dance, and she did not refuse a second time. The sight of the two crusty merfolk twirling around set everybody to laughter.

After much merriment, the impromptu ball drew to a close, and the merpeople began to swim home.

"I wish you well, my dear, I heartily wish you well," said Aunt Marsh to Meg, as she hugged her niece good-bye. She added to the bridegroom, as he led her to her oyster sleigh, "You've got a treasure. See that you deserve her."

"That is the prettiest wedding I've been to for an age, Kenn. I don't see why, for there wasn't a bit of style about it," observed Mrs. Sirena Moffin to her husband, as their sleigh pulled them away.

"Laurie, my lad, if you ever want to indulge in this sort of thing, get one of those Marsh mergirls to plan it for you. I would be perfectly satisfied," said Mr. Laurence, nestling himself into a cushion to rest his tail from its celebratory exertions.

"I'll do my best to gratify you, sir," was Laurie's unusually dutiful reply, as he carefully removed the sea-flower Jo had tucked into his armlet.

The couple's little cave was not far away, and the only honeymoon trip they would have was the short swim to it. When Meg and John were ready to leave, her merfamily gathered about them. They said 'good-bye', as tenderly as if she had been going to tour the Coastline.

"Don't feel that I am separated from you, Marmee dear. Or that I love you any less for loving John so much," she said, clinging to her mother, with a little sob for a moment. "I will swim over to visit every day, Father. Expect to keep my old place in all your hearts, though I am married. Beth is going to stay with me a great deal. You other mergirls must drop in now and then to laugh at my housekeeping struggles. Thank you all for my happy wedding day. Good-bye, good-bye!"

The Marsh merfamily hovered at the end of the garden, watching with faces full of love and hope and tender pride as Meg swam away. Her long pink hair billowed out behind her, turquoise flowers glittering in its wave. Most beautiful of all was the way she held her husband's hand. The merfamily knew the two of them would be happy forever.

CHAPTER 27

Acting Sociable

"Swim along, Jo, it's time."

"For what?"

"You don't mean to say you have forgotten that you promised to make half a dozen visits with me today?" asked Amy with a frown.

"I've done a good many rash and foolish things in my life, but I was never fool enough to say I'd make six visits in one day. A single one upsets me for a week."

"Yes, you did, it was a bargain between us. I was to finish the portrait of Beth for you, and you were to go properly with me, and return our neighbors' visits."

Jo hated visits of the formal sort, and never made any until Amy compelled her with a bargain, bribe, or promise. In the present instance there was no escape. So she gave in, pulled on her gloves with a sniff of resignation, and told Amy the victim was ready.

"Jo Marsh, you are perverse enough to provoke an angelfish! You don't intend to make calls in that state, I hope," cried Amy, surveying her with amazement.

"Why not? I'm neat and cool and comfortable, quite proper for swimming about outside. If merpeople care more for my outfit than they do for me, I don't wish to see them."

"Oh, dear!" sighed Amy, "Please at least shine your tail a little bit."

"What's wrong with my tail?"

Amy did not reply to her sister except to hand her a jar of scale polish. Jo pulled her gloves back off and opened the jar. An hour later the mergirls swam out the door with gleaming green tails.

"Now, Jo dear, the Chesters consider themselves very elegant merpeople. So I want you to put on your best deportment. Don't make any of your abrupt remarks, or do anything odd, will you? Just be calm, cool, and quiet, that's safe and merladylike. You can easily do it for fifteen minutes," said Amy, as they approached the first set of caves.

"Let me see. 'Calm, cool, and quiet', yes, I think I can promise that. I've played the part of a prim young mermaid on the stage, and I'll play it perfectly here. My acting powers are great as you will see. So be easy in your mind, my merchild."

Amy looked relieved, but naughty Jo took her at her word. During the first visit she perched gracefully composed, each scale correctly placed. She was calm as a drowsy Hot Season current, cool as a saltwater ice slush, and as silent as a gorge.

In vain Mrs. Chester alluded to Jo's 'charming story scroll'. The Chester mergirls tried to begin conversation about parties, picnics, and the opera. Each and all were answered by a smile, a wave of her hand, and a demure "Yes" or "No" with no elaboration.

In vain Amy mouthed the word 'talk' to Jo. She tried to draw her out, and administered covert pokes with the back of her tail fin. Jo hovered as if blandly unconscious of it all, with deportment entirely calm, cool, and quiet.

"What a haughty, uninteresting creature that oldest Miss Marsh is!" was the unfortunately audible remark of one of the mermaids, as the door closed upon their guests. Jo laughed noiselessly all through the tunnel back outside. Amy looked disgusted at the failure of her instructions. She very naturally laid the blame upon Jo.

"How could you mistake me so? I merely meant you to be dignified and composed, and you made yourself perfect ice and stone. Try to be sociable at the Anglers'. Gossip as other mergirls do. Be interested in dress and flirtations and whatever nonsense comes up. They move in the best society, and are valuable persons for us to know. I wouldn't fail to make a good impression there for anything."

"I'll be agreeable. I'll gossip and giggle, and have horrors and raptures over any trifle you like. I rather enjoy this, and now I'll imitate what is called 'a charming mergirl'. I can do it. See if the Anglers don't say, 'What a lively, nice creature that Jo Marsh is!"

Amy felt anxious, as well she might, for when Jo started her dramatics there was no knowing where she would stop. Amy's face was a picture of forced composure, as she watched her sister float into the next drawing room. Jo kissed all the young mermaids with effusion, and smiled graciously upon the young mermen. Then she joined in the chat with a spirit which amazed the beholder.

Things went well until Mrs. Angler asked Jo where she got the pretty mint green ribbon she wore to the picnic. Theatrical Jo, instead of mentioning the place where she bought it two years ago, answered with unnecessary zest, "Oh, Amy painted it. You can't buy those soft shades, so we paint ours any color we like. It's a great comfort to have an artistic sister."

"Isn't that an original idea?" cried Miss Angler, who found Jo great fun.

"That's nothing compared to some of her brilliant performances. There's nothing the merchild can't do. Why, she wanted a pair of rainbow shells for Sirena Gardinia's wedding to the Moffin merman. So she just painted her stained white ones the loveliest stripes you ever saw. They looked exactly like the real shells," added Jo, with pride in her sister's accomplishments. Poor Amy wished she could disappear into the seaweed cushion—and take Jo with her.

"We read a news-scroll with an adventure story of yours the other day, and enjoyed it very much," observed the elder Miss Angler. She wished to compliment the literary mermaid, but any mention of her stories had a bad effect on Jo. She either grew rigid and looked offended, or changed the subject with a brusque remark, as now. "Sorry you could find nothing better to read. I write rubbish because it sells, and ordinary merpeople like it."

Jo immediately saw her mistake in the look on Miss Angler's face. Miss Angler had truly 'enjoyed' the story. Jo's answer was not grateful or complimentary, but left the poor Angler stumbling for words. Jo so feared to make the matter worse, that she suddenly 'remembered' it was time to leave. She rose with an abruptness that left three mermaids swaying in her wake.

"Amy, we must swim off. Good-bye, dears. Do come and see us. We are pining for a visit. I don't dare to ask you, Mr. Angler, but if you should come, I don't think I will have the heart to send you away."

Jo said this with such an exaggeratedly gushing style, that Amy darted out of the room as rapidly as possible. Amy strongly desired to laugh and sob at the same time.

"Didn't I do well?" asked Jo, with a pat on her own back as they swam away.

"Nothing could have been worse," was Amy's crushing reply. "What possessed you to tell those stories about the ribbon and the shells and the paint?"

"Why, it's funny, and amuses merpeople. They know we are poor, so it's no use pretending that we are not."

"You needn't go and tell them all our private ways, and expose our poverty in that perfectly unnecessary manner. You haven't a bit of proper pride, and never will learn when to hold your tongue and when to speak," said Amy despairingly.

"How should I behave here?" Jo asked humorously, as they approached Aunt Marsh's grand cave dwelling.

"Just as you please. I scrub my hands of you," was Amy's short answer.

They found Aunt Caldwell with Aunt Marsh. The two old mermaids were absorbed in some very interesting subject. They dropped it as the mergirls swam in. Their conscious looks betrayed that they had been talking about their nieces.

Jo was not in a good humor, as she did not feel appreciated for her sociable efforts. She nestled down and sulked, tapping her tail fin aggravatingly on the floor.

Amy, however, kept her focus on being pleasant. Her amiable spirit was felt at once, and both aunts 'my deared' her affectionately.

"How are your Coastline lessons swimming along?" asked Aunt Caldwell, nibbling on a cake.

"Quite well, Auntie," answered Amy. "It's such a lovely language."

"Not at all," put in Jo decidedly. "I hate to be forced to learn another language when it takes so much effort to master my own."

"It's a pleasure to mingle with creatures from all over the Ocean. What wonderful stories they can tell. Some do not appreciate this," observed Aunt Marsh. She looked over her spectacles at Jo, who rocked on her tail, with a somewhat morose expression.

If Jo had only known what happiness wavered in balance for one of them, she would have turned angelfish in a minute. She deprived herself of several years of pleasure with her next statement, and received a timely lesson in the art of choosing her words.

"I don't like mingling. I'd rather be about my own business, and be perfectly independent."

"Ahem!" coughed Aunt Caldwell softly, with a look at Aunt Marsh.

"I told you so," said Aunt Marsh, with a decided nod to Aunt Caldwell.

Mercifully unconscious of what she had done, Jo turned up her chin with her nose stuck up in the water. Her revolutionary attitude was anything but inviting.

Aunt Marsh said to Amy, "You are quite strong and well now, dear, I believe? Eyes don't trouble you any more, do they?"

"Not at all, thank you, ma'am. I'm very well, and mean to do great things next Cold Season."

"Good mergirl!" said Aunt Marsh, with an approving pat on the head, as Amy politely added jam to the tarts.

Polly squalled:

"Stuck in a cave. Stuck in a cave."

He pressed his knobsnout into Jo's face with such impertinence that it was impossible not to laugh.

"Most observing parrotfish," said the old merlady.

"Come along, Amy." Jo rose to swim home, feeling more strongly than ever that visits had a bad effect on her constitution. Amy kissed both the aunts, and the mergirls departed. They left behind them the impression of sweet and sour, an impression which caused Aunt Marsh to say, as they vanished...

"You'd better do it, Coralee. I'll supply the sand dollars."

And Aunt Caldwell to reply decidedly, "I certainly will, if her father and mother consent."

A week later a letter-in-a-bottle came from Aunt Caldwell. Mrs. Marsh's face brightened so much when she read it that Jo and Beth demanded what the glad tidings were.

"Aunt Caldwell is going abroad next month, and wants..."

"Me to go with her!" burst in Jo, floating out of her cushion in an uncontrollable rapture.

"No, dear, not you. It's Amy."

"Oh, Mother! She's too young, it's my turn first. I've

wanted it so long. It would do me so much good, and be so altogether splendid. I must swim along with Aunt Caldwell!"

"I'm afraid it's impossible, Jo. Auntie says Amy, decidedly, and it is not for us to dictate when she offers such a favor."

"It's always so. Amy has all the fun and I have all the work. It isn't fair, oh, it isn't fair!" cried Jo passionately.

"I'm afraid it's partly your own fault, dear. When Aunt spoke to me the other day, she regretted your blunt manners and stiff attitude. Here she writes, as if quoting something you had said—'I planned at first to ask Jo, but as she doesn't 'like mingling', and has no use for 'the Coastline language', I think I won't venture to invite her. Amy is more sociable, will make a good companion for Flo, and receive gratefully any help the trip may give her.'"

"Oh, my tongue, my abominable tongue! Why can't I learn to choose my words?" groaned Jo, remembering the words which had been her undoing. When she had heard the explanation of the quoted phrases, Mrs. Marsh said sorrowfully...

"I wish you could have swum along. There is no hope of it this time, so try to bear it cheerfully. Don't sadden Amy's pleasure by reproaches or regrets."

"I'll try," said Jo, scrunching her face hard while retrieving the satchel that she had joyfully set adrift. "I'll act just like her, and try not only to seem glad, but to be so, and not grudge her one minute of happiness. It won't be easy, for it is a dreadful disappointment."

"Jo, dear, I'm very selfish, but I couldn't spare you. I'm glad you are not going quite yet," whispered Beth, embracing her, satchel and all. Beth's touch was so clinging and her face so loving that Jo felt comforted. Yet she still wished to swim up to Aunt Caldwell and beg to be taken to the Coastline with her whole soul.

By the time Amy swam in, Jo was able to take her part in the merfamily jubilation, although not quite as heartily as usual. The young mermaid herself received the news as tidings of great joy. She sank into a solemn sort of rapture. Then she fell to packing at once. Into travel nets went art boards and squid ink, by-passing such practicalities as outfits and sand dollars.

"It isn't a mere pleasure trip to me, mergirls," she said impressively, as she scraped her best palette. "It will decide my career. If I have any artistic genius, I will find it out at the Coastline, and will do something to prove it."

"Suppose you haven't?" said Jo, weaving away, with a twitchy tail, at the new armlets which were to be handed over to Amy.

"Then I will return and teach drawing for my living," replied the aspirant for fame, with philosophic composure. But she made a wry face at the prospect. She scraped away at her palette as if bent on vigorous measures before she gave up her hopes.

"No, you won't. You hate hard work, and you'll marry some rich merman, and swim back to ride the fins of luxury all your days," said Jo.

"Your predictions sometimes come to pass, but I don't believe that one will. I sure wish it would, for if I can't be an artist myself, I should like to be able to help those who are," said Amy. She smiled as if the part of a mermaid of great generosity would suit her better than that of a poor drawing teacher.

"Hum!" said Jo, with a sigh. "If you wish it you'll have it, for your wishes are always granted—mine never."

"Would you like to swim along?" asked Amy, thoughtfully rubbing a bit of shiny paint over her tail.

"Rather!"

"Well, in a year or two I'll send for you, and we'll breathe real sky air, and carry out all the plans we've made so many times."

"Thank you. I'll remind you of your promise when that joyful day comes, if it ever does," returned Jo. She accepted the vague but magnificent offer as gratefully as she could.

There was not much time for preparation, and the cave was in a ferment until Amy was off. Jo bore up very well until Amy's sleigh started off to the caravan. Then she retired to her refuge, the attic, and sobbed until she couldn't sob any more.

Amy likewise bore up stoutly until she dismounted her sleigh at the caravan. She choked back sobs as she boarded a hermit shell as large as their kitchen, pulled by a giant lobster. It suddenly washed over her that a whole Ocean was soon to roll between her and those who loved her best. She clung to Laurie, who carried in her heaviest net, saying with a sob...

"Oh, take care of them for me, and if anything should happen..."

"I will, dear, I will, and if anything happens, I'll swim there and comfort you," whispered Laurie, little dreaming that he would be called upon to keep his word.

So Amy rode away to the Coastline, which is always new
and beautiful to young eyes. Her father and friend watched
the giant lobsters start forward on their spindly legs. The
enormous shells they pulled followed after them. They
fervently hoped that gentle fortunes would befall the happy-
hearted mergirl. She waved at them until the caravan passed
out of the coral reef, and empty water was all they could see.

CHAPTER 28

From the Coastline

COASTLINE, COVINGTON

Dearest merfamily, Here I nestle at a front window of the Blue Shark Hotel, Covington. It's not a fashionable place, but Uncle Caldwell stopped here years ago, and won't stay anywhere else. However, we don't mean to stay long, so it's no great matter. Oh, I can't begin to tell you how I enjoy it all! I never can, so I'll only give you bits out of my note-scroll, for I've done nothing but sketch and scribble since my voyage started.

Aunt and Flo felt poorly all the entire trip. The bobbing and rocking of our caravan shell made their heads quite addled. They liked to be let alone, and so I nestled into the back and painted what I saw out the windows. Such colorful fish and what rapturous fashions! I wish Beth could have seen them. As for Jo, she would have tried to swim out the window and perch atop the caravan, hanging on for dear life and dear adventure!

It was all heavenly, but I was glad when we finally rumbled to a halt. The ocean is so much bluer here. It's a lighter color all around. I will never forget how strange it looked when I first swam about in it. I kept blinking and shaking my head.

The plants and rocks are different too. Not so much tall kelp, but plenty of brilliant algae and anemones. Also, baby turtles! Oh they are so adorable when they first swim into the sea.

It's very late, but I can't post this letter-in-a-bottle without telling you what happened last evening. Who do you think swam in, as we were just finishing supper? Laurie's Coastline friends, Fred and Frank Waverly! I was so surprised, for I shouldn't have recognized them without introductions. Both are long mermen with emerald green tails. Fred is handsome in the Coastline style. Frank's arm—the one the shark tore—has healed completely, except for a nasty scar. They had heard from Laurie where we were to be, and floated over to invite us to visit their caves.

They swam along to the theater with us after supper. We had such a good time. Frank devoted himself to Flo, and Fred and I talked as if we had known each other all our days. Tell Beth that Frank inquired about her, and was sorry to hear of her ill health. Fred laughed when I spoke of Jo, and sent his 'respectful compliments to the trickiest mermaid.' Neither of them had forgotten Laurie's picnic, or the fun we had there. What ages ago it seems, doesn't it?

Aunt is rapping on the door shells the third time, so I must stop and join her. I really feel like a fine Coastline mermaid. I'm wearing a braided neck ribbon, and have baby turtles painted on my tail. I long to see you all, and in spite of my nonsense am, as ever, your loving...

AMY

VERA HARBOR

Dear mergirls,

In my last I told you about our Covington visit, how kind the Waverlys were, and what pleasant parties they made for us. I enjoyed the trips to the Coastline Museum more than anything else. I saw the paintings of the greatest Coastline artists, and was much inspired. We 'did' Covington to our heart's content, thanks to Fred and Frank. I'm sorry to leave them. Coastline merpeople cannot be outdone in hospitality, I think. The Waverlys hope to meet us in Vera Harbor next Cold Season. I shall be dreadfully disappointed if they don't, because Grace and I are great friends. The merboys are very nice too, especially Fred.

Well, we were hardly settled here in Vera Harbor, when Fred turned up again, saying he had come for an early holiday to enjoy the harbor. Aunt Caldwell looked sober at first, but he was so cool about it she couldn't say a word. And now we get on nicely, and are very glad he's here. He is fluent in Coastline, and I don't know what we should do without him. Uncle doesn't know ten words. He insists on talking the Deep Ocean dialect very loud, as if it would make merpeople understand him. Aunt's Coastline pronunciation is old-fashioned. Flo and I, though we flattered ourselves that we knew a good deal, find that we don't. Fred makes life much easier for us.

Such delightful times as we are having! Sight-seeing from morning until night, and meeting with all sorts of droll adventures. If the water is rough, I spend the day in the Art Museum, reveling in pictures. Jo would turn up her naughty nose at some of the finest, because she has no soul for art. I have one, and I'm cultivating my eye and my taste as fast as I can.

Our rooms are high on the side of a cliff, and nestled on the balcony, we look up and down a long, brilliant thoroughfare. It is so pleasant that we spend our evenings talking there when too tired with our day's work to swim out. Fred is very entertaining. He is altogether the most agreeable young merman I ever knew—except Laurie, whose manners are more charming. I wish Fred was dark-haired, for I don't fancy light-haired mermen. However, the Waverlys are very rich and come of an excellent merfamily. So I won't find fault with their yellow hair, as my own is yellower.

I keep my diary, and try to 'remember correctly and describe clearly all that I see and admire', as Father advised. It is good practice for me, and with my sketch-scroll will give you a better idea of my tour than these scribbles.

I embrace you tenderly, your Amy

VERA HARBOR

My dear Mamma,

Having a quiet hour before we leave for Ruby Reef,

I'll try to tell you what has happened. Some of it is very important, as you will see.

The trip to the shore was perfect, and I'd enjoyed it with all my might. Get Father's old guide-scrolls and read about it. I haven't words beautiful enough to describe it.

That night, back at our cave, was peaceful until about midnight. Flo and I were awakened by the most delicious music outside our windows. We nestled underneath them and hid behind the curtains. Sly peeks outside showed us Fred and the students singing away in the night waters. It was the most romantic thing I ever saw—and the music was fit to melt a heart of stone.

When they were done, we threw some sea-flowers out the window to them. They fought over the petals, and kissed their hands to the invisible mermaids. Then they went swimming away laughing.

Next morning Fred showed me one of the crumpled sea-flowers in his vest pocket. He looked very sentimental. I laughed at him, and told him I didn't throw it, but Flo did. This seemed to disgust him, for he tossed it out of the window, and turned sensible again. I'm afraid I'm going to have trouble with that merboy. It begins to look like it.

(Kayla said once she hoped Fred would marry soon, and I quite agree with her that it would be well for him.)

Vera Harbor has been delightful. I've seen all sorts of important looking statues and artifacts. There was one of a mermaid holding a double-sided trident. I didn't like to ask who she was, as everyone knew it or pretended they did. I wish Jo would tell me all about it. I ought to have read more, for I find I don't know anything, and it mortifies me.

Now comes the serious part, for it happened here, and Fred has just left us. He has been so kind and jolly that we all got quite fond of him. I never thought of anything but a traveling friendship until the serenade night. Since then I've begun to feel that the garden swims and balcony chit chat were something more to him than fun.

Now I know Mother will shake her tail, and the mergirls say, "Oh, the mercenary little fish!", but I've made up my mind. If Fred asks me, I will accept to marry, though I'm not madly in love. I like him, and we get on comfortably together. He is handsome, young, clever enough, and very rich—ever so much richer than the Laurences. I don't think his merfamily would object. I should be very happy, for they are all kind, well-bred, generous merpeople, and they like me.

Fred, as the eldest twin, will have the Covington estate, I suppose, and such a splendid one it is! A city cave in a fashionable thoroughfare. It's not so showy as our big caves in the Deep Ocean, but twice as comfortable. It's full of solid luxury, such as Coastline merpeople believe in. I like it, for it's genuine. I've seen the place, the merfamily jewels, and portraits of their second cave in the wilds outside town. Oh, it would be all I should ask! I may be mercenary, but I hate poverty, and don't mean to bear it a minute longer than I can help. One of us *must* marry well. Meg didn't, Jo won't, Beth can't yet, so I will, and make everything okay all round.

I wouldn't marry a merman I hated or despised. You

may be sure of that. Though Fred is not my model hero, he does very well. In time I should get fond enough of him if he was very fond of me.

So I've been turning the matter over in my mind the last week, for it was impossible to help seeing that Fred liked me. He said nothing, but little things showed it. He never swims out with Flo. He always gets on my side of the sleigh or table. He looks sentimental when we are alone, and frowns at any other merman who ventures to speak to me.

Last evening we swam over to explore the ruins just outside the harbor. Well, at least all of us but Fred, who was to meet us there after checking at the Post Office for letters-in-bottles. We had a charming time poking about the ruins: the tumble down walls covered in algae; the statues with arms and fins broken off; the benches the Mer King carved long ago for his many daughters. I liked the great terrace best, for the view was divine. While the rest went to see the rooms inside, I sat there trying to sketch the sea lion's head on the wall. Wild seaweed crowned it in orange and green. I felt as if I'd slipped into a romance, sitting there, listening to the soft currents, and waiting for my lover. I was like a real story-scroll mergirl. I had a feeling that something was to happen and I was ready for it. I didn't feel blushy or quaky, but quite cool and only a little excited.

By-and-by I heard Fred's voice, and then he swam at a hurl through the great arch to find me. He looked so troubled that I forgot all about myself, and asked what the matter was. He said he'd just got a letter-in-a-bottle begging him to swim home, for Frank was in another shark accident.

Fred was darting off at once to the night caravan and only had time to say goodbye. I was very sorry for him, worried for Fred, and disappointed for myself. Then he said, as he shook hands in a way that I could not mistake, "I will soon swim back to you. You won't forget me, Amy?"

I didn't promise, but I looked at him, and he seemed satisfied. There was no time for anything but goodbyes, for he was off in an hour, and we all miss him very much. I know he wanted to speak to me about our future. I think, from something he once hinted, that he had promised his father not to do anything of the sort yet a while. He is a rash merboy, and the old merman dreads a Deep Ocean daughter-in-law. We will soon meet again, and then, if I don't change my mind, I'll say "Yes, thank you," when he says "Will you, please?"

Of course this is all *very private*, but I wished you to know what is developing. Don't be anxious about me. Remember that I am your 'prudent Amy', and be sure I will do nothing rashly. Send me as much advice as you like. I'll use it if I can. I wish I could see you for a good talk, Marmee. Love and trust me.

Ever your AMY

CHAPTER 29

Arrivals & Departures

Laurie swam into Meg and John's kitchen one Saturday, nearly a year after their wedding. He was received with a clash of jingle shells. Nanna-pus clapped seven of them in sheer joy, somersaulting through the room.

"What's happened? Did *it* happen?" asked Laurie in a loud whisper.

"Oh yes it happened. Doubly happy too," with this somewhat mysterious reply, Nanna-pus darted out of the room, chuckling ecstatically.

Presently Jo appeared, proudly bearing an armful bundled in a delicate night wrap. Her face was very sober, but her eyes twinkled, and there was an odd sound in her voice of repressed emotion of some sort.

"Shut your eyes and hold out your arms," she said invitingly.

Laurie floated precipitately into an alcove, and put his hands behind him. "No, thank you. I'd rather not. I will drop it or smash it, as sure as fate."

"Then you shan't see your godson," said Jo decidedly, turning as if to go.

"I will, I will! Only you must be responsible for damages." Obeying orders, Laurie heroically shut his eyes while something was put into his arms. A peal of laughter from Jo, Mrs. Marsh, Nanna-pus, Beth and John caused him to open them the next minute. Laurie found himself holding two merbabies instead of one.

"...Or your goddaughter," continued Jo.

"Twins!" was all he said for a minute. Then he turned to the mermaids with an appealing look that was comically piteous. He begged, "Take 'em quick, somebody! I'm going to laugh, and I will drop 'em."

Jo rescued the merbabies, swishing her tail back and forth to rock them in the water. She carried one on each arm, as if already initiated into the mysteries of baby-tending. Laurie laughed until he sobbed.

"It's the best joke of the season, isn't it? I wouldn't have told you, for I set my heart on surprising you. I flatter myself that I've done it," said Jo, when she finished swishing.

"I never was more staggered in my life. Isn't it fun? A merboy and a mergirl? What are you going to name them? Let's have another look. Help me, Jo, for upon my life it's one too many for me," answered Laurie.

"Aren't they beauties?" said the proud father, beaming upon the two squirming tails and four reaching arms.

"Most remarkable merchildren I ever saw. Which is which?" and Laurie bent to examine the prodigies.

"We put a black ribbon on the merboy and a red on the mergirl, Coastline fashion, so you can always tell. Besides, one has violet eyes and one brown. Kiss them, Uncle Laurie," said Jo teasingly.

"I'm afraid they mightn't like it," began Laurie, with unusual timidity in such matters.

"Of course they will, they are used to it now. Do it this minute, sir!" commanded Jo, fearing he might propose a proxy.

Laurie screwed up his face and obeyed with a gingerly peck at each little cheek. This produced another laugh, and made the merbabies squeal.

"There, I knew they didn't like it! That's the merboy. He has brown eyes like his father" cried Laurie, delighted with a slap in the face from a tiny green tail.

"He's to be named John Laurence, and the mergirl Margaret, after mother and grandmother. We'll call her Daisy, so as not to have two Megs. I suppose the merboy will need a nickname too. Maybe Johnny?" said Beth, with aunt-like interest.

"Name him Demi-john, and call him Demi for short," said Laurie.

"Daisy and Demi, just the thing! I knew Laurie would do it," cried Jo clapping her hands.

Laurie certainly had done it that time, for the merbabies were 'Daisy' and 'Demi' to the end of their childhoods.

After hours of love and laughter, Laurie and Jo swam home together from the Brooke's little cave.

"What a happy life," mused Laurie.

"Like a story-scroll," said Jo. "Perfectly adorable merbabies. A perfect mixture of mother and father."

"A mixture of black hair and lavender hair would be even cuter," said Laurie, strangely wistful.

Jo looked at her black-haired friend and twisted her own lavender locks around her finger. "It certainly would not," she retorted at last.

"You can't say *certainly* not," said Laurie, slowing to hover in place on the thoroughfare.

Jo gazed into his dark eyes, which were so full of tenderness that they scared her. "Yes, I can!" she cried. With a powerful push of her tail, she propelled herself away from him. She did not stop until she reached her cave. Even then she closed the door behind her without turning to see if Laurie had followed.

The next few days Jo decidedly avoided Laurie. She seemed distant to her merfamily, as if pondering a deep project. She was only truly present when she visited with Daisy and Demi.

Then, all at once, the normal light returned to her eyes, and she sought out her mother in the parlor. Jo had made up her mind.

"You asked me the other day what my wishes were. I'll tell you one of them, Marmee," Jo began, as they wove together. "I want to go away somewhere this Cold Season for a change."

"Why, Jo?" and her mother looked up quickly, as if the words suggested a double meaning.

With her eyes on her work, Jo answered soberly, "I want something new. I feel restless and anxious to be seeing, doing, and learning more than I am. I brood too much over my own small affairs, and need stirring up. I'd like to expand my horizons."

"Where will you expand into?"

"To Pink City. I had a bright idea yesterday, and this is it. You know Mrs. Kiana wrote to you for some respectable young mermaid to teach her merchildren. I think I should suit if I tried."

"My dear, go out to service in that great boarding cavern!" and Mrs. Marsh looked surprised, but not displeased.

"It's not exactly going out to service, for Mrs. Kiana is your friend—the kindest soul that ever lived—and would make things pleasant for me, I know. Her merfamily is separate from the boarders, and no one knows me there. Don't care if they do. It's honest work, and I'm not ashamed of it."

"Nor I. But your writing?"

"All the better for the change. I will see and hear new things, get new ideas. Amy and Meg have new things happening in their lives. I haven't any new material of my own to work with."

"I have no doubt of it, but are these your only reasons for this sudden decision?"

"No, Mother."

"May I know the others?"

Jo looked up and Jo looked down, then said slowly, with sudden color in her cheeks. "I may be mistaken but—I'm afraid—Laurie is getting too fond of me."

"Then you don't care for him in the way it is evident he begins to care for you?" Mrs. Marsh looked anxious as she put the question.

"Mercy, no! I love the dear merboy, as I always have, and am immensely proud of him, but as for anything more, it's out of the question."

"I'm glad of that, Jo."

"Why, please?"

"Because, dear, I don't think you are suited to one another. As friends you are very happy. You can forgive your frequent quarrels, but I fear you would both rebel if you were mated for life. You are too much alike and too fond of freedom. Not to mention your hot tempers and strong wills. I'm afraid you won't get on happily together in a relation which needs infinite patience, as well as love."

"That's just the feeling I had, though I couldn't express it. I'm glad you think he is only beginning to care for me. It would trouble me sadly to make him unhappy. I couldn't fall in love with the dear merboy merely out of gratitude, could I?"

"You are sure of his feelings for you?"

The color deepened in Jo's cheeks as she answered. She bore the mingled pleasure, pride, and pain of a young mergirl first speaking of lovers. "I'm afraid it is so, Mother. He hasn't straight out declared it, but he hints at it, and watches me often. I think I had better swim off before it comes to anything."

"I agree with you, and if it can be managed, you will get to seek your own fortunes in Pink City."

Jo looked relieved, and after a pause, said, smiling, "How Mrs. Moffin would wonder at your lack of management, if she knew. We are purposefully avoiding a marriage with that rich, neighborly merboy. She can rejoice that her Ariel may still hope."

"Ah, Jo, mothers may differ in their management, but the hope is the same in all—the desire to see their merchildren happy. Meg is so, and I am content with her success. You I leave to enjoy your adventures. Amy is my chief care now, but her good sense will help her. For Beth, I indulge no hopes except that she may be well. She seems so much brighter since Daisy and Demi, doesn't she?'

"Yes, I believe she's taking quite well to being an aunt," said Jo.

Mrs. Marsh nodded and smiled. "It's good of the Laurence's to send their sleigh for her when she's too worn to make the trip to Meg's cave."

Jo's thoughts returned to her neighbor. "Let us say nothing about Pink City to Laurie until the plan is settled. I'll swim off before he can collect his wits and be tragic. He's been through so many little trials of the sort, he's used to it, and will soon get over his lovelornity."

Jo spoke hopefully, but could not shake the fear that this 'little trial' would hurt her friend. Perhaps Laurie would not get over his 'lovelornity' as quickly and easily as she'd like him to.

The Pink City plan became real, for Mrs. Kiana gladly accepted Jo, and promised to make a pleasant place for her. The teaching job would make her financially independent. She could turn her leisure time into writing. The new scenes and society would be both useful and agreeable. Jo liked the prospect and was eager to swim off to new waters. The home cave was growing too stale and narrow for her adventurous spirit.

When all was settled, the time arrived to tell Laurie. Jo did so with fear and trembling, but to her surprise he took it very quietly. He had been graver than usual of late, but very pleasant. When she jokingly accused him of turning his tides, he answered soberly, "So I am, and I mean these ones to stay turned."

Jo was very much relieved that one of his virtuous moods should be in full swing just then. She made her preparations with a lightened heart, and hoped she was doing the best for all.

"Two things I leave in your special care," she said to Beth, the night before she left.

"You mean your scrolls?" asked Beth.

"No, our niece and nephew. Be very good to them, won't you?"

"Of course I will, but I can't fill the place of two aunties. You'll miss them, won't you?"

"Yes, truly," said Jo with a sore heart. "And take care of our Laurie too."

"I'll do my best, for your sake," promised Beth, nestling her sister into a hug.

When Laurie said good-bye, he whispered meaningfully, "I won't forget you, Jo. Enjoy Pink City, and return to tell me all about it."

CHAPTER 30

From Pink City

PINK CITY, COOL SEASON

Dear Marmee and Beth,

I'm going to write you a whale-long scroll. I've got heaps to tell, though I'm not a fine young merlady traveling on the Coastline. When I lost sight of Father's dear old face, I felt a trifle lonesome aboard the caravan. I might have sobbed, if a mermaid with four small merchildren hadn't distracted me. I amused myself by tearing off bits of kelp crisp and floating it over to them every time they began to scream.

Mrs. Kiana welcomed me so kindly I felt at ease at once, even in that big cavern full of strangers. She gave me a funny little back cave parlor—all she had left. There is an oven in it, and a nice marble table below a surprisingly large window. I can nestle down and comfortably ink here whenever I like. A fine view of Pink City atones for the many tunnels it takes to swim to my parlor. I took a fancy to my rooms on the spot.

(Pink City does live up to its name. All my life you've told me how it is carved into a mountain of amethyst. Words can't capture how it glistens. It would etch its mark on the hardest heart.)

The nursery, where I am to teach and weave for the merfamily, is a pleasant room. It is next to Mrs. Kiana's private parlor. The two little mergirls are pretty merchildren. They are rather spoiled, I fancy, but they took to me after telling them *The Seven Naughty Cod*. I've no doubt I will make a model governess.

I may have my meals with the merchildren, if I prefer their quarters to the great cavern table. For the present I do, for I am shy, though no one will believe it.

"Now, my dear, make yourself at home," said Mrs. Kiana in her motherly way. "I'm swishing about morning to night, as you may suppose with such a cavernous merfamily. A great anxiety will be off my mind if I know the merchildren are safe with you. My private parlor is always open to you, and your own will be as comfortable as I can make it. There are some pleasant merpeople in the house if you feel sociable. Your evenings are always free. Swim to me if anything goes wrong, and be as happy as you can. There's the shells clattering for the afternoon cakes, I must dash off and attend to them." And off she swam, leaving me to settle myself in my new surroundings.

As I swam down the tunnels soon after, I saw something I liked. The tunnels are very long in this enormous boarding cave. As I hovered waiting at the head of the third one for a little mergirl to struggle through, I saw a merman come along behind her. He asked her if he could help her with the heavy load she carried. She looked so relieved. He swam it all the way up, and settled it down at a nearby door. Then he glided away, saying, with a kind nod and a Coastline accent, "It goes better so. The little tail is too young to have such heaviness."

Wasn't it good of him? I like such things, for as Father says, trifles show character. When I mentioned it to Mrs. Kiana that evening, she laughed, and said, "That must have been Professor Bhaer. He's always doing things of that sort."

Mrs. Kiana told me he was from the Coastline, very learned and good, but hadn't two spare sand dollars to his name. He gives lessons to support himself and two little orphan nephews—Krill and Rio—whom he is educating here. His sister willed it so. She married a merman from the Deep Ocean, and wants her children raised in Pink City. Not a very romantic story, but it interested me. I was glad to hear that Mrs. Kiana lends him her parlor for some of his scholars. There is a glass door between it and the nursery, and I mean to peep at him, and then I'll tell you how he looks. He's almost forty, so it's no harm, Marmee.

After supper and a go-to-bed romp with the little mergirls, I attacked the big work satchel. Then had a quiet evening chatting with my new friend. I will keep a journal-letter, and send it once a week, so goodnight, and more another time.

Nothing has happened to write about, except a visit to Miss Narwhal. She has a room full of pretty things, and is very charming. She showed me all her bits and baubles. Then she asked me if I would sometimes go with her to lectures and concerts, as her escort, if I enjoyed them. She put it as a favor, but I'm sure Mrs. Kiana has told her about us, and she does it out of kindness to me. I'm as proud as a puffer, but such favors from such merpeople don't grieve me, and I accepted gratefully.

When I got back to the nursery, there was such an uproar in the parlor on the other side of the glass door. I looked in, and there was Mr. Bhaer swimming in circles, with Mrs. Kiana's daughter Tina on his back. Her second daughter, Charisma, was leading him with a long ribbon. Meanwhile her third daughter, Minnie, fed two small merboys dulse cakes. The merboys roared and ramped in cages built of seaweed cushions.

"We are playing zoo," explained Charisma.

"Dis is mine giant lob'er!" added Tina, holding on by the Professor's hair.

"Mamma always allows us to do what we like Saturday afternoon, when Krill and Rio come, doesn't she, Mr. Bhaer?" said Minnie.

The 'giant lobster' sat up, looking as much in earnest as any of them. He said soberly to me, "I give you my word it is so, if we make too large a noise you will say Hush! to us, and we go more softly."

I promised to do so, but left the glass door open and

enjoyed the fun as much as they did. A more glorious
frolic I never witnessed.

They played squid and soldiers, then danced and
sang. When they grew tired at last, they all nestled about
the Professor. He told charming stories of baby turtles
hatching on beaches. Or of the 'big white moon' that
one can see if one pops one's head out of the Ocean. I
wish Deep Ocean merfolk were as simple and natural as
Coastline merfolk, don't you?

I'm so fond of writing, I should go inking on forever
if motives of economy didn't stop me. Though I've used
a thin kelp scroll, I tremble to think of the postage this
letter-in-a-bottle will need.

Pray forward Amy's letters-in-bottles as soon as you
can spare them. My small news will sound very flat after
her splendors, but you will like them, I know. Is Laurie
studying so hard that he can't find time to write to his
friends? Take good care of him for me, Beth, and tell me
all about the merbabies, and give heaps of love to everyone. From your faithful Jo.

P.S. On reading over my letter, it strikes me as rather
Bhaery. I am always interested in odd merpeople, and I
really had nothing else to write about. Bless you!

MIDDLE OF COLD SEASON

A Happy New Year to you all, my dearest merfamily,
which of course includes Mr. L. and a young merman by
the name of Laurie. I can't tell you how much I enjoyed
your Sea Queen's Day satchel, for I didn't get it until
night and had given up hoping. Your letter-in-a-bottle

came in the morning. You tricky creatures sent the satchel to arrive later, meaning it for a surprise.

I was a bit troubled. I didn't think you would forget me, but I suspected you had. I felt sad as I lounged in my room after afternoon cakes. When the big, silty, battered-looking satchel was brought to me, I just hugged it and twirled. It was so homey and refreshing that I sunk down to the floor and read and ate and laughed and cried, in my usual absurd way.

The things were just what I wanted, and all the better for being made instead of bought. Beth's new 'ink holder' was capital, and Nanna-pus's box of hard ginger-kelp crisp will be a treasure. I'll be sure and wear the nice black vest you sent, Marmee, and read carefully the scrolls Father has marked. Thank you all, heaps and heaps!

Speaking of scrolls reminds me that I'm getting rich in that line, for on New Year's Day Mr. Bhaer gave me a fine volume of poetic stories. It is one he values much, and I've often admired it. So you may imagine how I felt when he brought it to me, inscribed "To Josephine Marsh, from your friend Friedrich Bhaer".

"You say often you wish a library. Here I gift you one, for in this roll are many scrolls in one. Read the poems well, and the stories will help you much. The study of character in this scroll will help you to read the Ocean. Then paint those in it with your pen."

I thanked him as well as I could, and talk now about 'my library', as if I had a hundred scrolls. I never knew how much there was in the poems of the Coastline before, but then I never had a Bhaer to explain them to me. Now don't laugh at his horrid name. It isn't pronounced either Bear or Beer, as Deep Ocean merfolk will say it. It's said something between the two, as only Coastliners can pronounce it. I'm glad you both like what I tell you about him, and hope you will know him some day. Father would admire his warm heart, and Mother his wise head. I admire both, and feel rich in my new 'friend Friedrich Bhaer'.

Not having many sand dollars, or knowing what he'd like, I got him several little things. I hid them about his parlor, where he would find them unexpectedly. They were useful, pretty, or funny. A new inkstand on his table... A little vase for his sea-flower, (he always keeps a sea-flower)... And a comb holder out of a purple shell. I made it like those Beth invented. A manta ray with a mouth for the opening, and black fins, woven tail, and beady eyes. It took his fancy immensely. He set it beside his deep sun crystal like it were a marble statue, so it was rather a failure after all. Poor as he is, he didn't forget a servant or a merchild in the whole boarding caverns. And not a soul here, from the laundry mermaid to Miss Narwhal forgot him. I was so glad of that.

They got up a masquerade, and had a jolly time New Year's Eve. I didn't mean to attend, having no costume. But at the last minute, Mrs. Kiana remembered some old mother-of-pearls. Miss Narwhal lent me lace and ribbons. So I dressed up as Nina, Princess of the Seven Seas, and sailed in with a mask on. No one knew me, for I disguised my voice. No one dreamed that I was the silent, haughty Miss Marsh (for they think I am very stiff and cool, most of them, and so I am to whippersnappers). I enjoyed it very much, and when we unmasked it was fun to see them stare at me. I heard one of the young mermen tell another that he knew I'd been an actress. In fact, he thought he remembered seeing me at one of the minor theaters. Meg will relish that joke. Mr. Bhaer was the Orca King, and Tina was his baby calf, a perfect little angelfish in his arms. To see them dance was 'quite a seascape', to use a Laurie-ism.

I had a very happy New Year, after all. When I thought it over in my chambers, I felt as if I was getting on a little in spite of my many failures. I'm cheerful all the time now, work with a will, and take more interest in other merpeople than I used to, which is satisfactory. Bless you all! Ever your loving... Jo

CHAPTER 31

Writing Stories

Jo was very happy in the social atmosphere about her. She was also very busy with the daily work that earned her keep and made it sweeter for the effort. Yet she still found time for literary labors.

She was shy about her stories, and kept her inking a secret from the others at the boarding cave. When she saw a wanted advertisement in the Weekly Volcano, a magazine-scroll that published short stories, she decided to take her chances.

She told no one, but concocted a 'sweet romance'. Then she dressed herself in her best shells, and boldly swam to the Weekly Volcano's editor, Mr. Dashwood.

Now the offices of this magazine scroll were disorderly alcoves. Bits and bobs floated everywhere. Three mermen lounged at desks, with their tail fins on the tables. Somewhat daunted by this reception, Jo hesitated on the threshold, murmuring in much embarrassment...

"Excuse me, I was looking for the Weekly Volcano office. I wished to see Mr. Dashwood."

Feeling that she must get through the matter somehow, Jo produced her story-scroll. Blushing redder and redder with each sentence, she blundered out fragments of a speech she'd prepared for the occasion.

"A friend of mine desired me to offer—a story—just as an experiment—would like your opinion—be glad to ink more if this suits."

While she blushed and blundered, Mr. Dashwood took the story-scroll. He unrolled it with a pair of rather dirty fingers, casting critical glances up and down the neat writing.

"Not a first attempt, I take it?" observing that the scroll was orderly, inked only on one side, and not tied up with a ribbon—sure sign of a novice.

"No, sir. My friend has had some experience, and got a prize for a tale in the *Baleen Banner*."

"Oh, did she?" and Mr. Dashwood gave Jo a quick look, which seemed to take note of everything she had on, from shells on her corset to her green gloves. "Well, you can leave it, if you like. We've more of this sort of thing on hand than we know what to do with at present. I'll run my eye over it, and give you an answer next week."

Now, Jo did *not* like to leave it, for Mr. Dashwood didn't suit her at all. Under the circumstances, there was nothing for her to do but leave the scroll and swim away. She did so looking particularly long and dignified, as she was apt to do when annoyed or abashed. Just then she was both. The knowing glances exchanged among the mermen told her that they considered the little fiction of 'my friend' a good joke. Then a laugh, produced by some inaudible remark of the editor, as he closed the door, completed her discomfiture. Half resolving never to return, she swam home. She worked off her irritation by weaving vigorously. In an hour or two she felt well enough to laugh over the scene and long for next week.

* * *

When she swam again to the offices for her answer, Mr. Dashwood was alone. He was much wider awake than before, so the second interview was much more comfortable than the first.

"We'll take this (editors never say I), if you don't object to a few alterations. It's too long, but omitting the passages I've marked will make it just the right length," he said, in a businesslike tone.

Jo hardly knew her own story-scroll, so crumpled and underscored were its lines and paragraphs. She felt as a tender parent might if asked to cut off her baby's tail in order that it might fit into a new cradle. When she looked closely at the marked passages, she was surprised to find that all the romance had been stricken out.

"But, sir, this is a sweet romance. You've only left in the crime parts with the villain."

Mr. Dashwoods's editorial gravity relaxed into a smile, for Jo had forgotten her 'friend', and spoken as only an author could.

"Sweet stories don't sell nowadays. Merfolk want to be scared. True crime is all we'll print." Which was not quite a correct statement, by the way.

"You think it would do with these alterations, then?"

"Yes, your villain is close enough to real life. We'll develop him more and say it happened," was Mr. Dashwood's affable reply.

"What do you—that is, what compensation—" began Jo, not exactly knowing how to express herself.

"Oh, yes, well, we give from twenty-five to thirty for things of this sort. Pay when it comes out," replied Mr. Dashwood, as if that point had escaped him. Such trifles do escape the editorial mind, it is said.

"Very well, you can have it," said Jo, handing back the story with a satisfied nod. After the dollar-a-column she made back in her little coral reef, even twenty-five seemed good pay.

"Should I tell my friend you will take another if she has one better than this?" asked Jo, unconscious of her little slip of the tongue, and emboldened by her success.

"Well, we'll look at it. Can't promise to take it. Tell her to make it gritty and criminal, and never mind the fluff.

What name would your friend like to put on it?" Mr. Dashwood asked in a careless tone.

"None at all, if you please, she doesn't wish her name to appear and has no pen name," said Jo, blushing in spite of herself.

"Just as she likes, of course. The tale will be out next week. Will you swim here for the sand dollars, or should I post them?" asked Mr. Dashwood, who felt a natural desire to know who his new contributor might be.

"I'll swim here. Good morning, sir."

As she darted off, Mr. Dashwood put his tail fin on the table with the graceful remark, "Poor and proud, as usual, but she'll do."

Following Mr. Dashwood's directions, Jo took the plunge into the frothy sea of true crime literature. She went to the news-scroll offices and poured over old happenings. They were miserable, tragic stories that did nothing for her imagination. She labored through her retellings, line by line, careful not to introduce any extra tenderness or fantasy.

Mr. Dashwood found her work suitable. She was soon regularly published at twenty-five sand dollars a week.

Though she delighted in the pay, Jo felt an ache in her heart. She hadn't time to ink out all the sweet romances and adventure stories bottled up inside her. Jo reminded herself that she'd come to the capital city in order to get new material. True crime was certainly nothing she'd thought of before. So she kept inking, telling herself that she would make the best of it.

As the weeks followed, one after another, Jo never lost her longing to write again with heart and passion. Quite unexpectedly, she found encouragement through a scroll-paper trident.

One evening Professor Bhaer floated in to give Jo a lesson in Coastline. He had a scroll-paper trident hanging on his back. Little Tina had pinned it there and he had forgotten to take it off.

Enjoying the sight of Mr. Bhaer dressed up like a warrior, Jo held her tongue. But before Mr. Bhaer could settle into the seaweed cushion, the trident fell from his back and drifted to the floor.

He caught the trident, laughing until he noticed the picture on one of its forks. He unrolled the scroll paper with regret, "I wish I had something other than this for the merchildren."

Jo glanced at the sheet and saw a scene from a true crime magazine. Two dead clown fish floated belly up on a busy thoroughfare.

"Yes," said Jo, "True crime isn't the best for merchildren. I grew up on stories of sweet romance and cozy adventure."

Jo had tried to hide her writing from him, because she was bashful about it, and not proud of her work. Mr. Bhaer, however, was quite observant and had guessed at her secret profession.

"Would you be able to ink out a story or two for my nephews?" he asked.

"You know that I write?"

"The ink is often on your hands."

"I must confess, I've been so busy inking for that magazine-scroll in your hand that I haven't had time to ink out any stories that I love."

"You write true crime?"

Jo nodded, turning crab-leg red.

"But you do not have your heart in it?" asked Mr. Bhaer.

"No, I haven't the time for stories with heart these days. All my effort goes into selling to the Weekly Volcano."

"Ah," he said, looking disappointed. He began to swim away, but then hovered in place and turned toward her. "May I speak freely, as a friend? A good friend?"

Jo felt her face redden even more, if it were possible. She was sensitive about her writing, and always felt judged by others for it. "Yes," she whispered.

"You have a good mind and good heart. Don't abandon them in the stale water of other people's interests." And with that, he swam away before she could answer.

* * *

It was a pleasant stay for Jo at Mrs. Kiana's boarding house, and a long one. She did not finish her work tutoring Charisma and Tina until late in the Warm Season.

Everyone seemed sorry when the time came for her to leave Pink City and return home. The merchildren were inconsolable, and Mr. Bhaer's hair stuck straight up all over his head. The merman always rumpled it wildly when he felt disturbed in mind.

"Going home? Ah, you are happy that you have a home to swim back to," he said, when she told him. Then he hovered apart, silently pulling his hair in the alcove.

Jo was departing on the early caravan, so she bade everyone in the boarding cavern goodbye the night before.

When Mr. Bhaer's turn came, she said warmly, "Now, sir, you won't forget to swim over and see us, if you ever travel our way, will you? I'll never forgive you if you forget, for I want you all to know my friend."

"Do you? Shall I swim to visit?" he asked, looking down at her with an eager expression which she did not see.

"Yes, come next month. Laurie graduates then, and you'd enjoy a Deep Ocean graduation ceremony. It will be something new for you."

"That is your best friend, of whom you speak?" he said in an altered tone.

"Yes, my merboy Laurie. I'm very proud of him and should like you to see him."

Jo looked up then, quite unconscious of anything but her own pleasure in the prospect of introducing them to one another. Something in Mr. Bhaer's face suddenly reminded her of the fact that Laurie wanted to be more than a 'best friend'.

She began to blush simply because she wanted to avoid the subject. The more she tried not to blush, the redder she grew. If it had not been for Tina in her arms, she didn't know what would have become of her. Fortunately the merchild was moved to hug her just then. So Jo managed to hide her face for an instant, hoping the Professor did not see it. But he did, and his own changed again from that momentary anxiety to a neutral expression, as he said cordially...

"I fear I shall not make the time for that, but I wish the friend much success, and you all happiness." And with that, he shook hands warmly, shouldered Tina, and swam away.

Later that night, after the merboys were nestled into

their night wraps, he floated about with a tired look on his face. Homesickness grew heavy in his heart.

"A cave and a companion are not for me. I must not hope it now," he said to himself, with a sigh that was almost a groan.

Early as it was, he was at the caravan next morning to see Jo off. Thanks to him, she began her solitary journey with the pleasant memory of a familiar face smiling farewell. He provided a bunch of purple zoas to keep her company, and best of all, the happy thought, "Well, the Cold Season's gone and Warm Season nearly with it. I haven't written stories with passion, I've earned no fortune, but I've made a friend worth having and I'll try to keep him all my life."

CHAPTER 32

Denied

Whatever his motive might have been, Laurie studied with purpose that year. He graduated college with honors, and gave the Coastline oration with grace and eloquence. They were all there, his grandfather—oh, so proud—Mr. and Mrs. Marsh, John and Meg, Jo and Beth. All exulted over him with the sincere admiration which young merfolk make light of at the time, but fail to win from the Ocean by any after-triumphs.

"I've got to stay here for this confounded, formal supper, but I will swim home early tomorrow. You'll come and meet me as usual, mermaids?" Laurie said, as the sisters gathered into the oyster sleigh after the joys of the day were over. He said 'mermaids', but he meant Jo, for she was the only one who kept up the old custom. She had not the heart to refuse her splendid, successful merboy anything, and answered warmly...

"I'll come, Laurie, and parade in front of you, playing 'Hail the conquering hero comes' on a jingle shell drum."

Laurie thanked her with a tender look that brought

sudden panic, "Oh, deary me! I know he'll say something, and then what will I do?"

Evening thoughts and morning work somewhat allayed her fears. She decided that she wouldn't be vain enough to think he would declare his love when she had given him every reason to know what her answer would be.

She swam out at the appointed time, hoping Laurie wouldn't do anything to make her hurt his poor feelings. A visit to Meg's, and a cuddle with Daisy and Demijohn, still further fortified her for the meeting with Laurie. Yet when she saw a stalwart, aquamarine figure looming in the distance, she had a strong desire to backflip and dart away.

"Where's the jingle shell drum, Jo?" called Laurie, as soon as he was within speaking distance.

"I forgot it." And Jo's fears calmed again, for that salutation could not be called lover-like.

She always used to take his arm on these occasions. This time she did not. He made no complaint, which was a bad sign. He talked about all sorts of faraway subjects, until they reached a little path that wove among the coral. Then he swam more slowly. He suddenly lost his fine flow of language, and now and then a dreadful pause occurred. To rescue the conversation from one of the gorges of silence into which it kept sinking, Jo said hastily, "Now you must have a good long holiday!"

"I intend to."

Something in his resolute tone made Jo look up quickly. She found him looking down at her with an expression that assured her the dreaded moment had arrived. She put out her hand with an imploring, "No, Laurie. Please don't!"

"I will, and you must hear me. It's no use, Jo. We've got

to have it out, and the sooner the better for both of us," he answered, getting flushed and excited all at once.

"Say what you like then. I'll listen," said Jo, with a desperate sort of patience.

Laurie was a young lover, but he was in earnest, and meant to 'have it out', if he died in the attempt. So he plunged into the subject with characteristic impetuosity, saying in a voice that would get choky now and then, in spite of his efforts to keep it steady...

"I've loved you ever since I've known you, Jo. Couldn't help it, you've been so good to me. I've tried to show you, but you wouldn't let me. Now I'm going to make you hear, and give me an answer. I can't live without one any longer."

"I wanted to save you this. I thought you'd understand..." began Jo, finding it a great deal harder than she expected. "I never wanted you to love me, and I swam away to keep you from it if I could."

"I thought so. It was like you, but it was no use. I only loved you all the more, and I worked hard to please you, and I gave up billiards and everything you didn't like, and waited and never complained, for I hoped you'd love me, though I'm not half good enough..." Here there was a choke that couldn't be controlled, so he decapitated seaflowers while he cleared his 'confounded throat'.

"You—you are, you're a great deal too good for me, and I'm so grateful for you, and so proud and fond of you. I don't know why I can't love you as you want me to. I've tried, but I can't rouse the feeling. It would be a lie to say I do when I don't."

"Really, truly, Jo?"

He hovered in front of her, and caught both her hands

in his. He waited for the answer with a look that she did not soon forget.

"Really, truly, dear."

They were deep among the coral now. When the last words slipped reluctantly from Jo's lips, Laurie dropped her hands and turned as if to swim away. Instead he sank at the base of a mighty elkhorn, and lay his head down on its coarse trunk. He lay so still that Jo was frightened.

"Oh, Laurie, I'm sorry, so desperately sorry. I wish you wouldn't take it so hard. I can't help it. You know it's impossible for merpeople to make themselves love other merpeople if they don't," said Jo inelegantly but remorsefully. She softly patted his shoulder, remembering the time when he had comforted her so long ago.

"They do sometimes," said a muffled voice from the elkhorn trunk.

"I don't believe it's the right sort of love, and I'd rather not try it," was the decided answer.

There was a long pause, filled with the *rat tat tat* of a nearby mantis shrimp breaking open clams. Thick seagrass rustled around them. Presently Jo said very soberly, as she perched on a ball of mushroom coral near the elkhorn, "Laurie, I want to tell you something."

Laurie grimaced as if he had been harpooned. He thrashed his tail back and forth, and said in a fierce tone, "Don't tell me that, Jo, I can't bear it now!"

"Tell what?" she asked, wondering at his temper.

"That you love that old merman."

"What old merman?" demanded Jo, thinking he must mean his grandfather.

"That foam-scum of a Professor you were always inking

about. If you say you love him, I know I will do something desperate." He looked as if he would keep his word, as he clenched his hands with a wrathful glint in his eyes.

Jo wanted to laugh, but restrained herself. She said passionately, for she too, was getting excited with all this, "Don't swear, Laurie! He isn't old, nor anything bad, but good and kind. He's the best friend I've got, next to you. Please don't slip into a fit. I want to be kind, but I know I will get angry if you abuse my Professor. I haven't the least idea of loving him *like that* or anybody else."

"But you will after a while, and then what will become of me?"

"You'll love someone else too, like a sensible merboy, and forget all this trouble."

"I can't love anyone else, and I'll never forget you, Jo. Never! Never!" with a smack of his tail on the sea floor to emphasize his passionate words.

"What will I do with him?" sighed Jo, finding that emotions were more unmanageable than she expected. "You haven't heard what I wanted to tell you. Nestle down and listen. I want to do what is right and make you happy," she said. She hoped to soothe him with a little reason, not knowing that reason is of little use in these matters of love.

Hearing a bit of hope in her words, Laurie threw himself down into the algae beside Jo's mushroom coral. He curled his tail fins around the base of the ball, and looked up at her with an expectant face. Now that arrangement was not conducive to calm speech or clear thought on Jo's part. How could she say difficult things to her merboy while he watched her with eyes full of love and longing? She gently turned his head away, averting his eyes. Then she said, as she ran her fingers through his coarse, black hair, "I agree with Mother that you and I are not suited to each other. Our quick tempers and strong wills would probably make us very miserable, if we were so foolish as to..." Jo paused a little over the last word, but Laurie uttered it with a rapturous expression.

"Marry—no, we wouldn't be miserable! If you loved me, Jo, I should be a perfect angelfish. I would do anything for you. Just tell me how to behave."

"No, I can't. I've tried and failed to fall in love with you. I won't risk our happiness by trying to change you. We don't agree and we never will. So we'll be good friends all our lives, but we won't go and do anything rash."

"Yes, we would agree if we get the chance," muttered Laurie rebelliously.

"Now do be reasonable, and take a sensible view of the case," implored Jo, almost at her wit's end.

"I won't be reasonable. I don't want to take what you call 'a sensible view'. It won't help me, and it only makes it harder. I don't believe you've got any heart."

"I wish I hadn't."

There was a little quiver in Jo's voice. Thinking it a good omen, Laurie turned round, bringing all his persuasive powers to bear. He said, in the wheedlesome tone that had never been so dangerously wheedlesome before, "Don't disappoint us, dear! Everyone expects it. Grandpa has set his heart upon it, your merpeople like it, and I can't get on without you. Say you will, and let's be happy. Do, do!"

Not until many seasons later did Jo understand how she had the strength to hold fast to her resolution. She had decided that she did not love her merboy, and never could.

It was very hard to do, but she held her course, knowing that delay was both useless and cruel.

"I can't say 'yes' truly, so I won't say it at all. You'll see that I'm right, by-and-by, and thank me for it..." she began solemnly.

"I'll be speared before I do!" and Laurie darted up from the algae, shaking with indignation at the very idea.

"Yes, you will see that I'm right!" persisted Jo. "You'll get over this after a while, and find some lovely, accomplished mermaid. She will adore you and make you a fine companion for your fine life. I shouldn't. I'm homely and awkward and odd. You'd be ashamed of me, and we should quarrel—we can't help it even now, you see—and I shouldn't like elegant society and you would. You'd hate my inking, and I couldn't get on without my stories. We would be unhappy, and wish we hadn't done it, and everything would be horrid!"

"Anything more?" asked Laurie, finding it hard to listen patiently to this prophetic burst.

"Nothing more, except that I don't believe I will ever marry. I'm happy as I am, and love my single life too well to exchange it for a merman."

"I know better!" broke in Laurie. "You think so now, but there'll come a time when you will care for somebody. You'll love him tremendously, and live and die for him. I know you will. It's your way. I will have to hover aside and watch." The despairing lover sank with such a gesticulation of the tail fin that it would have been comical, if his face had not been so tragic.

"Yes, I will live and die for him, if a merman ever manages to make me love him, and you must manage it the best you can!" cried Jo, losing patience with poor Laurie. "I've done my best, but you won't be reasonable. It's selfish of you to keep wheedling for what I can't give you. I will always be fond of you, very fond indeed, as a friend, but I'll never marry you. The sooner you believe it the better for both of us—so now!"

That speech was like a tempest blast. Laurie looked at her a minute as if he did not quite know what to do with himself. Then he turned sharply away, saying in a desperate sort of tone, "You'll be sorry some day, Jo."

"Oh, where are you swimming off to?" she cried, for his face frightened her.

"To the deepest, darkest trench!" was the consoling answer.

For a minute Jo's heart stood still, as he propelled himself down the path toward the gorge. Yet Laurie was not one of the sort who are conquered by a single failure. He had no thought of a melodramatic plunge, but some blind instinct led him to swim close to the edge. Jo choked back sobs as she watched the poor fellow disappear into the distance. She felt as if she had murdered some innocent thing and buried it deep in a dark kelp forest.

"Now I must go and prepare Mr. Laurence to be very kind to my poor merboy. Dear me, this whole situation is dreadful."

Being sure that no one could do it as well as herself, she swam straight to Mr. Laurence. She told the difficult story bravely through, and then broke down, sobbing. The kind old merman, though sorely disappointed, did not utter a reproach. He knew even better than Jo that love cannot be forced. So he shook his head sadly and resolved to carry his merboy out of harm's way.

That evening, when Laurie returned to the cave, his grandfather met him with open arms. "My merboy," said the old merman, "This home cave will do you no good. You need time and distance. Swim off to the Coastline for a long tour." Surprised, Laurie pushed away from his grandfather. He studied the old merman's eyes. They were full of such love and sincerity that all Laurie could do was pull the old merman close and quietly agree.

Beth's Secret

When Jo had first returned home from her work in Pink City, she had been struck with the physical changes in Beth. No one spoke of them or seemed aware of them. They had come too gradually to startle those who saw her daily, but to eyes sharpened by absence, they were very plain.

Jo's concerns began when she first saw her sister's face. It was not any paler and only a little thinner than when Jo had seen her last. Yet there was a strange, transparent look about it, as if the mortal was being slowly melted away. The immortal shone through the frail flesh with an indescribably pathetic beauty. Jo saw and felt it, but said nothing at the time. Soon the first impression lost much of its power. Beth seemed happy, and no one appeared to doubt that she had recovered from her bout with scale-breaker fever six years ago. Jo became distracted with other things, and for a couple of seasons forgot her fear.

But when Laurie had left for the Coastline, and peace prevailed again, the vague anxiety returned to haunt her.

Beth was not well, and Jo knew it. When Jo proposed a trip to the thermal springs in Pink City, Beth had thanked her heartily, but begged not to travel so far away from home. Another little visit to the thermal springs the next town over would suit her better. So Jo took Beth down to the quiet place, where she could rest two weeks in the healing water, and let the hot springs color her pale cheeks.

It was not a fashionable place, but even among the few merpeople there, the mergirls did not make friends. They spent the weeks living for one another. Beth was too shy to enjoy society, and Jo too wrapped up in her to care for anyone else. So they were all in all to each other. They swam from spring to spring, quite unconscious of the curiosity they aroused in those about them. They were the strong sister and the feeble one, always together, as if they felt instinctively that a long separation was not far away.

They felt the goodbye approaching, yet neither spoke of it. Often between ourselves and those nearest and dearest to us there exists a reserve which it is very hard to overcome. Jo felt as if a curtain had fallen between her heart and Beth's. There seemed something sacred in the silence, and she waited for Beth to speak.

She wondered, and was thankful also, that her parents did not seem to see the changes in Beth that she saw. During the quiet weeks when the weakness grew so plain to her, she inked nothing of it to those at home. She believed that Beth's failing health would tell its own story when she swam back no better.

Jo wondered still more if her sister already guessed the hard truth. What thoughts were passing through her mind during the long hours when she lay on the warm rocks with her head in Jo's lap?

One day Beth told her. Beth lay so still on the thermal rocks that Jo thought she was asleep. Jo put down her scroll and studied her with wistful eyes, trying to see signs of hope in the faint color on Beth's cheeks. But she could not find enough to satisfy her, for the cheeks were very thin. The hands seemed too feeble to hold even the rosy little shells they had been collecting. It came to her then more bitterly than ever that Beth was slowly drifting away from her. Jo's arms instinctively tightened their hold upon the dearest treasure she possessed. For a minute her eyes were too dim for seeing. When they cleared, Beth was looking up at her so tenderly that there was hardly any need for her to say, "Jo, dear, I'm glad you know it. I've tried to tell you, but I couldn't."

There was no answer except her sister's cheek against her own, not even sobs, for when most deeply moved, Jo did not sob. She was the weaker sister then, and Beth tried to comfort and sustain her. Beth wrapped her arms about her and tried to soothe her with the words she whispered in her ear.

"I've known the truth about me for a good while, dear, and now I'm used to it. It isn't hard to think of or to bear. Try to see it so and don't be troubled about me, because it's best, indeed it is."

"Is this what made you so unhappy in the Cool Season, Beth? You did not feel it then and keep it to yourself so long, did you?" asked Jo, refusing to see or say that it was best.

"Yes, I gave up hoping on a long life then, but I didn't

like to own it. I tried to think it was a sick fancy, and would not let it trouble anyone. But when I saw you all so well and strong and full of happy plans, it was hard to feel that I could never be like you, and then I was miserable, Jo."

"Oh, Beth, and you didn't tell me, didn't let me comfort and help you? How could you shut me out, bear it all alone?"

Jo's voice was full of tender reproach. Her heart ached to think of Beth's solitary struggle to learn how to say goodbye to health, love, and life.

"Perhaps it was wrong, but I tried to do right. I wasn't sure, no one said anything, and I hoped I was mistaken. It would have been selfish to frighten you all when Marmee was so anxious about Meg, and Amy away, and you so happy with Laurie—at least I thought so then."

"I don't care what becomes of anybody but you, Beth. You must get well."

"I want to, oh, so much! I try, but every day I lose a little, and feel more sure that I shall never gain it back. It's like the tide, Jo, when it turns, it goes slowly, but it can't be stopped."

"It shall be stopped. Your tide must not turn so soon. Nineteen is too young, Beth. I can't let you drift away. I'll work and pray and fight against it. I'll keep you in spite of everything. There must be ways. It can't be too late," said poor Jo rebelliously, for her spirit was far less resigned than Beth's.

Simple, sincere merpeople seldom speak much of their death. Beth could not explain the resignation that gave her courage to give up life. She had no words for the patience that let her cheerfully wait for death. She could only sob out, "I try to be willing," while she held fast to Jo, as the first bitter wave of this great sorrow broke over them together.

By and by Beth said, with recovered serenity, "You'll tell them this when we swim home?"

"I think they will see it without words," sighed Jo, for now it seemed to her that Beth's health sunk lower every day.

"Perhaps not. I've heard that the merpeople who love best are often blindest to such things. If they don't see it, you will tell them for me. I don't want any secrets, and it's kinder to prepare them. Meg has John and the merbabies to comfort her, but you must support Father and Mother, won't you, Jo?"

"If I can. But, Beth, I don't give up yet. I'm going to believe that it is a sick fancy, and not let you think it's true," said Jo, trying to speak cheerfully.

Beth lay a minute thinking. Then she said in her quiet way, "I don't know how to express myself, and shouldn't try to anyone but you. I can't speak out except to my Jo. I only mean to say that I have a feeling I was never intended to live long. I'm not like the rest of you. I never made any plans about what I'd do when I grew up. I never thought of being married, as you all did. I couldn't seem to imagine myself anything but little, blue-tailed Beth, floating about at home. I never wanted to swim away into my own adventures, and the hard part now is leaving you all. I'm not afraid to swim out alone, but it seems as if I should be homesick for you even in the afterlife."

Jo could not speak. For several minutes there was no sound but the hiss of the thermal water and popping bubbles. An iridescent jellyfish glided by, glimmering like purple diamonds. Beth watched it until it vanished, and her eyes were full of sadness. A flat, brown sole came rustling over the rocks. It came quite close to Beth, and looked at her with a gray eye. It nestled down on a rock beside them, rippling in delight with the heat. Beth smiled and felt comforted. The tiny thing seemed to offer its small friendship and remind her that a pleasant Ocean was still to be enjoyed.

"Dear little sand sole! See, Jo, how tame it is. I like them better than the jellyfish. They are not so wild and handsome, but they seem happy, confiding little things. I used to call them my fish last Hot Season. Mother said they reminded her of me—busy, plain-colored creatures, always near the floor. You are the jellyfish, Jo, strong and wild, so full of your own colors, floating far out to sea, and happy all alone. Meg is the homey cichlid, tending her young. Amy is like the sword fish, trying to advance herself, but bumping its nose on the way. Our little Pokes! Remember the name? She's so ambitious, but her heart is good and tender. No matter where she swims, she never will forget our home cave. I hope I will see her again, but she seems so far away."

"She is coming Warm Season next, and I intend that you will be all ready to see and enjoy her. I'm going to have you well and rosy by that time," began Jo, feeling that of all the changes in Beth, the talking change was the greatest. It seemed so easy for her to share her heart. Beth thought aloud in a way quite unlike the bashful merchild she once was.

"Jo, dear, don't hope any more. It won't do any good. I'm sure of that. We won't be miserable, but enjoy being together while we wait. We'll have happy times, for I don't suffer much, and I think the tide will go out easily, if you help me."

Jo leaned down to kiss the tranquil face, and with that silent kiss, she dedicated herself soul and scale to Beth.

Jo was right. There was no need of any words when they got home, for Father and Mother saw plainly now what they had prayed to be saved from seeing. Tired with her short journey, Beth swam off at once to bed. When Jo swam to her parents in the parlor, she found that she would be spared the hard task of telling Beth's secret. Her father hovered with his face toward the deep sun crystal, and did not turn as she swam in. Her mother stretched out her arms as if for help, and Jo floated over to comfort her without a word.

CHAPTER 34

Two Drawings

Laurie went to Ruby Reef intending to stay a week, and remained a month. He was tired of wandering about alone. Amy's familiar presence seemed to give a homelike charm to the foreign scenes in which she bore a part. Amy was very glad to see him now, and quite clung to him. He was the representative of the dear merfamily for whom she longed more than she would confess. They naturally took comfort in each other's society and were much together. They rode, swam, danced, or dawdled, for at Ruby Reef no one can be very industrious during holidays.

While they amused themselves in the most careless fashion, they formed new opinions about each other. Amy rose daily in the estimation of her friend, but he sank in hers. Laurie made no effort of any kind, but just let himself drift along as comfortably as possible. He felt that he could not change the opinion she was forming of him. He rather dreaded the eyes that seemed to watch him with such half-sorrowful, half-scornful surprise.

"All the rest have gone cockle hopping for the day. I preferred to stay at home and ink letters-in-bottles. They are done now, and I am going to the south side of the reef to sketch. The reds are said to be brilliant there. Will you swim along with me?" said Amy, as she joined Laurie one lovely day when he lounged in as usual, about noon.

"Well, yes, but isn't it rather warm for such a long swim?" he answered slowly. The cool rocks in the salon looked inviting compared to the hot waters about.

"I'm going to have the little oyster sleigh drawn up for us," answered Amy. "You'll have nothing to do on the way except feel the water in your hair."

"Then I'll go with pleasure."

It was a lovely ride to the south side, along winsome thoroughfares rich in the picturesque scenes that delight beauty-loving eyes. Here an ancient ruin. There a row of shops, full of colorful wares. Merchildren played in front of squat stone caves. Gnarled elkhorn corals twisted up into the light blue water, and sea-flowers of all sorts bloomed on the ocean floor.

The closer Amy and Laurie rode to the south side, the more reds appeared in the blossoms. First ruby, and then scarlet. Sparkling crimson and deep maroon. The floor of the reef itself was the brightest truest of reds. Yet all of these sights could not turn Amy's attention from her friend.

"Laurie, when are you going to your grandfather?" Amy asked, as she settled herself on a bench-like scarlet coral.

"Very soon."

"You have said that a dozen times within the last three weeks."

"I dare say, short answers save trouble."

"He expects you, and you really ought to swim to him."

"Hospitable creature! I know it."

"Then why don't you do it?"

"Natural depravity, I suppose."

"Natural indolence, you mean. It's really dreadful!" and Amy looked severe.

"Not so bad as it seems, for I should only plague him if I went, so I might as well stay and plague you a little longer. You can bear it better. In fact I think it agrees with you excellently," and Laurie composed himself in a bed of burgundy finger corals.

Amy shook her head and arranged her art board with a sigh of resignation. She had made up her mind to lecture 'that merboy' and in a minute she began again.

"What are you doing just now?"

"Watching crustaceans."

"No, no. I mean what do you intend and wish to do?"

"Eat lunch, if you'll allow me."

"How provoking you are! I will only allow you to eat early on condition that you let me put you into my sketch. I need a subject."

"With all the pleasure in life. How will you have me, full length or three-quarters, on my head or my tail fins? I should respectfully suggest a recumbent posture. Then put yourself in also and call it *Doing nothing is doubly sweet.*"

"Stay as you are, and eat all our lunch if you like. I intend to work hard," said Amy in her most energetic tone.

"What delightful enthusiasm!" and he nestled down with entire satisfaction.

"You look like a young warrior dressed for burial," she

said, carefully tracing the aquamarine tail sharply defined against the burgundy finger coral.

"Wish I was!"

"That's a foolish wish, unless you have spoiled your life. You are so changed, I sometimes think—" there Amy stopped. Her half-timid, half-wistful look, more significant than her unfinished speech.

Laurie saw and understood the affectionate anxiety which she hesitated to express. Looking straight into her eyes, he said, just as he used to say it to her mother, "It's all right, ma'am."

That satisfied her and set at rest the doubts that had begun to worry her lately. It also touched her, and she showed that it did, by the cordial tone in which she said...

"I'm glad of that! I didn't think you'd been a very bad merboy, but I fancied you might have wasted money at gambling. Or got into some of the scrapes that young mermen seem to consider a necessary part of a foreign tour. Come perch beside me on the coral bench and 'let us be friendly', as Jo used to say when we nestled into our cushions and told secrets."

Laurie obediently slipped into position beside her. He began to amuse himself by weaving a garland of the ruby sea-flowers that grew behind them.

"I'm all ready for the secrets." He glanced up with a decided expression of interest in his eyes.

"I've none to tell. You may begin."

"Haven't one to bless myself with. I thought perhaps you'd had some news from home."

"You have heard all that has come lately. Don't you hear

often? I fancied Jo would send you barrels of letters-in-bottles."

"When do you begin your great work of art?" he asked, changing the subject abruptly after another pause. He had been wondering if Amy knew his secret and wanted to talk about it.

"Never," she answered, with a despondent but decided tone. "I fear that I shall never be a great artist."

"And what will you do if you give up on your talent, if I may ask?"

"Polish up my other talents, and be an ornament to society, if I get the chance."

"Good! And here is where Fred Waverly comes in, I fancy."

Amy preserved a discreet silence, but there was a conscious look in her downcast face. Laurie sat up and said gravely, "Now I'm going to play brother, and ask questions. May I?"

"I don't promise to answer."

"Your face will, if your tongue won't. You aren't a mermaid of the world enough yet to hide your feelings, my dear. I heard rumors about Fred and you last year. It's my private opinion that if he had not been called home so suddenly and detained so long, something would have come of it. Don't you think?"

"That's not for me to say," was Amy's grim reply, but her lips smiled. There was a traitorous sparkle of the eye which betrayed that she knew of Fred's interest in her.

"You are not engaged, I hope?" and Laurie looked very elder-brotherly and grave all of a sudden.

"No."

"But you will be, if he swims back and proposes, won't you?"

"Very likely."

"Then you are fond of old Fred?"

"I could be, if I tried."

"But you don't intend to try until the proper moment? Bless my soul, what a well of prudence! He's a good fellow, Amy, but not the merman I fancied you'd like."

"He is rich and has delightful manners," began Amy, trying to be quite cool and dignified. She felt a little ashamed of herself, in spite of the sincerity of her intentions.

"I understand. Sea queens can't get on without sand dollars. So you mean to make a good match, and start in that way? Quite right and proper, as the Ocean goes, but it sounds odd from the lips of one of your mother's mergirls."

"True, nevertheless."

A short speech, but the quiet decision with which it was uttered contrasted curiously with the young speaker. Laurie felt this instinctively and nestled himself down again in the finger corals. He felt a sense of disappointment which he could not explain. His look and silence, as well as a certain inward self-disapproval, ruffled Amy. She resolved to deliver her lecture to him without delay.

"Do you want to know what I honestly think of you?"

"Pining to be told," answered Laurie.

"Well, I despise you."

If she had even said 'I hate you' in a petulant or coquettish tone, he would have laughed and rather liked it, but the grave, almost sad, accent in her voice made him open his eyes, and ask quickly...

"Why, if you please?"

"Because, with every chance for being good, useful, and happy, you are faulty and miserable."

"Strong language, fair mermaid."

"If you like it, I'll continue."

"Pray do, it's quite interesting."

"I thought you'd find it so. Selfish merpeople always like to talk about themselves."

"Am I selfish?" the question slipped out involuntarily and in a tone of surprise. The one virtue on which Laurie prided himself was generosity.

"Yes, very selfish," continued Amy, in a calm, cool voice, twice as effective just then as an angry one. "I'll show you how, for I've studied you while we were frolicking, and I'm not at all satisfied with you. Here you have been visiting the Coastline for nearly six months. You've done nothing with it but waste time and sand dollars and disappoint your friends."

"Isn't a fellow to have any pleasure after a four-year college grind?"

"You don't look as if you have much pleasure. At any rate, you are none the better for it, as far as I can see. I said when we first met that you had improved. Now I take it all back. I don't think you half so nice as when I left you back at our little home reef. You have grown abominably careless. You like gossip, and waste time on frivolous things. With money, talent, position, health, and beauty—you've given up on life! But it's the truth, so I can't help saying it, with all these splendid things to use and enjoy, you can find nothing to do. Instead of being the merman you ought to be, you are only..." there she stopped, with a look that had both pain and pity in it.

"Saint Laurence of Self-Pity," added Laurie, blandly finishing the sentence. But the lecture began to take effect. There was a wide-awake sparkle in his eyes now. A half-angry, half-injured expression replaced the former indifference.

Neither spoke for several minutes. Laurie floated in the algae, staring at his tail fins. Amy put the last touches to the hasty sketch she had been working at while she talked. Presently she passed it to him, merely saying, "How do you like that?"

He looked and then he smiled, as he could not well help doing, for it was capitally done. A long, indolent figure on the algae, with a listless face, half-shut eyes, and one hand holding a crispy kelp sandwich.

"How well you draw!" he said, with a genuine surprise and pleasure at her skill, adding, with a half-laugh, "Yes, that's me."

"As you are. This is as you were." Amy laid another sketch beside the one he held.

It was not nearly so well done, but there was a life and spirit in it which atoned for many faults. It recalled the past so vividly that a sudden change swept over the young merman's face as he looked. It was a rough sketch of Laurie taming a seahorse. Every line of the active figure, resolute face, and commanding attitude was full of energy and meaning. There was a suggestion of arrested motion, of strength, courage, and youthful buoyancy. It contrasted sharply with the supine grace of the *'Doing nothing is doubly sweet'* sketch. Laurie said nothing but as his eye went from one to the other, Amy saw him flush up. He folded his lips together as if he read and accepted the little lesson she had given him. That satisfied her, and without waiting for him to speak, she said, in her sprightly way...

"Don't you remember the day you tamed the orange seahorse, and we all watched? Meg and Beth were frightened, but Jo clapped and somersaulted. I hovered at the hedge and drew you. I found that sketch in my portfolio the other day, touched it up, and kept it to show you."

"Much obliged. You've improved immensely since then, and I congratulate you. May I venture to suggest that five o'clock is the dinner hour back with your aunt and uncle?"

Laurie rose as he spoke, returning the pictures with a smile and a bow. He tried to resume his former easy, indifferent manner, but it was an affectation now. The reminder of how vibrant he had been was more efficacious than he would confess. Amy felt the coldness in his manner, and said to herself...

"Now, I've offended him. Well, if it does him good, I'm glad. If it makes him hate me, I'm sorry, but it's true. I can't take back a word of it."

They laughed and chatted all the way home, but both felt ill at ease. The friendly frankness was disturbed. Despite their apparent gaiety, there was a secret discontent in each heart.

"Will we see you this evening?" asked Amy, as they parted at her aunt's door.

"Unfortunately, I have an engagement," and Laurie bent as if to kiss her hand, in the Coastline fashion, which suited him better than many mermen. Something in his face made Amy say quickly and warmly...

"No, be yourself with me, Laurie. Let's part in the good old way. I'd rather have a Deep Ocean handshake than all the sentimental salutations near the shore."

"Goodbye, dear," and with these words, uttered in the tone she liked, Laurie left her, after a handshake almost painful in its heartiness.

Next morning, instead of the usual visit, Amy received a

letter-in-a-bottle. It made her smile at the beginning and sigh at the end.

> My Dear Mentor, Please make my farewell to your aunt, and exult within yourself. I have taken your drawings to heart and swum home to my grandpa, like the best of merboys. A pleasant Cold Season to you! I think Fred would be benefited by a spirited mermaid like you. Tell him so, with my congratulations.
> Yours gratefully, Laurie

"Good Laurie! I'm glad he's swum home," said Amy, with an approving smile. The next minute her face fell as she glanced about the empty room. She added, with an involuntary sigh, "Yes, I am glad, but how I will miss him."

CHAPTER 35

Beth Moves On

eth's declining health was bitter to those who loved her. The first days were the most difficult, but time softened the flavor. They accepted the inevitable and tried to bear it cheerfully. A tender affection binds households together in times of trouble. The Marsh merfamily felt this special comfort. They put away their grief, and each did his or her part toward making Beth's last year a happy one.

The pleasantest room in the caves was set apart for Beth. They gathered everything she loved most into it, her potted sea-flowers and her miniature harp—even her doll collection and the old catfish. Father's best scrolls found their way there. So did Mother's springiest seaweed cushion, Amy's favorite painting, and Jo's best stories. Every day Meg brought her merbabies to blow bubble kisses for Aunty Beth. John quietly set apart a few sand dollars, that he might enjoy supplying Beth with any sweets she craved. Old Nanna-pus never wearied of concocting dainty dishes to tempt a capricious appetite.

Here, cherished like a chest of treasure, nestled Beth, tranquil and busy as ever. Nothing could change her sweet, unselfish nature. Even while preparing to leave life, she tried to make it happier for those who should remain behind.

The feeble fingers were never idle. One of her pleasures was to make little things for the merchildren daily passing in front of their caves. She wove little armlets for their dolls. She strung tiny shell corsets and carved miniature combs. The dolls of their neighborhood never looked better. If Beth had wanted any reward, she found it in the bright little faces always turned up to her window. The merchildren brought their dolls to hold to the glass, displaying their new outfits. Sweet little letters-in-bottles often arrived for her full of thumbprints and gratitude.

The first few months were very happy ones, and Beth often used to look around, and say, "How beautiful this is!" They all nestled together in her sunny room, the merbabies squirming and playing on the floor. Mother and sisters worked near, and father read, in his pleasant voice, from wise old scrolls. The old scrolls were rich in comforting words. Grace and comfort is as applicable now as when written centuries ago.

This peaceful time was preparation for the sad hours to come. The day came when Beth said the weaving fiber was 'so heavy', and put it down forever. Talking wearied her, faces troubled her, and pain claimed her for its own. Her tranquil spirit was sorrowed by the ills that vexed her feeble flesh.

Ah me! Such heavy days, such long, long nights, such aching hearts and imploring prayers. Those who loved her best were forced to see the thin hands stretched out to them, to hear the bitter cry, "Help me, help me!" and to feel that there was no help.

The sad struggle of the serene soul against its fate was mercifully brief. The natural rebellion ended, and the old peace returned more beautiful than ever. With the wreck of her frail body, Beth's spirit grew strong. Though she said little, those about her sensed that she was ready. They saw that the first of them who would visit the afterlife was the best suited for it.

Jo never left her for an hour after Beth told her, "I feel stronger when you are here." She slept on a cushion along the wall, waking often to feed, lift, or wait upon her sister. Beth seldom asked for anything, and 'tried not to be a trouble'. All day Jo hovered in the room, prouder of the comfort she brought Beth than of any honor her life ever brought her.

These hours were precious to Jo, and helpful to her. In them her heart received the teaching that it needed. Lessons in patience were so sweetly taught that she could not fail to learn them. She learned charity for all. She grew the lovely spirit that can forgive and truly forget unkindness. She knew the loyalty to duty that makes the hardest tasks easy. She found the sincere faith that fears nothing, but trusts the strength of love.

Often when she woke, Jo found Beth reading well-worn little scrolls. She heard her singing softly, to beguile the sleepless night. Jo would lie watching her with thoughts too deep for sobs. She felt that Beth, in her simple, unselfish way, was weaning herself from her life. Beth prepared herself for the afterlife by quiet prayers and the music she loved so well.

Seeing this did more for Jo than the wisest scrolls, the sweetest songs, and the most hearty prayers. For with a heart softened by the tenderest sorrow, she recognized the beauty of her sister's life. Beth was uneventful, unambitious, yet full of the genuine virtues which 'smell sweet, and blossom in the silt'. She possessed the virtues that make a life truly successful, however short.

One night Beth looked among the scrolls to find something to make her forget the weariness and the pain. Out fell a little scroll she did not recognize. It was scribbled over in Jo's handwriting. The title caught her eye, and the jagged look of the lines made her sure Jo had inked it with passion.

"Poor Jo! She's fast asleep, so I won't wake her to ask permission. She shows me all her things, and I don't think she'll mind if I look at this", thought Beth. She glanced at her sister, who slept with her emerald tail tucked beneath her.

MY BETH

Nestled patient in her alcove,
Till the blessed time to part,
A serene and saintly presence,
Comforts every troubled heart.
Ocean joys and hopes and sorrows,
Settle on the silty floor,
Of the deep and darkest passage.
Where she slips to Evermore.

O my sister, passing from me,
Out of Ocean care and strife,
Leave me, as a gift, those virtues,
Which have beautified your life.
Dear, bequeath me that great patience,
Which has power to sustain,
A cheerful, uncomplaining spirit,
In its prison-cave of pain.

Give me, for I need it sorely,
Of that courage, wise and hale,
Which has made the course of duty,
Brilliant round your true-blue tail
Give me that unselfish nature,
That with charity divine,
Can pardon wrong for love's dear sake—
Meek heart, forgive me mine!

Thus our parting daily loses,
Something of its bitter pain,
And while learning this hard lesson,
My great loss becomes my gain.
For the touch of grief will render,
My wild nature more serene,
Give to life new inspirations,
A new trust in the unseen.

Henceforth, my love, my Beth,
The first to leave of sisters four,
My beloved, friendly mermaid,
Wait for me in Evermore,

Blurred and blotted, faulty and feeble as the lines were, they brought Beth inexpressible comfort. Her one regret had been that she had done so little. This seemed to assure her that her life had not been useless, that her death would not bring the despair she feared. As she sat with the scroll rolled between her hands, Jo awoke. She yawned and floated over to her.

"I'm so happy, dear. See, I found this and read it. I knew you wouldn't care. Have I been all that to you, Jo?" Beth asked, with wistful, humble earnestness.

"*Oh*, Beth, so much, so much!" and Jo's tail fin flicked up and down to mark her sincerity.

"Then I don't feel as if I'd wasted my life. I'm not so good as you make me, but I have tried to do right. And now, when it's too late to even begin to do better, it's such a comfort to know that someone loves me so much. Someone feels as if I'd helped them."

"More than any one in the Ocean, Beth. I used to think I couldn't let you leave, but I'm learning to feel that I don't lose you. You'll be more to me than ever. Death can't part us, though it seems to."

"I know it cannot, and I don't fear it any longer. I'm sure I will be your Beth still, to love and help you more than ever. You must take my place, Jo, and be everything to Father and Mother when I've left. They will turn to you. Don't fail them. If it's hard to work alone, remember I will never forget you, even in the afterlife. Love is the only thing that we can carry with us when we leave, and it makes the end of life so easy."

"I'll try, Beth." Then and there Jo felt the blessed solace of a belief in the immortality of love.

So the Warm Season days came and went. The Ocean grew slower, the plants greener. The sea-flowers blossomed fairly early. The little Hot Season fish came back in time to nuzzle Beth's window in goodbye.

Beth, like a tired but trustful merchild, clung to the hands that had led her all her life. Father and Mother guided her tenderly through to the afterlife, and gave her up in love.

Seldom except in story-scrolls do the dying utter memorable words or see visions. Those who have seen many departing souls know that to most the end comes as naturally and simply as sleep. As Beth had hoped, the 'tide went out easily', and peacefully in the night. On her mother's bosom, where she had drawn her first breath, she quietly drew her last. She bore no farewell but one loving look, and one little sigh.

When morning came, for the first time in many seasons, Jo's place was empty, and Beth's room was very still. But the heart-of-the-seas blossomed at the window, and the little Hot Season fish continued their vigil behind the glass. They peeked in at the still figure of the blue-tailed mermaid, as if blessing her journey. Beth's merfamily, those who loved her best, smiled through their sobs. They gave thanks that Beth was well at last.

CHAPTER 36

Beginning in Bottles

Our story goes back in time to the Coastline, where Amy's lecture did Laurie good. He traveled back to his grandfather in the Deep Ocean. Laurie was so devoted to him that the old merman declared that the Ruby Reef had improved him wonderfully. Laurie had better try it again.

There was nothing the young merman would have liked better, but whales could not have dragged him back after the scolding he had received. Whenever the longing grew very strong, he fortified his resolution. He repeated the words that had made the deepest impression—"I despise you."

Laurie turned the matter over in his mind and brought himself to confess that he had been selfish and morose. He had been besieged by a great sorrow. The battle was long and painful, but by now he felt that his affections were quite dead. Jo wouldn't love him, but he might make her respect and admire him. He would do something which would prove that a mermaid's 'No' had not spoiled his life.

He had always meant to do something with his life. Amy's distaste for him was quite unnecessary. He had only been waiting until the aforesaid affections were decently healed. That being done, he felt that he was ready to 'hide his stricken heart, and still toil on'.

Laurie resolved to embalm his love-sorrow into music. The great sirens of old, when they had a joy or a grief, put it into a song. Like them, Laurie would compose a Requiem which should harrow up Jo's soul and rend the scales of every hearer.

So the next time the old merman found Laurie getting restless and moody and ordered him off to the Coastline, Laurie went to Covington instead of Ruby Reef. He had musical friends there to bolster him. He sank into work with the firm determination to distinguish himself. Yet he could not produce his vision. Perhaps his sorrow was too vast to be embodied in music. Or perhaps the music was too ethereal to uplift a mortal woe. Whatever the case, he soon discovered the Requiem was beyond him at present.

Then he tried an opera, for no project seems impossible at its beginning. Here again unforeseen difficulties beset him. He wanted Jo for his heroine. He called upon his memory for tender recollections and romantic visions of his love. But memory turned traitor, and he could only recall Jo's oddities and faults. His memory would only show her in the most unsentimental aspects. He envisioned her combing night wraps with a frown, closing him out of the attic, or swimming away from him. An irresistible laugh spoiled the pensive picture he was endeavoring to paint. Jo wouldn't be put into the opera at any price. He had to give her up with a "Bless that mergirl, what a torment she is!" and a clutch at his hair, as became a distracted composer.

He looked about him for another and less intractable damsel to immortalize in melody. His memory produced one with the most obliging readiness. This phantom wore many faces, but it always had curly, golden hair. She was ensconced in a diaphanous current. She floated before his mind's eye in a pleasing chaos of glow blooms, rainbow shells and purple jellyfish. He did not give the complacent wraith any name, but he took her for his heroine. He grew quite fond of her, as well he might, for he gifted her with every gift and grace in the Ocean. He escorted her, unscathed, through trials which would have annihilated any mere mermaid.

Thanks to this inspiration, he got on swimmingly for a time. Gradually the work lost its charm. He forgot to compose while he hovered musing, pen floating away from him. He took to swimming about the city to refresh his mind, which was in a somewhat unsettled state that season. He did not do much, but he thought a great deal and was conscious of a change of some sort going on in spite of himself. "It's genius bubbling, perhaps. I'll let it bubble, and see what comes of it," he said. He suspected in secret that it wasn't genius, but something far more common.

Whatever it was, it bubbled to some effect. He grew more and more discontented with his desultory life, and began to long for some real and earnest work. He finally came to the wise conclusion that everyone who loved music was not a composer. Returning from a grand opera, splendidly performed at the Grand Mer Theater, Laurie looked over his own music. He sang some of his favorite parts, and found them lacking. He said soberly to himself...

"My heart isn't in this! Neither is my talent. I won't compose any longer. Now what will I do?"

That seemed a hard question to answer, and Laurie began to wish he had to work for his daily kelp crisp. Now if ever, occurred an eligible opportunity for being 'miserable and selfish', as Amy had put it. He had plenty of sand dollars and nothing to do. The poor fellow had temptations enough, but he withstood them well. As much as he valued liberty, he valued good faith and confidence more. His promise to his grandfather, and his desire to look honestly into the eyes of the mermaids who loved him, and say "All's well," kept him safe and steady.

Laurie thought that the task of forgetting his love for Jo would absorb all his powers for years. To his great surprise he discovered it grew easier every day. He refused to believe it at first, and got angry with himself. Laurie couldn't understand why his heart wouldn't ache. The wound persisted in healing with a rapidity that astonished him. Instead of trying to forget, he found himself trying to remember. He had not foreseen this turn of affairs, and was not prepared for it. He was disgusted with himself, surprised at his own fickleness. He held a mixture of disappointment and relief that he could recover from such a tremendous blow so soon. He was reluctantly obliged to confess that the merboyish passion was slowly subsiding. It became a more tranquil sentiment, very tender, and a little sad and resentful still. The resentment was sure to pass away in time. Soon he would have only a brotherly affection for the lost mermaid, an affection which would last unbroken to the end of his days.

As the word 'brotherly' passed through his mind in one of his reveries, he smiled and seized a cork and bottle. He inked a final supplication to Jo. He told her that he could not settle to anything while there was the least hope of her changing her mind. Couldn't she, wouldn't she—and let him swim home to her and be happy?

While waiting for an answer, he did nothing, but he did it energetically, for he was in a fever of impatience. The answer arrived at last. It settled his mind effectually on one point, for Jo decidedly couldn't and wouldn't love him. She was wrapped up in Beth, and never wished to hear the word love again. Then she begged him to be happy with somebody else—to always keep a little alcove of his heart for his loving sister Jo. In a postscript she asked him not to tell Amy that Beth was worse. Amy was returning to the Deep Ocean in the Warm Season, and there was no need of saddening the remainder of her stay. Laurie must write to Amy often, and not let her feel lonely, homesick or anxious.

"So I will, at once. Poor little mermaid. It will be a sad travel home for her, I'm afraid." Laurie opened his desk, as if writing to Amy had been the proper conclusion all along.

But he did not ink a letter-in-a-bottle that day. As he rummaged out his best scrolls, he came across something which changed his purpose. Tumbling about the desk, among bills, passports, and business documents, were several of Jo's letters-in-bottles. In another compartment were three bottles from Amy. Each had a blue ribbon delicately tied about the neck. With a half-repentant, half-amused expression, Laurie gathered up all Jo's bottles. He corked them tightly and stacked them away under the desk. He hovered for a minute, and then swam out to visit a graveyard. Though not overwhelmed with affliction, he felt as if there had been a funeral. This seemed a more proper way to spend the rest of the day than in writing letters-in-bottles to a charming young mermaid.

The letter-in-a-bottle posted very soon, however, and was promptly answered. Amy was homesick, and confessed it in the most delightfully confiding manner. The correspondence flourished famously. Letter-in-bottles sailed to and fro with unfailing regularity all through the season. Laurie wanted desperately to swim to Ruby Reef, but would not visit until he was asked. This was something she was not willing to do just then. She was having experiences of her own which made her wish to avoid the quizzical eyes of 'our merboy'.

Fred Waverly had returned. He proposed the question to which she had once decided to answer, "Yes, thank you." Now she said, "No, thank you," kindly but steadily. When the time came to marry a merman just for his riches, her courage failed her. She found that something more than money and position was needed to satisfy her. New longings filled her heart, which was now full of tender hopes and fears.

The words, "Fred is a good fellow, but not at all the merman I fancied you would ever like," kept returning to her. Laurie's face returned to her too. She remembered her declaration, "I will marry for money." It troubled her, and she wished she could take it back. She didn't want Laurie to think her a heartless, mercenary creature. She didn't care to be a queen of society now half so much as she did to be a mermaid loved. She was so glad he didn't hate her for the dreadful things she said. He took them so beautifully and was kinder than ever. His letters-in-bottles were such a comfort. The bottles from her merfamily were very irregular and not half so satisfactory as his.

It was not only a pleasure, but a duty to answer him. The poor merboy was forlorn. He needed comforting since Jo persisted in being stony-hearted. Amy thought that Jo ought to have made an effort and tried to love him. It couldn't be very hard. Many merpeople would be proud and glad to have such a dear merboy care for them. But Jo never would act like other mermaids, and so there was nothing for Amy to do but be very kind and treat him like a brother.

If all brothers were treated as well as Laurie was by Amy, they would be a much happier race of beings than they are. Amy never lectured now. She asked his opinion on all subjects, she was interested in everything he did. She made charming little presents for him, and sent him two letters-in-bottles a week. Her scrolls were full of sisterly confidences and captivating sketches of the Coastline.

Few brothers have their letters-in-bottles carried about in their sister's satchels. Sisters don't usually sob over their correspondence when short, or kiss them when long. We will not hint that Amy did any of these fond and foolish things. She certainly did grow a little pale and pensive that season. She lost much of her relish for society, and swam out sketching alone a good deal. She never had much to show when she floated home. She was studying nature, I dare say, while she nestled for hours, tail tucked under her, on the corals at Vera Harbor. She absently sketched any fancy that occurred to her. Once it was a black-haired warrior upon a seahorse. Another time a handsome merboy asleep in the finger algae. She drew a curly haired mermaid in gorgeous array, promenading down a ballroom on the arm of a brown-skinned merman. Both of their faces were blurred, according to the latest fashion in art. Safe, but not altogether satisfactory.

Her aunt thought that she regretted her answer to Fred. Finding denials useless and explanations impossible, Amy left her to believe what she liked. She took care that Laurie should know that Fred had swum off to Pink City. That was all, but he understood it. He looked relieved, as he said to himself, with a venerable tone...

"I was sure she was better than him. Poor merman! I've been through it all, and I can sympathize."

With that he heaved a great sigh. Then, as if he had discharged his duty to the past, he put his tail fins up on the table. He leaned back and enjoyed Amy's letter-in-a-bottle luxuriously.

While these changes were going on abroad, trouble had arrived at the home caves. But the letter-in-a-bottle telling that Beth's health was failing never reached Amy. When the bottle found her, her sister already rested beneath the Ocean floor. The sad news met her at Vera Harbor. The heat had driven them from Ruby Reef at the beginning of the Hot Season.

She bore the news with courage, and quietly accepted her merfamily's wishes. They told her that she should not shorten her time at the Coastline. It was too late to say goodbye to Beth. She had better stay, and let absence soften her sorrow. But her heart was very heavy. She longed to be with her loved ones in their cave dwelling. Every day she looked wistfully across the corals, waiting for Laurie to swim to her and comfort her.

He did swim to her very soon. The Marsh merfamily had posted them letters-in-bottles on the same day. He was in Covington, and it took longer for his to reach him. The moment he read it, he packed his travel net and bade adieu to his friends. He swam off fast as he could to keep his promise, with a heart full of joy and sorrow, hope and suspense.

CHAPTER 37

Ending at the Harbor

Laurie knew Vera Harbor well. As soon as his caravan arrived, he darted to the edge of the town. Amy's Aunt and Uncle had rented a holiday cave overlooking the harbor.

The housekeeper was in despair that the whole merfamily had swum off to the City Center. "But no, the blonde mermaid might be in the rock garden. If the young, visiting merman would nestle down, a flash of time should present her."

But the visiting merman could not wait even a 'flash of time'. In the middle of the housekeeper's speech, he darted off to find the blonde mermaid himself.

A pleasant, private rock garden bordered the wilds of the harbor outside the city. Fallen stones of white, gray and black created a fence of sorts, and anemones sprouted every-where. At the back lay an enormous boulder, the size of three whales. In it was a bench, carved from the rock and plaited with mother-of-pearl. Amy often rested here to read or work, or console herself with the beauty all about her.

She perched here that day, leaning her head on her hand, with a homesick heart and heavy tail. She thought of Beth and longed for Laurie. She wondered why he did not swim to her. Lost in the sadness of her thoughts, she did not hear the ripple as he crossed into the garden. Nor did she see him pause as he neared the large rock with her mother-of-pearl bench.

He floated still for a minute looking at her with new eyes. The tender side of Amy's character blossomed openly. Everything about her mutely suggested love and sorrow. She clutched a blotted scroll to her chest, and a black ribbon tied up her hair. She bore a mermaidly pain and patience in her face well beyond her years. If he had any doubts about the reception she would give him, they were set at rest the minute she looked up and saw him. She scattered everything in the waters around her and swam to him, exclaiming in a tone of unmistakable love and longing...

"Oh, Laurie, Laurie, I knew you'd swim to me!"

I think everything was said and settled then, as they floated together quite silent for a moment. The dark head bent down protectingly over the light one. Amy felt that no one could comfort and sustain her so well as Laurie. Laurie decided that Amy was the only mermaid in the Ocean who could fill his heart. He did not tell her so, but she was not disappointed. Both felt the truth, were satisfied, and gladly left the rest to silence.

In a minute Amy drifted back to her bench, while Laurie gathered up the scattered scrolls. He noted the romantic sketches and his well-worn letters-in-bottles. Good omens, so he thought, for the future. As he nestled down beside her, Amy felt shy again. She turned crab-red at the recollection of her impulsive greeting.

"I couldn't help it. I felt so lonely and sad, and was so very glad to see you. It was such a surprise to look up and find you floating in front of me. I was beginning to fear you wouldn't arrive," she said, trying in vain to speak quite naturally.

"I started swimming the minute I heard. I wish I could say something to comfort you for the loss of dear little Beth, but I can only feel, and..." He could not get any further, for he too turned bashful of a sudden, and did not quite know what to say. He longed to cuddle Amy's head into his shoulder and tell her to have a good sob. He did not dare, and so took her hand instead. He gave it a sympathetic squeeze that was better than words.

"You needn't say anything. This comforts me," she said softly. "Beth is well and happy in the afterlife, and I mustn't wish her back. I do dread the return to the Deep Ocean, much as I long to see my merfamily. We won't talk about it now, because it makes me sob. I want to enjoy you while you stay. You needn't swim right back, need you?"

"Not if you want me, dear."

"I do, so much. Aunt and Flo are very kind, but you seem like one of my little merfamily. It would be so comforting to have you for a little while."

Amy spoke and looked so endearing that Laurie forgot his bashfulness all at once. He gave her just what she wanted —the comfort she was used to and the cheerful conversation she needed.

"Poor little soul, you look as if you'd grieved yourself half sick! I'm going to take care of you. Come and swim about with me. The current is too chilly for you to sit still," he said, in the half-caressing, half-commanding way that Amy liked. He tucked a loose curl behind her ear and drew her arm through his. The two of them began to swim up and down the anemone laden rocks. He felt more at ease in motion, and Amy found it pleasant to have a strong arm to lean upon. He was a familiar face to smile at her, and a kind voice to talk delightfully for her alone.

The quaint old rock garden had sheltered many pairs of lovers. It seemed expressly made for romance. It was so secluded behind the tumble of rocks. The anemones massaged the slow water, whisking away the couple's words as they talked. For an hour this new pair swam and laughed, or rested on the marble bench. They enjoyed the sweet influences which gave such a charm to time and place. When an unromantic dinner shell clanged for them, Amy felt as if she left her burden of sorrow behind her.

The moment Aunt Caldwell saw the mergirl's altered face, she realized a new truth. She exclaimed to herself, "Now I understand it all—the merchild has been pining for young Laurence. Bless my heart! I never thought of such a thing."

With praiseworthy discretion, the good merlady said nothing. She betrayed no sign of enlightenment, but cordially urged Laurie to stay. She begged Amy to enjoy his society, because it would do her more good than so much solitude. Amy was a model of docility. As her aunt was a good deal occupied with Flo, she was left to entertain her friend. The little mermaid did so with more than her usual success.

At Ruby Reef, Laurie had lounged and Amy had

scolded. At Vera Harbor, Laurie was never morose. He was always swimming, dancing, or studying in the most energetic manner. Amy admired everything he did and followed his example as far and as fast as she could. He said the change was owing to the climate, and she did not contradict him. She was glad to share the same excuse for her own recovered health and spirits.

The invigorating waters did them both good. Much exercise worked wholesome changes in minds as well as bodies. They seemed to get clearer views of life and duty up there near the shore. The shallow waters washed away desponding doubts and delusive fancies. The quick tides brought in tender hopes and happy thoughts. The troubles of the past fell from them and sunk to the Ocean floor. They bobbed their heads out of the water at night, to stare at the moon. The grand silver circle seemed to look down upon them saying, "Little merchildren, love one another."

In spite of the new sorrow, it was a very happy time. It was so happy that Laurie could not bear to disturb it by a word. It took him a little while to recover from his surprise at the cure of his first love. He had firmly believed that it would also be his last and only love. He consoled himself for the seeming disloyalty. It would have been impossible to love any other mermaid but Amy so soon and so well. His first wooing had been of the tempestuous type. He looked back upon it as if through a hazy swirl of silt, with a feeling of compassion blended with regret. He was not ashamed of it, but put it away as one of the bitter-sweet experiences of his life. The kind of experience for which he could be grateful when the pain was over. His second wooing, he resolved, should be as calm and simple as possible. There was no need to have a similar scene of declaration as he had attempted with Jo. Amy sensed that he loved her. She knew it without words and had given him his answer long ago.

It all came about so naturally that no one in either of their merfamilies could complain. He knew that everybody would be pleased, even Jo.

When our first attempt at passion has been crushed, we are apt to be wary and slow in making a second trial. So Laurie let the days pass, enjoying every hour. He left to chance the utterance of the word that would put an end to the first and sweetest part of this new romance.

He had rather imagined that the denouement would take place at a romantic dinner in a quiet cove. It would occur in the most graceful and decorous manner. It turned out exactly the reverse, for the matter was settled in the rough sea near the land, and a few blunt words.

Now, Vera Harbor is very close to the land. It borders a shallow harbor, from where it draws its name. The merfolk can play there at night, unnoticed. Amy and Laurie had been dancing around the harbor all the evening.

They had been laughing and splashing, whispering secrets and playing chase. Amy caught Laurie just as they thrust their heads up out of the water. Lightning flashed, and the rain began with a thunderclap. They held each other, delighting in the salt and the storm. Laurie wrapped his arms about her with an expression in his eyes that made her say hastily, merely for the sake of saying something...

"You must be tired. Let's swim back and rest awhile."

"I'm not tired, but we may sink back under the water, if you like," answered Laurie, as he leaned close to her ear to speak over the thunder.

Feeling that she had not mended matters much, Amy nodded shyly and shivered. He pulled her closer.

"How well we float together, don't we?" said Amy, who objected to silence just then.

"So well that I wish we might always float together. Will you, Amy?" Laurie asked very tenderly.

"Yes, Laurie," Amy answered, very low.

Then they both looked to the vast night sky, enjoying the air and the rain on their faces. They unconsciously added the perfect portrait of love and happiness. A mermaid and merman floating together in perfect harmony, in a stormy harbor.

CHAPTER 38

Surprises

Jo was alone in the evening, nestled into the seaweed cushion, gazing at the deep sun crystals, and thinking. This was her favorite way to spend quiet hours. She used to lie there with Beth's little dolls, planning stories or dreaming dreams. She could lose herself in tender thoughts of the sister who never seemed far away. No one disturbed her.

This evening her face looked tired, grave, and rather sad. Tomorrow was her birthday. She was thinking how fast the years swam by, how old she was getting, and how little she seemed to have accomplished. Almost twenty-five, and nothing to show for it. Jo was mistaken in that. There was a good deal to show, and by-and-by she saw this, and was grateful for it.

"An old, single mermaid, that's what I'm to be. A lonely literate, with a pen for a spouse and a satchel of scrolls as merchildren. Twenty years from now I'll enjoy a morsel of fame, perhaps. But I'll be ancient and won't be able to enjoy it. Solitary, and can't share it. Independent, and don't need it. Well, I needn't be a sour angelfish nor a selfish squid. I dare say, solitary mermaids are very comfortable when they get used to it, but..." and there Jo sighed, as if the prospect was not inviting.

Jo must have fallen asleep, for suddenly Laurie's ghost seemed to float before her. It was a substantial, lifelike ghost. It leaned over her with the very look Laurie used to wear when he felt a strong emotion but tried to hide it.

Jo lay staring up at him in startled silence, until he bowed and took her hand. Then she knew him, and darted up, sobbing joyfully...

"Oh my Laurie! Oh my Laurie!"

"Dear Jo, you are glad to see me, then?"

"Glad! My blessed merboy, words can't express my gladness. Where's Amy?"

"Your mother has got her down at Meg's little cave. There was no getting my wife out of those merbabies' clutches."

"Your what?" exclaimed Jo. Laurie uttered those two words with an unconscious pride and satisfaction which betrayed him.

"Oh, mackerels! Now I've done it," and he looked so guilty that Jo was down on him faster than a shark.

"You've swum off and got married!"

"Yes, please, but I never will again." He rolled over to float on his back. His upside-down countenance was full of mischief, mirth, and triumph.

"Actually married?"

"Very much so, thank you."

"Mercy on us. What dreadful thing will you do next?" Jo sank into her cushion with a gasp.

"A characteristic, but not exactly complimentary, congratulation," Laurie observed aloud, upside-down and grinning.

"What can you expect, when you sneak in like a burglar and drop a net such as that? Right yourself, you ridiculous merboy, and tell me all about it."

Laurie flipped himself head-up tail-down, and said with a vain attempt at dignity…

"Don't I look like a married merman?"

"Not a bit, and you never will. You've grown bigger and scalier, but you are the same whale calf as ever."

"Now really, Jo, you ought to treat me with more respect," began Laurie, who enjoyed it all immensely.

"How can I, when the mere idea of you, married and settled, is so irresistibly funny that I can't keep sober!" answered Jo, smiling so infectiously that they had another laugh. "Now, start right, and tell me how it all happened. I'm pining to know."

"Well, I did it to please Amy," began Laurie, with a twinkle that made Jo exclaim…

"Fib number one. Amy did it to please you. Go on, and tell the truth, if you can, sir. How did you ever get Aunt to agree?"

"It was hard work, but between us, we talked her over, for we had heaps of good reasons on our side. There wasn't time to ink home for a blessing. We were so absorbed in one another we were of no mortal use apart. We had to get married before we died of love."

"When, where, how?" asked Jo, in a fever of interest and curiosity, for she could not imagine their wedding.

"Six weeks ago, at the Deep Ocean ambassador's office

in Vera Harbor. It was a very quiet wedding of course, for even in our happiness we didn't forget dear little Beth."

Jo took his hand at the memory of Beth. Laurie gently nodded at the dolls, which he remembered well.

"Why didn't you let us know afterward?" asked Jo, in a quieter tone, after they paused for a silent minute.

"We wanted to surprise you. Oh it's so delightful to be married. My faith! Wasn't it love among the harbor rocks!"

Laurie seemed to forget Jo for a minute, and Jo was glad of it. The fact that he told her these things so freely assured her that he had forgiven and forgotten. She tried to draw away her hand, but Laurie held it fast. As if he guessed her thoughts, he said, with a mermanly gravity she had never heard in him before...

"Jo, dear, I want to say one thing, and then we'll put it aside forever. As I told you in my letter-in-a-bottle, I never will stop loving you. The love is decidedly altered, and I have learned to see that it is better so. Amy and you changed places in my heart, that's all. I think it was always meant to be, and would have come about naturally, if I had waited. I was a merboy then, headstrong and tempestuous. It took a hard lesson to show me my mistake. For it was a great mistake, Jo, as you said. I found it out after making a fool of myself.

"When I saw Amy in Vera Harbor, everything seemed to settle all at once. You both got into your right places in my heart. You are in your proper place, a sister's place. I can honestly share my heart between sister Jo and wife Amy, and love them dearly. Will you believe me, and go back to the happy old times when we first knew one another?"

"I'll believe it, with all my heart, but, Laurie, we never

can be merboy and mergirl again. The happy old times can't come back, and we mustn't expect them. We are merman and mermaid now, with sober work to do. Playtime is over, and we must give up romping. I'm sure you feel this. I see the change in you, and you'll find it in me. I will miss my merboy, but I will love the merman as much and admire him more. He's grown into what I hoped he would. We can't be little playmates any longer, but we will be brother and sister. We'll care for and help one another all our lives, won't we, Laurie?"

He did not say a word, but took up the second hand she offered him. He laid his face down on both her palms for a minute. He felt that out of the death of a merboyish passion, there had risen a friendship to bless them both.

"This last year has been such a hard one that I feel forty."

"Poor Jo! We left you to bear it alone, while we were swimming and playing along the Coastline. You are worn. I can see it. You've had a great deal to bear, and had to bear it all alone. What a selfish fish I've been!" and Laurie pulled his coarse hair, with a remorseful look.

Amy's voice interrupted before Jo could reply. Her call floated up from the rooms below, "Where is she? Where's my dear Jo?"

A moment later, in poured the whole merfamily, including old Mr. Laurence and Nanna-pus. Everyone was hugged and kissed all over again. After several vain attempts, the wanderers were nestled down to be looked at and exulted over.

Mr. Laurence, hale and hearty as ever, was quite improved by his merboy's success in love. The crustiness seemed to be nearly gone. His old-fashioned courtliness had received a polish which made it kindlier than ever. It was good to see him smile at 'my merchildren', as he called the young pair. It was better still to see Amy pay him the daughterly duty and affection which completely won his old heart. It was best of all to watch Laurie revolve about the two, as if never tired of enjoying the pretty picture they made.

The minute Meg laid her eyes upon Amy, she concluded that her little sister was a most elegant mermaid. Jo watched the pair and thought, "How well they look together! I was right. Laurie has found the accomplished mermaid who will suit him better than clumsy old Jo. She'll be a pride, not a torment to him." Mrs. Marsh and her husband smiled and nodded at each other with happy faces. Their youngest had done well, not only in material things, but in love, confidence, and happiness.

Amy's face was full of the soft shimmer which speaks of a peaceful heart. Her voice had a new tenderness in it. The cool, prim way she carried herself was changed to a gentle dignity. No false affectations marred it. The cordial sweetness of her manner was more charming than the new beauty or the old grace.

"Love has done much for our little mergirl," said her mother softly.

"She has had a good example before her all her life, my dear," Mr. Marsh whispered back. He looked lovingly at the worn face and gray head beside him.

"Blessed me!" muttered old Nanna-pus. "She is as beautiful as a betta's tail. Our little Amy all grown-up into a grand mermaid." The beloved octopus sobbed with joy.

Little Daisy found it impossible to keep her eyes off her 'pitty aunty'. She attached herself like a barnacle to her aunt's tail. Demi paused to consider the new relatives before he accepted them. Laurie knew how to produce an unconditional surrender. The tiny merboy was won over by a set of driftwood toys from the Coastline.

How the reunited merfamily did talk! First one, then the other, then all burst out together—trying to tell the history of three years in half an hour. It was fortunate that jam and algae tarts were at hand to produce a lull and provide refreshment. They would have been faint if they had gone without nourishment much longer.

Such a happy procession floated down into the little dining room! Mr. Marsh proudly escorted the new Mrs. Laurence. Mrs. Marsh as proudly leaned on the arm of 'my son' Laurie. The old merman took Jo, with a whispered, "Beth would have loved to be here." A glance at the empty alcove by the sun crystals made Jo whisper back, "I'm sure she is here, in her own way, and is happy for us."

The twins swam behind, reveling at their own sweet liberty. The youngsters were quite overlooked in the celebration. They took every opportunity to snatch limed sea apples from the cupboards. They stuck their fingers in the jam, put kelp crisp in each other's hair, and broke into Amy's best tail polish. At last the little rascals attached themselves to 'Dranpa', who hadn't his spectacles on.

Amy, who was handed about like refreshments, returned to the parlor on Father Laurence's arm. The others paired off as before, and this arrangement left Jo companionless. She did not mind it at the minute, for she lingered to answer Nanna-pus's thoughtful inquiry.

"Do you suppose Mrs. Amy Laurence will continue to paint now that she's married?"

"Shouldn't wonder if she painted with the finest squid inks and emerald studded brushes. Laurie thinks nothing too good for her," answered Jo with infinite satisfaction.

"What happiness!" declared Nanna-pus, who pumped her eight appendages and darted off after the crowd.

Jo hovered back for a minute as her merfamily vanished into the parlor. A sudden sense of loneliness washed over her so strongly that she drifted against the cave wall. She had no one to lean upon. It was as if every friend had deserted her, even Laurie.

If she had known what birthday gift was swimming nearer and nearer with every minute, she would not have said to herself, "I'll sob a little sob tonight in my clam shell bed. It won't do to be dismal now." She straightened her shell corset and tightened her armlets. She mustered all the courage she would need to swim into the parlor and be jolly. Yet before she could swim in, the door shells rattled with a great *clap clap clap.*

She opened with hospitable haste, and startled as if another ghost had come to surprise her. There floated a long, bearded merman with a bouquet of glow blooms.

"Oh, Mr. Bhaer, I am so glad to see you!" cried Jo. She grabbed his hand with the sea-flowers as if she feared the Ocean would swallow him up before she could pull him indoors.

"And I am glad to see Miss Marsh. But no, you have a party," and the Professor paused as the sound of voices and singing drifted out to them.

"No, we haven't. Only the merfamily. My sister and

friends have just swum home, and we are all very happy. Swim in, and make one of us."

Though a very social merman, I think Mr. Bhaer would have swum decorously away to return later. Yet how could he when Jo yanked him into the cave by both arms and shut the door behind him? Perhaps her face had something to do with it. She forgot to hide her joy at seeing him. Her frank happiness proved irresistible to the solitary merman. The exuberant welcome far exceeded his boldest hopes.

"If I will not be clumsy—in the way—I will so gladly see them all. Have you been ill, my friend?"

He put the question abruptly, for, as Jo hung up his cloak, he saw her profile and noticed a change in it.

"Not ill, but tired and sorrowful. We have had trouble since I saw you last."

"Ah, yes, I know. My heart was sore for you when I heard that." He took her hands into his, with a sympathetic face. Jo felt as if no comfort could equal the look of the kind eyes, or the grasp of the big, warm hand.

When Jo swam into the parlor, leading her friend by his big hand, all eyes beheld them with surprise.

"Father, Mother, this is my friend, Professor Bhaer," Jo said with irrepressible pride and pleasure.

CHAPTER 39

Empty Hands

I f the stranger had any doubts about his welcome, they were set at rest by the cordial reception he received. Everyone greeted him kindly, for Jo's sake at first, but very soon they liked him for his own. Mr. Bhaer had the face of a traveler who knocks at a strange door, and when it opens, finds himself at home. Meg's merchildren went to him like walruses to clams, establishing themselves on each side of his tail. They pulled at his hair, spun his armlets around backward, and investigated his satchel. He took the juvenile audacity as a funny game. Mr. Marsh felt that he had found a kindred spirit, and the mermaids nodded in approval to one another. Silent John listened and enjoyed the talk, but said not a word, and Mr. Laurence found it impossible to swim off to sleep.

If Jo's attention had not been otherwise engaged, Laurie's behavior would have amused her. A faint twinge, not of jealousy, but something like suspicion, caused him to hover aloof at first. He observed the newcomer with brotherly circumspection. But it did not last long. He got interested in spite of himself, and before he knew it, was drawn into the circle. Mr. Bhaer talked well in this genial atmosphere, and did himself justice.

Over the next few days, Laurie and Amy set up their cave, decorating and planning a blissful future. They surrounded themselves with marble tables, magenta fixtures, and the bride's beautiful paintings. Meanwhile, Mr. Bhaer and Jo were enjoying a setting of a different sort. They took long swims through the coral reef, over tiger seagrass and through wild waters.

By the second week, everyone knew perfectly well what was going on. Yet everyone tried to look as if they were stone-blind to the changes in Jo's face. They never asked why she sang about her work, or fixed her lavender hair three times a day. It was quite evident that Professor Bhaer was giving the mermaid lessons in love.

Jo, however, could not sink into love gently. She sternly tried to quench her feelings, but failing to do so, she led a somewhat agitated life. She was afraid of being laughed at for surrendering. She'd made so many and vehement declarations of independence. Laurie was her special dread, but thanks to Amy's prodding, he behaved himself in public. Privately, he laughed himself to sleep. He looked forward to the days when he could tease Jo openly about her Professor. He was sure they would be here soon.

For a fortnight, this Professor came and went with lover-like regularity. Then he stayed away for three whole days and made no contact. This caused everybody to look sober, and Jo to become pensive, at first, and then—alas for romance—very cross.

"Disgusted, I dare say, and swam home as suddenly as

he swam here. It's nothing to me, of course. But I should think he would have bid us goodbye like a proper merman," she said to herself.

Too agitated to nestle down in the attic, or even to go out for a leisurely swim, Jo threw on her cloak and darted out the door. She pumped her tail, hurling herself toward their little city. She crashed right into the chest of a familiar merman.

"We thought you swam away," said Jo hastily, backing away from their collision. She was equal parts embarrassed and exuberant, and cupped her face to hide her joy.

"Did you believe that I should swim away with no farewell to those who have been so kind to me?" he asked so reproachfully that she felt as if she had insulted him by the suggestion, and answered heartily...

"No, I didn't. I knew you were busy about your own affairs, but we rather missed you, Father and Mother especially."

"And you?"

"I'm always glad to see you, sir."

In her anxiety to keep her voice quite calm, Jo made it rather cool. The frigid little monosyllable at the end seemed to chill the Professor. His smile vanished, as he said flatly...

"I thank you, and I swim to you one more time before I leave."

"You are leaving, then?"

"I have no longer any business here. It is finished."

"Successfully, I hope?" asked Jo, for that short reply of his held the bitterness of disappointment.

"I ought to think so. I have opened a way to me by

which I can make my kelp crisp and give my nephews much help."

"Tell me, please! I like to know all about the—the merboys," said Jo eagerly.

"That is so kind. I gladly tell you. My friends find for me a place in a college where I can teach and earn enough to make life good for Krill and Rio. For this I should be grateful, should I not?"

"Indeed you should. How splendid it will be to have you doing what you like, and be able to see you often, and the merboys!" exclaimed Jo.

"Ah! But we will not meet often, I fear. This place is at the Coastline."

"So far away!" said Jo, her spirits sinking.

"Now will we swim to your parents?" he asked, as if the words were very pleasant to him.

"Yes, it's late, and I'm *so* tired." Jo's voice was more pathetic than she knew. Mr. Bhaer was swimming away. He only cared for her as a friend. It was all a mistake, and the sooner it was over the better.

Mr. Bhaer saw the corners of her mouth turn down, even though she turned her head away. The sight seemed to touch him very much. He suddenly stooped down and asked in a tone that meant a great deal, "Heart's dearest, why do you sob?"

Jo answered, with an irrepressible quaver, "Because you are swimming away."

"Ach, that is so good!" exclaimed Mr. Bhaer. "Jo, I have nothing but much love to give you. I swam here to see if you could care for me. I waited to be sure that I was something more than a friend. Am I? Can you make a little place in your heart for old Fritz Bhaer?" he added, his words tumbling out all at once.

"Oh, yes!" said Jo, folding both hands over his. She looked at him with an expression that plainly showed how happy she would be to swim through life beside him.

It was certainly proposing under difficulties. The two of them had paused in the middle of the busy thoroughfare that led to the city. Oyster sleighs passed them on either side. Seahorses snorted at them for being in the way. They could not indulge in tender remonstrations in the middle of so much commotion.

Passers-by probably thought them a pair of silly lovers, which in fact, they were. Little they cared what anybody thought. They were enjoying the happy hour that seldom comes but once in any life. This is the magical moment which bestows youth on the old, beauty on the plain, and wealth on the poor. The Professor looked as if he had conquered a kingdom, and the Ocean had nothing more to offer him in the way of bliss. Jo floated beside him, feeling as if her place had always been there. She wondered how she ever could have chosen any other future. Of course, she was the first to speak—intelligibly, I mean. The emotional remarks which followed her impetuous "Oh, yes!" were not of a coherent or reportable character.

"Why didn't you tell me all this sooner?" asked Jo bashfully.

"I had a wish to tell something the day I said goodbye in Pink City, but I thought the handsome friend was betrothed to you. So I spoke not. Would you have said 'Yes', then, if I had spoken?"

"I don't know. I'm afraid not, for I didn't have any heart just then."

"Prut! That I do not believe. I must be happy now, because some questions will never need answered."

"One does. Tell me what brought you here to our little reef, at last, just when I wanted you?"

"This," and Mr. Bhaer took a little worn scroll out of his satchel.

Jo unrolled it and looked much abashed. It was one of her own contributions to a magazine-scroll that paid for poetry.

"How could that bring you to me?" she asked, wondering what he meant.

"I found it by chance. I knew it by the names and the initials. I also knew it that you write again with your true heart. There was one little verse that seemed to call me to you. Read and find it."

IN THE ATTIC

Four little nets all in a row,
Slung on pegs, and worn by time,
All fashioned and filled, long ago,
By merchildren now in their prime.
Four little names, one on each sack,
Inked out by a merboyish hand,
Within each old and winsome pack,
Histories of the happy band,
Once playing here, and pausing oft,

To tip and twirl gleefully,
Dancing in the attic loft,
In our soft and happy sea.

"Meg" on the first net, smooth and fair.
I look in with loving eyes,
For slipped in here, with well-known care,
A goodly gathering lies,
The record of a peaceful life—
Baubles of a mergirl grown,
Silver corset, scrolls to a wife,
A single glove, a bridal gown.
Ah, happy mother! Well I know
You sing the contented melody,
A lullaby ever warm and low,
In our soft and happy sea.

"Jo" on the next, scratched and worn,
And within a motley store,
Of headless dolls, of school-scrolls torn,
Fish and fins that speak no more,
Half-writ poems, stories wild,
Bottled letters, warm and cold,
Diaries of a bright merchild,
Hints of a mermaid early old,
A mermaid in a lonely cave,
Hearing, as an inner plea,
"Wait, my love, and love you'll have,"
In our soft and happy sea.

My Beth! the silt is always swept
From the net that bears your name,
As if by loving eyes that wept,
By careful hands that often came.
The silver bell, so seldom rung,
The little cap which last she wore,
The music she'd composed and sung
The miniature harp upon the floor.
The songs she sang, without lament,
When she set her spirit free,
Forever is her courage lent,
In our soft and happy sea.

Within the last net's braided form,
Legend now both fair and true
A painted, black-haired mer in storm,
Sings out "Amy" in letters blue.
Within lie combs that pinned her hair,
Brushes that have drawn their last,
Faded flowers laid with care,
A tail fin mold she used to cast,
A wish for how her life should be,
How her wishes were surpassed,
In our soft and happy sea.

Four little nets all in a row,
Sanded with silt, and worn by time,
Four mermaids, taught by weal and woe
To love and labor in their prime.
Four sisters, parted for an hour,
None lost, one only gone before,

Made by love's immortal power,
Nearest and dearest evermore.
Lives whose music long shall ring,
Songs whose life shall ever be,
Sisters are a blessed thing,
In our soft and happy sea.

"It's very bad poetry, but I felt it when I wrote it, one day when I was very lonely, and had a good sob on a night wrap. I never thought it would go where it could tell you tales," said Jo.

"Yes," he answered earnestly. "I read that, and I think to myself, she writes from her true heart. That heart has a sorrow, she is lonely. She would find comfort in true love. I have a heart full—full for her. Will I not swim up and say, 'If this is not too poor a thing to give for what I hope to receive, take it from me in exchange?'"

"And so you came to find that it was not too poor a gift, but the one precious thing I needed," whispered Jo.

"I had no courage to think that at first, heavenly kind as was your welcome to me. But soon I began to hope, and then I said, 'I will have her if I die for it,' and so I will!" cried Mr. Bhaer, with a defiant nod. Just then a large hermit crab crawled past, carrying a dozen passengers and sloshing mightily. The wake pushed the lovers off-balance. The Professor wrapped his arms tightly about Jo. They bounced off a starfish and three grumpy dolphins on their way to safety.

Jo thought the rescue was splendid, and resolved to be worthy of her sea prince.

"What made you stay away so long?" she asked presently. She found it so pleasant to ask confidential questions and get delightful answers. She could not keep silent.

"It was not easy, but I could not find the heart to take you from that so happy a merfamily. How could I ask you to give up so much for a poor old merman, who has no fortune but a little learning?"

"I'm glad you are poor. I couldn't bear a rich husband," said Jo decidedly, adding in a softer tone, "Don't fear poverty. I've known it long enough to lose my dread and be happy working for those I love. Don't call yourself old—forty is the prime of life. I couldn't help loving you if you were seventy!"

The Professor found this so touching that he would have sobbed if he wasn't so occupied with laughing for joy.

"I may be strong-minded, and no one can say that's a disadvantage to our love. I'm to carry my share, Fritz, and help to earn our cave. Make up your mind to that, or I'll never agree to marry you," she added resolutely.

"Ah! You give me such hope and courage. I have nothing to give back but a full heart and these empty hands," said the Professor, quite overcome.

Jo never, never would learn to be proper. When he said that as they floated beside the thoroughfare, she slipped both hands into his and whispered tenderly, "Not empty now." Then she leaned in and kissed him in front of everyone. It was dreadfully improper, but she would have done so even if the Ocean Queen were watching. She was very far sunk into love indeed, and quite regardless of everything but her own happiness.

Though it came in such a very simple disguise, their next task was the crowning moment of both their lives.

They turned from the gaping crowd and swam hand-in-hand to the Marsh's cave dwelling. They slipped into the glow and warmth and peace waiting to receive them. With a glad "Welcome home!", Jo led her lover in, and shut the door.

CHAPTER 40

Merboys

For a year Jo and her Professor worked and waited, hoped and loved. They met occasionally. They posted voluminous letters-in-bottles. Laurie said their correspondence accounted for the rise in the price of squid ink. The second year began rather soberly. They felt no nearer to marriage, and Aunt Marsh died suddenly. But when their first sorrow was over—for they loved the old merlady in spite of her sharp tongue—they found they had cause for rejoicing. She had left her grand cave dwelling to Jo, which made all sorts of joyful things possible.

"It's a fine old cave, and will bring a gorge-full of sand dollars. Of course you intend to sell it," said Laurie, as they were all talking the matter over some weeks later.

"No, I don't," was Jo's decided answer, as she stroked the elderly parrotfish, whom she had adopted, out of respect to his former mistress.

"You don't mean to live there?"

"Yes, I do."

"But, it's an immense cave dwelling, and will take more

than a gorge of sand dollars to keep it in order. The garden and orchard alone need two or three merpeople to work them, and farming isn't in Bhaer's line, I take it."

"He'll put his tail to it, if I propose it."

"And you expect to live on the produce of the place? Well, that sounds paradisiacal, but you'll find it desperate hard work."

"The crop we are going to raise is a profitable one," and Jo laughed.

"Of what is this fine crop to consist, ma'am?"

"Merboys. I want to open a school for little merboys—a good, happy, homelike school. I will take care of them and Fritz will teach them."

"What a perfect 'Jo' plan! Isn't that just like her?" cried Laurie, appealing to the merfamily, who looked as much surprised as he.

"I like it," said Mrs. Marsh decidedly.

"So do I," added Bhaer. He welcomed the thought of trying his own methods of teaching young merfolk.

"It will be an immense responsibility for Jo," said Meg, stroking Demi's head, her one all-absorbing merboy.

"Jo can do it, and be happy in it. It's a splendid idea. Tell us all about it," said Mr. Laurence. He longed to lend the lovers his tail, but knew that they would refuse his help.

"I knew you'd admire me for it, Father. Amy does too —I see it in her eyes, though she prudently waits to turn it over in her mind before she speaks. Now, my dear merpeople," continued Jo earnestly, "just understand that this isn't a new idea of mine. It is a long cherished plan. Before my Fritz came, I used to think what I'd do when I'd made my fortune and no one needed me at home. I dreamed of renting a big cave, and picking up some poor, forlorn little merboys who hadn't any mothers. I'd take care of them and make life jolly for them before it was too late. I see so many swimming into difficult futures for lack of help at the right minute. I love so to do anything for them. I seem to feel their wants, and sympathize with their troubles, and oh, I should so like to be a mother to them!"

Mrs. Marsh held out her hand to Jo, who took it, smiling. Jo continued on in the old enthusiastic way, which they had not heard for a long while.

"I told my plan to Fritz at once. He said it was just what he would like to do and agreed to try it when we got rich. Bless his dear heart, he's been doing it all his life—helping poor merboys, I mean, not getting rich, that he'll never be. Sand dollars don't stay in his satchel long enough to pile up. But now, thanks to my good old aunt, who loved me better than I ever deserved, I'm rich. At least I feel so.

"We can live at the grand cave perfectly well, if we have a flourishing school. It's just the place for merboys. It is big, and the coral fixtures are strong and sturdy. There's plenty of room for dozens inside, and splendid grounds outside. They could help in the garden and orchard. Such work is healthy, isn't it, sir? Then Fritz could train and teach in his own way, and Father will help him. I can feed and nurse and dote on and scold them, and Mother will be my standby.

"I've always longed for lots of merboys. Now I can fill my big cave full of them and revel in the little fishies to my heart's content. Think what luxury—my own estate and a school of merboys to enjoy it with me."

As Jo waved her hands and gave a sigh of rapture, the

merfamily went off into a whirl of merriment. Mr. Laurence laughed until his face turned blue.

"I don't see anything funny," she said gravely, when she could be heard. "Nothing could be more natural and proper than for my Professor to open a school, or for me to reside in my own grand cave."

"She's speaking as a grand mermaid already," said Laurie, who regarded Jo inheriting Aunt Marsh's social position as a capital joke. "But may I inquire how you intend to support the establishment? If all the pupils are little bottom-feeders, I'm afraid your crop won't be profitable in a sand dollar sense, Mrs. Bhaer."

"Now don't be a drag on the mood, Laurie. Of course I will have rich students, also—perhaps begin with such altogether. Then, when I've got a start, I can take in a poor student or two. Rich merpeople's merchildren often need care and comfort, as well as poor. I've seen unfortunate little creatures left to fend for themselves. Rich merboys neglected in every sense except material.

"I've a special interest in such young merboys. I won't just see them as clumsy tails, mischievous arms, and rowdy minds. I will show them that I see their warm, honest, well-meaning merboys' hearts. I've had experience, too, for haven't I brought up one merboy to be a pride and honor to his merfamily?"

"I'll testify that you tried to do it," said Laurie with a grateful look.

"And I've succeeded beyond my hopes. Here you are, a steady, sensible merman of business. You do heaps of good with your sand dollars. You are not merely about business. You love good and beautiful things, enjoy them yourself, and let others go halves, as you always did in the old times. I am proud of you, Laurie, for you get better every year. Everyone feels it, though you won't let them say so. Yes, and when I have my school, I'll just point to you, and say 'There's your model, my merboys.'"

Poor Laurie didn't know where to look, for, merman though he was, something of the old bashfulness came over him. This burst of praise made all faces turn approvingly upon him.

"I say, Jo, that's rather too much," he began, just in his old merboyish way. "You have all done more for me than I can ever thank you for, except by doing my best not to disappoint you. You have rather cast me off lately, Jo, but I've had the best of help, nevertheless. So, if I've got on at all, you may thank these two for it." He laid one hand gently on his grandfather's head, and the other on Amy's golden one, for the three were never far apart.

"I do think that families are the most beautiful things in all the Ocean!" burst out Jo, who was in an unusually up-lifted frame of mind just then. "When I have one of my own, I hope it will be as happy as the three I know and love the best. If John and my Fritz were only here, it would be quite a moment of paradise," she added more quietly. She swam to her room that night after a blissful evening of merfamily counsels, hopes, and plans. Her heart was so full of happiness that she could only calm it by floating beside the empty shell bed near her own, and thinking tender thoughts of Beth.

It was a very astonishing year altogether. Things seemed to happen in an unusually rapid and delightful manner. Almost before she knew where she was, Jo found herself married and settled at Aunt Marsh's cave. Then a merfamily of six or seven merboys sprung up like sponges, and flourished surprisingly. They were poor merboys as well as rich. Mr. Laurence was continually finding some touching case of destitution. He begged the Bhaers to take pity on the merboy. Then he regularly donated for his support. In this way, the sly old merman got around proud Jo's refusal of help. He furnished her with the style of merboy in which she most delighted.

How Jo did enjoy her 'school of merboys'. How also poor, dear Aunt Marsh would have lamented had she been there. Her prim, well-ordered grand estate was filled with lively merboys. There was a sort of poetic justice about it, after all. The old merlady had been the terror of the merboys for miles around. Now it became a sort of merboys' paradise.

It never was a fashionable school, but it was just what Jo intended it to be—'a happy, homelike place for merboys, who needed teaching, care, and kindness'. Every room in the grand cave was soon full. Every little plot in the garden soon had its owner. A regular menagerie appeared in barn and stables, for pet fish were allowed. And three times a day, Jo smiled at her Fritz from the head of a long table lined on either side with happy young faces.

The merboys turned to her with affectionate eyes, confiding words, and grateful hearts. She did not tire of them, though they were not angelfish, by any means. Some of them caused both Jo and Fritz much trouble and anxiety. Her faith in the good in the heart of the naughtiest merchild gave her patience and success.

The friendship of the merboys was very precious to Jo.

She treasured their droll or touching little confidences. There were slow merboys and bashful merboys, feeble merboys and riotous merboys, merboys that lisped and merboys that couldn't swim. Each one was a treasure, a pearl in his berth.

Yes, Jo was a very happy mermaid there, in spite of hard work, much anxiety, and a perpetual racket. She enjoyed it heartily and found the applause of her merboys more satisfying than any praise in the Ocean. Now she told her stories to her school of enthusiastic believers and admirers. As the years went on, two little merboys of her own came to increase her happiness—Ronan, named for Grandpa, and Theodore, a happy-go-lucky merbaby. He seemed to have inherited his papa's happy temper as well as his mother's lively spirit. How they ever grew up alive in that whirlpool of merboys was a mystery to their grandma and aunts. Yet little Ronan and Theodore flourished like wild seagrass. Their companions loved and served them well.

CHAPTER 41

Harvest Time

There were a great many holidays at Jo's grand cave dwelling. One of the most delightful was the yearly sea apple harvest. The Marshes, Laurences, Brookes, and Bhaers turned out in full force and made a party of it. Five years after Jo's wedding, one of these fruitful festivals occurred.

It was a perfect Cool Season day. The water was full of an exhilarating freshness which made the spirits float. The old orchard wore its holiday attire. Orange zoas and crimson algae-blooms fringed the rockweedy walls. Sea bugs slipped briskly in the seagrass, and clams chirped like Coast-line orators. Mantis shrimp were busy with their small harvesting. The last, lingering little Hot Season fish bid their adieux from the corals in the lane. Every sea apple stood ready to be plucked. Everybody was there. Everybody laughed and sang, swam up and somersaulted down. Every-body declared that there never had been such a perfect day or such a jolly set to enjoy it. They gave themselves up to the simple pleasures as if there were no such things as care or sorrow in the Ocean.

Mr. Marsh glided placidly about, chatting with Mr. Laurence. The two old mermen enjoyed the sight of the youngsters at play. The Professor darted up and down the rows of sea apples, leading his school of merboys. Laurie devoted himself to the littlest ones, carrying his small daughter in a comfy net on his back. Mrs. Marsh and Meg nestled among piles of plucked sea apples, sorting the contributions that kept pouring in. Amy, with a motherly expression on her face, painted the various groups into memory. A tiny turquoise ring sparkled on her brush hand.

Jo was in her element that day. She swished about, with her lavender hair braided back, and her shell corset twisted at a lopsided angle. Her merbaby was tucked under her arm, ready for any lively adventure which might turn up.

At four o'clock a lull took place. The sea apple pickers rested, swapping laughs and lightening hearts. Then Jo and Meg, with a detachment of the bigger merboys, spread out supper on a large rock. An out-of-door meal was always the crowning joy of harvest day.

When no one could eat any more, the Professor proposed a blessing, which was customary at such festivals —"Aunt Marsh, bless her!" The good merman, who never forgot how much he owed her, led all the little merboys in a hearty cheer.

"Now, Grandma's sixtieth birthday! Long life to her, with three times three!"

That was given heartily, as you may well believe, and the cheering once begun, was hard to stop. Everybody's health was blessed, from Mr. Laurence to the astonished catfish. Demi, as the oldest grandchild, then presented Grandmother Marsh with various gifts. They were so numerous that they were transported to the festive scene in an oyster sleigh.

Funny presents, some of them, but what would have been defects to other eyes were ornaments to Grandma's. The merchildren's gifts were all their own. Every stitch Daisy's little fingers had put into the armlets she wove was better than embroidery to Mrs. Marsh. Demi offered a miracle of mechanical skill, though the innovative jewelry case wouldn't shut. Jo's little Ronan gave a seaweed cushion with lumps in it that Grandma declared were soothing. No paragraph of the costly scroll Amy's merchild gave her was so fair as that on which appeared in tipsy capitals, "To dear Grandma, from her little Beth Laurence."

During the ceremony the merboys had mysteriously disappeared. When Mrs. Marsh tried to thank her merchildren, she broke down in sobs. Laurie quietly offered her his shoulder, while the Professor suddenly began to sing. Then, from behind the piles of plucked sea apples, voice after voice took up the words. The merboys sang with all their hearts a little song that Jo had written, and Laurie set to music. The Professor trained his merboys to present it with the best effect. They popped their heads out from behind the piles in time to the music. This was something altogether new, and it proved a grand success. Mrs. Marsh couldn't get over her surprise, and insisted on shaking hands with every one of the young choir.

After this, the merboys dispersed for a final adventure, leaving Mrs. Marsh and her daughters nestled around the supper rock.

"I don't think I ever ought to call myself 'unlucky Jo' again. My greatest wishes have been so beautifully gratified," said Mrs. Bhaer.

"And yet your life is very different from the one you pictured so long ago. Do you remember our youthful fancies?" asked Amy, smiling as she watched Laurie and John playing waterball with the merchildren.

"Yes, I remember," said Jo, "I never wanted to grow up, but I'm so glad that I did. Life as a merchild is not half so stimulating as being an author, a mother, and the head of a school. Who would have thought that being a full-grown mermaid would be so glorious?"

"My fancies were the most nearly realized of all. I dreamed of splendid things, to be sure. In my heart I knew I would be satisfied if I had a little cave, and John, and some dear merchildren like these. I'm the happiest mermaid in the Ocean," said Meg. She laid her hand on her merboy's head, with a face full of tender and devout content.

"My life is very different from what I hoped, but I would not alter it. I've begun to plan a statue of a merbaby, and Laurie says it will be the best thing I've ever done. I think so, myself, and mean to do it in marble, so that, whatever happens, I may at least keep the image of my little angelfish."

As Amy spoke, she held back tender sobs. Sleeping in her arms was her merbaby. Her one well-beloved daughter was a frail little creature. The dread of losing her was heavy on the parents. One love and sorrow bound mother and father closely together. Amy's nature was growing sweeter, deeper, and more tender. Laurie was growing more serious, strong, and firm. Both were learning that beauty, youth, good fortune, even love itself, cannot keep care and pain, loss and sorrow, from the most blessed because...

Into each life some sadness must settle,
Some waters must be cold and dreary.

"She is growing better, I am sure of it, my dear," said Mrs. Marsh. Tenderhearted Daisy cuddled in to lay her rosy cheek against her little cousin's pale one.

"You do cheer me, Marmee, and so does Laurie," replied Amy warmly. "I can't love him enough. In spite of my one sorrow, I can say with Meg, 'I'm a happy mermaid.'"

"There's no need for me to say it, for everyone can see that I'm far happier than I deserve," added Jo. She glanced from her good husband to her chubby merchildren. "Fritz is getting gray and stout. I'm growing as thin as a squid leg and am thirty. We never will be rich. In spite of these unromantic facts, I have nothing to complain of, and never was so jolly in my life."

"Yes, Jo, I think your harvest will be a good one," began Mrs. Marsh, frightening away a big green sea bug that was scaring Jo's merbaby Theodore.

"Not half so good as yours, Mother. We never can thank you enough for the patient planting and plucking you have done," exclaimed Jo, with the loving impetuosity which she never would outgrow.

"I hope there will be a sweeter and sweeter pile to pluck every year," said Amy softly.

"A pile deep as a gorge, but I know there's room in your heart for it, Marmee dear," added Meg's tender voice.

Touched to the heart, Mrs. Marsh could only stretch out her arms to gather her merchildren and grandchildren to herself. She said, with face and voice full of motherly love, gratitude, and humility…

"Oh, my little mermaids, however long you may live, I never can wish you a greater happiness than this!"

There's More

Thanks for joining the Marsh merfamily under the sea...

If you loved the book and have a spare moment, I would be so thankful if you left a short review where you found it. Reviews make a whale-sized difference in helping new readers discover the book.

Thanks to each of you who take the time to review. As Jo would say, "You're capital!"

The fun isn't over yet...

Curl up with a free bonus chapter, *Daisy and Demi*, when you sign up to my Notes and News. You'll also get updates on new releases, giveaways and other exclusive content.

Grab your bonus chapter at https:// meganloiswhitehill.com/stayintouch/

Daisy and Demi

I have not done my duty as a Marsh merfamily historian, unless I devote a chapter to the next generation.

If there ever were a pair of twins in danger of being utterly spoiled by adoration, it was the twin Brookes. Of course Meg and John's merbabies were the most remarkable ever born. They swam at eight months— performing full backflips not two weeks later. They spoke fluently at twelve months. At  two-years-old they behaved with a propriety which charmed all beholders....

Curl up with their cute antics for free now:
    https://meganloiswhitehill.com/stayintouch/

Over one-hundred and fifty years have passed since the first publication of Little Women. The original was released in two volumes; the first in 1868 and the second in 1869. Since then it has been loved and treasured by millions of people— and if merfolk existed, I'd like to think they'd treasure it too.

Alcott's original explored many themes faced by Civil War era American women: patriarchy, poverty, sickness, and saying goodbye forever to those you love. Recent TV and film adaptations have leaned heavily on Jo's dissatisfaction with being a woman in a world where men have the best opportunities. So much so that Jo's tomboy nature has become synonymous with her character arc.

What would Jo's character arc look like in an ocean that has never known patriarchy? A world where a girl has no reason to be jealous of a boy? These were questions I asked myself as I sat down to retell her story under the sea. Patriarchy does not translate into a world of powerful mermaids, and it had to be left on the cutting floor.

Thankfully, Alcott's original "book Jo" came to the

rescue. Book Jo is a passionate character who struggles to learn how to direct her anger. Book Jo does not want to endure the inevitable changes growing-up brings to relationships. She wants Meg to stay home, Beth to survive, and Laurie to remain an innocent friend forever. Book Jo also wants to be a boy. Unlike recent films, I've brought the focus of her arc squarely onto the first two, and left the latter behind.

Fans who know Jo only by the films may find this unexpected. I assure you that anger-management and saying goodbye are elements of Alcott's original Josephine March.

I've done my best to preserve the sweet, heart-touching tone of the original. May you fall in love with Meg, Jo, Beth, and Amy again for the first time. I certainly did.

If you aren't ready to say goodbye to them yet, you can curl up with free bonus content at https://meganloiswhitehill.com/stayintouch/

Acknowledgments

A hearty thanks to everyone who influenced, inspired and labored with me on this book.

First, many thanks to Louisa May Alcott. I hope that wherever you are, you are happy. I hope I have preserved the emotional truth of your original in my translation to "Mermaid World."

Thank you to my husband and to my mother, for always believing in me—listening to me often and providing food when needed.

Thank you to my sister, who forced me to read *Little Women* when I was a young Jo who turned up her nose at sentimental books.

Thank you to the mentors who've inspired me from afar: Michael La Ronn, Abbie Emmons, and Alexa Donne. Your books, videos, and podcasts kept me going on long, dark nights.

Thank you to my illustrator, Andrea Vásquez A., for your beautiful imagination. Thank you also to Maddy D. and Ashley Lavadinho for beta reading, and to my proofreader, Vidhipssa Mohan. All mistakes are my own.

Lastly and most of all, thank you to my niece—the little woman who asked me for a good mermaid book for her birthday.

Driven by wild curiosity and a passion for the enchanted, Megan Lois Whitehill can't stop making up imaginary worlds. When her niece asked her for a 'good mermaid book', she started retelling classics as adventures under the sea.

Megan has traveled to over 14 countries and lived abroad. She loves tasting new foods, exploring new biomes, and hearing an area's legends. She holds a Master's Degree in Applied Linguistics, and—quite frankly—loves words. All of these experiences add richness and depth to her stories. Committed to her craft, Megan writes in a spirit of cozy, creative, and goodhearted fun. Nestle back and escape awhile.

When she isn't writing, you'll find her enjoying a sauna, over-thinking movie plots, or restoring vintage teddy bears. She lives in Pennsylvania with one husband and two parakeets.